Available in February 2010
from Mills & Boon® Intrigue

Branded by the Sheriff
by Delores Fossen
&
The 9-Month Bodyguard
by Cindy Dees

The Sharpshooter's Secret Son
by Mallory Kane
&
Fury Calls
by Caridad Piñeiro

Snowbound with the Bodyguard
by Carla Cassidy
&
Lady Killer
by Kathleen Creighton

Small-Town Secrets
by Debra Webb

Wild Hunt
by Lori Devoti

Protecting His Witness
by Marie Ferrarella

"Where's your daughter right now?" Beck asked.

His tone alone would have alarmed her, but there was more than a sense of urgency in his expression.

"Aubrey's with her nanny. Why?"

"Because I was just trying to put myself in the killer's place. If he came here to scare you off and it didn't work, then what will he do next?" His stare was a warning.

Faith's heart dropped to her knees.

Beck took a step towards her. "He might try to use your daughter to get to you."

"Oh, God." Faith grabbed her phone and prayed that it wasn't too late to keep her baby safe.

THE 9-MONTH BODYGUARD

She breathed his name. "Austin… trust me. I know wild. And you're not it."

He quirked a brow. "Hey! I'm as wild as the next guy."

Her laughter tinkled around him like silver bells. "No, you're not. You're Mr Law-and-Order, do-the-right-thing guy."

If only Silver knew some of the things he'd done in his life. He could tell her about missions so daring they'd curl her toes. He couldn't count the number of times he'd dived into death-defying stunts without a second thought. "You have no idea what wild really is, little girl," he snorted.

"Oh yeah? Are you going to show me?"

Man, he was tempted. Really, really tempted. But from somewhere deep inside him, a kernel of the self-control she'd accused him of reared its ugly head. "Honey, you couldn't handle it."

Her expression suddenly softened, and her gaze grew serious. Aww, jeez. Did she have to go all feminine and sweet on him? That was so much harder to resist than the brazen hussy…

First published in Great Britain 2010
Harlequin Mills & Boon Limited,
Eton House, 18-24 Paradise Road, Richmond, Surrey TW9 1SR

Branded by the Sheriff © Delores Fossen 2009
The 9-Month Bodyguard © Harlequin Books S.A. 2009

Special thanks and acknowledgement are given to Cindy Dees for her
contribution to the LOVE IN 60 SECONDS mini-series.

ISBN: 978 0 263 88198 1

46-0210

Harlequin Mills & Boon policy is to use papers that are natural, renewable
and recyclable products and made from wood grown in sustainable forests.
The logging and manufacturing processes conform to the legal environmental
regulations of the country of origin.

Printed and bound in Spain
by Litografia Rosés S.A., Barcelona

BRANDED BY
THE SHERIFF
BY
DELORES FOSSEN

THE 9-MONTH
BODYGUARD
BY
CINDY DEES

MILLS & BOON

BRANDED BY
THE SHERIFF

BY
DELORES FOSSEN

Imagine a family tree that includes Texas cowboys, Choctaw and Cherokee Indians, a Louisiana pirate and a Scottish rebel who battled side by side with William Wallace. With ancestors like that, it's easy to understand why Texas author and former air force captain **Delores Fossen** feels as if she were genetically predisposed to writing romances. Along the way to fulfilling her DNA destiny, Delores married an air force top gun who just happens to be of Viking descent. With all those romantic bases covered, she doesn't have to look too far for inspiration.

To Debbie Gafford, thanks for always being
there for me.

Chapter One

LaMesa Springs, Texas

A killer was in the house.

Sheriff Beck Tanner drew his weapon and eased out of his SUV. He hadn't planned on a showdown tonight, but he was ready for it.

Beck stopped at the edge of the yard that was more dirt than grass. He listened for a moment.

The light in the back of the small Craftsman-style house indicated someone was there, but he didn't want that someone sneaking out and ambushing him. After all, Darin Matthews had already claimed two victims, his own mother and sister. Since this was Darin's family home, Beck figured sooner or later the man would come back.

Apparently he had.

Around him, the January wind whipped through the bare tree branches. That was the only sound Beck could hear. The house was at the end of the sparsely populated County Line Road, barely in the city limits and a full half mile away from any neighboring house.

There was a hint of smoke in the air, and thanks to

a hunter's moon, Beck spotted the source: the rough stone chimney anchored against the left side of the house. Wispy gray coils of smoke rose into the air, the wind scattering them almost as quickly as they appeared.

He inched closer to the house and kept his gun ready.

His boots crunched on the icy gravel of the driveway. No garage. No car. Just a light stabbing through the darkness. Since the place was supposed to be vacant, he'd noticed the light during a routine patrol of the neighborhood. Beck had also glanced inside the filmy bedroom window and spotted discarded clothes on the bed.

The bedroom wasn't the source of the light though. It was coming from the adjacent bathroom and gave him just enough illumination to see.

Staying in the shadows, Beck hurried through the yard and went to the back of the house. He tried to keep his footsteps light on the wooden porch, but each rickety board creaked under his weight. He knew the knob would open because the lock was broken. He'd discovered that two months earlier when he checked out the place after the murder of the home's owner.

Beck eased open the door just a fraction and heard the water running in the bathroom. "A killer in the shower," he said to himself. All in all, not a bad place for an arrest.

He made his way through the kitchen and into the living room. All the furniture was draped in white sheets, giving the place an eerie feel.

Beck had that same eerie feeling in the pit of his stomach.

He'd been sheriff of LaMesa Springs for eight years,

since he'd turned twenty-four, and he'd been the deputy for the two years before that. But because his town wasn't a hotbed for serious crime, this would be the first time he'd have to take down a killer.

The thought had no sooner formed in his head when the water in the bathroom stopped. He had to make his move now.

Beck gripped his pistol, keeping it aimed.

He nudged the ajar bathroom door with the toe of his boot, and sticky, warm steam and dull, milky light spilled over him.

Since the bathroom was small, he could take in the room in one glance. Outdated avocado tile—some cracked and chipped. A claw-footed tub encased by an opaque shower curtain. There was one frosted glass window to his right that was too small to use to escape.

Beck latched on to the curtain and gave it a hard jerk to the left. The metal hooks rattled, and the sheet of yellowed vinyl slithered around the circular bar that supported it.

"Sheriff Beck Tanner," he identified himself.

But his name died on his lips when he saw the person standing in the tub. It certainly wasn't Darin Matthews.

It was a wet, naked woman.

A scream bubbled up from her throat. Beck cursed. He didn't know which one of them was more surprised.

Well, she wasn't armed. That was the first thing he noticed after the "naked" part. There wasn't a gun anywhere in sight. Just her.

Suddenly, that seemed more than enough.

Water slid off her face, her entire body, and her midnight-black hair clung to her neck and shoulders.

Because he considered himself a gentleman, Beck tried not to notice her small, firm breasts and the triangular patch of hair at the juncture of her thighs.

But because he was a man, and because she was there right in front of him, he noticed despite his efforts to stop himself.

"Beckett Tanner," she spat out like profanity. She swept her left hand over various parts to cover herself while she groped for the white towel dangling over the nearby sink. "What the devil are you doing here?"

Did he know her? Because she obviously knew him.

Beck examined her face and picked through all that wet hair and water to see her features.

Oh, hell.

She was obviously older than the last time he'd seen her, which was…when? Just a little more than ten years ago when she was eighteen. Since then, her body and face had filled out, but those copper brown eyes were the same.

The last time he'd seen those eyes, she'd been silently hurtling insults at him. She was still doing that now.

"Faith Matthews," Beck grumbled. "What the devil are *you* doing here?"

She draped the towel in front of her and stepped from the tub. "I own the place."

Yeah. She did. Thanks to her mother's and sister's murders. Since her mother had legally disowned Faith's brother, the house had passed to Faith by default.

"The DA said you wanted to keep moving back quiet," Beck commented. "But he also said you wouldn't arrive in town until early next month."

Beck figured he'd need every minute of that month,

too, so he could prepare his family for Faith's return. It was going to hit his sister-in-law particularly hard. That, in turn, meant it'd hit him hard.

What someone did to his family, they did to him.

And Faith Matthews had done a real number on the Tanners.

"I obviously came early." As if in a fierce battle with the terry cloth, she wound the towel around her.

"I didn't see your car," he pointed out.

She huffed. "Because I took a taxi from the Austin airport, all right? My car arrives tomorrow. Now that I've explained why I'm in my own home and how I got here, please tell me why you're trespassing."

She sounded like a lawyer. And was. Or rather a lawyer who was about to become the county's new assistant district attorney.

Beck had tried to convince the DA to turn down her job application, but the DA said she was the best quali-fied applicant and had hired her. That was the reason she was moving back. She wasn't moving back alone, either. She had a kid. A toddler named Aubrey, he'd heard. Not that motherhood would change his opinion of her. That opinion would always be low. And because LaMesa Springs was the county seat, that meant Faith would be living right under his nose, again. Worse, he'd have to work with her to get cases prosecuted.

Yeah, he needed that month to come to terms with that.

"I'm *trespassing* because I thought your brother was here," he explained. "The clerk at the convenience store on Sadler Street said he saw someone matching Darin's description night before last. The Rangers are still ana-lyzing the surveillance video, and when they're done, I

figure it'll be a match. So I came here because I wanted
to arrest a killer."

"An *alleged* killer," she corrected. "Darin is innocent." The towel slipped, and he caught a glimpse of her
right breast again. Her rose-colored nipple, too. She
quickly righted the towel and mumbled something
under her breath. "Before I got in the shower, I checked
the doors and windows and made sure they were all
locked. How'd you get in?"

"The back lock's broken. I noticed it when I came
out here with the Texas Rangers. They assisted me with
the investigation after your mother was killed."

Her intense stare conveyed her displeasure with his
presence. "And you just happened to be in the neighborhood again tonight?"

Beck made sure his scowl conveyed some displeasure, too. "As I already said, I want to arrest a killer. I
figure Darin will eventually come here. You did. So
I've been driving by each night on my way home from
work to see if he'll turn up."

She huffed and walked past him. Not a good idea.
The doorway was small, and they brushed against each
other, her butt against his thigh.

He ignored the pull he felt deep within his belly.

Yes, Faith was attractive, always had been, but she'd
come within a hair of destroying his family. No amount
of attraction would override that.

Besides, Faith had been his brother's one-night
stand. She'd slept with a married man, and that encounter had nearly ruined his brother's marriage.

That alone made her his enemy.

Faith snatched up her clothes from the bed. "Well,

now that you know Darin's not here, you can leave the same way you came in."

"I will. First though, I need to ask some questions." In the back of his mind, he wondered if that was a good idea. She was only a few feet away…and naked under the towel. But Beck decided it was best to put his discomfort aside and worry less about her body and more about getting a killer off the streets.

"When's the last time you saw your brother?" he asked, without waiting to see if she'd agree to the impromptu interrogation.

With a death grip on the towel, she stared at him. Frowned. The frown deepened with each passing second. "Go stand over there," she said, pointing to the pair of front windows that were divided by a bare scarred oak dresser. "And turn your back. I want to get dressed, and I'd rather not do that with you gawking at me."

It was true. He had indeed gawked, and he wasn't proud of it. But then he wasn't proud of the way she'd stirred him up.

"Strange, I hadn't figured you for being modest," he mumbled, strolling toward the windows. He could see his SUV parked out front. It was something to keep his focus on, especially since he didn't want to angle his eyes in any direction in case he caught a glimpse of her naked reflection in the glass.

"Strange?" she repeated as if this insult had actually gotten to her. "I'd say it's equally *strange* that Beckett Tanner would still be making assumptions."

"What does that mean?" he fired back.

Her response was a figure-it-out-yourself grunt. "To answer your original question, I haven't seen Darin in nearly a year." Her words were clipped and angry. "That's in the statement I gave the Texas Rangers two months ago. I'm sure you read it."

Heck, he'd memorized it.

The part about her brother. Her sister's ex. Her estranged relationship with all members of her family. When the Rangers had asked her if Aubrey's father, Faith's own ex, could have some part in this, she'd adamantly denied it, claiming the man had never even seen Aubrey.

All of that had been in her statement, but over the years he'd learned that a written response wasn't nearly as good as the real thing.

"You haven't seen your brother in a long time, yet you don't think he's guilty?"

Silence.

Beck wished he'd waited to ask that particular question because he would have liked to have seen her reaction, but there wasn't any way he was going to turn around while she was dressing.

"Darin wouldn't hurt me," she finally said.

He rolled his eyes. "I'll bet your mother and sister thought the same thing."

"I don't think he killed them." Her opinion wasn't news to him. She had said the same in her interview with the Texas Rangers. "My sister's ex-boyfriend killed them."

Nolan Wheeler. Beck knew him because the man used to live in LaMesa Springs. He was as low-life as they came, and Beck along with the Texas Rangers had been looking for Nolan, who'd seemingly disappeared after giving his statement to the police in Austin.

Well, at least Faith hadn't changed her story over the

past two months. But then Beck hadn't changed his theory. "Nolan Wheeler has alibis for the murders."

"Thin alibis," Faith supplied. "Friends of questionable integrity who'll vouch for him."

"That's more than your brother has. According to what I read about Darin, he's mentally unstable, has been in and out of psychiatric hospitals for years, and he resented your mom and sister. On occasion, he threatened to kill them. He carried through on those threats, though I'll admit he might have had Nolan Wheeler's help."

"Now you think my brother had an accomplice?" Faith asked.

He was betting she had a snarky expression to go along with that snarky question. "It's possible. Darin isn't that organized."

Or that bright. The man was too scatterbrained and perhaps too mentally ill to have conceived a plan to murder two women without witnesses or physical evidence to link him to the crimes. And there was plenty of potential for physical evidence since both victims had been first shot with tranquilizer darts and then strangled. Darin didn't impress him as the sort of man who could carry out multistep murders or remember to wear latex gloves when strangling his victims.

Beck heard an odd sound and risked looking in her direction. She was dressed, thank goodness, in black pants and a taupe sweater. Simple but classy.

The sound had come from her kneeling to open a suitcase. She pulled out a pair of flat black shoes and slipped them on. Faith also took out a plush armadillo before standing, and she clutched onto it when she faced him head-on. She was about five-six. A good eight inches shorter than he was, and with the flats, Beck felt as if he towered over her.

"My brother has problems," she said as if being extra mindful of her word choice. "I don't need to tell you that we didn't have a stellar upbringing, and it affected Darin in a negative way."

It was the old bad blood between them that made him want to remind her that her family was responsible for the poor choices they'd made over the years.

Including what happened that December night ten years ago.

Even now, all these years later, Beck could still see Faith coming out of the Sound End motel with his drunk brother and shoving him into her car. She, however, had been as sober as a judge. Beck should know since, as a deputy at that time, he'd been the one to give her a Breathalyzer. She'd denied having sex with his brother, but there'd been a lot of evidence to the contrary, including his own brother's statement.

"You got something to say to me?" Faith challenged.

Not now. It could wait.

Instead, he glanced at the stuffed baby armadillo. It had a tag from a gift shop in the Austin airport and sported a pink bow around its neck. "I heard you had a baby." Because he was feeling ornery, he glanced at her bare ring finger.

"Yes." Those copper eyes drilled into him. "She's sixteen months old. And, no, I'm not married." The corner of her mouth lifted. Not a smile of humor though. "I guess that just confirms your opinion that I have questionable morals."

He lifted a shoulder and let it stand as his response about that. "You think it's wise to bring a child to LaMesa Springs with a killer at large?"

She mimicked him by lifting her own shoulder, and she let the seconds drag on several moments before she continued. "I have a security company rep coming out first thing in the morning to install some equipment. Once he's finished, I'll call the nanny and have her bring my daughter. We'll stay at the hotel until I have some other repairs and updates done to the house." She glanced around the austere room before her gaze came back to his. "I intend to make this place a home for her."

That's what Beck was afraid she was going to say. This wasn't just about her new job. It was Faith Matthews's homecoming. Something he'd dreaded for ten years. "Even with all the bad memories, you still want to be here?"

Her mouth quivered. "Ah. Is this the part where you tell me I should think of living elsewhere? That I'm not welcome here in *your* town?"

He took a moment with his word selection as well. "You being here will make it hard for my family."

She had the decency to look uncomfortable about that. "I wish I could change that." And she sounded sincere. "But I can't go back and undo history. I can only move forward, and being assistant DA is a dream job for me. I won't walk away from that just because the Tanners don't want me here."

He could tell from the resolve in her eyes that he wasn't going to change her mind. Not that he thought he could anyway. At least he'd gotten his point across that there was still a lot of water under the bridge that his brother and she had built ten years ago in that motel.

But there was another point he had to make. "Even with security measures, it might not be safe for you or your daughter. The man who killed your mother and sister is still out there."

Oh, she was about to disagree. He could almost hear the argument they were about to have. Maybe that wasn't a bad thing. A little air clearing. Except the old stench was so thick between them that it'd take more than an argument to clear it.

She opened her mouth. At the exact moment that Beck caught movement out of the corner of his eye.

Outside the window.

Front yard.

Going on gut instinct, Beck dove at Faith and tackled her onto the bed. He lifted his head and saw the shadowy figure. And worse, it looked as if their *visitor* had a gun pointed right at Faith and him.

Chapter Two

Faith managed a muffled gasp, but she couldn't ask Beck what the heck was going on. The tackle onto the bed knocked the breath from her.

She fought for air and failed. Beck had her pinned down. He was literally lying on her back, and his solid weight pushed her chest right into the hard mattress.

"Someone's out there," Beck warned. "I think he had a gun."

Just like that, she stopped struggling and considered who might be out there. None of the scenarios that came to mind were good. It was too late and too cold for a neighbor to drop by. Besides, she didn't have any nearby neighbors, especially anyone who'd want to pay her a friendly visit. Plus, there was Beck's reaction. He obviously thought this might turn dangerous.

She didn't have to wait long for that to be confirmed.

A sound blasted through the room. Shattering glass. A split-second later, something thudded onto the floor.

"A rock," Beck let her know.

A rock. Not exactly lethal in itself, but the person who'd thrown it could be a threat. And he might have a weapon.

Who had done this?

Better yet, why was Beckett Tanner sheltering her? He had put himself in between her and potential danger, and once she could breathe, Faith figured that maneuver would make more sense than it did now.

Because there was no chance he'd put himself in real harm's way to protect her.

"Get under the bed," Beck ordered. "And stay there."

He rolled off her, still keeping his body between her and the window. Starved for air, Faith dragged in an urgent breath and scrambled to the back side of the mattress so she could drop to the floor. She crawled ben̲ and a few dead and obviously not been a g

Worse, Faith didn't know why she'd decided at the last minute to stay. Her plan had been to check in to the hotel, to wait for the renovations to be complete and for the new furniture to arrive. But after stepping inside, she thought it was best to exorcise a few demons before trying to make the place "normal." So she'd sent the cab driver on his way, made a fire to warm up the place and got ready for bed.

Now someone had hurled a rock through her window.

There was another crashing sound. Another spray of glass. Another thud. Her stomach tightened into an acidy knot.

Beck got off the bed as well. Dropping onto the floor and staying low, he scurried to what was left of the window and peeked out.

"Can you see who's out there?" she asked.

He didn't answer her, but he did take a sliver-thin cell phone from his jeans pocket and called for backup. For some reason that made Faith's heart pound even harder. If this was a situation that Beck Tanner believed he couldn't handle alone, then it was *bad*.

She thought of Aubrey and was glad her little girl wasn't here to witness this act of vandalism, or whatever it was. Faith also thought of their future, how this would affect it. *If* it would affect it, she corrected. And then she thought of her brother. Was he the one out there in the darkness tossing those rocks? It was a possibility—a remote one—but Beck wouldn't believe it to be so remote.

Her brother, Darin, was Beck's number one murder suspect. She'd read every report she could get her hands on and every newspaper article written about the murders.

She didn't suspect Darin, though. She figured her sister's ex, Nolan Wheeler, was behind those killings. Nolan had a multipage arrest record, and her sister had even taken out a temporary restraining order against him.

For all the good it'd done.

Even with that restraining order, her sister, Sherry, had been murdered near her apartment on the outskirts of Austin. Their mother's death had happened twenty-four hours later in the back parking lot of the seedy liquor store where she worked in a nearby town. The murder had occurred after business hours, within minutes of her mother locking up the shop and going to her car. And even though Faith wasn't close to either of them and hadn't been for years, she'd mourned their loss and the brutal way their lives had ended.

Still staying low, Beck leaned over and studied one

of the rocks. It was smooth, about the size and color of a baked potato, and Faith could see that it had something written on it.

"What does it say?" she asked when Beck didn't read it aloud.

His hesitation seemed to last for hours. "It says, 'Leave or I'll have to kill you, too.'"

Mercy. So it was a threat. Someone didn't want her moving back to town. She watched Beck pick up the second rock.

Beck cursed under his breath. "It's from your brother."

Faith shook her head. "How do you know?"

"Because it says, 'I love you, but I can't stop myself from killing you. Get out,'" Beck grumbled. "I don't know how many people you know who both love you and want you dead. Darin certainly fits the bill. Of course, maybe he just wrote the message and had Wheeler toss it in here for him."

She swallowed hard, and the lump in her throat caused her to ache. God. This couldn't be happening.

Faith forced herself to think this through. Instead of Nolan being Darin's accomplice, Nolan himself could be doing this to set up her brother. Still, that didn't make it less of a threat.

"Listen for anyone coming in through the back door," Beck instructed.

There went her breath again. If Beck had been able to break in, then a determined killer or vandal would have no trouble doing the same.

Because she had to do something other than cower and wait for the worst, Faith crawled to the end of the bed where she'd placed her suitcase. After a few run-ins with Nolan Wheeler, she'd bought a handgun. But she didn't have it with her. However, she did have pepper spray.

She retrieved the slender can from her suitcase and inched out a little so she could see what was going on. Beck was still crouched at the window, and he had his weapon ready and aimed into the darkness.

With that part of the house covered, she shifted her attention to the bedroom door. From her angle, she could see the kitchen, and if the rock thrower took advantage of that broken lock, he'd have to come through the kitchen to get to them. Thankfully, the moonlight piercing through the back windows allowed her to see that the room was empty.

"You don't listen very well," Beck snarled. "I told you to stay put."

She ignored his bark. Faith wouldn't make herself an open target, but she wanted to be in a position to defend herself.

"Do you see anyone out there?" she barked back.

She clamped her teeth over her bottom lip to stop the trembling. Not from fear. She was more angry than afraid. But with the gaping holes in the window, the winter wind was pushing its way through the room, and she was cold.

"No. But if I were a betting man, I'd say your brother's come back to eliminate his one and only remaining sibling—you."

"Maybe the person outside is after you?"

He glanced back at her. So brief. A split-second look. Yet, he conveyed a lot of hard skepticism with that glimpse.

"You're the sheriff," she reminded him. "You must

have made enemies. Besides, my mother and sister have been dead for over two months. If that's Darin or their real killer out there, why would he wait this long to come after me? It's common knowledge that I was living in Oklahoma City and practicing law there for the past few years. Why not just come after me there?"

"A killer doesn't always make sense."

True. But there were usually patterns. Her mother and sister's killer had attacked them when they were alone. He hadn't been bold or stupid enough to try to shoot them with a police officer nearby. Of course, maybe the killer didn't realize that the car out front belonged to Beck, since it was his personal vehicle and not a cruiser. Therefore he wouldn't have known that Beck was there. She certainly hadn't been aware of it when she had been in that shower. Talk about the ultimate shock when she'd seen him standing there.

Her, stark naked.

Him, combing those smoky blue eyes all over her body.

"Dreamy eyes," the girls in school had called him. Dreamy eyes to go with a dreamy body, that toast-brown hair and quarterback's build.

Faith hadn't been immune to Beck's sizzling hot looks, either. She'd looked. But the looking stopped after the night he'd given her a Breathalyzer test at the motel.

A lot of things had stopped that night.

And there was no going back to that place. Even if those dreamy looks still made her feel all warm and willing.

"I hope you're having second and third thoughts about bringing your daughter here," Beck commented. He still had his attention fastened to the front of the house.

She was. But what was the alternative? If this was

Darin or her sister's slimy ex, then where could she take Aubrey so she'd be safe?

Nowhere.

That was a sobering and frightening thought.

But Beck was right about one thing. She needed to rethink this. Not the job. She wasn't going to run away from the job. However, she could do something about making this a safe place for Aubrey. And the first thing she'd do was to catch the person who'd thrown those rocks through her window.

She could start by having the handwriting analyzed. Footprints, too. Heck, she wanted to question the taxi driver to see if he'd told anyone that he'd dropped her off at the house. Someone had certainly learned quickly enough that she was t███████████████

"I think the guy's gotten away by now," Faith let Beck know.

He didn't answer because his phone rang. Beck glanced at the screen and answered with a terse, "Where are you right now?" He paused, no doubt waiting for the answer. "Someone in front of the house threw rocks through the window. Check the area and let me know what you find."

Good. It was backup. If Nolan Wheeler or whoever was still out there, then maybe he'd be caught. Maybe this would all be over within the next few minutes. Then she could deal with this adrenaline roaring through her veins and get on with her life.

Faith waited there with her fingers clutched so tightly around the pepper spray that her hand began to cramp. The minutes crawled by, and they were punctuated by silence and the occasional surly glance from Beck.

He still hated her.

She could see it in his face. He still blamed her for that night with his brother. Part of her wanted to shout the truth of what'd happened, but he wouldn't believe her. Her own mother hadn't. And over the years she'd convinced herself that it didn't matter. That incident had given her a chip on her shoulder, and she'd used that chip and her anger to succeed. Coming back here, getting the job as the assistant district attorney, that was her proof that she'd risen above the albatross of her family's DNA.

"It's me," someone called out, causing her heart to race again.

But Beck obviously wasn't alarmed. He got to his feet and watched the man approach the window.

"I see some tracks," the man announced. "But if anybody's still out here, then he's freezing his butt off and probably hiding in the bushes across the road."

The man poked his face against the hole in the window, and she got a good look at him. It was Corey Winston. He'd been a year behind her in high school and somewhat of a smart mouth. These days, he was Beck's deputy. She'd learned that during her job interview with the district attorney.

Corey's insolent gaze met hers. "Faith Matthews." He used a similar tone to the one Beck had used when he first saw her. "What are you doing back in LaMesa Springs?"

"She's going to be the new assistant district attorney," Beck provided.

That earned her a raised eyebrow from Corey. "Now I've heard everything. You, the ADA? Well, you're not off to a good start. You breeze into town, your first night back, and you're already stirring up trouble, huh?"

The *huh* was probably added to make it sound a little less insulting. But it only riled her more. She'd let jerks like Corey, and Beck, run her out of town ten years earlier, but they wouldn't succeed this time.

She would continue full speed ahead, and if that included arresting her own brother, she'd do it and carry out her lawful duties. Of course, because of a personal conflict, the DA himself would have to prosecute the case, but she would fully cooperate. It helped that she had been estranged from her mother and sister. That wouldn't help with Darin. It would hurt. But duty had to come first here.

Beck reholstered his gun and glanced around at the glass on the floor. "Secure the scene," he told Corey. "Cast at least one of the footprints, and I'll send it to the lab in Austin. We might get lucky."

"You think it's worth it?" Corey challenged. But his defiance went down a notch when Beck stared at him. "It just seems like a lot of trouble to go through considering this was probably done by those Kendrick kids. You know those boys have too much time on their hands and nobody at home to see what they're up to."

"There's a killer on the loose," Beck reminded him.

That reminder, however, didn't stop Corey from scowling at Faith before he turned from the window and got to work. He grumbled something indistinguishable under his breath.

Beck looked at her then. He wasn't exactly sporting a scowl like Corey, but it was close. "I need you to come with me to my office so I can take a statement."

It was standard operating procedure. Something that needed to be done, just in case it had been the killer outside that window. Besides, she didn't want to be alone in the house. Not tonight. Maybe not ever. She would truly have to rethink making this place a home for Aubrey.

Faith grabbed her purse and got ready to go.

"I don't believe it was the Kendrick kids who threw those rocks," Beck said to her.

That stopped her in her tracks. "You think it was Darin?" she challenged.

"If not Darin, then let's play around with your assumption, that your mom and sister's killer was Sherry's ex, Nolan Wheeler." He hitched his thumb toward the broken glass. "If Nolan was outside that window tonight, he could want to do you harm."

She shook her head. "Stating the obvious here, but if that's true, why wait until now?"

"Because you were here, alone. Or so he thought. You were an easy target."

Faith zoomed in on the obvious flaw in his theory. "And his motive for wanting me dead?"

"Maybe Nolan thinks you'll use your new job to come after him for the two murders. He might even think that's why you've come back."

She opened her mouth to deny it, but she couldn't. In fact, that's exactly the way Nolan would think.

Other than in confidence to her boss, Faith hadn't announced to anyone in Oklahoma that she had accepted the job in LaMesa Springs.

Not until this morning.

This morning, she'd also called LaMesa Springs'

DA to tell him she would be arriving. She had arranged for renovations and a security system for the house. She'd made lots and lots of calls, and anyone could have found out her plans.

Anyone, including Nolan.

"Where's your daughter right now?" Beck asked. His tone alone would have alarmed her, but there was more than a sense of urgency in his expression.

"Aubrey's still in Oklahoma with her nanny. Why?"

"Because I was just trying to put myself in Nolan's place. If he came here to scare you off and it didn't work, then what will he do next?" His stare was a warning. "If he's got an accomplice or if it was his accomplice who just tossed those rocks, that means one of them could be here in LaMesa Springs and the other could be in Oklahoma."

Her heart dropped to her knees.

Beck took a step toward her. "Either Darin or Nolan might try to use your daughter to get to you."

"Oh, God."

Faith grabbed her phone from her purse and prayed that it wasn't too late to keep Aubrey safe.

Chapter Three

By Beck's calculation, Faith had been pacing in his office for three hours while she waited for her daughter to arrive. Even when she'd been on the phone, which was a lot, or while giving her official statement to him, she still paced. And while she did that, she continued to check her delicate silver watch.

The minutes were probably dragging by for her.

They certainly were for him.

Beck tried to keep himself occupied with routine paperwork and notes on his current cases. Normally he liked keeping busy. But this wasn't a normal night.

Faith Matthews was in his office, mere yards away, and sooner or later he was going to have to break the news to his family that she'd returned. Since it was going on midnight, Beck had opted for later, but he knew, with the gossip mill always in full swing, that if he didn't tell his father, brother and sister-in-law by morning—early morning, at that—then they'd find out from some other source.

As if she knew what he was thinking, Faith tossed him a glance from over her shoulder.

Despite the vigor of her pacing, she was exhausted. Her eyes were sleep-starved, and her face was pale and tight with tension. On some level he understood that tension.

Her daughter might be in danger, and she was waiting for the little girl to arrive with her nanny and the Texas Ranger escort from the Austin airport. Beck hadn't had the opportunity to be around many babies, but he figured the parental bond was strong, and the uncertainty was driving Faith crazy.

"You're staring at me," she grumbled.

Yeah. He was.

Beck glanced back at his desk, but the glance didn't take. For some stupid reason, his attention went straight back to Faith. To her tired expression. Her tight muscles. The still damp hair that she hadn't had a chance to dry after her shower.

Noticing her hair immediately made him uncomfortable. But then so did Faith. Dealing with a scrawny eighteen-year-old was one thing, but Faith was miles away from being that girl. She was poised and polished, even now despite the damp hair. A woman in every sense of the word.

Hell. That made him uncomfortable, too.

"I figure you're having second thoughts about accepting the ADA job," he grumbled, hoping conversation would help. It was a fishing expedition since she'd kept her thoughts to herself the entire time she had been waiting for her daughter and the nanny to arrive.

"You wish," she tossed at him. "The DA and the city council want me here, and I have to just keep telling myself that not everyone in town hates me like the Tanners."

Okay. No second thoughts. Well, not any that she

would likely voice to him. She had dug in her heels, unlike ten years ago when she'd left town running. Part of him, the part he didn't want to acknowledge, admired her for not wavering in her plans. She certainly hadn't shown much backbone or integrity ten years ago.

She flipped open her cell phone again and pressed redial. Beck didn't have to ask who she was calling. He knew it was the nanny. Faith had called the woman at least every half hour.

"How much longer?" Faith asked the moment the woman apparently answered. The response made her relax a bit, and she seemed to breathe easier when she added, "See you then."

"Good news?" he asked when she didn't share.

"They'll be here in about fifteen minutes." She raked her hair away from her face. "I should have just gone to the airport to meet them."

"The Texas Rangers didn't want you to do that," Beck reminded her, though he was certain she already knew that. The Ranger lieutenant and her new boss, the DA, had ordered her to stay put at the sheriff's office.

The order was warranted. It was simply too big of a risk for her to go gallivanting all over central Texas when there might be a killer on her trail.

"So what's the plan when your daughter arrives?" Beck asked.

"Since the Texas Rangers said they'll be providing security, we'll check in to the hotel on Main Street." She didn't hesitate, which meant, in addition to the calls and pacing, she'd obviously given it plenty of thought. "Then tomorrow morning, I can start putting some security measures in place."

He'd overheard her conversations with the Rangers about playing bodyguard and the other conversation about those measures. She was having a high-tech security system installed in her childhood home. In a whispered voice, she'd asked the price, which told Beck that she didn't have an unlimited budget. No surprise there. Faith had come from poor trash, and it'd no doubt taken her a while to climb out of that. She probably didn't have money to burn.

She made a soft sound that pulled his attention back to her. It was a faint groan. Correction, a moan. And for the first time since he'd seen her in the shower, there was a crack in that cool composure.

"I have to know if you're a real sheriff," she said, her voice trembling. "I have to know if it comes down to it that you'll protect my daughter."

Because the vulnerable voice had distracted him, it took him a second to realize she'd just insulted the hell out of him.

Beck stood and met her eye-to-eye. "This badge isn't decoration, Faith," he said, and he tapped the silver star clipped to his belt.

She just stared at him, apparently not convinced. "I want you to swear that you'll protect Aubrey."

Riled now, Beck walked closer. Actually, too close. No longer just eye-to-eye, they were practically toe-to-toe. "I. Swear. I'll. Protect. Aubrey." He'd meant for his tone to be dangerous. A warning for her to back down.

She didn't. "Good."

Faith actually sounded relieved, which riled him even more. Hell's bells. What kind of man did she think he was if he wouldn't do his job and protect a child?

Or Faith, for that matter?

And why did it suddenly feel as if he wanted to protect her?

Oh, yeah. He remembered. She was attractive, and mixed with all that sudden vulnerability, he was starting to feel, well, protective.

Among other things.

"Thank you," she added.

It was so sincere, he could feel it.

So were the tears that shimmered in her eyes. Sincere tears that she quickly blinked back. "For the record, I'm a good lawyer. And I'll be a good ADA." Now she dodged his gaze. "I have to succeed at this. For Aubrey. I want her to be proud of me, and I want to be proud of myself. I'll convince the people of this town that I'm not that same girl who tried to run away from her past."

She turned and waved him off, as if she didn't want him to respond to that. Good thing. Because Beck had no idea what to say. He preferred the angry woman who'd barked at him in the shower. He preferred the Faith that'd turned tail and run ten years ago.

This woman in front of him was going to be trouble.

His brother had once obviously been attracted to her. Beck could see why. Those eyes. That hair.

That mouth.

His body started to build a stupid fantasy about Faith's mouth when thankfully there was a rap at his door. Judging from Corey's raised eyebrow, he hadn't missed the way Beck had been looking at Faith.

"What?" Beck challenged.

Corey screwed up his mouth a moment to indicate

his displeasure. "I took a plaster of one of the footprints like you said. It's about a size ten. That's a little big for one of the Kendrick kids."

Beck had never believed this was a prank. Heck, he wasn't even sure it was a scare tactic. Those rocks had been meant to send Faith running, and Beck didn't think the killer was finished.

"I'll send the plaster and the two rocks to the Rangers lab in Austin tomorrow morning." With that, Corey walked away.

Realizing that he needed to put some distance between him and Faith, Beck took a couple of steps away from her.

"My brother wears a size-ten shoe," Faith provided.

He stopped moving away and stared at her again. "So does your sister's ex, Nolan."

She blinked, apparently surprised he would know that particular detail.

"Even though the murders didn't happen here in my jurisdiction, I've been studying his case file," Beck explained.

Another blink. "I hope that means you're close to figuring out who killed my mother and sister."

"I've got it narrowed down just like you do." He shrugged. "You think it's Nolan. I think it's your brother, Darin, working with Nolan. The only other person I need to rule out is your daughter's father."

She folded her arms over her chest. Looked away. "He's not in the picture."

"So you said in your statement to the Rangers, but I have to be sure that he's not the one who put those rocks through the window."

"I'm sure he has no part in this," she snapped. "And that brings us back to Darin and Nolan. Darin really doesn't have a motive to come after me—"

"But he does," Beck interrupted. "It could be the house and the rest of what your mother owned."

Faith shook her head. "My mother disowned Darin four years ago. He can't inherit anything."

"Does your brother know that?"

"Darin knows." There was a lot emotion and old baggage that came with the admission. The disinheritance had probably sparked a memorable family blowup. Beck would take her word for it that Darin had known he couldn't benefit financially from the murders.

"That leaves Nolan," Beck continued. "While you were on the phone, I did some checking. Your sister, Sherry, lived with Nolan for years, long enough for them to have a common-law marriage. And even though they hadn't cohabited in the eighteen months prior to her death, they never divorced. That means he'd legally be your mother's next of kin…if you and your daughter were out of the way."

Her eyes widened, and her arms uncrossed and dropped to her sides. "You think Nolan would kill me to inherit that rundown house?"

"Not just the house. It comes with three acres of land and any other assets your mother left. She only specified in her will that her belongings would go to her next of kin, with the exclusion of Darin."

"The land, the house and the furniture are worth a hundred thousand, tops," she pointed out.

"People have killed for a lot less. That's why I alerted every law-enforcement agency to pick up Nolan the moment he's spotted. I want him in custody so I can question him."

That caused her to chew on her bottom lip, and Beck wondered if she was ready to change her mind about staying in town. "I have to draw up my will ASAP. I can write it so that Nolan can't inherit a penny. And then I need to let him know that. That'll stop any attempts to kill me."

Maybe.

Unless there was a different reason for the murders.

The front door opened, and just like that, Faith raced out of his office and into the reception area. Corey was at the desk, by the dispatch phone, and Faith practically flew right past him to get to the three people who'd just stepped inside.

A Texas Ranger and a sixtysomething-year-old Hispanic woman carrying a baby in pink corduroy overalls and a long-sleeved lacy white shirt. Aubrey.

Faith pulled the little girl into her arms and gave her a tight hug. Aubrey giggled and bounced, the movement causing her mop of brunette hair to bounce as well.

Beck hadn't really known what to expect when it came to Faith's daughter, but he'd at least thought the child would be sleeping at this time of night. She wasn't. She was alert, smiling, and her brown eyes were the happiest eyes he'd ever seen.

"Sgt. Egan Caldwell," the Ranger introduced himself first to Beck and then to Faith.

"Sheriff Beck Tanner."

"Marita Dodd," the nanny supplied. Unlike the little girl, this woman's dark eyes showed stress, concern and even some fear. She was petite, barely five feet tall, and a hundred pounds, tops, but even with her demure size and sugar-white hair, she had an air of authority about her. "Aubrey's obviously got her second wind. Unlike the rest of us."

"Ms. Matthews," the Ranger said to Faith. "Could I have word with you?" He didn't add the word *alone,* but his tone certainly implied it.

"Of course." After another kiss on the cheek, Faith passed the child back to the nanny, and she and Sgt. Caldwell went to the other side of the reception area to have a whispered conversation.

Beck watched Faith's expression to see if she was about to get bad news, but if her brother had been caught or was dead, then why hadn't the Ranger told Beck as well? After all, Beck was assisting with the case.

"I really have to go the ladies' room," Marita Dodd said. That brought Beck's attention back to her.

"Down the hall, last room on the right," Beck instructed.

But Marita didn't go. She glanced at Aubrey, then at Faith, and finally thrust Aubrey in his direction. "Would you mind holding her a minute?"

Beck was sure his mouth dropped open. But if Marita noticed his stunned response, she didn't react. Aubrey reacted though. The little girl went right to him. Straight into his arms.

And then she did something else that stunned Beck.

Aubrey grinned and planted a warm, sloppy kiss on his cheek.

That rendered him speechless and cut his breath. Man. That baby kiss and giggle packed a punch. In that flash of a moment, he got it. He understood the whole parent thing and why men wanted to be fathers.

He got it, and he tried to push it aside.

This was the last child on earth to whom he should have an emotional response.

Aubrey babbled something he didn't understand and cocked her head to the side as if waiting for him to reply. She kept those doe eyes on him.

"I don't know," Beck finally answered.

That caused her to smile again, and she aimed her tiny fingers at the Ranger vehicle parked just outside the window. "Tar," she said as if that explained everything.

"Car?" Beck questioned, not sure what he was supposed to say.

"Tar," she repeated. Then added, "Bye-bye."

Another smile. Another kiss that left his cheek wet and smelling like baby's breath. And she wound her plump arms around his neck. The child obviously wasn't aware that he was a stranger at odds with her mother.

Beck was having a hard time remembering that, too.

Well, he was until he heard Faith storming his way. Her footsteps slapped against the hardwood floor. "Aubrey," she said, taking the child from his arms.

While Beck understood Faith's displeasure at having him hold her baby, Aubrey showed some displeasure, too.

"No, no, no," Aubrey protested and reached for Beck again. She waggled her fingers at him, a gesture that Beck thought might mean "come here."

"This won't take but another minute," the Ranger interjected. He obviously wasn't finished talking to Faith.

Faith huffed. Aubrey continued to struggle to get back to Beck, and she clamped her small but persistent hand onto the front of his shirt. They were still in the middle of the little battle when the phone rang. The deputy, Corey, answered it, but immediately passed the phone to Beck.

"It's your brother," Corey announced.

Great. This was not a conversation Beck wanted to have tonight.

Faith practically snapped to attention, and despite Aubrey's protest, she carried the child back across the room and resumed her conversation with the Ranger.

"Pete," Beck greeted his brother. "What can I do for you?"

"You can tell me if what I heard is true," Pete stated. "Is Faith Matthews back in town?"

Because he was going to need it, Beck took a deep breath. "She's here."

With that, Faith angled her eyes in his direction. Hearing his brother's voice and seeing Faith was a much-needed reminder of the past.

"Why did she come back?" Pete didn't ask in anger. There was more dread in his voice than anything else.

"She's the new assistant district attorney. I didn't tell you sooner because I didn't think she was coming until next month. It wasn't my decision to hire her. It was the DA's."

"It's for sure? The DA actually hired her?"

"Yeah. It's for sure."

"Then I'll have a chat with him," Pete insisted.

Beck had already had that chat, and the DA wouldn't budge. Pete wouldn't, either. His brother would talk and argue with the DA, too, but in the end the results would be the same—Faith would still be the new ADA.

"In the meantime, you do whatever it takes to get

Faith Matthews away from here," Pete continued. "I don't want her upsetting Nicole."

Nicole, Pete's wife of nearly a dozen years. This would definitely upset her. Nicole was what his grandmother would have called high-strung. An argument would give Nicole a migraine. A fender bender would send her running to her therapist over in Austin.

This would devastate her.

"There's a lot to be resolved," Beck told his brother.

"What does that mean?"

Heck, he was just going to say it even though he knew Faith would overhear it. "It means Faith might change her mind about staying."

Yeah, that earned him a glare from her. He hadn't expected anything less. But then she glared at whatever the Ranger said, too. Her glare was followed by a look of extreme shock. Wide eyes. Drained color from her cheeks. Her mouth trembled, and he wasn't thinking this was a fear reaction. More like anger.

"I'll call you back in the morning," Beck continued with his brother. "In the meantime, get some sleep."

"Right." With that final remark, Pete hung up.

Beck hung up, too, and braced himself for the next round of battle he was about to have with Faith. But when he saw her expression, he rethought that battle. No more shock. Something had taken the fight right out of her.

Sgt. Caldwell stopped talking to Faith and made his way back to Beck. "I got a call on the drive over here. The crime lab reviewed the surveillance disk you sent us. The one from Doolittle's convenience store. They were able to positively identify your suspect."

Beck let that sink in a moment. Across the room

while holding a babbling happy baby, Faith was obviously doing the same.

"So Darin Matthews was in LaMesa Springs?" Beck clarified.

The Ranger nodded. "We can also place him just five miles from here. About four hours ago, he filled up at a gas station on I-35."

Everything inside Beck went still. "Any reason he wasn't arrested?"

"The clerk thought Darin looked familiar, but he didn't make the connection with the wanted pictures in the newspaper until Darin had already driven away. But the store had auto security feeds to the company that monitors them, and that means we had fast access to the surveillance video. That's how we were able to make such a quick ID."

So Darin had come back, and he might have thrown those rocks with the threatening messages through Faith's window. "You didn't see Nolan Wheeler on either surveillance feed?" Beck asked.

"No. But that doesn't mean he wasn't there. He could have been out of camera range."

Beck snared Faith's gaze. "Does this mean you're leaving?"

She didn't jump to defend herself. Her mouth tightened, she kissed the top of Aubrey's head and looked at Sgt. Caldwell. "They want me to be bait."

Beck repeated that, certain he'd misunderstood. "Bait?"

"An enticement," the Ranger clarified. "We believe there's only one person who can get Darin Matthews to surrender peacefully, and that's his sister."

True. But Beck could see the Texas-size holes in this

so-called plan. "She's got a kid. Being bait isn't safe for either of them."

Sgt. Caldwell nodded. "We're going to minimize the risks."

"How?" Beck demanded.

"By making her brother think he can get to her. No matter where she goes, she'll be in danger. Her baby, too. My lieutenant thinks it's best if we make a stand. Here. Where we know Darin is."

Beck cursed under his breath, but he bit off the rest of the profanity when he realized Aubrey was smiling at him. "So what's the plan to keep her and that little girl safe?"

"The lieutenant wants to set up a trap to lure Darin back. We'll alert all the businesses in town and the surrounding area to be on the lookout for Matthews. Meanwhile, we'll put security measures in place for Ms. Matthews's house while she's at the hotel tonight."

"Her house?" Beck questioned. He didn't like anything about this plan. "You honestly expect her to stay there after what happened tonight? Someone threw rocks through her window."

Another nod. "She won't actually be staying at the house. She'll just make an appearance of sorts, but we'll tell everyone in town that's where she'll be staying."

Beck felt a little relief. "So Faith and her daughter will be going to a safe house?"

The sergeant glanced back at Faith, and it was she who continued. "Not exactly. I can't live in a safe house for the rest of my life, and Darin won't be able to find me if I'm hidden away. So the Rangers want to set up a secure place for Aubrey and the nanny. I'll be there, too, while making appearances at my house to coax out Darin. Obviously, we can't have Aubrey in harm's way, but my brother would know something was up if Aubrey's in one location and I'm in another. So we have to make it look as if she's with me even though she'll be far from danger." She paused, moistened her lips. "I'm hoping it won't take long for my brother to show, especially since he's already in the area."

So she agreed with this plan. But for someone in agreement, she certainly didn't seem pleased about it.

"If it weren't for Aubrey, I would have never gone along with this," she stated.

Confused, Beck shook his head. "Excuse me?"

"She means the protective custody issue," Sgt. Caldwell explained.

Beck sure didn't like the sound of this. "What about it? She doesn't want to be in the Rangers' protective custody?"

"No." Faith hesitated after her terse answer. "I don't want Aubrey to be in yours."

"Mine?" Beck felt as if someone had slugged him.

"Yours," Caldwell verified. "The Rangers will continue to provide you assistance on the case, but with a possible suspect in your jurisdiction, this is now your investigation, Sheriff Tanner."

"What are you saying exactly?"

The Ranger looked him straight in the eyes. "I'm saying we'll need your help. We can't risk it being leaked that Ms. Matthews really isn't staying at her place. And we can't keep her real whereabouts concealed if she's in the hotel for any length of time. There are too many employees there who could let it slip."

Beck's hands went on his hips. "So where do you propose her daughter and she go?"

"First, to the hotel to give us time to set up some security. Then, when everything's in place, they can go to your house. Her daughter will be in your protective custody." The Ranger didn't even hesitate.

It took Beck a moment to get his jaw unclenched so he could speak. "Let me get this straight. I'll become a bodyguard and babysitter in my own home?"

Sgt. Caldwell gave a crisp nod. "Protecting the child will be your primary task." The Ranger glanced at Faith again. Frowned. Then turned back to Beck. "Ms. Matthews has refused to be in your protective custody."

Her left eyebrow lifted a fraction when Beck's attention landed on her. "Yet you'd trust me with your daughter?" Beck asked.

"This wasn't her idea," Sgt. Caldwell interjected, though Faith had already opened her mouth to answer. "I had to convince her that this was the fastest and most efficient way to keep the child safe. And as for her not being in your protective custody, well, you can call it what you want, but it won't change what you have to do."

Beck stared at the Ranger. "And what exactly do I have to do?"

Sgt. Caldwell stared back. "Once we have this plan in place, Faith and her daughter's safety will be *your* responsibility."

Chapter Four

This was not the homecoming Faith had planned.

From the window of the third-floor "VIP suite" of the Bluebonnet Hotel, she stared down at the town's equivalent of morning rush hour. Cars trickled along the two-lane Main Street flanked with refurbished antique streetlights. The sidewalks were busy but not exactly bustling as people walked past the rows of quaint shops and businesses. Many of the townsfolk stopped to say "Good morning."

There were lots of smiles.

She wanted to be part of what was going on below. She wanted to dive right into her new life. But instead she was stuck inside the hotel, waiting for "orders" from Beck and the Texas Rangers, while one of Beck's deputies guarded the door to make sure no one got in.

The three-room suite was a nice enough place with its soothing Southwest decor. Her and Aubrey's room was small but tastefully decorated with cool aqua walls and muted coral bedding. Marita's room was similar, just slightly smaller, and the shared sitting room had a functional, golden-pine desk and a Saltillo tile floor.

It reminded Faith of a gilded cage.

Of course, anything less than getting on with her new life would feel that way.

She forced herself to finish the now cold coffee that room service had delivered an hour earlier. She already had a pounding headache, and without the caffeine, it would only get worse. She had to be able to think clearly today.

What she really needed was a new plan.

Or a serious modification of the present one.

Aubrey was now in Beck's protective custody and he was responsible for her safety. Right. What was wrong with this picture?

She went back to the desk, sank down onto the chair and glanced at the notes she'd made earlier. It was her list of possible courses of action. Unfortunately, the list was short.

Option one: she could immediately leave LaMesa Springs, and go into hiding. But that would be no life for Aubrey. Besides, she had to work. She couldn't live off her savings for more than six months at most.

Faith crossed off option one.

Option two: she could arrange for a private bodyguard. Again, that would eat into her savings, but it was a short-term solution that she would definitely consider. Plus, she knew someone in the business, and while things hadn't worked out personally between them, she hoped he could give her a good deal.

And then there was option three, and it would have to be paired with option two: try to speed up her brother's and Nolan's captures. The only problem was that other than making herself an even more obvious target, she wasn't sure how to do that. Maybe she could make an appeal on the local TV or radio stations? Or maybe she could just step foot inside her house a few times.

She already felt like a target anyway.

Frustrated, she set her coffee cup aside and grabbed a pen, hoping to add to the meager list. She sat, pen poised but unmoving over the paper, and she waited for inspiration to strike. It didn't.

The bedroom door opened, and Marita came out. Behind her toddled Aubrey, dressed in a pink eyelet lace dress, white leggings and black baby saddle oxfords. Just the sight of her instantly lightened Faith's mood.

"'i," Aubrey greeted her. It was her latest attempt at "hi" and she added a wave to it.

"Hi, yourself." Faith scooped her up in her arms and kissed her on the cheek.

"She ate every bite of her oatmeal," Marita reported. "And getting to bed so late doesn't seem to have bothered her." Marita patted her hand over a big yawn. "Wish I could say the same for my old bones."

"Yes. I'm sorry about that."

"Not your fault." Marita went to the window and looked out. "You warned me that some folks in this town wouldn't open their arms to you." She paused. "Guess Sheriff Tanner is one of those folks."

It wasn't a question, but Faith knew the woman wanted and deserved answers. After all, Marita had essentially been part of her family since Faith had hired her fifteen months ago as Aubrey's nanny. Faith had gotten Marita through an employment agency, but their short history together didn't diminish her feelings and respect for Marita.

"I left town ten years ago because of a scandal," Faith said, hoping she could get this out without emotion straining her voice. "Beck saw me coming out of a motel with his brother, Pete. His married brother. Word quickly got around, and his brother's wife attempted suicide because she was so distraught. Beck blames me for that."

Marita turned from the window, folded her arms over her chest and stared at Faith. "You *were* with the sheriff's married brother?"

Aubrey started to fuss when she spotted the stuffed armadillo on the settee, and Faith eased her to the floor so she could go after it.

"I was with him at the hotel." But Faith shook her head. She wasn't explaining this to Beck, who would challenge her every word. Marita would believe her. "But I didn't have sex with him. It didn't help that I couldn't tell the whole truth." She lowered her voice so that Aubrey wouldn't hear, even though she was much too young to understand. "It also didn't help that there were used condoms in the motel room. And when Beck found us, Pete was groping at me."

Marita made a sound of displeasure. "Beck was an idiot not to see what was really going on. You're not the sort to go after a married man." She glanced at the papers on the desk and frowned again. "Is that what I think it is?" Marita pointed to the document header, Last Will and Testament.

"I wrote it this morning." She noted the shocked look on Marita's face. "No, I'm not planning to die anytime soon. I just need to let someone know that he won't inherit anything in the event of my demise."

Faith didn't have time to explain that further because her cell phone rang. Since she was expecting several important calls, she answered it right away.

"Zack Henley," the caller identified himself. "I'm the driver who took you from the airport to LaMesa Springs last night. You left a message with my boss saying to call you, that it was important."

"It is. I need to know if you told anyone that you'd taken me to my house."

"Told anyone?" he repeated. He sounded not only surprised but cautious.

Faith rephrased it. "Is it possible that someone in LaMesa Springs learned that you had driven me to my house?"

He stayed quiet a moment. "I might have mentioned it to the guy at the convenience store."

That grabbed her attention. "Which guy and which convenience store?"

"Doolittle's, I think is the name of it."

The same store where her brother had been sighted. "And who did you tell about me?"

"I didn't tell, exactly. I mean, I didn't go in the place to blab about you, but the guy asked me what a cab driver was doing in LaMesa Springs, and I told him I'd dropped someone off on County Line Road. He asked who, and I told him. I knew your name because you paid with your credit card, and you didn't say anything about keeping it a secret."

No. She hadn't, but she also hadn't expected to be threatened with those tossed rocks. Or with the possibility that her brother had been the one to do the threatening. "Describe the person you spoke to."

"What's this all about?" he asked.

"Just describe him please." Faith used her courtroom voice, hoping it would save time.

"I don't remember how he looked, but he was the clerk behind the counter. A young kid. Maybe nineteen or twenty. Oh, yeah, and he had a snake tattoo on his neck."

She released the breath she didn't even know she'd been holding and jotted down the description. That wasn't a description of her brother. But it didn't mean this clerk hadn't said something to anyone else. Or her brother could have even been there, listening.

"Thank you," she told the cab driver.

Faith hung up and grabbed the Yellow Pages so she could find the number of the convenience store. She had to talk to that clerk. But before she could even locate the number, there was a knock at the door. Faith reached for her pepper spray, only to remind herself that there was a deputy outside and that a killer probably wouldn't knock first.

"It's me, Beck," the visitor called out.

Faith groaned, unlocked the door and opened it. It was Beck all right. Wearing jeans, a blue button-up and a walnut-colored, leather rodeo jacket. The jacket wasn't a fashion statement, though on him it could have been. It was as well-worn as his jeans and cowboy boots.

"My deputy needed a break," Beck explained. He didn't move closer until Aubrey came walking his way.

"'i," Aubrey said, grinning from ear to ear. It was

adorable. But in Faith's opinion that cuteness was aimed at the wrong person.

Beck, however, obviously wasn't able to resist that grin either because he smiled and stepped around Faith to come inside the suite.

"Is she ever in a bad mood?" he asked, keeping his focus on Aubrey.

"Wait 'til nap time," Marita volunteered. Unlike Aubrey's cheerfulness, Marita's voice had an unfriendly edge to it.

When Aubrey began to babble and show Beck the armadillo, he knelt down so that he'd be at her eye level. "That's a great-looking toy you got there."

"Dee-o," Aubrey explained, giving him her best attempt to say "armadillo." She put the toy right in Beck's face and didn't pull it back until he'd kissed it.

Aubrey giggled and threw her arms around Beck's neck as if she'd known him her entire life. The hug was brief, mere seconds, before she pulled back and pointed to the silver badge he had clipped to his belt.

"See?" Aubrey said. "Wanta see."

And much to Faith's surprise, Beck unclipped it and handed it to her so she could "see."

Frustrated with the friendly exchange, Faith shut the door with more force than necessary. Beck seemed to become aware of the awkward situation, and he stood.

"We need to talk," he told her, suddenly sounding very sherifflike.

That was obviously Marita's cue to give them some privacy, so she came across the room and picked up Aubrey. However, she stopped and looked at Beck.

"Maybe this time you'll be willing to see the truth," she snarled. She took the badge from Aubrey and handed it back to him.

"What does that mean?" Beck asked, volleying confused glances between Faith and Marita.

"Nothing," Faith said at the same time that Marita said, "She wasn't with your brother that night. Faith's not like that."

And with that declaration which would be hard to explain, Marita started walking. Aubrey waved and said, "Bye-bye," before the two disappeared into the bedroom.

"Don't ask," Faith warned him.

"Why not?"

"Because you won't believe me."

He lifted his shoulder. "What's not to believe? Didn't you tell me the truth ten years ago?"

"I told you I hadn't slept with your brother. That's the truth."

"He said otherwise."

She huffed and wondered why she was still trying to explain this all this time later. "Pete was drunk, and he lied, maybe because he was too drunk to know the truth. Or maybe because he didn't want you to know what'd really happened. I didn't seduce him, and I didn't take him to that motel. The only thing I tried to do was get him out of there."

Faith stopped when she noted his stony expression. "You know what? Enough of this. I don't owe you anything." To give herself a moment to calm down, she went to the desk and glanced at the notes she'd taken earlier. "I need to question a clerk at Doolittle's convenience store. The cabbie who drove me home told this clerk that I was in town. I want to find out who else knew so I can figure out who threw those rocks."

Beck just stared at her.

Unnerved and still riled, Faith continued, "You said we had something to discuss, and I don't think you meant personal stuff."

"Why would Pete lie about being with you?" He walked closer, stopping just a few inches away.

Why didn't he just drop this? "Ask him. For now, stick to business, *Sheriff*."

"The personal stuff between us keeps interfering with the business."

He caught her arm when she started to move away. Faith looked down at his grip, but he didn't let go of her. He kept those gunmetal-blue eyes nailed to her, and though she hadn't thought it possible, he got even closer. So close that she could smell coffee and sugar on his breath.

Faith hiked up her chin and met his gaze. "Be careful," she warned. She meant her voice to sound sharp and stern. It didn't quite work out that way.

Because something changed.

With his hand on her, with him so close, old feelings began to tug at her. She'd once been hotly attracted to him. A lifetime ago. But those years suddenly seemed to melt away.

She was still attracted to him. And this time, she didn't think it was one-sided.

She was toast.

"The Rangers installed some security equipment at your house," Beck said. His voice wasn't strained. Nor angry. He sounded confused, and the subject didn't fit the slow simmer in the air.

"Good," she managed to answer. She tried to step away, but he held on. And she didn't fight him.

She was obviously losing her mind.

"The Rangers dressed like security technicians so anyone looking wouldn't realize the authorities had staked out the place." He paused. His jaw muscles stirred. "There. That's what I came to say. Now, let's finish this." He shook his head. Cursed. Shook his head again. And finally, he let go of her and took a step back. "This can't happen between us."

"You're right. It can't."

Neither of them looked relieved.

And neither of them looked as if they believed it.

That tug inside her pulled harder. So hard that she moved away and returned to the window. She needed a few deep breaths before she could continue. "I want a different plan than the one the Rangers came up with."

He paused. Nodded. Nodded again. "I'm listening."

It took her a moment to realize that was all he was going to say. "Well, I don't *have* a different plan," she admitted. "I just *want* one."

"Welcome to the club. I sat up most of the night trying to make a list of options."

She huffed and glanced at her list. "Since Sgt. Caldwell made it clear that the Rangers don't have the manpower to provide protection for Aubrey, Marita and me, I was thinking of hiring a private bodyguard from Harland Securities in San Antonio. A friend owns the company."

"Ross Harland," Beck provided. "I've heard of him. He's your friend?"

"We used to date." Though she had no idea why she'd just told him that, especially since things hadn't ended that well between Ross and her. Ross might not even want to talk to her, but that wouldn't stop her from trying. "I plan to call him this morning and ask if he can help."

"You mean so that Aubrey and you won't be in my protective custody?"

Suddenly, that made her feel a little petty, but she pushed the uncomfortable feeling aside. Who cared if he was insulted that she would look elsewhere for protection? "You said yourself the personal stuff keeps getting in the way."

His jaw muscles went to war. "I swore I'd protect Aubrey, and I will. I'll protect you and Marita, too. There's not enough personal stuff in the world to ever stop me from doing my job."

She believed him. More than she wanted to.

Their eyes met again, and something circled around them. A weird intimacy. Something forged with all the emotion of the bad blood. And this bizarre attraction that had reared its hot, ugly head.

Faith forced herself to look away. To move. She shook off the Beck Tanner hypnotic effect and reached for the phone to call Ross Harland. She pressed in the number to his office, hoping she remembered it correctly, and the call went straight to voice mail. It was still before normal duty hours.

"Ross, this is Faith," she said. "Please call me. I'm in LaMesa Springs, and my cell-phone service is spotty so if you can't get through, you can reach me at the Bluebonnet Hotel."

She read off the number of the hotel phone and her

room number and clicked the end call button just as the door to the suite burst open. The movement felt violent. And suddenly so did the air around them.

The woman who rushed into the room was Nicole Tanner.

Beck's sister-in-law. Pete's wife.

Faith hadn't seen the woman since the night of the motel incident, but Nicole hadn't changed much. Sleek and polished in her high-end, boot-length, black duster, London blue pants and matching top. Her shoulder-length honey-blond hair was perfect. Not a strand out of place. She looked like the ideal trophy wife.

Except for her eyes and face.

The tears had cut their way through her makeup, leaving mascara-tinged streaks on her porcelain cheeks.

"Nicole, what are you doing here?" Beck demanded.

"Taking care of a problem I should have taken care of years ago."

And with that, Nicole took her hand from her coat pocket and aimed a slick, silver handgun right at Faith.

Chapter Five

Hell.

That was Beck's first thought, right after the shock registered that his sister-in-law had obviously gone off the deep end. Now he had to diffuse this situation before it turned deadly.

Beck stepped in front of Faith. He didn't draw his weapon, though that was certainly standard procedure. Still, he couldn't do that to Nicole.

Not yet anyway.

He lifted his hands, palms out, in a backup gesture. "Nicole, put down that gun."

Nicole shook her head and swiped away her tears with her left hand. "I can't. I have to make her leave."

Beck could hear Faith's raw breath and knew she was afraid, but that didn't stop her from leaving the meager cover he'd provided her. She stepped out beside him.

"Get back," he warned her. "Nicole's not going to shoot me," he added. But he couldn't say the same about what she might do to Faith. He didn't want his sister-in-law to do anything stupid, and he didn't want bullets flying with Aubrey just in the next room.

He didn't want Faith hurt, either.

"I'm not leaving," Faith said, though her voice trembled slightly.

Man, it took courage to say that to an armed woman. Ill-timed courage.

"Let me handle this," he insisted. He then fastened his attention to Nicole. "You have to put the past behind you. Faith won't cause you any more trouble."

Nicole's hysteria increased. "She already has caused more trouble. Pete's been up all night talking about her. You know how he is when he gets upset. He shuts me out, and he drinks too much."

Beck did know. Like Nicole, Pete had a low tolerance for certain kinds of stress, and Faith's return would have set him off.

"Put down the gun, Nicole," Beck tried again. "And I'll talk to Pete."

"It won't do any good. I have to make Faith leave before it destroys my marriage."

"Your marriage?" Faith spat out. She obviously didn't intend to let him handle this in his own way. "You have a gun pointed at me, and my daughter is just one room away. You're endangering her as well as Beck, and yet your top priority is saving your marriage?"

Nicole blinked. She probably hadn't expected this. Faith hadn't stood up for herself ten years ago. "My marriage is in trouble because of you."

"No," Faith countered. "Your marriage is in trouble because of your cheating husband. Now, put down that gun, or I'll take it away from you myself."

Since this was quickly getting out of hand, Beck moved in front of Faith again. The new position wouldn't last long. Faith was already trying to maneuver herself to his side, but Beck didn't let that happen. It was a risk. He didn't want to push Nicole into doing something even more stupid.

"Give me the gun," he insisted. Beck didn't bolt toward her. He kept his footsteps even and unhurried. No sudden moves.

But Beck was just about a yard away when there was movement in the hall, just outside the suite. Nicole automatically glanced over her shoulder, and that split-second distraction was all Beck needed. He lunged at Nicole, snagged her by the wrist and latched on to the gun. The momentum sent them flying, and they landed against the two men who'd just arrived.

His brother, Pete, and his father, Roy.

"What the hell's going on here?" Pete shouted.

"I'm disarming your wife," Beck snarled. He took control of the gun and stepped back just in case anyone else decided to try to make a move toward Faith.

Pete shot Nicole a glance. Not of disapproval, either. The corner of his mouth actually lifted as if he were pleased that Nicole was in the process of committing a felony.

"I tried to get her to leave," Nicole volunteered.

"Well, this probably wasn't the way to go about it," her father-in-law interjected.

Good. Father was being reasonable about this. Beck needed another voice of support since Faith's and his didn't seem to be enough.

He checked Nicole's gun and discovered that it wasn't loaded. Beck showed Faith the empty chamber, causing her to groan again.

"I wanted to scare her into leaving," Nicole explained. "I didn't want to actually hurt her."

Well, that was something at least, but it didn't make this situation less volatile.

With emotion zinging through the air, his father and Pete stood side by side, and Pete glared at Faith. Roy only shook his head and mumbled something under his breath. The men were the same height, same weight, and with the exception of some threads of gray in Roy's hair, they looked enough alike to be brothers. That probably had something to do with the fact that Roy had only been eighteen years old when Pete was born.

Beck glanced back at Faith. He could tell she wasn't about to back down despite being outnumbered.

"Before this gets any worse, I want everyone to know that I'm not Beck right now. I'm *Sheriff* Tanner, and this is not going to get violent."

"Then she's leaving." That from Pete, and it was a threat aimed at Faith. Their father caught onto Pete's arm and stopped him from moving any closer.

"No. I'm not," Faith threatened right back. "Maybe it is time for an air clearing. For the truth. I'd planned to do it anyway, just not this soon."

That got everyone's attention, and the room fell silent.

Faith pointed to Pete. "I didn't sleep with you ten years ago. Or any other time."

There it was. The finale to the conversation that Faith and he were having shortly before Nicole arrived.

Beck pushed aside his own surprise and checked out the responses of the others. Nicole went still, the muscles in her arms going slack. The reactions of his father and brother, however, went in different directions.

Pete's face flushed with anger, and it seemed as if Father had been expecting her to say just that. He didn't look surprised at all.

"You were drunk," Faith reminded Pete. "All the years I've told myself that maybe you actually didn't lie about what happened, that you simply couldn't remember what you'd done, but now I'm not so sure."

"I didn't lie." Pete's voice was low and tight. Dangerous.

Faith walked closer. "Well, it wasn't me in that motel room with you. It was my sister, Sherry."

"Sherry," Beck mumbled. Since Sherry had been the town's wild child, he didn't have any trouble believing that, but apparently two members of his family did: Pete and Nicole. His father was still just standing there as if all of this was old news.

And maybe it was to him.

Had his father known the truth this whole time?

Nicole shook her head. "If that's true, why didn't you say so sooner? No one put a gag on you when you were outside the motel."

All attention turned back to Faith.

She pulled in a long breath. "I didn't say anything because Sherry's boyfriend, Nolan, would have killed her if he'd found out she cheated on him with your husband or with any other man, for that matter."

That made sense, and it also made Beck wonder why he hadn't thought of it sooner. But he knew why—he'd believed his brother.

"So why were you even there that night?" Nicole questioned Faith again. Judging from her expression, she wasn't buying any of Faith's account.

Faith took another breath. "When you came to the motel and started pounding on the door, Sherry called me. She was terrified word would get out that she'd been with Pete. I came over, hid on the side of the building and waited for you to leave. Then I took Sherry out of there. I was trying to get your husband out, too, when you and Beck showed up and accused me of seducing Pete."

"That's not the way I remember things," Pete insisted.

"Then your memory is wrong," Faith insisted right back.

Pete rammed his finger against his chest. "Why would I lie about which Matthews sister I'd slept with when I was drunk?"

"Only you can answer that, Pete." Faith volleyed glares at each one of them. "I want you all out of here. Now. If not, I intend to call the Texas Rangers and have you arrested."

He understood Faith's desire to be rid of his kin, but that riled Beck. Of course, he was already riled about this entire situation, so that was only frosting on the cake. "I don't need the Rangers to handle this," he assured Faith. "Do you want to file charges against Nicole?"

That earned him a fierce look from Pete, a raised eyebrow from his father and a surprised gasp from Nicole. Why, Beck didn't know. Nicole couldn't have possibly thought brandishing a gun, even an unloaded one, wouldn't warrant at least a consideration of arrest.

"I won't file charges at the moment," Faith said, pointing at Nicole. "But let's get something straight. I won't have you anywhere near my daughter or me with a weapon again. Understand?"

"But you ruined my life. *You*. It wasn't Sherry in that motel room. If it'd been your sister, my husband would have said so."

"Get them out of here," Faith mumbled, and she turned and walked into the adjoining room.

She didn't slam the door. She closed it gently. But Beck figured if she'd been wrongly accused and run out of town, that had to be eating away at her. Now add this latest incident with Nicole, and, oh, yeah, Faith was no doubt stewing.

"Go home, Nicole," Pete told his wife.

When Nicole didn't move, Roy caught onto his daughter-in-law's arm and led her toward the door. "I'm sorry about this, Beck. We'll talk later."

Beck nodded his thanks to his father and turned back to unfinished business. "Did you sleep with Faith or not?"

Pete glanced away. "What does it matter?"

Beck cursed under his breath. "That's not an answer to my question."

"Because it's not a question you should be asking. I'm your brother, for heaven's sake."

"Being my brother doesn't mean I'll gloss over your indiscretions. Especially if that indiscretion has put the blame on the wrong woman for all these years."

Pete looked him straight in the eye. "I was with Faith that night, not Sherry."

For the first time, Beck was seriously doubting that his brother had told the truth. But if he was lying, why? What could be worse than letting everyone, especially Nicole, believe he'd had sex with Faith? Unless fear of Nolan did play some part of this. The problem was his brother wasn't usually the sort to fear anyone.

"So what happens now?" Pete asked. "Faith just stays in town like nothing ever happened?"

Beck didn't want to mention that Faith, Aubrey and the nanny would soon be going to his house. And that they were in his protective custody. Besides, he didn't want anyone to know that his place was now essentially a safe house for the three. He wanted to get Faith, Aubrey and Marita in there without anyone else noticing. Or knowing about it. That would mean hiding them in the backseat of his car, parking in his garage and getting them inside only after the garage door was closed.

Of course, there was the other part to the plan. The part he could tell Pete since he needed the gossip mill working for the bait plan to succeed.

"Faith plans to stay at her mother's old house," Beck informed him, and he watched carefully for his brother's reaction. There wasn't much of one, just a slight shift in his posture. "I tried to talk her out of it, but she insisted on staying there."

"Then she's an idiot," Pete declared. "Her brother's a killer, and he's out on the loose. Anything could happen to her at that house."

And it wasn't a surprise that Pete didn't seem torn up about that. He probably wanted Darin to go after Faith.

Beck nodded and tried to appear detached from the situation. He realized, much to his disgust, that he wasn't detached. He didn't like this plan, and he didn't like that he'd just used his brother to set it into motion.

"You need to leave," Beck said, unable and unwilling to keep the anger from his voice. "See to your wife and make sure she doesn't come anywhere near Faith again."

Beck practically shoved his brother out the door, and he locked it. He made a mental note to keep it locked in case Nicole or Pete returned for round two. He needed to do some damage control from round one first.

Because once Faith gave it some thought, she just might file those charges against Nicole.

And if so, he'd have to arrest his own sister-in-law. Beck didn't want to speculate what kind of powder keg that would create between Pete, Nicole and Faith.

The phone on the desk rang. Figuring that Faith was still too shaken to answer it, Beck snatched it up. "Sheriff Tanner," he answered.

He was greeted with several seconds of silence, and for a moment Beck thought this might be another threat, similar to the rocks.

"Ross Harland," the caller finally said. "I'm returning Faith's call."

Beck glanced at the closed bedroom door. "She's, er, indisposed at the moment."

"Is she okay?" It didn't sound like a casual question, which might mean this guy, this former boyfriend, still had feelings for her.

"Faith's fine, but she had a rough morning. And a rough night, too."

"What happened?" Another noncasual question.

Beck didn't intend to get into specifics, but for anyone who knew Faith, her background was no doubt common knowledge. "Faith's brother is suspected of murder and is still at large. Aubrey and Faith might be in danger because of him."

"Who's Aubrey?"

That caused Beck to pause a moment. "Faith's daughter."

"A daughter?" He sounded shocked.

"I figured you knew."

"No. Faith and I dated for a year or so, but we stopped seeing each other nearly two years ago."

He didn't want to, but Beck quickly did the math. Aubrey was sixteen months old, which meant she'd been conceived a little over two years ago.

Right about the time Faith had been with Ross Harland.

Beck mentally groaned. Had Faith kept it from this man that he'd fathered a child?

"How can I help Faith?" Harland asked.

The question stunned Beck. Here, Beck had just told him in a roundabout way that he likely had a daughter, and Harland hadn't even asked about Aubrey. Certainly Harland could do the math as well. And that riled Beck to the core. If Aubrey had been his child, he'd sure as hell want to know, and he'd want to be part of her life.

"I'm not sure you can help," Beck answered, trying not to launch into a rant about how Harland should step up to the plate and be a man. "But Faith wanted to ask about getting a bodyguard for Aubrey."

Harland made a sound of understanding. "Well, I do have someone on staff who might work. Her name is Tracy Collier, and she's trained as both a nanny and a bodyguard. How old is Faith's daughter?"

Now the guy might finally get it. "Sixteen months."

"Good. I was hoping we weren't dealing with a newborn here."

"No. Not a newborn." Beck hesitated, wondering how much he should say and knowing he couldn't stop himself. He had to know, because despite Faith's denial, her past lover could have a part in this. "I thought you might be Aubrey's father."

"Me? Not a chance."

Beck had to hesitate again. This conversation was getting more and more confusing. "But you were with Faith about the time Aubrey was conceived."

"Look, I don't know what Faith told you about our relationship, and I'm not even sure it's any of your business, but there's no way that child could be mine."

"Birth control isn't always effective," Beck pointed out.

He cursed. "I want to talk to Faith."

"Like I said, she's indisposed. She'll have to call you back. And for the record, she never said you were Aubrey's father. I just put one and one together."

"Well, you came up with the wrong answer. Faith and I weren't lovers."

Beck nearly dropped the phone. "Not lovers? And you were together for a year?"

"Her choice. Not mine. Now, what the hell does this have to do with your investigation, Sheriff?"

Maybe nothing. Maybe everything. "Faith doesn't believe her brother is trying to kill her, and it's possible the danger is linked to someone in her past. When relationships go bad, situations can turn dangerous. Aubrey's father might have some part in this."

"Well, I don't know who he is, but he must be someone pretty damn special."

"What do you mean?"

Harland cursed again, and he stayed silent so long that Beck thought maybe the call had been dropped.

"Ask Faith why we never slept together," Harland finally said.

"Excuse me?" Beck said because he didn't know what else to say.

"You heard me. If you want answers, ask her." And with that, Harland hung up.

Beck glanced at the phone and then at Faith's bedroom door. He didn't know what the devil was going on, but he intended to find out.

Chapter Six

"Beck Tanner asked you *what?*" Faith demanded.

There was a groan from the other end of her cell-phone line. "He thought I was your daughter's father," Harland explained.

Faith slowly got up from the bed where she'd been sitting and started to pace across the guest room in Beck's house. "What did you say?"

"The truth, that the child couldn't be mine because we were never lovers."

Faith didn't groan, but she squeezed her eyes shut a moment and silently cursed a blue streak.

"The sheriff said this was pertinent to the investigation," Ross added. "He said he wanted to be certain that none of your previous relationships could have a part in you being in danger."

"Maybe, but he had no right to ask you about our sex life." Or the lack thereof. Mercy, she did not want to explain this to Beck.

The truth could ultimately put Aubrey in danger.

"Anyway, the bodyguard I'm sending over is Tracy Collier," Ross continued, obviously opting for a less volatile subject. "She's one of my best. She should be there any minute, and she's yours for as long as you need her."

"Thanks, Ross," Faith managed to say. She did appreciate this, truly, but it was hard to be thankful when Beck might learn the truth.

"I'm sorry I told Sheriff Tanner anything about our relationship," Ross continued. "Should I phone him and have a little chat with him?"

It wouldn't be a chat. More like a tongue-lashing. "No. I'll do that myself." She thanked her old friend again and ended the call.

How dare Beck ask Ross a question like that, and he hadn't even had the nerve to tell her. But then he hadn't exactly had a chance, she reluctantly admitted. Like her, he'd been tied up all day planning to make Aubrey as safe as possible.

And they had succeeded. For now, anyway.

She, Marita and Aubrey were at Beck's house on the edge of town, and it appeared that no one had been aware of the move. Beck had literally sneaked them out the back of the hotel and into his place. Once the bodyguard arrived, then the plan was for a Texas Ranger to pull backup bodyguard duty while she and Beck made an appearance at her own house.

But first, she wanted to let Beck have it for that phone conversation with Ross.

Faith jerked open the guest-room door and stormed toward the family room, where she could hear voices. Beck's house was large, especially for a single guy: three bedrooms, three baths and an updated gourmet kitchen. A real surprise. When Beck had given them the whirlwind tour, she'd wanted to ask if he actually used the brick-encased, French stove or the gleaming, stainless cookware on the pot rack over the butcher's block island. But she hadn't said a word, because she hadn't wanted to intrude on his personal life.

He obviously hadn't felt the same about hers.

She nodded to Sgt. Sloan McKinney, a Texas Ranger who was sipping coffee while he stood by the kitchen door. Faith went straight to the family room and stopped dead in her tracks. Her temper didn't exactly go cold, but it did chill a bit when she saw what was going on. Marita was talking to a tall brunette. The bodyguard, no doubt. But it wasn't the bodyguard who snared her attention. Aubrey was on the floor, sitting in Beck's lap while he read *Chicka Chicka Boom Boom* to her.

Beck looked up at Faith, and his smile dissolved. Maybe because she looked angry. And was. And maybe because he knew the reason for her anger.

He'd changed clothes since they'd arrived and was now wearing black jeans and a white, button-up, long-sleeve shirt. Anything he could have worn would have made him look hot. But sitting there with Aubrey made him look hot and…extraordinary. It wasn't just his good looks now. It was that whole potential fatherhood thing. Beck seemed totally natural holding a child. Her child. And that created a bizarre ripple of emotions.

She had to remind herself to hang on to the anger.

"We'll go to your house when I'm done with the story," Beck let her know. Aubrey didn't take her eyes off the brightly colored pages.

"Faith, this is Tracy Collier," Marita said.

Faith shook the woman's hand. "Thank you for coming."

"No problem. Ross said it was important."

Yes, and Faith owed him for that. But not for what he'd volunteered to Beck.

"Sheriff Tanner checked my ID," Tracy volunteered. "And he ran a background check on me before I arrived." She didn't sound upset. More amused.

"She checked out clean," Beck informed Faith.

Though she was upset with him, she couldn't find fault with the extra security steps he'd taken with Tracy. But how could any man look that hot while jabbering nonsensical words like *chicka, chicka?*

Marita and Tracy resumed their conversation about sleeping arrangements. Apparently, Tracy had decided to take the sofa in the family room since it was near the front door. The Ranger would have a cot near the back door. Good. The arrangement gave Faith a little reassurance about leaving Aubrey, but it would still be tough.

Babbling, Aubrey tried to repeat the last line of the book that Beck read. He then did something else that shocked Faith. He brushed a kiss on Aubrey's forehead. There was genuine affection in his eyes. Aubrey's eyes, too.

Aubrey gave Beck a hug.

Beck's gaze met Faith's again, and he went from affection to a little discomfort. With Aubrey in his arms, he stood and walked to Faith.

"Ready to go to your house?" he asked.

No, but she was ready for that conversation. And ready to get her mind off Beck as a potential father.

Marita came to take Aubrey, and Faith gave the little girl a kiss. "Mommy won't be long."

Aubrey babbled something, reached for Beck again, but Marita moved her away. Faith gave her a nod of thanks.

"You don't want me reading to Aubrey," Beck mumbled.

"Yes. I mean, no." Since she was starting to feel petty again, she headed toward the garage. "I'm just surprised, that's all."

"Me, too. But it's hard not to get attached to her."

"Oh, that should make your family really happy," she snarled.

He didn't respond to that. They went into the garage, got into his SUV. Even though the windows were tinted and it was dusky dark outside, he still had her slip down low in the seat so that none of his neighbors, or a killer, would spot her coming out of his place.

On the backseat, there was a doll wrapped in a blanket. Faith already knew what she would do with that doll. She'd carry it into her house so that anyone watching would think it was Aubrey. The little detail had been Beck's idea because he said he didn't want anyone questioning why Faith wouldn't have her daughter with her at her house, especially since everyone in town likely knew about the child's arrival the night before.

Beck looked down at her. "You talked to Ross Harland," he said. Apparently, that was an invitation to start the argument he guessed they were about to have.

"You had no right to ask him those questions," Faith accused.

"I beg to differ. You don't think your brother is guilty. But I'm trying to figure out the identity of a killer. Your previous relationships are relevant." He pulled out of the garage and immediately hit the remote control clipped to his visor to shut it. He didn't pull away from the house until the door was fully closed.

Faith just sat there. Stewing. And waiting. She didn't have to wait long.

"Harland said he couldn't possibly be Aubrey's father," Beck continued. "I don't guess you intend to tell me who is."

"No." She didn't even have to think about her answer.

"That's what I figured you'd say, though I don't have a clue why you'd keep something like that a secret. I'm repeating myself here, but I'm trying to find a killer, Faith."

"And knowing Aubrey's father won't catch that killer."

He cursed under his breath. "I had a friend at the FBI fax me a copy of Aubrey's birth certificate. The father's name isn't listed. Just yours."

That had been intentional, and it would stay that way. Her silence must have let him know that because he didn't say anything else about it. Silently, he drove through LaMesa Springs and down Main Street—Faith could tell from the tops of the streetlights, but she was too low in the seat to actually see anything.

"No one seems to be following us," he explained, checking the rearview and side mirrors. He made the turn into the hotel and went to the back parking lot. Beck glanced all around them. "You can sit up now. I want people to think I picked you up here."

"But what if someone on the hotel staff blabs that I wasn't here all afternoon?"

"No one knows. There's been a Do Not Disturb sign

on the door and strict orders that no one goes into the room. Later, I'll phone the manager and tell him that I've moved you guys to your house."

Even though it was the plan, it still sent a chill over her. After that call, she'd officially be bait.

"So it was really Sherry in the motel with Pete?" Beck asked as he drove away from the parking lot. Except it didn't sound like a question.

But Faith answered it as if it'd been one. "What did your brother say?"

"He lied."

She glanced at him, and even in the darkness she had no trouble seeing his expression. A mixture of emotions. "How do you know that?"

"Because I could see it in his eyes."

Faith blew out a long breath. "Why didn't you see it ten years ago?"

"Because I wasn't looking. I just accepted what he told me as gospel."

"You accepted it because you already believed the worst about me."

He took a moment to answer. "Yes, and it's probably too little, too late, but I'm sorry."

She nearly laughed. For years, she'd wanted that apology. She'd wanted Beck to know the truth. But it seemed a hollow victory since she couldn't enjoy it. Well, not now anyway. But once the danger had passed it would no doubt sink in that this moment had been monumental.

Faith frowned.

She certainly hadn't expected an apology from Beck to feel so darn good. Maybe because she'd already written him off. She hoped it had nothing to do with this crazy attraction between them.

"I'll work on my father and Nicole," he continued, taking the final turn to her house. Even though the curtains all appeared to be closed, some lights were on. "Pete, too, eventually. Once they've accepted that you were the scapegoat in this, then your life here should be a little smoother."

"Thank you." That was a gift she certainly hadn't expected so soon. Then it hit her. "You're doing this for Aubrey."

"In part," he readily admitted. "I don't want her to feel any resentment from anyone. But I'm doing it for me, too. Because it's the right thing to do, and since Sherry is dead, I think this will help my family get past the hurt. You know that old saying—the truth will set you free."

"Not always," she said under her breath.

They came to a stop outside her house, directly in front of the porch. All she had to do was go up the steps, and she'd be inside.

Beck glanced at her again, and for a moment she thought he might have heard her and was going to question it. He didn't. He just looked at her.

He opened his mouth. Closed it. Shook his head. But he didn't explain why he was suddenly speechless. Instead, he picked up the doll, handed it to her and motioned for her to get out.

"Make it quick but not too obvious that you're trying to hurry," he instructed.

Faith did. While clutching the doll, she got out of the SUV and went inside to find Sgt. Caldwell waiting for them.

Beck and he exchanged handshakes. "Let's hope we catch a killer tonight," Beck greeted him.

"We'll do our best." The Ranger pointed to the security keypad by the door. "Before I leave, I want to go over the updates. There are external motion detectors that'll alert you if anyone comes within twenty feet of the house."

"What about windows?" Beck asked.

"All doors and windows are wired for security, and if anything's tripped, the alarm will go off, and the keypad will light up the problem area."

Faith was certain she looked confused. "But won't the alarm scare off Darin if he shows?" She propped the doll against the wall.

"No. The alarm will be a series of soft beeps. You shouldn't have any trouble hearing them, but they won't be loud enough to be heard from outside."

Beck's cell phone rang, and he stepped aside to answer it.

"The keypad's easy to work," Sgt. Caldwell continued. "Just press in the numbers one, two, three and four to arm it after I leave. Oh, and don't stand directly in front of any windows."

She had no plans for that. "If Darin shows, how fast can you respond?"

"Less than two minutes. I'll be nearby, parked several streets over. I don't want to be any closer, because if he sees me, it might scare him off."

"Two minutes," she repeated. "I hope that's fast enough to catch him."

Sgt. Caldwell lifted his shoulder. "Best case scenario is that your brother will call you first before he shows up. If that happens, just stay on the line with him and have Beck contact us so we can make a trace."

Faith nodded. "I don't want Darin hurt."

"We'll try our best. But it might not be possible. For that matter, it might not even be your brother who shows up."

"Nolan Wheeler," she provided.

Yes, he might have tossed those rocks through the window. And if so, if he was the one who arrived on her doorstep, then he could be arrested and questioned. It wouldn't tie up the loose ends with her brother, but she believed it would get a killer off the street.

Beck ended his call and rejoined them. One glance at him, and Faith knew something was wrong.

"That was the manager of the convenience store," Beck explained.

She held her breath, waiting for him to say her brother had been spotted again.

"Not Darin," Beck clarified, obviously understanding the concern in her body language. "This is about the taxi driver who stopped there after dropping you here at your house. When the clerk asked him what he was doing in LaMesa Springs, the driver told him."

Which confirmed what the taxi driver told Faith. "Let me guess—Nolan Wheeler was in the store?"

Beck shook his head. Paused. "No, but my father was."

"Your father?" she mumbled.

She didn't have to clarify what that meant. If his father knew, then so had Nicole and Pete. And after that stunt Nicole had pulled in her hotel room, Nicole could have been the one who'd thrown those rocks.

Beck looked away from her and handed Sgt. Caldwell his car keys. "I turned off the porch light. Figured it'd help in case someone's already watching the place."

And that person would believe it was Beck leaving. That's why Beck had changed his clothes, so that he would be dressed like the Ranger. Since no one knew the Ranger was there, the killer or her brother would think Faith was alone and vulnerable. Well, she wouldn't be alone, but the vulnerable part still applied.

"This could end up lasting all night," the Ranger reminded him.

Faith had considered that, briefly. What she hadn't considered was staying in the house alone with Beck. That suddenly didn't seem like a smart idea. But she couldn't let something like attraction get in the way of catching the person responsible.

"Good luck," Sgt. Caldwell said, heading for the door. He turned off the light in the entry as well and waited until Beck and Faith stepped into the shadows before he walked out. She immediately went to the door, locked it and set the security alarm.

"I'll talk to my dad," Beck promised. "I'll see if he repeated any information he got from the taxi driver. Plus, the rocks and foot casting are still at the crime lab. Either might give us some evidence."

"If it's Nicole who threw those rocks, I intend to file charges for that and the empty gun incident." Faith couldn't let the woman continue her harassment. Of course, if it was Nicole, there was a problem with the size-ten shoeprint that'd been found. Though maybe that print had been left earlier by someone not involved in this.

"If it's Nicole, I'll arrest her."

Faith caught his gaze. And saw the determination there. The pain, too. She also saw concern for her, so she thought it best if she stepped away from him.

Keeping in the shadows, she walked into the living room. Someone had taken the sheets from the furniture, and the sofa and recliner had a stack of bedding and pillows on them. This was where she and Beck were supposed to sleep. If sleep was even possible.

Beck would only be a few feet away from her.

With that overdue apology out of the way, there didn't seem to be so many old obstacles standing between them. Too bad. Because it made her remember a time when she'd lusted after him.

Who was she kidding?

She was still lusting after him. At least she was when she wasn't riled at him.

He followed her into the living room and caught onto her arm. The contact surprised her so much that she jumped. Faith reeled around, expecting him to do God knows what, but he merely repositioned her farther away from the window. He let go of her quickly, but then looked down at his hand as if that brief touch had caused him to feel something more.

"You might as well just go ahead and slap me," he said.

"For what?" she asked cautiously.

"For what I'm about to say."

Oh. With both curiosity and some fear, she considered the possibilities of what he might say. Maybe he wanted a discussion about the attraction. Or to discuss something about the touch that was still tingling her arm. Maybe he even intended to kiss her. Could that have been wishful thinking on her part?

"What?" she prompted when he didn't continue. Mercy. Her voice had way too much breath in it. She sounded like a lovesick schoolgirl.

"It has to do with the conversation I had with Ross Harland."

Oh, that. Faith hated that she'd anticipated anything not dealing with the case.

Beck moved closer to her again. Too close. "He was so adamant about not being Aubrey's father that I figured he was telling the truth about you two not having had sex." His voice was smooth and easy. No pressure, no expectations. He shrugged. "You can slap me for asking, and I doubt you'll answer, but at least tell me if Ross Harland might have anything to do with the murders."

That easy drawl took away some of the sting. "He doesn't."

He nodded. That was it. Beck's only reaction. He even seemed to believe her, which he should, since it was the truth.

The silence came. It was suddenly so quiet she could hear her own heartbeat in her ears. Seconds passed. Very slowly. While Beck and she just stood there and stared at each other.

"Is Ross Harland gay?" Beck finally asked.

She had no idea why that made her laugh, but it did. Maybe because Beck had lost the battle with curiosity after all. "No. He's not gay. And I don't know whether to be angry or flattered that you'd want to know so much about my sex life."

"Be flattered," he said, his voice all sex and sin.

She was. Flattered and suddenly very warm.

He leaned in, letting his mouth come very close to hers. Breath met breath. Her heart kicked into overdrive. So did her body.

She knew she should say something flippant and move away. But she didn't. "Beck," she warned.

But it sounded more like an invitation than anything else.

He didn't back away. Didn't heed her warning. He moved in for the kiss. His mouth brushed against hers. It was gentle. Nonthreatening. No demands.

It hit her like a boulder.

Faith felt the jolt. New sensations mixed with old ones that she thought she would never feel again. Leave it to Beck and his mouth to accomplish the impossible.

She leaned into him. Deepening the kiss with the pressure. He slid his hand around her neck, easing her closer. Inch by inch. Slowly, as if to give her a chance to escape. Beck was treating her like fine crystal.

And that kiss was melting her.

Faith heard herself moan. She felt the strength of his body. The fire was instant. The impact was so hard that she nearly lost her breath. She'd apparently already lost her mind. But then she broke the intimate contact and stepped back.

"I don't kiss a lot," she said, the words rushing out.

He cocked his head to the side. "Well, you should because you're good at it."

"No. I'm not." She didn't know what to do with her hands so she folded them over her chest.

His easy expression faded a bit. By degrees. Until it was replaced by confusion.

"I like to kiss," she clarified. Well, she liked to kiss

Beck, anyway. "But kissing leads to other things. Like sex. Which we aren't going to have."

He lifted his left eyebrow. "You're right. Our relationship is too complicated for sex."

"Yet you still kissed me."

He shook his head, cursed under his breath and dragged his hand through his hair. "I don't know why. Maybe because I haven't been able to get you out of my mind since I saw you naked in the shower. But I know that kiss can't go any further than it just did."

She blinked. "You honestly believe that?"

"I have to believe it. We can't deal with the alternative right now. Aubrey's safety has to come first. Then this investigation. Once we catch this killer, then we can…talk. Or kiss. Or do something we'll really regret like have great sex."

But he waved off that last part. Too bad she couldn't wave off the effect it had on her body. The image of them having sex sizzled through her.

"So *this* is on hold," he continued. "Unless there's something you want to tell me now."

She wanted to. But it wasn't that easy. The truth would give him some answers. More questions, too. And it would open Pandora's box.

Beck was right. Aubrey's safety came first.

Faith was about to repeat that, but a blast tore through the room.

Chapter Seven

Someone had fired a shot at them.

The moment the sound of the bullet registered, Beck reacted.

He hooked his arm around Faith's waist and dragged her to the floor. She was already headed in that direction anyway, and they landed on the pile of sheets that'd been removed from the furniture. That cushioned their fall a little, but the new position didn't take them out of the line of fire.

Another bullet came at them and slammed into the wall just above their heads.

Hell.

Beck drew his weapon. "We have to move."

But where and how?

His initial assessment of the situation wasn't good. There'd been no broken glass, and that meant no broken windows. And no tripped motion detector, either. So the shooter had to be more than twenty feet away from the house and was literally shooting through the wall.

Probably with a high-powered rifle.

But it was the accuracy of the shot that caused Beck's

stomach to knot. Both bullets had come entirely too close, especially considering there was no way the shooter could have a visual on them.

So, was the guy pinpointing them through some kind of eavesdropping device or had he managed to rig surveillance cameras that had given him an inside view of the house?

The third shot slammed into the wooden floor next to them and sent splinters flying. That was it. They couldn't stay there any longer.

"Let's go." Beck latched on to Faith's arm and got them running out of the living room. He needed to put another wall between them and the shooter.

Staying low, they raced toward the kitchen, the nearest room, but the shooter stayed in pursuit, and the bullets continued. Each blast followed them, tracking them as they made their way across the living room.

Beck shoved Faith ahead of him so that his body would give her some small measure of protection. It wasn't enough. They needed a barrier, something wide and thick. He spotted the fridge. It was outdated and fairly small, but he hoped the metal would hold back those bullets. He hauled Faith in front of it and shoved her to the linoleum floor.

The bullets didn't stop.

They tore through the kitchen drywall and shattered the tiny window over the kitchen sink. That set off the alarm, and the soft beeps began to pulse through the room. If the shooter moved to the back of the house, they'd be sitting ducks with that broken window.

"Call Sgt. Caldwell," Beck instructed Faith. He

handed her his cell phone and kept his gun ready just in case the shooter decided to bash through a window or door and try to come into the house.

Beside him, he felt Faith trembling, and her voice trembled, too, as she made the call to the Ranger and told him that someone was shooting at them from the front of the house. She asked him to come immediately.

Faith had no sooner made that request when the angle of the shots changed.

The next two rounds came right at the refrigerator. The bullets slammed into the metal but thankfully didn't exit out the front. The accuracy of the shots, however, told Beck that the gunman wasn't just using a high-powered, long-range rifle but that it was likely equipped with some kind of thermal scope or camera.

That thermal device could be a deadly addition.

It was no doubt picking up their body heat, and that heat had given away their exact location. That's why the shots were aimed so closely at them.

Faith ended her call with the Ranger. Even though the overhead light wasn't on, there was enough moonlight for Beck to see the terror on her face.

"Aubrey," she said, flipping open the phone again. She frantically stabbed in the numbers, and a moment later over the deafening blasts, she said, "Marita, is Aubrey okay?"

Beck hadn't been truly afraid until that moment. Faith was silent, and he watched her expression, praying that the gunfire had been only for them and a second shooter hadn't gone to his house to make a simultaneous attack there.

"They're fine," she finally said. Faith let out a hoarse sob. Fear mixed with relief.

Beck shared that relief. For just a moment. And then the anger took over. How dare this shooter put Faith through this. This was a blatant attempt to kill her, but the fear of harm to her child was far, far worse.

"I'll get this guy," Beck promised her.

The shots stopped.

Just like that, there were no more blasts. The only sounds were their sawing breaths, the hum of the central heating and the beeps from the security alarm.

"Is it over?" Faith asked.

He caught onto her arm to stop her from trying to get up. "Maybe."

Beck left it at that, but her widened eyes let him know that she understood. This could be a temporary cease-fire, a lure to draw them out away from the fridge.

Or it could mean the shooter was moving to the back of the house.

Where he'd have a direct shot to kill them.

"We'll stay put," he said, not at all sure of his decision. It was a gamble either way.

"I want to go to Aubrey," Faith mumbled.

"I know. So do I."

Waiting was hell, but this was the best way he knew to keep Faith alive.

His cell phone rang, the sound slicing through the room. Faith quickly answered it.

"Sgt. Caldwell's nearby," she relayed to him a moment later. "He'll turn on his sirens and an infrared scanner."

The sirens started to sound almost immediately. They would almost certainly scare off a shooter, if the shooter was still around, that is. But maybe, just maybe, the infrared would help Caldwell spot the shooter so he could be apprehended and arrested.

Beck wanted to be outside, to help with the search. He wanted to be the one to catch this piece of slime. But he couldn't leave Faith because the shooter could use that opportunity to go after her.

So he waited. It seemed endless. But it was probably only a couple of minutes before the phone rang again. This time, Beck grabbed it and answered it.

"It's Caldwell," the Ranger said.

"Did you get him?" Beck snapped.

"No. Nothing showed up on the infrared."

Beck groaned. This couldn't happen. They couldn't let this guy get away.

"I'm taking Faith back to my house to stay with the Ranger there and the bodyguard," he told the Ranger. "And then I'm going after this SOB."

FAITH CHECKED THE TIME on the screen of her cell phone. It was ten o'clock. Not that late, but Beck had been out looking for the shooter for well over an hour.

Each minute had seemed like an eternity.

She paced in the family room but kept her movements light so she wouldn't disturb Marita and Aubrey, who were already in bed and hopefully sleeping. Aubrey certainly was. Faith had verified that just five minutes earlier when she peeked in on them in the guest room. Marita had her eyes closed, but Faith doubted the woman was truly asleep.

The shooting had put them all on edge.

Tracy was on the sofa, reading. The Ranger, Sgt.

McKinney, was standing guard in the kitchen. Everything was quiet, but the tension was thick enough to taste.

Where was Beck? And why hadn't he checked in?

The silence was driving her crazy. She was imagining all sorts of things. Like he was lying somewhere shot. Or that he was being held hostage.

Because she was so caught up in those nightmarish thoughts, the sound of the phone ringing caused her to jump. "Hello?" Faith said as quickly as she could get the phone to her ear.

Silence.

That brought on some more horrible thoughts, and then she checked the caller ID. The person had blocked their number, and there was no reason for Beck to have done that.

"Who is this?" she asked.

Her alarmed tone obviously alerted Tracy, who got to her feet. She put her hand on the butt of the pistol that rested in her shoulder holster.

"It's me," the caller finally said.

Faith had no trouble recognizing that voice.

Nolan Wheeler.

Her stomach dropped to her knees from the shock of hearing him, but she welcomed this call. It was the first contact she'd had in years with a man she thought was a cold-blooded killer.

"Nolan," Faith said aloud so that Tracy would know what was going on. Tracy reacted. She went racing into the kitchen to tell Sgt. McKinney. Hopefully, they could do something to trace this call and pinpoint Nolan's location. "Did you take shots at me tonight?"

"Me? Of course not." He used his normal cocky tone,

but that didn't mean he was telling the truth. "I called about Sherry."

"What about her? She's dead. And I think you might be responsible."

"Not a chance. I didn't want her dead. She owed me money. Lots of it."

Faith was instantly skeptical. "How did that happen? You've never been one to have extra cash to lend anyone."

"I didn't exactly lend it to her. She stole my car and left a note, saying she was in a bind. She needed cash and needed it fast."

"Did she say why she needed money?" Faith asked.

"To gussy up." Nolan snickered. "Said she had to impress somebody, and she needed to look her best and that she'd pay me back. Killing her wouldn't get me the money so I've got no motive."

"What about the house? Did you think you could inherit it? Because you can't. I made a will, and there's no way you can ever inherit anything that's mine."

He made a tsk-tsk sound. "But I can inherit what's mine. Well, what was Sherry's anyway. Half of the place should have been hers after your mother was killed. Guess what, Faith? I want that half."

She fought to hang on to her temper. Flying off the handle now wouldn't solve anything. Besides, she wanted to give the Ranger more time to locate Nolan.

"Sherry and you separated eighteen months before her death," Faith reminded him. Even though their marriage was common law, Nolan probably did have a right to half of whatever Sherry owned. "And after the hell you put her through, you don't deserve anything from her estate."

"In the eyes of the law, I do. And you know the law, don't you?"

"I know it well enough that you won't see a penny."

"Oh, I want more than pennies," Nolan gloated. "A lot more. So here's the deal. You give me a hundred thousand dollars, and I'll go away."

Oh, mercy. "That's more than the place is worth, and besides, I don't have that kind of money."

"Then get it. Bye, Faith."

"Wait!" she said in a louder voice than she'd anticipated. This call couldn't end yet. "I need to know about Darin. Have you seen him?"

Nolan took his time answering. "He's around."

That was chilling, and despite the simple answer, it sounded like some kind of threat. "Where?"

"Don't worry about your brother. He can take care of himself."

"I'm not so sure of that, especially if you're manipulating him in some way." And if Nolan was in contact with her brother, then he was almost certainly manipulating him. "Where are you, Nolan?"

"Just get me that money," he said, ignoring her question.

Faith tried again. "Where are you?"

"I'm closer than you think, sweet cakes."

With that, Nolan hung up.

Faith looked in the doorway of the family room, where Tracy and the Ranger were standing. Sgt. Mc-Kinney took her phone and relayed the numbers to someone on the other end of his own cell-phone line.

A moment later, the sergeant shook his head. "The guy was using a prepaid cell phone. We couldn't trace it."

Faith didn't have time to groan because she heard the garage door open. Beck was home. And she raced to meet him. One look at his face, however, told her that he didn't have any better news than she did.

Beck took off his muddy cowboy boots and dropped them on the laundry-room floor. "I couldn't find the shooter."

Because he looked exhausted and beyond frustrated, Faith motioned for him to go into the family room so he could sit down. He smelled like the woods and sweat, and there were bits of dried leaves and twigs on his clothes.

"What about the shell casings?" Sgt. McKinney asked. "Caldwell called and said you'd found some at the scene."

"We did. They're Winchester ballistic silver tips." Beck looked at her. "They're used for long-range shooting. Coupled with what was probably a thermal camera or scope, I'm guessing the shooter had what we call a hog rifle. It's used for hunting wild hogs or boars at night."

"This type of weapon is rare?" she asked hopefully.

"Not around here. I know of at least a half dozen people who own one. Wild boars can be dangerous to people and livestock so they're usually hunted when they show up too close to the ranches."

Maybe Nolan had gotten his hands on one of these rifles. "Nolan Wheeler called a few minutes ago," she filled him in. "We couldn't trace the call."

The fatigue vanished. The concern returned. "What did he want?"

"Money. A hundred grand to be exact. He wants me

to give him more than half of my inheritance. But he didn't tell me how I could find him."

I'm closer than you think.

She pushed aside the chill from remembering Nolan's final remark. "He'll call back." Faith was certain of that. "He'll want that cash. And maybe we can use it to draw him out."

Beck hesitated a moment. Then nodded. "But you won't be the one who's drawing him out. No more playing bait."

Faith was still too shaky to argue with him. Nor did she argue when Beck reached out and pulled her closer. That was all it took. That bit of comfort. And Faith felt the tears well up in her eyes.

"I could use a cup of coffee," Tracy said, and she hitched her shoulder toward the kitchen. "Why don't you join me?" she asked Sgt. McKinney.

Faith didn't mind the obvious ploy to leave her and Beck alone because the tears started to spill down her cheeks.

"I'm sorry," she mumbled.

Beck pulled her even closer to him and closed his arms around her. She took everything he was offering her, even though it was wrong. Beck had been through that shooting, too, and he wasn't falling apart.

"I'm not ashamed of crying," she said, wiping away the tears with the back of her hand. Beck wiped away the other cheek. "But I wish I wasn't doing this in front of you."

"Why?" With his fingers still on tear-wiping duty, he caught her gaze, and the corner of his mouth hitched. "Because I'm the enemy?"

"No. Because you're Beckett Tanner."

The smile didn't fully materialize, and his fingers stayed in place. Warm on her cheek. "What would that have to do with it?"

"I always wanted to impress you. Or at least get your attention in a good way." She blamed the confession on the adrenaline crash and the fatigue.

"You succeeded. You got my attention. Even back then, before you left town." He slid his fingers down her cheek to her chin and lifted it slightly. As if he were readjusting it for a kiss. "You were about sixteen, and I saw you coming out of the grocery store on Main. You were wearing this short red dress. Trust me, I noticed."

Faith was stunned. "So why didn't you ask me out or something?"

"Because you were sixteen and I was twenty. The term *jailbait* comes to mind. I decided it'd be best to wait a couple of years."

For a moment, she got a glimpse of what life could have been if there hadn't been the incident at the motel. Of course, Beck's family would have never accepted her, and besides, the attraction would have run its youthful course and burned out.

She looked at him again.

Maybe not.

His mouth came to hers. Just a brush of his lips, and then he pulled back. When his gaze met hers again, the trip down memory lane was over. He drew her into his arms again. But it had nothing to do with kisses or sex. He eased her onto the sofa and simply held her.

For some reason, it seemed more intimate than a real kiss.

"I'm a good cop," he said, his voice hardly more than a whisper. "But I've made mistakes. I nearly let you get killed tonight."

So he was feeling guilty, too. "You couldn't have known that was going to happen."

"Yes, I did. I should have nixed that bait plan right from the start."

"It worked out all right," she assured him. Though they both knew that was a lie. They'd have nightmares about this for years. "I would just leave town, but I'm afraid this monster will follow me."

He made a sound of agreement.

Faith's phone rang again. She jolted. Her body was still on full alert. The caller had blocked the number.

"Nolan again," she mumbled. She answered the call and held the phone between Beck and her so he could hear as well.

"Hello, Faith."

It was a man all right. But not Nolan.

"Darin?" Though it wasn't a question. She knew it was her brother's voice. "God, I've been so worried about you. Where are you?"

"I can't say." He sounded genuinely sad about not being able to tell her that detail. "I called to warn you. You're in danger."

"Yes. From Nolan." She moved to the edge of the sofa. "I think he tried to kill me tonight."

"Maybe. But watch out for the Tanners. You can't trust them, Faith. They want to hurt you."

She wasn't exactly surprised after what had happened at the hotel. "Who, Nicole Tanner?"

"All of them. The whole family. If Sherry was alive,

she'd tell you the same. It's about those letters. Something went wrong with the letters."

Now she was surprised. "Darin, I don't understand— what letters? What do you mean?"

He stayed silent for several long moments. "Just be careful."

"Don't go," she said when she thought he was about to hang up. "I want to see you. Can we meet somewhere?"

That earned her a sharp look from Beck.

"No meeting," Darin insisted. "Not yet. It isn't safe. Not for you. Not for Aubrey."

"Aubrey?" Her breath practically froze in her throat.

Beck had a slightly different response. She saw the anger wash over him, and he tried to take the phone. She shook her head and eased her hand over the receiver. "He'll hang up if he knows you're listening," she mouthed.

"Aubrey's in danger because of the letters," Darin continued a moment later.

"Who has these letters?" Faith asked. "Nolan?"

"I don't know. Maybe."

If those letters contained something sinister, then Nolan was almost certainly involved. "Then I need to find him. Where is he?"

"He's here in LaMesa Springs."

Here.

I'm closer than you think.

And that meant Darin was probably in town, too.

"Yes, but where in LaMesa Springs?" Faith pressed.

"He's in the attic."

Faith flattened her hand over her chest to steady her heart. *Mercy, was Nolan here at Beck's house?* "What attic?" And she held her breath, waiting.

"At the house. Your house. He said the lock on the back door was broken so he went inside and climbed into the attic so he could wait for you. He got there before the cops and Rangers and then stayed quiet so they wouldn't hear him moving around."

"Darin?" Faith forced herself to talk. Nolan could be dealt with later. "I want to see you. Please."

But she was talking to herself. Her brother had already hung up.

Beck pulled out his own phone and jabbed in some numbers. Since the room was so quiet, Faith had no trouble hearing the man who answered. It was Sgt. Caldwell.

"Are you still at the Matthews house?" Beck asked the Ranger.

"Yeah. Why?"

"Check the attic. But be careful. One of our suspects, Nolan Wheeler, might be up there."

"I'll call you back," Caldwell let him know.

Beck hung up and looked at her. "Do you know anything about those letters Darin mentioned?"

She shook her head. This wasn't something she wanted to discuss right now. She wanted to know what was going on in that attic. But at least the conversation would keep her mind off the wait. Plus, this was important. "It sounded as if he believed they were connected to your family."

"Yeah, it did. But this is Darin, remember? He might not be mentally stable right now. Still," Beck continued before she could say anything, "I'll call my father in the morning and set up a meeting. I want to ask him about the convenience store anyway."

With everything else that was going on, she'd nearly forgotten about that. "I think it's pretty clear that he told Pete and maybe even Nicole that I was back in town. After all, your brother called you when I was still at your office. That was only a couple of hours after the rock throwing incident."

He mumbled another "yeah" and checked his watch.

"Sgt. Caldwell will be careful," she said more to herself than Beck.

But she prayed nothing went wrong and that the Ranger didn't get hurt. Besides, her brother could have been wrong. Beck was right about Darin possibly being delusional. God knows how much of what he said was real or a product of his mental illness.

Beck's phone rang, and he answered it immediately. He clicked on the speakerphone function.

"There's no one in the attic," Sgt. Caldwell explained. "But someone's been here. There's a discarded fast-food bag and graffiti."

"Kids maybe?" Beck asked.

"I don't think kids did this." His comment and tone upped the chill coursing through her. "I used my camera phone to take some pictures of the walls. I'm sending four of them to you now."

Beck went to the phone menu and pressed a few buttons. The first picture started to load on the screen.

Yes, it was definitely the attic. And though she couldn't see the fast-food bag the sergeant had described, she could see the wall that he'd captured in the photograph. Someone had taken red paint—at least she hoped it was paint—and written on the rough wood planks.

It was a calendar of sorts, crudely drawn squares, some blank, some with writing inside. The dates went back to a month earlier. She couldn't make out the writing and motioned for Beck to go to the next picture. It was the square with the date November 11th.

Inside the box someone had written:

Sherry dies.

Faith swallowed hard. That was indeed the day Sherry had been killed. But anyone who knew her sister would have had that information.

The next picture showed the date. November 12th. The caption inside:

Annie dies.

Her mother's name was Annie, and like the previous caption, it was correct. Her mother had been murdered then.

Picture three was dated January 12th with the words:

Faith's homecoming.

Yes, she had come home then. And someone had thrown rocks through her window.

God, had Nolan been there that whole time, waiting for her, watching her? The security had been set up to keep anyone from getting in, but what if he was already inside?

Beck clicked another button and the final picture loaded. There was a date: January 14th.

Tomorrow's date.

And beneath it were two words that caused her to gasp.

Faith dies.

Chapter Eight

Faith was not going to die today.

Beck wouldn't let that happen.

It riled the hell out of him to think of the death threat that'd been left in her attic. It had shaken Faith to the core. Immediately after seeing those pictures on the phone, she'd sat motionless in his arms while he rattled off how he was going to put an end to this.

The handwriting and fast-food bag would be analyzed. That was a given. As would the shell casings collected from the attack the night before. But there was something else Beck could do. He could keep Faith away from her house. If he didn't let her out of his sight, he could protect her.

He hoped that'd be enough.

So, after giving her all the assurance he could, he'd sent her off to bed, where he was sure she hadn't gotten any sleep. He certainly hadn't. But that didn't matter. He could sleep later. Right now, he had to solve the case. The devil was in the details, and there was one detail he could further investigate.

He'd already called his father at the family ranch and

asked about the encounter with the taxi driver at the convenience store and the mysterious letters that Darin had mentioned to Faith. His father had become defensive, saying that it wasn't a good time to talk, but Beck didn't think it was his imagination that his dad was confused about those letters. Surprised, even. Maybe that meant his family had nothing to do with any potential evidence.

Maybe.

Since Pete and Nicole also lived on the grounds of the ranch, Beck would extend his questions to them and have that chat about giving Faith a much-needed break.

Beck got up from the kitchen table and poured himself another cup of coffee. He could hear the TV in the family room, where Tracy was having her breakfast. She was alone since the Ranger had left to assist with the processing of the crime scene at Faith's house. Beck had wanted to be part of that, but not at the expense of leaving Faith and Aubrey.

Before he could return to his seat and his case notes, he heard soft uneven footsteps. A moment later, Aubrey appeared. She was wearing a yellow corduroy dress and no shoes, just socks with lace at the tops.

She smiled and waved at him.

Just like that, the weight of the world seemed to leave his shoulders. "Good morning," he told her.

She babbled something with several syllables and went straight to him. "Up, up," she said.

Beck set his coffee aside and out of her reach, and he picked her up. Aubrey rewarded him with a hug and kiss on the cheek.

"She's faster than she used to be," Marita said, hurrying in. The nanny stopped and eyed them. "And she seems to think you're her new best friend."

There was worry in the woman's tone. Beck understood that. Faith had probably told her about their bitter past, but as far as Beck was concerned, that wasn't going to play a part in how he felt about his new best friend.

"Anything come back on that stuff you found in her attic?" Marita asked, helping herself to a cup of coffee. "Faith just told me about all of that while she was getting dressed."

So that's where she was. Beck had hoped she was still in bed. "We'll try to link the writing to Nolan Wheeler."

Marita flexed her eyebrows and had a sip of coffee. "Or Faith's brother."

Beck nodded and realized that Aubrey was studying him with those intense, cocoa-brown eyes. The little girl finally reached out and pinched his nose. She giggled. And Beck wondered how anyone could be in a bad mood around this child.

From the doorway, Faith stepped into view, studying him. She'd put on a pair of dark brown pants and a coppery top that was nearly the same color as her eyes. She'd pulled her shoulder-length hair into ponytail, a style that made him think of fashion models.

And kissing her neck.

He frowned, hating how he couldn't control those thoughts that kept popping into his head.

"I fixed some eggs," Beck let Marita and Faith know. He considered asking Faith how she was, but he knew the answer. Her eyes said it all. She was troubled and weary. Fear and adrenaline could do that.

Marita went to the stove and lifted the lid to a terra-cotta server. "This looks good. Really good."

"I put in a little smoked sausage and Asiago cheese." He got a little uncomfortable when both women stared at him. "I left some plain for Aubrey. If she can eat eggs, that is. I wasn't sure."

Great. Now he was babbling and sounding like a contestant on some cooking or parenting show.

Thankfully, Marita quit staring at him as if he had a third eye. She dished up some eggs and sampled them. "Mmm. A man who can cook. I think I'm in love," she joked.

"It's a hobby," Beck explained.

Faith smiled. An actual real smile. And that made all of his discomfort worth it. He wasn't embarrassed about his hobby, but it wasn't exactly something a man with his true Texas upbringing liked to brag about. Barbecuing steaks was one thing, but stove cooking and a cowboy image didn't always mesh.

It didn't take long, however, for Faith's smile to fade. "Anything new on the investigation?"

Yeah. And it was news she wasn't going to like. "There were no prints on the rocks and no match on the shoe impression. The sole was too worn to come up with anything distinguishable. Also, the track could have been there a day or two. It wasn't necessarily made by the rock thrower."

Faith stayed quiet, processing that information.

Aubrey pointed to the window, obviously wanting to go closer and look out, but Beck moved her farther away from it. The danger was just too great to do normal things, and if a gunman could shoot into Faith's house, he could do the same to Beck's if he found out Faith and Aubrey were there. He couldn't let that happen.

Marita dished up a small plate of plain eggs, took a spoon from the drawer and reached for Aubrey. "Why don't I feed this to her in the family room so you two can talk?"

When the nanny took Aubrey from him, Beck immediately felt the loss. So did Aubrey—her mouth tightened into a rosebud pout as Marita carted her away.

"You look…disappointed," Faith commented.

"I think being around Aubrey makes me think about being a father. I'm thirty-two. Guess this weird, gut feeling is the equivalent of my biological clock ticking."

Great. Now he was talking biological clocks after his cooking babble. He might have to go wrestle a longhorn to get back his manly image.

Faith lifted an eyebrow. "You want to be a father?"

Her astonished expression and tone stung. "You don't think I'd be a good dad?"

"No. I think you'd be very good at it." Faith walked closer and poured some coffee. She smelled like peach-scented shampoo. "I'm just a little surprised, that's all."

Another shrug. He tipped his head to the family room where he could hear Aubrey babbling. "What can I say? I've decided I want a child."

Actually, he wanted Aubrey.

Why did he feel such a strong connection to that little girl? Maybe because he was starting to feel a strong connection to Aubrey's mother.

Beck looked at Faith then, just as her gaze landed on him. Uh-oh. There it was again. The reminder of that kiss.

She moistened her lips, causing his midsection to clench. He had to move away from her, or he was going to kiss her again. But Faith beat him to it. She leaned in and brushed her mouth over his.

"Mmm," she mumbled. That sound went straight through him. "I shouldn't want you."

He smiled. God knows why. There wasn't anything to smile about. He was getting daddy fever, and he wanted Faith in his bed. Or on the floor.

Location was optional.

Because he was crazed with lust, Beck did something totally stupid. He hooked his arm around her waist and eased her to him. Body against body. It was a good fit. The heat just slid right through him.

"Does saying 'I shouldn't want you' make you want me less?" he asked, making sure it sounded like a joke.

"No." That wasn't a joking tone. A heavy sigh left her mouth. "It's complicated, Beck."

He was aware of that. But something was holding her back other than what'd happened in their past. "Want to tell me about it?"

He saw the hesitation in her eyes. "You'll want to sit down for this," she finally said.

Beck silently groaned. This sounded like trouble.

Before either of them could sit at the kitchen table, he heard the doorbell. It was almost immediately followed by a knock.

Beck snatched his gun from the top of the fridge. "Take Marita and Aubrey and go into the bedroom," he instructed.

Faith gave a shaky nod and started toward the family room. She didn't have to go far. Marita was carrying

Aubrey, and she was headed back into the kitchen. Tracy was right on their heels.

"Try to keep Aubrey quiet," Faith told them. She began to pick up the toys that'd been left in the room.

There was another ring of the doorbell. Another knock. Beck hurried to see who his impatient visitor was, but before he could get to the door, the key slid into the lock. He took aim. The door flew open.

His father was standing there.

Pete was behind him.

"Hell." Beck lowered his gun and cursed some more. His father had obviously not waited and used his emergency key to get in. "It's not a good time for a visit. We'll have to get together later."

His father eyed the gun. Then Beck. But Pete looked past Beck, and his attention landed on Faith. She had various toys clutched in her hands and was apparently headed to the bedroom. She froze.

"What's she doing here?" Pete demanded.

His father didn't let Beck answer, and he gave Pete a sharp warning look. "Maybe this is a good thing. She can probably clear up some of this mess."

Beck had no idea what *mess* his father was talking about, but he had a massive problem on his hands. His family now knew Faith's whereabouts, and unless he could convince them to keep quiet—and trust them to do so—then he was going to have to find a new location to use as a safe house. But he'd have to do that later. Right now, he needed to deal with the situation.

"What's this about?" Beck asked.

His father and brother stepped in and shut the door. "When you called earlier, you wanted to know if I knew anything about some letters that had to do with Sherry Matthews," Roy said. "Well, I do."

Beck was poleaxed. This was another unwanted surprise. Beck had expected his father to have no idea about that particular subject. "What do you mean?"

Roy pulled out a large manila envelope he had tucked beneath his arm. "These letters."

Beck placed his gun on top of the cabinet that housed the TV. Hoping this wasn't something that would lead to his father's arrest, he grabbed a Kleenex from the box on the end table, and he used a tissue so that he wouldn't get his prints on what might be evidence.

Still clutching the toys, Faith walked closer and watched as Beck took out the letters.

"Two and a half months ago, Sherry came out to the ranch to see Pete and me," Roy explained. "He wasn't there so I talked to her alone. She wanted money."

"Two and a half months ago?" Beck repeated. "That was just a couple of weeks before she was murdered."

"A week," Roy corrected. "She was very much alive when she left, but she said she was in big trouble. That she owed someone some money."

"Nolan," Faith supplied. "She called me about that same time, and I told her I couldn't lend her any more. I told her to work it out with Nolan."

"She didn't," Roy informed her. "Sherry said if Pete didn't give her ten grand in cash, then she was going to tell Nicole that she was having an affair with him. She said she'd tell Nicole she was having an affair with me, too."

Beck felt every muscle in his body go stiff. He waited for his father to deny it. He didn't. But Pete did.

"They were bald-faced lies," Pete volunteered.

"Sherry didn't wait around to say those lies to my face. She left, and a day later, the first letter arrived."

Roy nodded. "When I came out of the grocery store, it was tucked beneath the windshield wiper of my truck." He pointed to the letter in question.

The envelope simply had "Pete and Roy" written on it. No "to" or "from" address. Still using the tissue as a buffer, Beck took out the letter itself. One page. Typed. No handwritten signature. No date. No smudges or obvious fingerprints.

However, the envelope had obviously been sealed at one time, and since it was the old-fashioned, lick-and-press kind, he might be able to have that tested for DNA to prove if Sherry had indeed sent it. At this point, he had no reason to doubt that she was the sender, but it was standard procedure to test that sort of thing.

Not that his family had followed procedure.

They should have brought the letters to him, and maybe he could have prevented the murders.

"I need that money," Beck read aloud. "You two owe it to me, and if I don't have that ten thousand dollars by Friday, I'm calling Nicole. Miss Priss won't be happy to hear you're both sleeping with me again, and this time I have proof. Sherry."

Again.

That word really jumped out at him. Maybe it was a reference to the motel incident. Or maybe this was something more recent. If his brother could lie about the first, he could probably lie about the second. But where did that leave his father? Had he slept with Sherry, too?

"Sherry called after the first letter," Pete explained.

"I told her I wasn't going to give her a dime. The next day, the second letter was in the mailbox."

The second letter was typed like the first, but this one contained a copy of a grainy photo. It appeared to be Pete, sleeping, his chest bare and a sheet covering his lower body. Sherry was also in the shot, and it was a photo she'd obviously taken herself since Beck could see her thumb in the image. She was smiling as if she knew that this photo would be worth big bucks.

"That's not me in the picture," Pete insisted. "It's some guy she got who looks like me."

Maybe. It wasn't clear. It, too, would have to be tested and perhaps could be enhanced to get a better image.

"This is your last chance," Beck read aloud from the second letter. "If I don't have the money by tomorrow at six o'clock, a copy of this picture will go to Nicole. Leave the cash with my mom at the liquor store."

"When he got the second letter, I told Pete that maybe we should just pay Sherry off," his father explained. "I didn't care what people thought about me, but I just didn't want Nicole involved in this."

Since blackmailers were rarely satisfied with one payoff, Beck ignored that faulty reasoning and went on to the third letter. It was similar to the others, but this time Sherry demanded fifty thousand dollars, not ten. There was no copy of a photo, only the threat to spill all to Nicole.

"Why didn't you tell me about these letters before?" Beck asked.

"Because I wouldn't let him," Pete spoke up. "I wanted to handle it myself. And I didn't want anyone to know. I didn't want this to get back to Nicole. All it would have taken is for one of your deputies to let it slip, and this wouldn't have stayed private very long."

"I wouldn't have shown this to my deputies." His family must have known that was true, which made Pete's excuse sound even less plausible. But Beck couldn't doubt Pete's motives completely. He would have done anything to prevent Nicole from knowing. His brother might have a loose zipper, but he was obsessed enough with his wife that he would do anything to keep her from being hurt.

Pete pointed to Faith. "I think she was in on this blackmail scheme of her sister's. I think she knew all about it."

"I didn't," Faith said at the same moment that Beck said, "She didn't."

His comment got him stares from all three. "Faith's been up-front with me about this case. Unlike you two," Beck added. "You should have come forward with these and told me about Sherry's visit."

Not that it would have helped him catch the killer. But it would have given Beck the whole picture. Of course, it would have also made his brother and father suspects in Sherry's and her mother's murders.

Hell.

First that gun incident with Nicole. Now this. He might have to arrest a Tanner or two before this was over.

"Faith's brainwashed you," his father decided.

"That's not brainwashing," Pete piped in. "She's using her body to blur the lines. It's what the Matthews women are good at."

Beck slowly laid the letter aside and stared down his brother. "How do you know that?"

"What the hell does that mean?" Pete's nostrils flared. "Were you having an affair with Sherry?"

Pete cursed. "I won't dignify that with an answer."

"Why, because it's true?"

Roy caught onto Pete's arm when his son started to bolt toward Beck. "If your brother says he wasn't sleeping with that woman, then he wasn't."

The denial didn't answer the questions. "Then why would Sherry say it? Why would she have that picture? And why would she try to blackmail you?"

"Because she's a lying tramp, just like her sister." Pete jabbed his finger at Faith again.

That did it. Beck was tired of this. He put the letters aside, went to the door and opened it. "Both of you are leaving now. Once I've processed these letters, I'll let you know if I'm going to file any charges against you."

"Charges?" his father practically yelled. "For what, trying to be discreet? Trying to protect my family from a liar and schemer?"

Beck reminded himself that he was speaking to his father and tried to keep his voice level. "The Rangers could construe this as obstruction of justice."

Roy looked as if he'd slugged him. "Don't do this, son. Don't choose this woman over your own family."

"It's not about Faith. I'm the sheriff. It's my job to investigate all angles of a double murder." He ushered them out, closed the door and locked it.

Faith dropped Aubrey's toys onto the floor. She blew out a long breath and rubbed her hands against the sides of her pants. "I always say I'm not going to let your family get to me."

But they had. And Beck hated that.

Even though she had her chin high and was trying to look strong, Beck went to her and pulled her into his arms. He brushed a kiss on her forehead.

"I didn't know Sherry tried to blackmail Pete and Roy," she volunteered. "I didn't know anything about the letters until Darin mentioned them last night."

"I believe you. If you'd known, you would have told me."

He felt her go stiff, and she eased back to meet his gaze. She shook her head, and he got the sinking feeling that he was about to hear another confession that would cause his blood pressure to spike.

"I have to move Aubrey," she said. "Now that your father and brother know she's here, she can't stay."

She was right. Keeping Aubrey safe had to be at the top of their list.

He nodded. "I have a friend who's the sheriff over in Willow Ridge. I'll call him and see if he can set up a place for all of you there."

"No. Not me. I can't go with her. The danger is tied to me, not her. If I get her away from me, then she'll be safe. But if she stays with me, she could be hurt."

Beck wanted to shoot holes in that theory, but he couldn't. "Are you sure you can be away from her?"

"No. I'm not. I'll miss her. But I can't risk another shooting with her around." She blinked back tears. "You can trust this friend?"

"I can trust him," Beck assured her.

He let go of her so he could start making the necessary arrangements. Beck walked toward his office, and Faith went into the bedroom to tell the others that they'd be moving.

She was keeping something from him.

Damn it.

Here, he'd just blasted his family for withholding evidence and information. He'd given Faith a *carte blanche* approval when defending her. But she obviously had some kind of secret. Was it connected to the murders?

It must at least be connected to Sherry or Darin.

And that meant he'd have to deal with it as soon as he made arrangements for the safe house. He also needed to call the bank and find out if his father or brother had recently withdrawn a large sum of money. Beck hated to doubt them, but he had to think like a lawman.

It was possible that one of them had taken the cash to Sherry to pay her off. Maybe an argument had broken out. Maybe one of them had accidentally killed Sherry. Then maybe Sherry's mother had been killed because she suspected the truth. Or might she have been a witness to her daughter's murder?

Beck groaned and scrubbed his hand over his face. Oh, man. He hated to even consider that, but it was possible. He only hoped it didn't turn out to be the truth.

His phone rang, and when he checked the caller ID screen, he saw that it was from the sheriff's office.

"It's me, Corey," his deputy greeted him when Beck answered. "You're never going to guess who just showed up here at your office."

After the morning from Hades that he'd just had, Beck was almost afraid to ask. "Who?"

"Our murder suspect, Nolan Wheeler. And he's demanding to see you and Faith. Now."

Chapter Nine

Faith could feel her heart breaking. Letting her daughter go was not what she wanted to do. She wanted Aubrey with her.

But more than that, she needed her child to be safe.

For that to happen, she had to say good-bye, even if it made her ache.

"It'll be okay," Beck assured her. Again. He'd been saying that and other reassuring things for the past three hours, since they'd started the preparations to move Aubrey and Marita to a safer location.

Faith wanted to believe him, especially since she didn't feel as if she had a choice. The killer had seen to that.

She kissed Aubrey again and strapped her into the car seat in Beck's SUV. Marita and Tracy were already seated, as was Sgt. Caldwell, who would be driving them to the sheriff's house in Willow Ridge. The Ranger had already promised her that he would take an indirect route to make sure no one followed. Every precaution would be taken. And he'd call her as soon as they arrived.

Faith's heart was still breaking.

Aubrey waved, first to Faith. Then to Beck, who was standing behind her. The little girl gave them both a grin, looked at Beck and said, "Dada."

Her words were crystal clear.

Faith stepped back and met Beck's gaze. "I have no idea why she said that."

He shrugged. "One of the books I read her yesterday had the word *daddy* in it. Guess she picked it up from there."

Relief washed through Faith. She didn't want Beck to think she'd coached Aubrey into saying that. Their lives were already complicated enough without adding those kind of feelings to the mix. But it was clear that her little girl was very fond of Beck.

Beck leaned in, kissed Aubrey's cheek. Faith added another kiss of her own, and Beck shut the door. They backed into the mudroom, and only then did the Ranger open the garage door.

Somehow, Faith managed not to cry when they drove away.

"We need to go to the station and deal with Nolan," Beck reminded her.

As much as she loathed the idea of seeing Nolan Wheeler, it'd get her mind off Aubrey, and would keep Nolan occupied while Aubrey was being transported to the new safe house.

"You don't have to see him," Beck said, heading toward the other vehicle, a police cruiser, that one of his deputies had driven over earlier. He had the manila envelope with Sherry's blackmail letters tucked beneath his arm, and he laid it on the console next to him. "You can wait in my office while I interrogate Nolan."

"Right," she mumbled. Faith got into the passenger's seat and strapped on the belt. "I'm doing this."

"You're sure?" Beck started the cruiser, drove out and closed the garage door behind him. "I told Corey to put Nolan in a holding cell and test him for gunshot residue. That was three hours ago. Nolan will be good and steamed by now that we didn't jump at his invitation to meet with him immediately."

Yes, but there was an upside to that. "With his short temper, maybe he'll be angry enough to tell us what we want to know."

And maybe that info would lead to an arrest. Preferably Nolan's. Faith wanted there to be enough physical evidence to prove Nolan had murdered her mother and sister. Then she could bring her little girl home and get on with her life.

Part of that included coming clean with Beck.

She needed to do that as soon as this meeting with Nolan was over and they had some downtime. She'd told Beck lies, both directly and by omission. He wouldn't appreciate that—it would put a wedge between them, just when they were starting to make some headway.

Faith touched her fingertips to her lips and remembered the earlier kiss. That kiss wasn't ordinary, but the truth was, it couldn't mean anything. It couldn't lead to something more serious. Still, she fantasized about the possibilities. What if all their problems were to magically disappear? And what if Beck could forgive her for lying to him?

Would they have a chance?

She silently cursed. She had enough on her plate without complicating things with a relationship.

"Having second thoughts?" Beck asked.

Faith looked at him. He glanced at her with those sizzling blue eyes and gave her a quick smile. He was very good with those smiles. They were part reassurance, all sex.

Wishing the attraction would go away wasn't working, and that meant she was fast on her way to a broken heart. She hadn't returned to town for that, but it seemed as inevitable as the white-hot attraction between them.

Beck pulled into a parking space directly in front of the back entrance to the sheriff's office. But he didn't reach for the door. He glanced around the parking lot before his eyes came back to her.

"I need to talk to you when we're done here," she said.

He stared at her, and for a moment she thought he was going to insist that conversation happen now. But he didn't. He glanced around the parking lot again and nodded. "Let's go inside. We'll talk later."

Beck ushered her into the break room and through the hall that led to the offices and the front reception.

Deputy Winston met them. "Glad you're here. Our *guest* is complaining."

"I'll bet he is," Beck commented. "What about the GSR test?"

"It was negative." Corey looked at her. "Probably means he wasn't the one who shot at you."

"Or it could mean he washed his hands in the past twelve hours," Beck disagreed.

Corey shrugged and hitched his thumb to the right. "I was watching the security camera and saw you drive up. I just took Nolan to the interview room. He's waiting for you."

Beck handed Corey the manila envelope. "I need you to process this as possible evidence in the Matthews murders. There are three letters inside. Use latex gloves when you handle them, then copy them and send the originals to the crime lab. I want the DNA analyzed and all the pages and envelopes processed for prints and trace."

Corey studied the envelope. "Where'd you get this?"

A muscle flickered in Beck's jaw. "My father and my brother. Once the letters are processed, I'll have them make official statements."

So there might be charges against his family members after all. Faith hated that Beck had to go through this and hated even more that she had to meet with Nolan. He wouldn't willingly give up anything that would incriminate himself. Still, a long shot was unfortunately their best shot.

Faith was familiar enough with the maze of rooms and offices that constituted the LaMesa Police Department. When she was sixteen, she'd had to come and pick up her mother after she'd been arrested for public intoxication. The holding cell had been in the center of the building, but this was Faith's first trip to the west corridor. The walls were stone-gray and bare, unlike Beck's office, which was dotted with colorful Texas landscapes, photos and books.

There were no books or photos in the interview room, either. Just more bare, gray walls and a heavy, metal table where Nolan was seated. Waiting for them.

Nolan stood when they entered, and Faith caught just a glimpse of his perturbed expression before it morphed into a cocky smile. The man hadn't changed a bit. His overly highlighted hair was too long, falling unevenly on his shoulders, and his stubble had gone several days past being fashionable. Ditto for his jeans, which were ripped at the knees and flecked with stains.

"You're looking good there, sweet cakes," he greeted her. Nolan's oily gaze slid over her, making her feel the urgent need to take a bath.

Faith didn't return his smile. "You're looking like the scum you are."

"Oh, come on." He pursed his mouth, bunched up his forehead and made a show of looking offended. "Is that any way to talk to your own brother-in-law?"

"My sister's abusive ex-live-in," she corrected. "You left a death threat for me in the attic of my house."

"It wasn't me. It was your brother." Nolan put his index finger near his right temple and made a circling motion. "Darin's loco."

Beck walked closer and stood slightly in front of her. Protecting her, again. Nolan didn't miss the little maneuver either. His cat green eyes lit up as if he'd witnessed something he might like to gossip about later.

"Have you two buried the hatchet?" Nolan asked.

"I rechecked your alibis for the nights of the murders," Beck said, ignoring Nolan's too-personal question. "They're weak."

Nolan shrugged and idly scraped his thumbnail over a loose patch of paint on the table. "I was at the Moonlight Bar in downtown Austin both times, nearly twenty miles from where Sherry lived. People saw me there."

"Yes, but those same people can't say exactly when you left. You had time to leave the Moonlight and get to both locations to commit both murders." Beck met him eye-to-eye. "So did you kill Sherry and Annie Matthews?"

"No." Nolan smiled again and sank back down onto the chair. "And you must believe that or I would have been arrested, not just detained."

"The day's not over," Beck grumbled. He pulled out a chair for Faith and one for himself. Both of them sat across from Nolan. "Where were you last night?"

"Any particular time that interests you?" Nolan countered.

"All night."

"Hmm. Well, I got up around noon, ate and watched some TV. Around six, I dropped by the Moonlight and hung out with some friends. I left around midnight."

Beck shook his head. "Can anyone confirm that?"

"Probably not." Nolan winked at her. "You really think I'd want to put a bullet in you? I've always liked you, Faith." Again, he combed that gaze over her.

The glare that Beck aimed at the man could have been classified as lethal. "I want your clothes bagged. My deputy will give you something else to wear."

Nolan lifted his left eyebrow. "And if I say no?"

"I'll make a phone call to Judge Reynolds and have a warrant here in ten minutes. Then I'll have you stripped and searched—thoroughly. Ever had a body cavity search, Nolan?"

For the first time since they'd walked into the room, Nolan actually looked uncomfortable.

"I also want a DNA sample," Beck added.

Faith felt her stomach tighten.

"Why?" Nolan challenged. "I heard there was no unidentified DNA at the crime scenes."

There wasn't, but there might be DNA in her attic. However, it wasn't the prospect of that match that was making her squirm.

"I want to make some DNA comparisons." Beck made it seem routine. "If you're innocent, you have nothing to worry about."

Nolan shifted in the chair. "Are you taking Darin's DNA and his clothes to test them for *comparisons?*"

"I would if I could find him."

"Maybe I can help you with that." Nolan let that hang in the air for several snail-crawling seconds. "He calls me a lot. And, no, you can't trace the number. He bought one of those cheapskate disposable phones. But when he calls again, I think I can talk him into meeting with you." Nolan was looking at her, not Beck, when he said that.

"If you believed you could arrange a meeting, then why haven't you already done it?" Faith asked.

"No good reason to."

"He's a murder suspect," Beck pointed out. "The police and the Rangers have been looking for Darin for two months."

"No skin off my nose." Nolan turned to her again. "But I'll do it. I'll set up a meeting, as a favor to you."

He probably thought this would make her more amicable about splitting the inheritance with him. And maybe she would be. If her brother was guilty. And if it got Darin off the street. But Faith wasn't at all convinced that Darin had committed these crimes.

"Set up the meeting if you can," Faith finally said. She stood. "Once I've talked with Darin, then and only then will I discuss anything else with you."

"Deal," Nolan readily agreed. "But one way or another, I'm getting that money. I don't care who I have to turn over to our cowboy cop friend here." Nolan flashed another smile before turning to Beck. "So am I free to go, after you get my clothes and my DNA?"

"Not just yet. Why don't you hang around for a while." It wasn't exactly a request.

Nolan's smile went south. "You can't hold me, Beckett Tanner. I got myself a lawyer, and she said there's not enough evidence for an arrest."

"Then I'll hold you here until your lawyer shows up," Beck informed him.

Faith didn't say anything until they were outside the room. "A good lawyer will have him out in just a few hours," she whispered.

"Well, that's a few hours that he won't be free to roam around and terrorize you." Beck walked to the reception, where Corey was waiting. "I want his clothes and his DNA, and I want it all sent to the crime lab ASAP."

"Will do. Are we locking him up?"

Beck nodded. "Until his lawyer shows. Maybe by then one of his alibis will fall through. The Rangers have put out feelers to see if anyone noticed Nolan leaving the bar in time to commit the murders. Or the shooting last night."

Corey grabbed an evidence kit from the supply cabinet behind him, and he strolled in the direction of the interview room.

Beck turned to Faith. "You really think Nolan can set up a meeting with your brother, or was that all hot air?"

"Maybe. Darin and Nolan aren't friends, but they did get along. Well, better than Nolan got along with the rest of us."

"Then maybe the meeting will pan out." Beck paused. "You flinched when I told Nolan I wanted a DNA sample."

"Did I?" Though she knew she had.

"You did." He blew out a deep breath and put his hands on his hips. "Nolan flirted with you in there. I thought there'd be more animosity. I thought I'd see more hatred in his eyes. But there wasn't any."

It took a moment for all that to sink in, and Faith was certain she flinched again. "What are you saying?"

But he didn't have time to answer. The front door flew open, and Nicole walked in. Faith automatically looked for a gun, but the woman appeared to be unarmed. Still, that didn't make this a welcome visit. She'd had more than enough of Beck's family today. Because of his father and brother's impromptu visit, Aubrey had had to go to a safe house.

"Her brother stole from me," Nicole announced.

That got Faith's attention, and she changed her mind about this visit. It might turn out to be a good thing. "You've seen Darin?"

But Nicole didn't answer her. Instead, she turned her attention to Beck. "That killer was at the ranch." She shuddered. "He was there and could have murdered us all."

"Let's go into my office," Beck suggested.

Faith silently agreed. Though they were the only ones in the reception area, it still wasn't the place to have a private discussion.

"I don't want to go into your office," Nicole insisted, and she wouldn't budge. "I want you to make her tell us where her creepy brother is so you can arrest him before he murders me like he did his mother and sister."

Beck held up his hands. "Faith doesn't know where Darin is. No one does. Now, what happened to make you think Darin wants to kill you, and what exactly did he steal?"

"He took a tranquilizer gun from the medical storage room in the birthing barn."

Faith pulled in her breath. A tranquilizer gun had been used to incapacitate both her mother and sister before they'd been strangled.

"I have proof," Nicole continued. She pulled a disk from her purse and slapped it onto the reception counter. "He's there, right on the security surveillance. He took it two and a half months ago, just days before the murders. He knew where it was because we've kept it in the same place for years, and as you well know, he used to work at the ranch part-time before all that mess at the motel."

Oh, mercy.

If this was true, it didn't sound good. Right up until the time of the murders, her brother had worked on and off as a delivery man for Doc Alderman, the town's only vet. The police had investigated the vet's supplies, but he could account for both of the tranquilizer guns in his inventory. Neither of those guns had prints or DNA from her brother. It was the bit of hope that Faith had clung to that Nolan had perhaps used a tranquilizer gun to set up Darin.

"And you just now noticed this tranquilizer gun was missing?" Faith asked.

Nicole still didn't look at her. She aimed her answer at Beck. "We haven't had to use it in ages. One of the ranch hands went in there to get it this morning to sedate one of the mares, and that's when we realized it was missing. Darin Matthews took it."

"That's on this disk?" Beck picked it up by the edges.

"It's there. It took me a while to find it. The security system in the storage room is motion-activated, and since the ranch hands hardly go in there, the disk wasn't full. I played it, and I saw Darin."

"You're sure it was him?" Beck asked before Faith could.

"Positive. You can see his face as clear as day."

"And you can see him take the tranquilizer gun?" Beck pressed.

Nicole dodged his gaze. "Not exactly. He moved in front of the camera, but what else would he have been doing in there?"

"Maybe delivering something for Dr. Alderman?" Faith immediately suggested. "Did you check with the vet to find out if he'd sent Darin out there to the ranch?"

"He had," Nicole said through clenched teeth. "Even though I'd told Alderman that I didn't want Darin any-where near us."

"So maybe Darin was just delivering supplies," Beck concluded.

"Then what happened to the tranquilizer gun?"

"It could have been misplaced. Or someone else could have stolen it."

Anger danced through Nicole's cool blue eyes. "You're standing up for her again."

"I'm standing up for the truth," Beck corrected.

Her perfectly manicured index finger landed against his chest. "You're standing up for the Matthews family. I don't understand why. You know what they've done to us. The cheating, the lies."

"Pete cheated that night, too," Beck countered.

The color drained from Nicole's face, and she dropped back a step. "I expected this from the likes of her. But not from you." And with that, Nicole turned on her heels and hurried out the door.

Faith stood there silently a moment and tried to hold on to her composure. "Thank you," she said to Beck.

He turned and faced her. But he seemed unmoved by her gratitude. "I'll look at this disk," he said, his words short and tight. "And if there's any hint that Darin or anyone else stole that gun, I'll send it to the crime lab."

She nodded. "I expected that. I never expected you to give my brother a free ride. If Darin's guilty, I'll do whatever's necessary to catch him, and I'll support your decision to arrest him."

He searched her eyes, as if trying to decide if she was telling him the truth. Then he motioned for her to follow him to his office.

Faith did, and her heartbeat sped up with each step. The moment he made it into his office, Beck turned around to face her again.

"After watching the way Nolan reacted to you, I need to know." But he didn't ask it right away. He waited a moment, with the tension thick between them. "Is Nolan Aubrey's father?"

There it was. The question she'd been dreading.

Well, one of them anyway.

"Is he Aubrey's father?" Beck demanded when she didn't answer.

Faith shook her head, stepped farther inside and shut the door. "Maybe."

"Maybe? Maybe!" That was all he said for several

seconds. Seconds that he spent drilling her with those intense and suddenly angry eyes. "You don't know who fathered your own child?"

"No, I don't."

Faith took a deep breath and braced herself for the inevitable fallout that would follow. "Because I'm not Aubrey's biological mother."

Chapter Ten

Beck dropped into the chair behind his desk, squeezed his eyes shut and groaned.

"I know, I should have told you sooner," Faith said. "But I had my reasons for keeping it a secret."

He slowly opened his eyes and pegged her gaze. "I'm listening." Though he was almost positive he wouldn't like what he heard.

Faith sat first. She eased into the chair as if it were fragile and might break. "Sixteen months ago, Sherry showed up at my apartment in Oklahoma. I hadn't seen her in months, but she was pregnant and needed money. I gave her what cash I had, and when she left, I realized she'd stolen my wallet. It had my ID and driver's license in it."

Beck didn't say a word because he'd already guessed how this had played out.

"The following day when Sherry went into labor, she used my name when she admitted herself to the hospital. She even put my name on Aubrey's birth certificate. I didn't know," Faith quickly added. "Not until after she checked out of the hospital two days later. She broke into my apartment and left Aubrey and a letter on my bed."

"Hell," he mumbled. He had guessed the part about Sherry being the birth mom. But not this. "She left a newborn alone?"

Faith nodded and swallowed hard. "Aubrey was okay. Hungry, but okay. Needless to say, I was a little shaken when I realized what Sherry had done."

Beck leaned closer, staring at her from across the desk. "Why didn't you tell anyone?"

"Because of the letter Sherry left. I have it locked away in a safety deposit box in Oklahoma if you want to read it for yourself. But Sherry told me in the letter that Aubrey would be in danger if her birth father found out she existed. 'He'll kill her,' Sherry wrote. 'You have to protect her. You can't tell anyone or she'll die.'" Faith shuddered. "I believed Sherry."

Yeah. Beck bet she had. He would have, too.

"You covered for your sister, again, just like you did ten years ago outside the motel with Pete."

Faith nodded. "I had to protect Aubrey. I loved her from the moment I laid eyes on her."

He understood that, too.

Beck wanted to be angry with Faith. He hated being lied to. He hated that she hadn't trusted him with something this important. But if their situations had been reversed, he might have done the same thing. All he had to do was look at the things he'd done to protect his own family.

"I'm sorry I let you believe she was mine." Faith swiped away a tear that slid down her cheek. "But she is mine, in every way that counts."

He didn't want to deal with Aubrey's paternity just yet. But he had to find out if this was connected to the case.

"Nolan could be the father," Beck said more to himself than to Faith. "But if he knew, he would have already tried to use her to get money."

Faith mumbled an agreement. "Sherry told me she'd kept her pregnancy a secret. That no one knew, except our mother and Darin. She left Austin when she starting showing and stayed in Dallas until the day before she came to see me."

Beck wasn't sure he could take Sherry's account at face value, but something must have happened to make her want to hide the pregnancy and her child. Or maybe the woman simply didn't want to play mother and conned Faith with that sob story. It felt real.

"If Aubrey's father is someone other than Nolan, he hasn't made any contact with me," Faith continued. "And if he'd talked to Sherry, she probably would have let me know. She was so worried about him finding out about Aubrey."

Beck thought that through. If Aubrey's birth father was the person responsible for the attempt to kill Faith, then why had he shot at her? If he wanted something— money, for instance—then why hadn't he gotten in touch with her so he could blackmail her?

"I don't think this is connected to the case," she added, her voice practically a whisper now.

"Maybe not, but we need to know for sure."

She shook her head and looked more than a little alarmed. "How can we do that without endangering Aubrey?"

"Do you have something of hers that would have her DNA on it?"

She stood, and he could see the pulse pounding on her throat. "I have her hairbrush in my purse, but I don't want her DNA tested. I believed Sherry when she said Aubrey could be in danger."

"I'm taking that threat seriously, too. But we have to know who Aubrey's father is. He could have killed Sherry and your mother. We have to rule him out as a suspect. Or else find him and arrest him."

"I know." A moment later she repeated it, and the fear and frustration made her voice ragged. "Sherry often had affairs with married men."

"And one of those men might not want the world to know he has a child." Beck stood, too, and walked closer to her. "So here's what we do. I'll package the hairbrush myself so that no one, including my deputies, will see it. Then I'll seal it and send it to the lab in Austin. I'll ask them to compare the DNA to Nolan's. And to mine."

Her eyes widened. "Yours?"

He obviously needed to explain this. "I'll ask Sgt. Caldwell to give the results only to me. But I want him to leak information that he did some DNA testing and that I'm Aubrey's father."

"What?" Her eyes widened even more.

From the moment the idea had popped into his head, he figured she'd be shocked. Still, this was a solution. Time would tell if the solution was a successful one. "If everyone believes I'm Aubrey's father, that'll stop Nolan or anyone else from being concerned that they've produced an unwanted heir."

With her eyes still wide, she shook her head. "Beck,

this could backfire. What happens when your family finds out?"

Oh, they would find out. No way to get around that. "They won't be happy about it, but it doesn't matter. This will keep Aubrey safe."

He hoped.

But there was another reason he wanted his DNA compared to Aubrey's. Beck was positive he wasn't the little girl's biological father, but he couldn't say the same for his brother. Or even his own father.

If Aubrey was his niece or his half-sister, then the test would prove it.

And if Aubrey was the primary motive for murder, that might mean there was a killer in his family.

FROM WHERE IT LAY on the coffee table, Beck's cell phone softly beeped again. An indication that he had voice mail. He didn't get up from the sofa and check it. Didn't need to. He'd already looked at the caller ID and knew the voice mails were from his father and brother.

He did check his watch though. It'd been six hours since he told Sgt. McKinney to get out the word that Beck was Aubrey's father. To make the info flow a little faster, Beck had told his deputy, Corey, the same necessary lie. The Rangers knew the truth. Corey didn't. He hoped Corey had leaked the little bombshell all over town, especially since Beck hadn't said anything about keeping it a secret.

Those two calls wouldn't be the only attention he'd get from his family. If he didn't answer their calls, they'd drop by for a visit—maybe even tonight. This time though, Beck had put the slide lock on. His father wouldn't be able to just walk inside as he'd done that morning. He'd also set the security system so if anyone tried to get in through any of the doors, the alarm would sound. Hopefully no one in his family would be desperate enough to try to crawl through a window.

He glanced at the numbers he'd written down when the bank manager had called him just minutes earlier. It was one of two other calls that brought bad news. Beck wasn't sure what to do about the second, but as for the first, he needed to investigate the bank figures from his father's account. Those numbers added up to trouble. They were yet another piece of a puzzle that was starting to feel very disturbing.

"Mommy misses you so much," he heard Faith say.

She was sitting on one of the chairs in the family room, just a few feet from him, with her phone pressed to her ear. She had her fingers wound in her hair and was doing some frequent chewing on her bottom lip. She was obviously talking to Aubrey, and it was the third call she'd made since the Ranger, Marita, Tracy and Aubrey had arrived at the safe house.

It wouldn't be the last.

This separation was causing her a lot of grief. Grief that Beck felt as well. But this arrangement was necessary. And hopefully only temporary. Once he'd caught the killer, then Faith could bring Aubrey home.

Wherever home was.

He doubted she could go back to her house, not with the attic death calendar and the shooting incident.

Faith got up from the chair and made her way to him. She held out the phone. "I thought you'd want to tell Aubrey 'Good night.'"

He did, but Beck knew all of this was drawing him closer and closer to a child that he should be backing away from. He needed to stay distanced and objective.

But he took the phone anyway. "Hi, Aubrey," he told her.

She answered back with her usual "'i'" and babbled something he didn't understand, but Beck didn't need to understand the baby words to know that Aubrey was confused. She was probably wondering why her mother wasn't there to tuck her into bed.

"Your mommy will be there soon," he added.

The next syllables he understood. She strung some Da-da-da's together. Such simple sounds. Sounds Aubrey didn't even comprehend, but they were powerful.

"Good night," he said and handed the phone back to Faith.

"Good night," she repeated to Aubrey. "I love you."

Faith hung up, stood there and blew out a long breath. "It's hard to be away from her."

Beck settled for a "yeah."

She put her phone on the coffee table next to his and then looked around as if she didn't know what to do with herself. "I cringe when I think of the prenatal care Sherry would have gotten when she was pregnant. She wouldn't have taken care of herself. But thankfully, Aubrey turned out just fine."

"You've done a good job with her. You're a good mother, Faith."

Her eyes came to his. "I'm sorry about lying to you. For what it's worth, I'd planned to tell you today."

He believed her. It riled him initially, but ultimately brought them closer.

Like now.

She stood there, just a few feet away, wearing dark jeans and a sapphire-blue stretch top, something she'd put on after showering when they'd returned from his office. Her hair was loose, falling in slight curls past her shoulder.

She looked like the answer to a few of his hot fantasies.

His body wanted him to act on the fantasies, to haul her onto his lap so he could kiss her hard and long. Of course, because this was his fantasy, the kiss would be just the beginning.

And all that energy would be misplaced because he needed to do everything to make sure there wasn't another attempt on her life.

Forcing his mind off her body, he picked up copies of the three blackmail letters and spread them out over the coffee table so that Faith could see them. "With everything else that's happened today, I haven't had a chance to go over these. They could be important."

She made a sound of agreement, sat down on the floor near his feet and picked up the first one. "I find it interesting that Sherry sent the letters to both your father and brother. By doing so, she implicates both, which means she could have had a recent affair with either of them."

"Or neither."

Faith didn't look offended by that. She stayed quiet a moment, apparently giving that some thought. "True, but then why would she think she could get money from them unless there'd been some kind of inappropriate relationship? Because Nicole hated Sherry so much and blamed her for her emotional problems, an affair with either would have upset her. Both Roy and Pete would have wanted to prevent Nicole from finding out."

She paused, and her gaze snapped to his. Her eyes widened. "The DNA tests," she said. "You wanted to compare Aubrey's DNA to yours so you'd know if Roy or Pete is Aubrey's father."

He nodded.

"Beck, this could be a nasty mess if one of them is."

He nodded again.

"Oh, mercy." She dropped the letter on the table and tunneled her hands through the sides of her hair again. "What happens if it's true, if one of them is a DNA match?"

"Then I'll deal with it." Which was his way of saying that he didn't know what he'd do. Still, he and Faith had to know the truth, and this was one way of getting it. DNA could also exclude his relatives and hone right in on Nolan.

Shaking her head, she leaped up from the floor. "I'm not giving up custody. I've raised Aubrey since birth. I love her—"

"You're not going to lose her," Beck promised, though he had no idea how he'd keep that promise. If necessary, he'd just continue the lie that he was Aubrey's father.

He felt as if he were anyway.

Because he was losing focus again, Beck forced himself to look at the letters. "The third letter is different from the other two," he continued.

It took her a moment to regain her composure, but then she glanced at all three letters. "Yes. Sherry asks for more money in the third one. Maybe because Nolan pressed her for more. Ironic, since his car was probably worth less than a thousand bucks. He would have tried to get everything he could from her, all the while threatening to go to the police to report her for car theft. With her priors, she would have gone to jail."

That made sense, but he wasn't sure that the rest of it did. "Why would Sherry have typed the letters, especially since she put her name on them, visited my father and told him what she wanted? These letters are physical evidence and prove attempted extortion."

Faith lifted her shoulder. "Who knows why Sherry did what she did. Maybe she thought she could bluff her way out of extortion charges if she was arrested. She could claim she didn't type the letters." Faith paused. "You think someone else did?"

Now it was Beck's turn to shrug. But he also stood so he could deliver this news when they were closer to eye level. "The bank manager called when you were on the phone with Aubrey. It took some doing, but he found that my father had taken money from his various investment accounts. A little here, a little there, but it all added up to ten grand."

She walked closer and stopped right in front of him. "That's the exact amount Sherry was demanding in the first two letters."

"Yes. And she might have gotten it." His father might have paid Sherry off. He'd deal with that later, after he'd put more of this together.

"But if your father gave her the money, then why the third letter?" Faith asked.

"My theory is that someone else might have continued the blackmailing scheme."

"You mean Nolan." She didn't hesitate.

Neither did he. "Or your brother. Or even your mother. All it would have taken is knowledge of Sherry's plan and a computer to type the letters."

She bobbed her head, took another deep breath. "Nolan could have done this, and when Sherry threatened to expose him, he could have killed her."

That's what Beck thought, too. Nolan could have killed Sherry's mother if the money had been left with her. She would have known Nolan had a part in the scheme.

Because he was watching her, he saw Faith go still. "Is Nolan still being held at the sheriff's office?"

Hell. He hated to tell her this. "No. His lawyer showed up, and he was released about a half hour ago."

"I see." The words were calm enough, but the emotion was there in her expression and in her body.

"If I can get just one person at the Moonlight Bar to say they saw Nolan leave early on any of the three nights in question, then I should have enough to ask the DA to take this to a grand jury."

"In the meantime, Nolan is a free man. And he might stay that way. There's enough reasonable doubt, especially with the security disk of Darin in that barn."

Her voice didn't crack. Her eyes didn't water. He didn't touch her, but he did move closer.

"Some homecoming," she mumbled. She tried to smile at him, but it turned into a stare that ran the gamut of emotions. "But at least we're on the same side."

Oh, yeah. And more. They'd moved from being enemies to being comrades. To being…something else that Beck knew he should avoid.

But he didn't.

When Faith stepped closer, he didn't step back. He

just watched her as she reached out and touched his arm lightly with the tip of her fingers.

"How badly would this screw things up?" she asked.

"Bad," he assured her.

She nodded. Didn't step back. She didn't take her caressing fingers from his arm.

"I'm not good at this." Her voice dropped to a silky whisper. "But I'll bet you are."

Beck couldn't help it. He smiled.

And reached for her.

Chapter Eleven

Beck's mouth came to hers, and just like that, Faith
melted. The intimate touch, the gentle I'm-in-control-
here pressure of his lips. The heat. They all combined
to create a kiss that went straight through her.

She couldn't move. Couldn't think. Couldn't
breathe. The kiss claimed her, just as Beck did when
he bent his arm around her waist and pulled her to him.
The sweet assault continued, and Faith could only hang
on for the ride.

Or so she thought.

But then he stopped and eased back just a bit. That's
when Faith realized her heart was pumping as if she
were starved for air. She blamed it on the intense heat
Beck had created with his kiss.

"You need a minute to rethink this?" he asked.

Did she?

Beck stood there, waiting. Breathing hard as well.
Looking at her.

Faith looked at him, too. At those sizzling blue eyes.
At that strong, ruggedly hot face. And she looked at his

body. Oh, his body. That was creating more firestorms inside her.

Because her right hand was already on his chest, she slid it lower and along the way felt his muscles respond. They jerked and jolted beneath her touch. It was amazing that she could do that to him.

Beck didn't touch her. He stood there with his intense eyes focused on her and his body heat sending out that musky male scent that aroused her almost as much as his kiss had done.

Her hand went lower, while their gazes stayed locked. A muscle flickered in his jaw. His heart was pounding. Hers, too. So much so that she wasn't sure if that was her own pulse in her fingertips or if it was Beck's.

When she made it to his stomach, she slipped her fingers inside the small gap between the buttons of his shirt and had the pleasure of touching his bare skin.

You can do this, she told herself. She wanted to do this.

"You still need time to think?" Beck asked her. She was surprised he could speak with his jaw clenched that tight.

"No." She eased her fingers deeper inside his shirt, loosening a button until it came undone. "I don't need any more time."

Before the last syllable left her mouth, he kissed her. It was hard and hungry. If it hadn't fueled the need inside her, it would have been overwhelming. Suddenly, she wanted to be overwhelmed. She wanted everything she knew Beck was capable of giving her.

With their bodies still facing each other, he scooped her up in his arms. Faith wrapped her legs around him, and he immediately started toward his bedroom. They bumped into some furniture along the way. And a wall. Neither of them were willing to break the kiss so they could actually see where they were going.

Beck used his foot to shove open the door. The room was dark, with only the moonlight filtering through the blinds and thin curtain.

Several steps later, Faith felt herself floating downward. Her back landed against his mattress. And Beck landed against her with his sex touching hers through the barrier of their jeans.

She didn't want any barriers. She kicked off her shoes and went after his shirt.

Beck went after hers, stripping it over her head and tossing it onto the floor.

Everything became urgent. Frantic. A battle against time. She cursed her fumbling fingers but then gave a sigh of pleasure when she got his shirt off and put her hands on him. He was all sinew and muscle. All man.

And for the moment, he was hers for the taking.

So Faith took.

She kissed his chest and explored some of those muscles. Not for long though. Beck had other ideas. He unhooked the clasp of her bra, and her breasts spilled out. He fastened his mouth onto her left nipple and sent her flying.

Mercy, was all she could think.

He kept kissing her breasts and lightly nipped her with his teeth; all the while he worked to get her jeans off. She worked to get his off, too, though she had to keep stopping to catch her breath.

Her jeans surrendered and landed somewhere on the floor where Beck tossed them. Faith shoved down his zipper. He shoved down her panties. And for only a moment, she felt the cool air on the inside of her thighs.

The coolness didn't last.

Beck kissed her. The heat from his mouth warmed her all right and had her demanding that he do something about the fire he'd created inside her.

He stood and rid himself of his boots and jeans. She wished the light had been on so she could see him better, but the moonlight did some amazing things to his already amazing body. The man was perfect.

Beck reached in the nightstand drawer and pulled out a foil-wrapped condom. Safe sex. She was glad he'd remembered. She certainly hadn't.

He tugged off his boxers while he opened the condom. She got just a glimpse of him, huge and hard, before he came back to her, moving between her legs.

Faith forced herself not to think. She wanted this to happen. With Beck. Right here, right now.

Their eyes met. The tip of his erection touched her in the most intimate way and sent a spear of pleasure through her. She gasped and gasped again when he pushed deeper.

Wow.

With just that pressure, that movement, that sweet invasion, she was certain this was as much of the tangle of heat that she could take. She felt on the verge of unraveling.

But Beck stopped.

In fact, he froze.

Faith wanted no part of that. She hooked her leg around his lower back and shoved him forward.

There was a flash of pain. But it was quickly overshadowed by a flood of pleasure.

Beck didn't move. He stayed frozen.

She focused, trying to see his face, and the confused expression she saw there probably matched her own. He had questions.

"You're a virgin?" he asked.

Now it was her turn to freeze. "Sort of."

Sort of? Sort of! She wanted to kick herself for that stupid response. And she wanted to kick herself again because the moment was gone. Even though the need was still there, racing through her, she knew this wasn't going to continue until Beck got an explanation.

She caught onto him when he tried to move off her. "I tried to have sex with my boyfriend in college, but it didn't work out. I panicked."

"You're twenty-eight," he reminded her. This time, he did move off her. He landed on his back next to her and groaned. "There would have been other opportunities since college."

"One other, a few years ago. I panicked then, too." Faith hesitated, wondering how much she should say, but since she'd already messed this up, she went for broke. "When I was fourteen, one of Sherry's drunk boyfriends sneaked into my bedroom one night and tried to rape me. He didn't succeed, obviously. Darin came in and hit the guy with an alarm clock. Anyway, it took me a long time to get over that."

Beck cursed under his breath. "You're over it now?" he asked, staring up at the ceiling.

"I'm over it." Beck seemed to have cured her. Amazing that he could do what therapy hadn't.

He turned on his side and faced her. "Why didn't you tell me before I got you onto this bed?"

"I didn't want to explain what'd happened in my past. I wanted to have sex with you. And besides, I didn't think you'd notice."

"I noticed." It sounded as if he'd worked hard to keep the emotion and maybe even some sarcasm out of his voice. "Did I hurt you?"

"No." Since that sounded like a lie, she tried again. "Just a little, that's all."

This time the cursing didn't stay under his breath. "I'm sorry."

"No need to be. I'm not."

He stared at her, groaned and looked up at the ceiling again. "You just turned my life upside down. Now I've got positive proof that my brother's been lying all these years about what happened in the motel. And everything I'd ever thought about you was wrong."

"You thought I was a slut." She put her hand over his mouth so he wouldn't have to confirm that. "Everyone did. Because everyone believed I was just like my mother and Sherry. Guilt by association. But the truth is, I went in the opposite direction. I didn't want to be anything like either of them."

He stayed quiet a moment, before he reached for her and pulled her to him gently, and just held her.

"I never wanted to be any woman's first lover," he said. "It was sort of a badge of honor for some guys in high school. Not me. I figured it created some kind of permanent bond that I wasn't sure I wanted."

That stung a little. Was he saying he was sorry this had happened? Apparently. Because he wasn't doing anything to continue what they'd started.

"You don't owe me anything, Beck," she assured him.

"Oh, I owe you. An apology for starters for the way I've treated you." He kissed the top of her head. Cursed softly. And looked down at her. "What the hell am I going to do with you now?"

Though he probably didn't want her to answer, she considered pointing out that they were naked on his bed. But a soft thump stopped her from saying anything. The small sound came from the direction of the window. It sounded as if someone had bumped against the glass.

Beck shot off the bed.

"Get down on the floor," he told her.

Her heart banged against her rib cage, and Faith did as he said. Beck ran into the bathroom and seconds later emerged with his boxers on. He gathered up his jeans and started to put them on while he reached for something in his nightstand drawer.

A gun.

That got her moving.

She hurriedly crawled around, collected her clothes and got dressed. Once Beck had on his jeans, shirt and boots, he raced to the window. Pressing himself against the wall, he peered out the edge of the blinds.

"Hell, someone's out there," he let her know.

Her heart banged even harder. "Who is it?"

"Can't tell. He's dressed all in black, and he's crouched down near the rosemary bush in the side yard."

A ringing sound sliced through the silence. It was her cell phone. She'd left it in the family room.

"Stay put," Beck instructed. But a moment later, he cursed again. "The guy looks like he's trying to sneak away."

Oh, mercy. She didn't want him to get away. If it was Nolan, they could use this to arrest the man for trespassing. If he had a weapon, even better, because they could possibly charge him with criminal intent.

Beck started for the bedroom door. "My cell's not in here either. Use the phone by the bed and dial nine-one-one. Ask for backup. But I don't want sirens. I want a quiet approach so we don't scare this guy off."

She dialed the number as he asked. The dispatcher answered right away, and she relayed what Beck had told her. The dispatcher said he would send the night deputy immediately.

"Are you thinking about going out there?" she asked Beck the moment she hung up.

"I need to catch this guy," was his uneasy answer.

The silence lasted several seconds. "I have another gun on the top shelf in the closet," he instructed. "Get it and then stay low while you follow me to the back door. Lock it when I leave and set the security system. I won't be long."

"You don't know that. This guy could shoot you."

"I'm the sheriff," he reminded her. Plus, if he could end this tonight, then Aubrey wouldn't be in danger.

Her little girl could come back home.

"I'm doing this," Beck insisted.

Faith considered arguing with him, but she knew it would do no good. She hurried to the closet and took the .38 from the shelf. They crouched down and hurried to the back door.

"Be careful," she told him. But that was it. All she had time to say.

"Six-eight-eight-nine," he explained, disarming the

security system so it wouldn't go off when he made his exit. He shoved a set of keys into his jeans pocket. "Lock the door, reset it and then get back into the bedroom. Stay on the floor. I'll let myself back in when I'm finished."

And just like that, he hurried out.

Faith followed his instructions to a tee, added a prayer that he would be okay, and headed to the bedroom. She hadn't even made it there when the house phone rang. Five rings and the answering machine kicked in.

"Sheriff Beck Tanner," the machine announced. "I'm not here, so leave a message. If this is an emergency, hang up and call nine-one-one."

She waited, her mind more on Beck than the caller. And then she heard the voice.

"Faith?"

It was Darin.

She scrambled across the room and picked up the phone. "Darin, it's me. I'm here."

"I'm here, too. Outside Beck's house. I need to see you. I have something to show you."

Oh, God. Beck was out there expecting to catch a killer. He might shoot Darin by mistake. Of course, there was that possibility that Darin was the killer.

"I'm in the yard," Darin continued. "By some rose-bushes. There's a window nearby."

So he wasn't by the rosemary. He'd moved from the side yard to the back, where Beck had just exited. They'd probably just missed each other. She needed to tell Beck what was going on, but he didn't have his cell phone with him.

"I won't hurt you," Darin promised. And for a moment,

she remembered her brother, the one who'd saved her from Sherry's drunken boyfriend. The brother she loved.

With the cordless phone in one hand and the gun gripped in the other, Faith crawled back toward the kitchen. Toward the window with the roses.

"What do you need to show me?" she asked Darin.

"Sherry had some pictures of her with a man. I found them, and I think they're important."

It was likely the photo that Sherry had sent Pete and Roy, the one that proved she'd had the affair that might earn her some blackmail money.

When she reached the kitchen window, Faith lifted her head a little and looked out. She didn't spot her brother. "Darin, listen. Beck's out there, and if he sees you, he might shoot first and ask questions later. So I want you to stay put. Don't run. Don't make any sudden moves."

She saw something then. Was that a shadow in the shrubs or was it Beck?

She couldn't tell.

"Stay down," she told her brother in a whisper. She waited until Darin had gotten to the ground. Then she opened the window several inches, and in a slightly louder voice, she said, "Beck?"

Nothing. Not even from the other end of the phone, and she wondered if Darin had hung up.

Faith lifted the window a little more. The shadow didn't move. "Beck?" she called out.

She waited. Not long. Seconds, maybe. And a swishing sound came right at her. It happened in the blink of an eye.

Something tore through the mesh window screen.

There was a stab in her neck. Sharp and raw. But she didn't even have time to scream.

Faith felt herself falling, losing consciousness, and there was nothing she could do to stop it.

BECK STAYED CLOSE TO the house so he could use it for cover in case something went wrong and so he could make sure no one got inside to go after Faith.

The figure he'd seen in the yard might be a kid playing a stupid game, but with everything else that'd happened in the past two days, he couldn't take the chance. He also didn't want to leave Faith alone much longer, so that meant he had to find this guy and take care of the situation—fast.

He hoped it was Nolan so he could arrest him. Or beat him senseless, whichever came first.

Hurrying but keeping his gun aimed and ready, Beck went to the front of the house and looked around the corner. No one was there so he moved across the porch toward the side yard where he'd first seen the figure.

He silently cursed when he didn't see anyone there.

Had Nolan or Darin gotten away?

From up the street, he saw a cruiser approaching. The siren was off, but the deputy had his headlights on. He turned them off when he was about a half block away, parked the cruiser and got out. It was Deputy Mark Gafford. Beck motioned that he was going to go back around the house.

Beck stepped down from the porch and into the side yard where his bedroom extended to just a few feet from that rosemary bush. He glanced inside the bedroom window but couldn't see Faith. Good. That hopefully meant the killer couldn't see her either.

With the deputy now covering his back, Beck got moving again. Staying in the shadows. Keeping watch. He half expected someone to ambush him at any moment. Because after all, Sherry and her mother had been ambushed. But with each step, he heard nothing, saw nothing.

Until he made it to the backyard.

Someone was on the back porch at the door, dressed all in black. Could it be the same shadowy figure that'd been in the rosemary?

"Hold it right there!" Beck called out. He ducked partly behind the corner of the house to use it as cover in case the person fired.

But there was no shot.

The person bolted off the porch and began to run.

"Stop!" Beck yelled.

The guy didn't. Beck jumped on the porch in pursuit. From the corner of his eye, he saw Faith. On the kitchen floor.

His heart fell to his knees.

He called out her name, the sound ringing through his head, and he got a glimpse of the darkly clad figure rounding the corner, out of Beck's sight.

Beck didn't chase after him. Instead, he raced to the back door, forgetting that it was locked. God, he had to get to her.

There was blood on her neck.

"Watch out for a gunman," Beck yelled to his deputy, hoping the man would hear him.

He fumbled through his pocket for his keys. It seemed to take an eternity before he got the right one into the lock. Finally, it opened, and despite the fact he'd triggered the security system and it started to blare, he ran to her.

She wasn't moving.

Trying to keep watch to make sure the gunman didn't return, Beck pressed his fingers to the side of her neck that wasn't bleeding.

He felt her pulse. It was faint. But it was there. She was alive.

For now.

He reached up, yanked the wall phone from its cradle and jabbed in nine-one-one.

"Sheriff Tanner," he said, the second the dispatcher answered. "Get an ambulance out to my place now. Faith Matthews has been shot."

He tossed the phone aside and checked her injury to see what he could do to help her. She wasn't bleeding a lot, and he soon realized why.

The injury wasn't from a bullet.

Beck reached down and plucked the tiny dart from her neck. And he felt both relief.

And fear.

Because someone had shot her with a tranquilizer gun.

Just the way her sister and mother had been shot, right before someone had murdered them.

Chapter Twelve

Faith forced her eyes open. No easy task, because her eyelids felt as heavy as lead. Actually, her entire body felt that way.

She glanced around and saw she was in a bed in a sterile white room. A hospital. That's when she remembered what had happened in Beck's kitchen.

Someone had shot her.

Her hand flew to her neck, to the thin bandage that was there. The skin beneath it was sore, but she wasn't actually in pain.

"Someone used a tranquilizer gun on you," a man said. "You're going to be okay." It was Beck. He was there. It was his voice she'd heard, and next to him stood Corey, his deputy.

"We didn't catch him," Beck added with a heavy, frustrated-sounding sigh.

"But you saved me. I didn't die," she mumbled.

Beck shook his head and walked closer. "You didn't die." His face was etched with worry, and judging from his bloodshot eyes, he hadn't slept in a while. Faith had no idea how long it might had been.

"How long have I been here?" she wanted to know.

Beck eased down on the side of the bed beside her and pushed her hair away from her face. His touch was gentle. "All night. It's nearly ten o'clock. There was enough tranquilizer in that dart to knock out someone twice your size. That's why you had to stay the night here in LaMesa Hospital."

"Ten o'clock?" That was too long. She had to find out who'd done this to her. She also had to check on Aubrey. Faith tried to get up, but Beck put his hand on her shoulder to make her lie back down.

"How are you feeling?" Corey asked.

So that it would speed things along and get her out of that bed, Faith did a quick assessment. Well, as quickly as her brain would allow. It felt as if her thoughts were traveling through mud. "I'm not in pain." She touched her throat and looked at Beck. "I guess you got to me before the killer could try to strangle me?"

"I got to you," Beck assured her, though that had not been easy for him to say. His jaw was tight again.

He was blaming himself for this.

Deciding to do something about that, Faith sat up. Beck tried to stop her again, but this time she succeeded. "How soon can I leave?"

He didn't look as if he wanted to answer that. "The doctor should be here any minute to talk to you."

She hoped he didn't hassle her about getting out of here. She wanted to get in touch with Marita and check on Aubrey. And her brother. She had to talk him into surrendering, or he was going to end up getting himself killed.

"Darin called me last night after you went outside,"

she explained to Beck. "He was there in your yard, but I don't think he's the one who shot me with the tranquilizer gun. I think someone else was out there."

Beck nodded. "There were two sets of tracks. I'm hoping I can match one of the sets to Nolan."

Good. That was a start and might finally lead to Nolan's arrest.

"I also had your neck photographed so the crime lab can compare your puncture wound to Sherry's and your mother's. The killer didn't leave the actual darts at those scenes so the lab can't make that comparison. But if the puncture wounds match, then we know the same person's responsible for all three attacks. Plus, they might be able to get some DNA from the dart I pulled from your neck."

And she prayed that DNA wouldn't belong to her brother. "Any sign of Darin or Nolan?"

Beck and Corey exchanged an uneasy glance. "No." Corey handed him an envelope that he'd been holding, and in turn Beck gave the envelope to her. "Darin left this by the rosebushes."

"Are these the pictures?" she asked, opening the envelope. "When he called last night, he said he had Sherry's pictures."

"And he obviously did," Corey mumbled. "I found them when I was processing the crime scene." He hitched his thumb toward the door. "I'll get back to the office and see if there's been any news about the case."

Faith waited until Corey was gone before she took out the first photograph. It was blurry and similar to the one in the blackmail letter. In the shot, there was a man lying asleep on a bed, and he was covered from the waist down with a white sheet. Maybe it was Pete, or even Roy, but it could have been Nolan with a wig.

In the second photo, someone had moved the sheet to expose the man's bare leg. Faith saw the spot on his thigh. A birthmark, she decided. She looked up at Beck for an explanation.

"Pete, my father and I all have that same birthmark."

Oh, no. Since she was dead certain that wasn't Beck in Sherry's bed, that left Roy and Pete. "The birthmark could be fake," she pointed out. "Nolan could have learned about the birthmark from Sherry and then painted it on to incriminate them."

Beck gave a crisp nod, an indication he'd already considered that. So why did he look as if that was a theory he didn't want to accept?

Faith tucked the second picture behind the third one. The last one. Again, it was a blurry shot, not of the man in the bed. This one was taken from long range, and it took Faith a moment to realize it wasn't Sherry.

It was a shot of her and Aubrey.

It'd been taken at the park about two months earlier. Right about the time the blackmail letters had been sent to Roy and Pete.

Faith drew in a sharp breath. "You think Sherry planned to use Aubrey to blackmail someone?"

But she didn't need an answer. She knew. This was exactly the kind of reckless thing Sherry would do.

"I have to go check on Aubrey," Faith insisted. She got out of the bed, and Beck looped his arm around her to steady her. If he hadn't, she would have fallen—her legs felt like pudding.

"Aubrey's fine," Beck assured her. "I talked to

Sheriff Whitley less than a half hour ago. No one has attempted to get into the safe house. You can't go check on her. It's too risky. Someone might try to follow you."

The disappointment was as strong as her concern for her daughter. But he was right. Faith couldn't take the danger to her child's doorstep. However, that didn't mean she had to stay put.

She was wearing a hospital gown, but Faith spotted her clothes draped over a chair. Wobbling a bit, she reached for the jeans and top.

Beck had her sit on the bed while he put on her jeans. It was a reminder that he'd done the exact opposite the night before when they were on his bed, and despite the hazy head and the punch of adrenaline, she remembered the heat they'd generated.

When she met Beck's gaze, she realized that he remembered it, too.

"Are you *really* okay?" he asked.

"I'm really okay." She was still wearing her bra, and he slipped off her gown and eased her stretchy blue top over her head so that she could put it on. "This wasn't your fault."

"Like hell it wasn't."

Because he looked as if he needed it, Faith put her arms around him. She would have done more. She would have kissed him for reassurance, both hers and his, if the door hadn't flown open.

Pete and Roy.

Apparently, there wasn't much security at the small-town hospital if anyone was allowed to march right into her room. That in itself was alarming enough. But her alarm skyrocketed when she spotted the blood on Roy's shirt. The man also had what appeared to be several fresh stitches on his forehead.

"Well, isn't this cozy?" Pete barked.

Faith stepped away from Beck as quickly as she could. But Beck didn't step away from her. He stood by her side and slipped his arm around her waist.

"What happened?" Beck asked his father.

Roy looked at her. "I had a run-in with your brother about a half hour ago."

Oh, God. "Are you hurt? Is Darin hurt?"

"My father's obviously hurt," Pete interjected before Roy could answer. "Darin is a sociopath and a killer."

"What happened?" Beck repeated, sounding very much like a cop now.

Unlike Pete, there was no anger in Roy's expression or body language. Just fatigue and spent adrenaline, something Faith could understand.

"I went out to the stables to check on a mare, and Darin was there," Roy explained. "He said he wanted to talk to me, but I didn't think that was a good idea. I grabbed my cell phone from my pocket to call you, and Darin tried to stop me." Roy lifted his shoulder. "I don't think he meant to hurt me. He just sort of lunged at me, and we both fell."

"Dad cut his head on a shovel and needed stitches," Pete supplied.

"What about Darin? What happened to him?" Beck wanted to know.

"He ran off, but I think he was hurt." Roy touched his wounded head and winced. "He was limping pretty badly."

As much as Faith hated to hear that, she hoped it would make Darin seek medical attention, and then maybe, finally, she could talk to him.

Roy looked at her. "I heard what happened to you. Could have been worse."

"Much worse," she supplied. "I'm sorry about what went on with my brother. He's scared, and he needs help."

"He needs to go back to the loony bin," Pete jabbed. "And maybe you do, too." But he didn't aim that last insult at her but rather Beck. "What's this I hear about you being the father of her kid?"

So the info had indeed been leaked, though it was ironic that the first question about it had come from Pete, the man who might very well be Aubrey's biological father. Faith didn't want to know what kind of problems that was going to create if he was. Of course, the alternatives were Roy and Nolan. Nolan was a jerk. Possibly even a killer. And Roy seemed too decent not to own up to fathering a child.

But then maybe Sherry hadn't told him.

"You didn't mention a word to us about the baby," Roy continued where Pete had left off. "Or about being with Faith."

"Because I knew you wouldn't approve." Not exactly a lie. They wouldn't have.

Pete's hands clenched into fists. "So you're saying it's true, that you are the kid's father?" But then he relaxed a bit. "Oh, wait. I get it. You slept with her on a down and dirty whim, and then she claimed you got her pregnant. And you actually believed her?"

Roy caught onto Pete's arm. "If Beck thinks the little girl is his, he must have a good reason to believe it."

"I do," Beck supplied. "I also have a good reason to believe that Pete lied ten years ago. You didn't sleep with Faith."

The anger flushed Pete's face. "You're taking her word over mine?"

"No. I'm taking what I know over what you said. I think you lied because you thought Nolan would pound you to dust if he found out you'd been with Sherry."

She expected Pete to return fire, but he didn't. He went still, and it seemed from his expression that he was giving it some thought. Several moments later, he scrubbed his hand over his face.

"I wasn't afraid of Nolan," Pete finally said. "And I don't remember what went on in that motel room."

Pete seemed to be on the brink of an apology, or at least an honest explanation, but Beck's cell phone rang. Pete shook his head again, and she could tell that he'd changed his mind about saying anything else.

"What?" Beck snapped at the caller.

That got everyone's attention. So did Beck's intensity. He cursed and slapped the phone shut.

"That was Nicole," he explained. "She said she just found a dead body in the west barn at the ranch."

BECK CAUGHT ONTO FAITH'S arm to stop her from bolting from the cruiser when he brought it to a stop in front of the west barn at his family's ranch.

"I have to see if it's Darin," she insisted.

Not that she needed to tell him that. From the moment he'd relayed Nicole's message, Faith had been terrified that the body belonged to her brother.

Beck figured it did, but he didn't say that to her.

Still, he couldn't discount the altercation Darin had had with Roy just an hour or so earlier. His father had even said that Darin was injured. Maybe he'd hit his head, and that had caused his death.

That wouldn't make it any easier for Faith to accept.

This was going to hurt, and Beck wasn't sure she would let him help pick up the pieces.

Nicole was there, standing in front of the dark red barn, waiting. There wasn't a drop of color in her face, despite the cold wind whipping at her.

"I have to go in first," he instructed Faith. He drew his weapon, just in case. "I have to do my job."

He didn't wait for her to acknowledge that. Behind him, Pete and Roy pulled up. And behind them was Corey. All three men barreled from their vehicles.

Beck got out and held out his hands to stop them from going any farther. "Corey, I need you to wait here with Faith. Pete and Dad, you wait with Nicole. As soon as I've checked it out, I'll let you know what's going on."

None of them argued, maybe because none of them were anxious to have a close encounter with a dead body.

"I couldn't see his face," Nicole volunteered. "But it's a man, and he's dead in the back stall. There's blood, a lot of it," she added in a hoarse whisper.

Pete pulled her into his arms, and Beck gave Corey one last glance to make sure he was guarding Faith. He was. So Beck went inside.

The overhead lights were on, so he had no problem seeing. The barn was nearly empty, except for a paint gelding in the first stall. He snorted when Beck moved past him. Beck walked slowly, checking on all sides of him.

With the exception of six stalls and a tack room at the back, there weren't many places a killer could hide.

If there was a killer anywhere around.

But Beck figured Darin would be the only person he'd find inside. That meant he'd have to interview his father about the fight he had with the man, and Beck only hoped that he had told the truth. He didn't want to find out his father had shot an unarmed man.

Beck spotted a pair of boots sticking out from the back stall. Judging from the angle, the guy was on his back. He wasn't moving, and there was a dark shiny pool of blood extending out from his torso. Nicole had been right—there was a lot of it. Too much for the person to have survived.

Keeping his gun ready and aimed, Beck went closer. There was a piece of paper on the open stall door. The top of the page was slightly torn where it'd been pushed against a raised nail head that was now holding it in place. Beck decided he would see what that was all about later, but first he needed to ID the body and determine if this person was truly dead or in need of an ambulance.

More blood was on the front of the man's shirt. And in his lifeless right hand, there was a .38. The barrel of the gun was aimed directly beneath his chin.

Yeah, he was dead.

Blood spatter covered his face, too, and it took Beck a moment to pick through what was left of the guy and figure out who this was.

"Hell," Beck mumbled.

He looked at the paper then. Hand-scrawled with just three sentences.

I killed them. God forgive me. I can't live with what I've done.

He left the note and body in place so the county CSI crew and the Rangers would have a pristine scene to process. That was if Nicole hadn't touched anything. He wanted them to find proof that this was indeed a suicide or if someone had staged it to look that way.

Everyone was waiting for Beck when he came back out, including Sgt. McKinney, the Ranger who was still investigating the tranquilizer gun incident from the night before. But it was Faith that Beck went to.

"It's not Darin," he told her.

Her breath broke, and she shattered. He felt the relief in her when he pulled her into his arms. "It's Nolan Wheeler."

Blinking back tears of relief, she looked up at him. "Nolan?" she repeated.

So did Pete and Nicole. "What was Nolan Wheeler doing here?" Pete asked.

"Apparently killing himself. There's a suicide note."

"I'll have a look," the Ranger insisted, going inside.

Faith shook her head. "Nolan committed suicide?"

Beck couldn't confirm that. "According to the note, he couldn't live with himself because of the murders he committed."

He saw the immediate doubt in Faith's eyes and knew what she was thinking. On the surface, Nolan wasn't the suicide type.

So did the man have some "help"?

"Why would he have done this?" Corey questioned.

Beck was short on answers. "Maybe he thought we were getting close to arresting him."

That was the only thing he could think of to justify

suicide. But why choose the Tanners' barn to do the deed? As far as Beck knew, Nolan wasn't familiar with the ranch.

"What were you doing in the barn?" he heard his brother ask Nicole.

Beck pushed aside his questions about Nolan because he was very interested in her answer.

Nicole, however, didn't seem pleased that all eyes were suddenly on her. "I was looking for my riding jacket. I thought I left it in there." Pete didn't jump to confirm her answer, so she sliced her gaze at Beck. "Why would I do anything to Nolan Wheeler? I hardly know him."

"You went to high school with him," Corey pointed out, earning him a nasty glare from both Pete and Nicole.

"I won't have Nicole accused of this or anything else," Pete snapped.

Nicole nodded crisply. "There's only one person here who had a reason to kill Nolan, and that's Faith."

Beck was about to defend her the way Pete had Nicole, but he spotted the Ranger walking back toward them. "I used my camera phone to take a picture of the suicide note and sent it straight to the crime lab. They'll compare it to Nolan's handwriting. We've got some samples on file that we've been comparing to the threats written in the attic."

"And did Nolan write those threats?" Faith wanted to know.

Sgt. McKinney shook his head. "The results are inconclusive, but we might have better luck with this suicide note since whoever wrote it didn't print."

Before the last word left the Ranger's mouth, Beck saw a movement out of the corner of his eye. He turned, automatically drawing his weapon. So did the Ranger and Corey. Pete shoved Nicole behind him.

Darin Matthews was walking straight toward them.

"Darin?" Faith called out.

Beck caught her arm to keep her from running toward her brother. Darin was limping and looked disheveled, maybe from the altercation he'd had with Roy.

"Don't shoot," Darin said. He lifted his hands in a show of surrender.

"Are you hurt?" Faith asked.

"Just my ankle. I think I sprained it when I was here earlier."

Roy took a step closer to the man. "You mean when I ran you off or when you killed Nolan?"

Darin froze, and his eyes widened. "Nolan's dead?" And he looked to Faith for confirmation.

"He's dead."

"I didn't do it. I came here because I've been sleeping in one of the barns while I've been in town looking for evidence to clear my name. I didn't kill anyone, and I didn't help Nolan do it, either." He took in a weary breath. "But I'm tired now. I need to rest."

"You'll have to get your rest at the sheriff's office," Beck let him know. He walked closer and patted Darin down. He wasn't armed, but in addition to the limp, there was a nasty gash on the back on his head. It was no longer bleeding, but it looked as if it could use some stitches.

The Ranger's cell phone rang, and he stepped aside to take the call.

"Darin will have to be cuffed," Beck let Faith know, and he kept a grip on her until after Corey had done that.

When he let go of her, Faith ran to Darin and hugged him. "I want to go with him."

Beck didn't even try to argue with her. He knew it would do no good. He motioned for Corey to get Darin into the cruiser. He and Faith would follow it, first to the emergency room and then to his office, where he'd eventually have to lock up Darin.

"I'll do whatever you need me to do," Darin insisted. He looked at Faith. "You're not in danger anymore. Nolan can't hurt you."

"And I'll help you," Faith promised. "I have attorney friends who can defend you if you're charged with anything. There's a lot of evidence, and when it's all examined and processed, I think it'll prove you're innocent."

Beck hoped the same thing.

Nicole walked closer to them. "Now that this is over, and the killer's been caught, there's no reason for Faith to stay at your house any longer. We can finally get back to the way things were."

Beck shook his head. "This case isn't settled." And Faith would stay with him until it was.

He didn't want to think beyond that.

"We might be one step closer to getting things settled," the Ranger announced, rejoining them. "That was the crime lab. We'll need to do more analysis, of course, but the handwriting expert says the suicide note appears to be a match to Nolan Wheeler's."

"So he did write that note," Nicole concluded.

Beck considered a different theory. "Perhaps he wrote it under duress?" While a gun was pointed to his head?

The Ranger shrugged. "Maybe, but according to

the expert, there are no obvious indications of hesitation. There probably would have been if he'd been forced to write it."

Well, that put a new light on things. Nolan had confessed to the murders in that note. Maybe Darin had been telling the truth about his lack of involvement? Maybe he wasn't a killer, and Nolan had been the one to orchestrate all of this so he could get the money from Sherry's blackmail scheme and her estate.

"We should go." Beck caught Faith's arm and led her toward his cruiser.

With her barely out of the hospital, he didn't like the idea of her having to accompany him to the station, but he didn't want her alone, either. Besides, she would want to be there when Beck questioned Darin. And when the questioning was done, the loose ends would be tied up into a neat little package.

So why did Beck have this uneasy feeling in the pit of his stomach?

Why did he feel that Faith was in even more danger than ever?

Chapter Thirteen

Faith's mind was racing. She was mentally exhausted after spending most of the afternoon with her brother. But she was also hopeful.

Because soon she'd get to see her little girl.

She'd already called Marita, and the nanny had told her they would be on their way back when they got everything packed up. With luck, Aubrey would be home within the next three hours.

Well, not home exactly. But back at Beck's house, where they'd stay another day or two until she could decide something more permanent.

She climbed out of the cruiser, went inside the house and into the kitchen. Because it suddenly seemed to take too much energy to go any farther, she leaned against the wall and tried to absorb everything.

So much had happened in the past twenty hours. Too much to grasp at once.

Nolan was dead and no longer a threat to Aubrey and her. Her brother was at the LaMesa Springs hospital receiving treatment for the head wound he'd gotten from the altercation with Roy. Once the doctor released him,

Darin would still have to undergo an intense interrogation. Maybe the evidence against him would even have to go to a grand jury. But Beck had promised her that Darin would be given fair treatment and that he personally was going to recommend that any assessment come from the county mental health officials.

Her brother might finally get the help he needed.

Beck came in behind her, took off his jacket and hung it on the hook on the mudroom door. "How's your neck?" he asked.

It took her a moment to realize what he meant. The tranquilizer dart wound. Even though it hadn't been that long since the injury, she'd forgotten all about it. "It's fine," she assured him.

The corner of his mouth lifted. A weary smile. "You're not feeling any pain because Aubrey will be here soon."

Faith couldn't argue with that, so she returned the smile. She took off her coat and hung it next to his. "Thank you for letting us stay with you."

It seemed as if he changed his mind a dozen times about what to say. "You're welcome."

His response was sincere, she didn't doubt that, but there was something else. Something simmering beneath the surface. "Your family won't like me being here. I'll make plans to leave tomorrow."

No smile this time. He took off his shoulder holster, and with the weapon inside, he placed it on top of the fridge. "No hurry. I don't want you to make any decisions based on my family. Truth is, I'm fed up with them. And I'd like for Aubrey, Marita and you to stay here for as long as you like. Or until at least we have everything sorted out with your brother. It's a big place, lots of room, and we can get to know each other better."

"You've known me for years," she pointed out.

He lowered his head. Touched his lips to hers. "But I want to know you *better.*"

The kiss was over before it even started. It was hardly more than a peck. But it slid through her from her lips all the way to her toes.

"That sounds sexual." Or maybe that was wishful thinking on her part.

"It is," he drawled. "But the invitation isn't good for tonight. Tonight, you'll rest, take a hot bath and spend time with Aubrey when she gets here. In a day or two, I'll work on getting you into my bed again."

There it was. More heat. She'd been attracted to men before but never like this. Nothing had ever felt like this. It scared her, but at the same time, she wanted more.

"Don't look at me like that," he warned.

She touched the front of his shirt with her fingertips. "Like what?"

"Like you want to get naked with me."

"Oh." Maybe she looked that way because that's exactly what she wanted. "I'm at a disadvantage here. I've spent my entire adult life pulling back from men. I don't know how to stop you from treating me like glass. I don't know how to make you take me the way you would a woman with lots of experience. I don't know how to seduce you."

He shrugged. "Breathe."

Faith blinked. "Excuse me?"

He leaned in, whispered in her ear, "This is all about

you, Faith. Just you. To seduce me, all you have to do is breathe and say yes."

"Yes." She pulled in a loud breath, and with that, his mouth came to hers.

This time, it wasn't a peck, it was a full-fledged kiss. His mouth moved over hers as if he knew exactly what to do to set her on fire.

It worked.

Faith leaned against him—until she could no longer do the thing that had set all of this into motion. She couldn't breathe. And she didn't care. She'd take Beck's kisses over breathing any day.

His left arm went around her waist, and he pulled her to him. The embrace was gentle. Unlike the kiss that had turned French and a little rough.

Faith broke the intimate contact so he could see her face. "No treating me like glass," she reminded him. "And I'd rather not rest tonight if you don't mind."

He stared at her, and she could see the debate that stirred the muscles in his jaw. "All right."

That was the only warning she got before he hoisted her up. Face-to-face. Body against body. And he delivered some of those kisses to the front of her neck and then into the V of her top.

Faith automatically wrapped her arms and legs around him. His sex touched hers and sent a shiver of heat dancing through her. She wanted him naked, now.

She went after his shirt as he carried her toward his bedroom. Buttons popped and flew, pinging on the floor, and her frenzy of need for him only fueled the fire. She got his shirt off and kissed his neck. Then his chest.

He made a throaty sound of approval and, off

balance, he rammed his shoulder into the doorjamb. Faith wanted to ask if he was okay, but he obviously was.

Beck kissed her even harder, and instead of taking her to the bed, he stopped just short of it, and with her pressed between him and the mattress, he slid them to the floor. While he kissed her blind, he unzipped her jeans and peeled them off her. Bra and panties, too, leaving her naked. He quickly covered her left nipple with his mouth.

The sensation shot through her.

His hand went lower, between her legs, and his fingers found her. He slipped his index finger through the slippery moisture of her body and touched her so intimately that Faith could have sworn she saw stars.

"Breathe," he reminded her.

She thought she might be breathing, but couldn't tell. The only thing she knew for sure was that she wanted him to continue with those slippery, clever strokes.

And he did.

He touched and created a delicious friction that brought her just to the edge.

Faith caught her breath and caught onto his hand. "You, inside me," she managed to say, though she didn't know how she'd gotten out the words. Speech suddenly seemed very complex and not entirely necessary.

She shoved down his zipper, which took some doing. He was huge and hard, making it difficult for her to free him from his jeans and boxers.

Even though her need was burning her to ash, she took a moment to fulfill a fantasy she'd had for years.

She got him out of those jeans, took Beck in her hand and slid her fingers down the length of him, all the while guiding him right to where she wanted him to go.

He reacted with a male sound deep within his chest. He buried his face in her hair. His breath, hot against his skin. His mouth, tense now, muffled a groan, and he kissed her. His tongue parted the seam of her lips as his hard sex touched the softness of hers.

Her vision blurred. She reached to pull him closer. Deeper into her. But he stopped and cursed.

"Condom," he gutted out.

Still cursing, he reached over, rummaged through his nightstand drawer and produced a condom. He hurried, but it still seemed an eternity. The moment he had it on, Faith pulled him back to her.

Despite the urgency that she could feel in every part of him, Beck entered her slowly. Gently. Inch by inch. While he watched her. That wasn't difficult to do since they were face-to-face with her straddling him. He was watching to see if he was hurting her.

He wasn't.

The only pain she felt was from the hard ache of unfilled need. A need that Beck was more than capable of satisfying.

She could see how much this gentleness was costing him. Beck didn't want to hold back anything, and Faith made sure he didn't. She thrust her hips forward.

Beck cursed again.

"It's better than I thought it'd be," she mumbled. A shock since she'd been positive it would be pretty darn good.

"Yeah," he said.

He stilled a moment to let her adjust to this intimate invasion, but the stillness only lasted a few seconds and a kiss. He moved, sliding into her. Drawing back. Then sliding in even deeper. Each motion took her higher. Closer. Until her focus honed in on the one thing she had to have.

Release.

Beck had taken her to this hot, crazy place. He'd made her feel things she'd only imagined. And he just kept making her feel.

He slid his hand between their bodies, and with him sliding in and out of her, he touched her with his fingers, matching the frenetic stokes of his sex. He kept touching. Kept moving. The need got stronger. Until she was sure she couldn't bear the heat any longer.

Beck seemed to understand that. He kissed her. Touched her. Went deep inside her. A triple assault. And it happened. In a flash. Her orgasm wracked through her, filling her and giving her primal release.

Breathe, Faith reminded herself. *Breathe.*

There were no barriers. No bad blood. Nothing to stop her from realizing the truth.

She was in love with Beckett Tanner.

WELL, FAITH WAS BREATHING all right.

Her chest was pumping as if starved for air, and each pump pushed her sweat-dampened breasts against his chest. There was a look of total amazement on her face.

She was practically glowing.

Beck knew he was somewhat responsible for giving her that look, and when his brain caught up with the now sated part of his body, he might try to figure out what he was going to do about that look. And about what'd just happened.

For now though, he just held her and tried not to make any annoying male grunts when the aftershocks of her climax reminded him that he was still inside her. Not that he needed such a reminder.

"That was worth waiting for," she mumbled.

He kissed her, tried to think of something clever to say and settled for another kiss. But he would have to address this sooner or later. Faith obviously wasn't a casual sex kind of person. Neither was he. But it suddenly felt as if he had more than a normal responsibility here. A commitment, maybe.

After all, he was her *first*.

He certainly hadn't expected to have that title once he was past the age of twenty. Maybe she'd have some emotional fallout from this.

Maybe even some regrets.

Beck realized she was staring at him. Her breathing had settled. There were no more aftershocks. But she had her head tilted to the side, and she was studying him.

"What?" he prompted.

"I'm just trying to get inside your head." She smiled. It was tentative. Perhaps even a facade. "Don't worry. This doesn't mean we're going steady or anything." Still smiling, she moved off him and stood.

Beck caught onto her hand before she could move too far from him. All in all, it wasn't a bad vantage point. He was still sitting. Looking up at her. She was naked. Beautiful. Glistening with perspiration. And his scent was on her.

He wanted her all over again.

"I need a drink of water," she let him know. She leaned down and kissed him. "Then I think I'll take a bath before Aubrey gets here."

He had some cleaning up to do, too, and rather than sit there and watch her dress, Beck got up, gathered his clothes from the floor and went into the adjoining bathroom.

While he cleaned up and put his jeans back on, he glanced at the tub. Should he run her a bath? Probably not. It would only lead to more sex. Once was enough for her tonight. Plus, despite her "going steady" remark, she had some feelings she needed to work through.

He certainly did.

The house phone rang, and he went back into the bedroom to answer it. "Sheriff Tanner."

"It's Corey. Is Darin Matthews with you?" His words were harried and borderline frantic.

That put a knot in Beck's stomach. "No. He's supposed to be at the hospital with you."

Corey cursed. "Darin was sedated so I went to the vending machine to get a Coke. When I got back, he wasn't in his bed. I guess he wasn't sedated as much as I thought. I've looked all through the building and the parking lot. He's not here."

Darin couldn't have gotten far with that injured leg. Beck hoped. Unless he stole a car.

"Don't put out an APB just yet, but if one of the Rangers is still around, let him know so he can look for him. Faith and I will drive around, too, and see if we can spot him. Darin's probably looking for her anyway."

"One more thing," Corey said before Beck could end

the call. "The Ranger lab in Austin put a rush on that DNA test you ordered. They faxed the results over, and the dispatcher brought it to me while I was looking for Darin."

Great. He needed those results, but he had to resolve this problem with Darin first. "The results will keep," Beck let him know.

Cursing under his breath, Beck hung up and reached for his boots. He should probably call Marita and Tracy and delay Aubrey's homecoming, just in case Darin had some kind of psychotic episode.

Beck reached for the phone again, but stopped when he heard the soft sound. A thud. He stilled and listened. But there wasn't another sound. Just the uneasy feeling that all was not right.

"Faith?" he called out.

Nothing.

That knot in his stomach tightened. Hell. Why hadn't she answered?

The answer that came to mind had him grabbing the gun from the nightstand.

Beck started for the kitchen.

Chapter Fourteen

Faith opened the cupboard and reached for a glass. But reaching for it was as far as she got.

The lights went out.

She heard footsteps behind her. Before she could pick through the darkness to see who was behind her, an arm went around her neck, putting her in a choke hold.

A hand clamped over her mouth, and she felt the cold steel of a gun barrel shoved against her right temple.

Oh, God. What was happening?

Nolan was dead. The danger was over. Who was this person, and what was going on?

She didn't wait for the answers. Faith rammed her elbow into her attacker's belly. She might as well have rammed it into a brick wall because other than a soft grunt, the person didn't react.

"What do you want?" she tried to say, but his hand muffled any sound.

Still, there were sounds. Footsteps, both his and hers, as he started to drag her in the direction of the back door. Beck would likely hear the sounds, even though he might still be on the phone dealing with the call that'd come in.

Once that call was finished, he would begin to wonder what was taking her so long to get a drink of water.

Then Beck would come looking for her.

And this person might shoot him.

He jammed the gun even harder against her temple when she started to struggle, and Faith had to try to come to terms with the fact that she might be murdered tonight. She thought of Aubrey, of her precious little girl. And of Beck. He would blame himself for this because he hadn't been there to protect her. But Faith didn't want him there. She wanted to live, but not at the expense of Beck being killed.

The man opened the back door, and cold air rushed inside, cutting what little breath she had. He tried to push her outside, but Faith dug in her heels. If he got her out of the house and away from Beck, he'd just take her to a secondary crime scene where he'd do God knows what to her.

But why?

And that brought her back to the question of whom.

Had Nolan hired someone to do this last deed? A way of reaching out from beyond the grave to settle an old score with her?

Of course, there was another possibility. One she didn't want to consider—maybe somehow her brother had gotten free. Maybe he really was a killer after all and had come to eliminate the last member of their family.

"Faith?" she heard Beck call out.

Her attacker froze for just a moment and then resumed the struggle to get her out the door. She tried to warn Beck, but her assailant's hand prevented that.

"What the hell's going on?" Beck called.

Though it was pitch-dark, she spotted him in the hallway opening just off the kitchen. She also saw him lift his gun and take aim.

The attacker stopped trying to shove her out the door, and he pivoted, placing her in front of him. He even crouched slightly down so that his head was partially behind hers.

She was now a human shield.

"Who are you?" Beck demanded. He squinted, obviously trying to adjust to the darkness. He reached out for the light switch on the wall next to him.

"Don't," her attacker growled. He kept his voice throaty and low, but there were no doubts that this was a man. A strong one. He had her in a death grip, and the barrel of the gun cut into her skin.

Beck didn't turn on the light, but he kept his gun aimed.

"I'm leaving with her," the man said. He was obviously trying to disguise his voice. That meant Beck and she probably knew him.

Inching sideways and with her still in front of him to block Beck's shot, the man started dragging her back to the door.

Faith didn't know whether to fight or not. If she did resist, he might just shoot Beck. However, the same might happen if she cooperated.

Beck inched closer as well, and because she was watching him, she saw his eyes widen. He didn't drop his gun, but he did lower it.

"Pete?" Beck called out.

The man's muscles went stiff, and he stopped. She heard every word of his harshly whispered profanity.

"What the hell do you think you're doing?" Beck demanded. He came even closer.

"Stop," the man said. Not a muffled whisper this time. She clearly heard his voice.

It was indeed Pete, Beck's brother.

"Well?" Beck prompted. "What the hell are you doing?"

"What's necessary." With that, Pete jammed the gun even harder against her. She could smell the liquor on his breath, but he wasn't drunk. He was too steady for that.

"What's necessary?" Beck spat out. "How did you even get in here?"

"You gave Dad the codes to disarm the security system and I used the key you gave me for emergencies. I didn't want you to be part of this," Pete said to Beck. "I wanted to take care of her before you noticed she was missing. She's a loose end."

Beck shook his head, and his expression said it all. He couldn't believe this was happening. "Put down your gun."

"I can't. I have to fix this." Pete groaned and took his hand from her mouth. "I've made a mess of my life."

"You can fix things the legal way," Beck insisted. His voice was calm, and he took another step toward them. "Put down the gun."

"It's too late for that. I killed them, Beck. I killed them all."

Oh, God. It was true. Pete was a killer, and he had her in his grips.

"You mean you killed Sherry and Annie?" Beck clarified.

"Yeah, I did. But it was all Sherry's fault. I swear she

tricked me into that affair. When I saw her at the Moon-light Bar, she came onto me, got me drunk and then took pictures of me when I was sleeping. She blackmailed me. And I gave her the money. I gave her exactly what she wanted—ten thousand dollars that I got from Dad's accounts. Look where it got me."

"Start from the beginning. What happened?" Beck asked.

"The beginning? I'm not sure when it all started. But killing Sherry was an accident. I swear. I used the tranquilizer gun from the stables and drugged her so I could reason with her. But the drug wore off too soon, and when she started struggling, I had to stran-gle her."

"It wasn't premeditated," Beck explained. "You could maybe plea down to manslaughter. That's why you need to put down the gun so we can talk."

"Talking's not going to save me. Sherry's death might not have been premeditated, but the others were."

Until that statement, Beck had managed to maintain some of his cop's persona, but the grim reality of Pete's confession etched his face with not just concern but shock. "What do you mean?"

"After I killed Sherry, I tried to get the money back so Dad and Nicole wouldn't find out, but Annie wouldn't give it to me. She said she wanted it and more. A lot more. She wanted fifty thousand dollars. That's when I had to kill her. I couldn't keep paying her off, and I knew she'd tell Nicole."

It was so hard for Faith to hear all of this. She hadn't been close to Sherry or her mother, but both of them had been killed for money. For greed. And to cover up an affair that Sherry had probably orchestrated just so she could blackmail Pete. If he hadn't been thinking from below the belt, Pete might have figured it out before things got this far.

"I thought after I killed Annie that it'd be over," Pete continued, his voice weary and dry. "But I got another letter demanding more money. I thought it came from Nolan. That's why I put a gun to his head and made him write that suicide note. But he insisted right up to the end that he hadn't sent any blackmail letters."

"You killed him anyway," Beck said. It wasn't a question.

"Nolan Wheeler deserved to die." Pete's voice was suddenly defiant. "He'd been skirting the law for years. I did the world a favor."

"The world might not agree," Beck countered. "I certainly don't. You killed three people, and you're holding a gun on your brother and the assistant district attorney. Where's the justice in that?"

Pete stayed quiet a moment. "It'll be my own form of justice. I can't let either of you live. Especially Faith. This afternoon there was another blackmail letter in the mailbox. She put it there. I know she did. There couldn't be anyone else."

"You don't know that. It could be one of Sherry's friends. Besides, Faith's been with me all day. She couldn't have put the letter in the mailbox."

"I don't believe you," Pete practically shouted. "You're covering for her because you're sleeping with her. You chose her over your own family."

"Maybe I did," Beck conceded. Unlike Pete, he kept his voice level and calm though Faith didn't know how he managed to do that. "But it's my job to protect her." He took another step toward them. "Put the gun down, Pete, and let's talk this out."

"No. No more talking. I'd wanted to do this clean and nearly succeeded last night. I got the tranquilizer in her, but then you came to the rescue. Just like tonight. But the difference is, tonight I'll kill you, too."

"I'm your brother," Beck reminded him. "Think what killing me would do the family."

"I can't think about that. I have to protect Nicole. She's my first and only concern. I have to make sure she never learns about any of this. The only way for that to happen is for you to die."

Pete re-aimed his gun.

At Beck.

Faith felt the muscles in Pete's arm tense. She saw the realization of what was about to happen on Beck's face. He couldn't shoot at his brother because he might hit her. Pete, however, had no concern about that since he intended to kill them both anyway.

She yelled for Beck to get down. With the sound of her voice echoing through the house, Faith turned, ramming her shoulder into Pete. He hardly budged from the impact, but it was enough to shake his aim.

The bullet that Pete fired slammed into the wall next to the fridge.

Beck lunged at them, and the hard tackle sent all three of them to the floor. Beck's own gun went flying, and it skittered across the floor. And the race was on to see which one would come up with Pete's gun.

Faith managed to untangle herself from the mix. She got to her feet and slapped on the light. Pete and Beck were practically the same size, and they were in a life-and-death struggle.

She waited until she spotted Pete's hand. And the gun. Faith went for it, dropping back to the floor, and she latched on to his wrist. Somehow, she had to keep that gun pointed away from Beck.

Beck drew back his fist and slammed it into Pete's face. The man was either tough as nails or the adrenaline had made him immune to the pain because he hardly reacted. In fact, Pete twisted his body and slammed his forearm into her jaw. The impact nearly knocked the breath from her, but somehow Faith managed to hang on to his wrist. She dug in her nails and clawed at any part of his flesh that she could reach.

Beck threw another punch. And another. The third one was the charm. Pete's head flopped back onto the tile floor. Dazed and bleeding from his mouth and nose, he groaned and mumbled something indistinguishable.

"The gun," Beck said.

Beck wrenched it from his brother's hand. He pulled in a hard breath and reached again, this time to roll Pete on his stomach so he could subdue him.

"Call nine-one-one," Beck told her.

"You're sure?" she asked, though she knew he had no choice. This was attempted murder. But Pete was still his brother. A lesser man would have wanted to try to resolve this without the law and tried to keep it a family secret.

Beck nodded. "I'm sure. Make the call."

She got up to do that, but before Faith even made it to her feet, the back door flew open, hitting her squarely in the back and sending her plummeting into Beck.

"Oh, my God," someone said.

Nicole.

Pete used the distraction of his wife's arrival to ram his elbow into Beck, and grab his gun.

Faith couldn't scramble away from him in time. Pete latched on to her hair and dragged her in front of him again.

"January fourteenth," Pete said as if in triumph. "Faith dies."

HIS BROTHER'S WORDS WERE like stabs from a switch-blade. It was the threat written in the attic. A threat Beck hadn't announced to anyone other than law enforcement, which meant Pete had been the one to paint that threat on Faith's attic walls.

Oh, man. Things had really gone crazy. And worse, it might turn deadly if he didn't do something now to stop all of this.

Beck's gaze connected with Faith's. She was scared. And shocked. But he could also see determination. She wasn't just going to stand there and let Pete kill them. She was a fighter, but this fight might cause Pete to pull that trigger even faster.

"Pete, what's going on?" Nicole asked.

Nicole looked at Beck, her eyes searching for a logical answer. But he couldn't give her one. There was no logic in any of this. Another of Pete's affairs had gotten him into trouble, and he'd been willing to kill to keep his secret.

"Pete killed Annie and Sherry Matthews. Nolan Wheeler, too," Beck explained to Nicole. "Now, he's going to put his gun down so we can deal with this."

Beck hoped.

"I killed them for you, Nicole," Pete insisted.

She gasped and stepped back. Good. So Nicole wasn't in on this. Maybe, just maybe, she could talk Pete into surrendering.

"Tell Pete to put his gun down," Beck instructed Nicole.

She gave a choppy nod. "Please, Pete. Do as Beck says."

"Faith's blackmailing me. She sent me a letter today. Left it in the mailbox—"

"No. She didn't." Nicole shook her head. "I sent the last two letters."

Beck hadn't thought there could be any more surprises tonight, but he'd obviously been wrong. "You?" he questioned. "Why?"

Tears filled Nicole's eyes. "Sherry called me two months ago and told me about her affair with Pete. She faxed me copies of the pictures of them together."

"Oh, God." Pete groaned. "I'm sorry. So sorry."

"I know." Nicole blinked back the tears, and her voice was eerily calm. "But I was upset, and I wanted to leave you—after I punished you. So, after Sherry and Annie were killed, I sent a third letter. This afternoon, I put the fourth one in the mailbox. I wanted you to suffer. I wanted you to think that your indiscretion would be punished for a long, long time."

Pete cursed. He glanced at Faith and then cursed some more.

"Faith didn't do anything wrong," Beck said. "You need to let her go."

"Yes," Nicole agreed. "Let her go. Let Beck handle this."

"I can't. Don't you see what has to happen here? I've already put the plan in place. I waited at the hospital until I could get Darin alone, and I forced him to leave with me. There are no security cameras in the entire place so it was easy. Then I left him on the side of the road about a mile from here."

"No," Faith mumbled.

Beck silently mumbled the same. With Darin hurt and possibility medicated, he shouldn't be out on his own on a cold winter night. It was a cliché, but he could literally die in a ditch somewhere.

"Darin will try to go home, but he won't have an alibi," Pete continued. "He'll be blamed for Beck's and Faith's murders. Then we can start over, Nicole. I swear, no more affairs."

That just pissed Beck off. His brother was willing to kill Faith and him rather than take responsibility for what he'd done. Somehow, he had to get Faith out of harm's way and subdue Pete.

"Do you hear yourself?" Beck snapped. "I knew you were self-centered and egotistical, but I had no idea you'd stoop to this. Think it through. You plan to kill me and Faith in front of Nicole? What kind of future can you have with that hanging over your heads?"

"Beck's right," Nicole added. "I could never stay with you after what you've done."

"You tricked me with those letters!" Pete shouted.

"Letters?" Nicole threw right back at him. "I didn't murder anyone. Nor would I. Did you honestly think I could live with a killer?"

Pete slowly aimed his attention at Nicole. The change in his brother's expression wasn't subtle. Rage sliced through his eyes, and the muscles corded on his face. "I did this all for you, and this is how you treat me?"

"You didn't do this for Nicole." Beck wanted to get Pete's attention off Nicole and Faith and back onto him. Because it looked as if his brother was about to start shooting at any minute. "You did this to cover up what you'd done. Well, the covering up has to stop."

"Who says?" He pushed Faith onto her knees and put the gun to the back of her head.

She looked up. Her eyes met Beck's. "I love you," she said, silently mouthing the words.

Oh, man. Oh. Man. That hit him, hard, but he knew he couldn't think about it. Later—and there would be a later—he'd deal with her confession.

A sound shot through the room.

Beck was certain he lost ten years of his life. It took him a moment to realize that Pete hadn't fired. The phone was ringing.

"Don't answer that," Pete ordered. "You," he said to Nicole. "Get down on the floor next to her."

Nicole frantically shook her head. "You're going to shoot me?"

"Yeah." This was no longer the voice of his brother. It was the voice of a cold, calculated killer. "I love you, Nicole. I always will. But I won't give up my life for you. I'm not going to jail for you."

The answering machine kicked in on the fifth ring. "Faith, it's Marita. Pick up."

"No," Faith whispered. She repeated it as Marita's cheerful voice poured through the room.

"I guess you're celebrating, but I wanted you to know we'll be there in about ten minutes. Aubrey's sacked out, but I'll wake her when we arrive so you can get some hugs and kisses."

Hell. Ten minutes. He couldn't have Marita, Tracy and especially Aubrey walking into this.

"I gave Marita an emergency key," Beck let Faith know. And that meant if they didn't answer the door, which they wouldn't be able to do at this point, then Marita might let herself in.

"You couldn't hurt a child," Beck told Pete, trying one last time to reason with him.

Pete met him eye-to-eye. "I'm fighting for my life. I can and will hurt anyone who gets in my way."

Beck believed him. This wouldn't end with a successful surrender. It would end only when he managed to stop Pete. He might even have to kill his own brother. But he would if it came down to that.

He wouldn't allow Pete to hurt anyone else.

"Go ahead," Beck instructed Nicole. "Get on the floor."

The tears were spilling down her cheeks now, and her eyes were wide with terror.

"Trust me," Beck added. "Get on the floor."

Nicole gave a shaky nod. Using her right hand to steady herself, she started to lower herself to her knees.

Beck waited.

Watching Pete.

His brother glanced at Nicole. Just as Beck had figured he would do. It was just a glance. But in that glance, Pete took his attention off Beck and Faith.

That was the break Beck had been waiting for.

He dove at Pete.

Though Beck was moving as fast as he could, everything seemed to slow to a crawl. He saw the split-second realization in Pete's eyes. And then Pete reacted. He didn't turn the gun on Beck.

But on Faith.

Pete lowered the barrel of the semiautomatic right toward the back of Faith's head.

And he fired.

Chapter Fifteen

Faith moved as quickly as she could, but she figured it wasn't nearly fast enough. She braced herself.

Death would come before she even knew if Beck had heard her. "I love you," she'd said. It might be the last time she ever had a chance to say that to anyone.

She was feeling and hearing way too much for Pete's bullet to have killed her. Instead, she realized that it'd smacked into the tile floor less than two feet from her.

Pete's bullet had missed her.

The sound of the fired shot was deafening, and it roared through her head, stabbing into her eardrums. It was excruciating, but since she could feel it, she knew she was very much alive.

So was Beck, thank God.

With his momentum at full speed, Beck crashed into Pete, and into her. Pete's gun dislodged from his hand and landed somewhere behind them.

"No!" Nicole yelled. She scrambled to the side to get away from the collision.

However, because Faith was directly in front of Pete, she wasn't so lucky. She was caught in the impact, again. Caught in the middle of the struggle. But this time, the stakes were even higher.

Aubrey was on her way there.

"Run!" Beck told her.

From the corner of her eye, she saw Nicole do just that. She threw open the back door and rushed out into the night. Maybe the woman would call the deputy. But as distraught as Nicole was, Faith couldn't rely on her for help. She and Beck had to stop Pete.

"Now!" Beck snarled to her. "Get out of here."

Faith wiggled her way out of the fight and somehow managed to get to her feet. But before she could run, Pete latched on to her ankle and tried to pull her back down. She fought, kicking at him, but he was pumped on adrenaline now and was fighting like a crazy man with triple his normal strength.

Then things got worse. The doorbell rang.

"We're here," Marita called out.

Marita's announcement nearly caused Faith to panic, but she forced herself to concentrate on the task. She gave Pete another hard kick, and that broke the vising grip he had on her. She felt him reach for her, and he groped at the floor.

Faith ran. But not out the back as Nicole had done.

Frantically, she looked around for Beck's gun. She didn't see it, and it took her a moment to figure out why.

Pete had it.

Oh, God.

Pete had the gun.

"Come in!" Pete shouted to Marita, dodging a fist that Beck had tried to send his way. "Beck needs help."

"No," Faith countered. "Stay back." And she hoped they'd heard her and would do as she said.

She looked around the floor for another weapon and remembered Beck's service pistol. Faith grabbed it from the top of the fridge where he'd put it right after they'd returned from seeing Darin.

"Stop!" she yelled.

Pete didn't. Neither did Beck. Pete managed to land a hard punch on Beck's jaw, and the momentum sent him backward. The two men weren't separated for long because Beck dove at him.

The doorbell rang again, and it was followed by a knock. "What's going on in there?" Tracy asked.

Faith hurried to him and held out his service revolver. Beck snatched it from her hand and got up off the floor.

Pete did the same.

And the two brothers met gun-to-gun.

"Don't," Beck warned, his voice a threatening growl.

The corner of Pete's mouth lifted. A twisted, sick smile. "You think a bullet can go through your front door?" He didn't wait for Beck to answer. "Because I do. God knows what a bullet would hit…"

Pete didn't have to aim in that direction. Faith realized his gun was already pointed there. Just to Beck's right. And that put it in line with the door.

Oh, God. That nearly brought Faith to her knees. Her baby was in danger.

"Try to warn them and I'll shoot through the door," Pete warned. "I have nothing to lose."

Faith didn't cower. "And you have nothing to gain from hurting my child."

"True. But it'll be nice to see you suffer."

Every inch of Beck was primed for the fight, and his face was dotted with sweat from the struggle. "Faith did nothing to you."

"Yes, she did. She came back. She made me think she'd written that blackmail letter. She made me believe I had to stop her. The woman's just bad luck, Beck. She always has been."

Faith saw Beck's finger tense on the trigger, and he had his attention fastened to his brother's own trigger finger. One move, and Beck would shoot him. Faith didn't doubt that. But what she did fear was that even if Beck shot him that Pete would still manage to shoot.

Aubrey could still be in danger.

She heard the scrape of metal, a key being inserted into a lock, and she glanced at the front door.

Just as it opened.

"No!" Faith shouted. And she automatically turned in the direction of the door. She had to block any shot that Pete might take.

She only made it one step before the bullet rang out.

BECK DIDN'T EVEN WAIT to see where Pete's bullet had hit.

Or who.

He couldn't think about that. Right now, he had to stop Pete from firing again. Each shot could be lethal.

Still, Beck couldn't stop the rage that roared through him. Pete had put Aubrey and Faith in danger. To save his own butt, his brother had been willing to hurt a child.

Beck grabbed Pete's right arm. He wanted to shoot his brother. To end this here and now. But Beck couldn't risk another shot being fired.

Not with Aubrey and Faith so close.

Faith yelled something, but the blood crashing in Beck's ears made it impossible to hear. Besides, Beck only wanted to concentrate on the fight.

Beck dropped his gun so he could use both hands to try to gain control of Pete. His brother was fighting him, trying to re-aim his gun in the direction of the door. Beck wasn't able to get his finger off the trigger.

Pete fired again. The shot landed somewhere in the ceiling, and white powdery plaster began to rain down on them. Good. As long as that shot wasn't near the others.

Beck heard the sound then. A cry.

Aubrey.

Every muscle in his body turned to iron. *God, was the child hurt?* Or maybe it was Faith who'd taken the bullet. Maybe both were injured. Hell. He could lose them and all because of his selfish SOB of a brother.

"You can't save them," Pete growled.

It was exactly what Beck needed to hear. Not that he needed a reminder of what was at stake, but his brother's threat was the jolt that gave Beck that extra boost of adrenaline. Nothing was going to stop him from saving Aubrey and Faith.

Nothing.

From the corner of his eye, Beck saw Faith running toward the front door. There was no color in her face, and she appeared to be trembling. But she was headed in Aubrey's direction. Hopefully, she'd take the child and run. He wanted them as far away from there as possible.

With both his hands clamped onto Pete's right arm and wrist, Beck used his body and strength to maneuver Pete backward. Toward the wall. Pete didn't go willingly. He cursed, kicked and spat at Beck, all the while using his left fist to pound any part of Beck that he could reach.

Beck slammed him against the wall. The impact was so hard that it rattled the nearby kitchen cabinets. Still, Pete didn't stop struggling. Beck didn't stop, either. He bashed Pete's right hand against the granite countertop. The first time he didn't dislodge the gun.

But the second time he did. Pete's gun fell onto the granite.

Even though he was unarmed, Pete was still dangerous. So Beck didn't waste even a second of time. He caught onto his brother's shoulder and whirled him around, jamming his face and chest against the wall between the cabinets and the mudroom door. There wasn't much room to maneuver, but Beck wanted to get Pete onto the floor, facedown, so he could better subdue him.

Pete didn't cooperate with that, either, but Beck had the upper hand. With his forearm against the nape of Pete's neck, he put pressure on the backs of his brother's knees until he could get him belly down onto the tile floor.

By the time it was done, both Pete and he were fighting for air. Both of them were covered in sweat and blood from their cuts and scrapes.

But it was finally close to being over.

"Faith, are you all right?" Beck called out.

Since he'd expended most of his breath in the fight, he had to repeat it before it had any sound. And then he waited.

Praying.

He didn't hear her say anything. No reassurance that she was okay. But he could hear footsteps. Frantic ones.

Something was going on in the living room. Before he could call out to Faith again, there was another sound.

The back door opened.

It was Nicole.

"Let Pete go," she said. Her voice was trembling as much as her hand.

And she had a gun in her hand.

Beck cursed. He didn't need another battle when he hadn't even finished the first one.

"Nicole," Pete said through his gusting breath. "I knew you'd come back for me."

"I didn't do this for you. What you did was stupid, Pete, but I can't let you go to jail. Despite what you've done, you're still my husband. Part of me still loves you." She turned her teary eyes to Beck and pointed the gun right at him. "I'm a good shot," she reminded him. "Now let him go."

"Go where? Pete's a killer. What if he turns his anger on you?"

"He won't. I'm the reason he killed."

"He could hurt someone else," Beck reminded her. "You'd be responsible for that."

"What do I care if Faith Matthews and her bastard child are hurt?" Her attention went back to Pete. "I'll get you out of this, and then we'll be even. I want you to leave and never come back."

That wouldn't be good enough. Beck knew Pete wouldn't stay away. As long as his brother was alive and free, Faith and Aubrey would be in danger.

"I can't let him go," Beck insisted.

"Then I'll have to shoot you," Nicole insisted right back.

And she would.

Beck could see it in her eyes.

She'd already crossed over and left reason behind. She was going to save Pete whether he deserved it or not.

Nicole adjusted her aim so that it was right at Beck's shoulder. She wasn't going for the kill, but it didn't matter. The shot could still be deadly, and even if it only incapacitated him, it would leave the others vulnerable.

Cursing under his breath, Beck readied himself to take evasive action. He'd roll to the right, dropping to Pete's side. It might cause Nicole to think twice about shooting. But then it would give Pete the opportunity to break free.

"Nicole!" someone yelled.

Faith.

Hell. She'd come back.

Nicole automatically looked in the direction of Faith's voice. Beck couldn't see her. She was behind him.

But he saw the movement of something flying through the air.

Nicole tried to adjust her aim. But it was too late. A coffee mug slammed right into Nicole's hand. Maybe it was the impact or the surprise of the attack, but Nicole dropped the gun.

Pete went after it.

So did Beck.

Both of them scrambled across the floor toward it.

Above them, Nicole moved as well. Faith, too. Beck could hear Faith's footsteps, and he knew she was going after Nicole.

And Faith might get hurt in the process.

Beck caught onto Pete and slammed him against the floor. Nicole reached down, to help Pete or get the gun. But reaching was as far as she got. Faith grabbed Nicole and with a fierce jerk, she yanked her back. It was the break that Beck needed. His hand clamped around the gun, and this time, he came up ready to fire.

"Move back," Beck told Faith.

Nicole reached for her to try to use her as a shield, but Faith darted across the room just out of Nicole's reach.

"Don't move," Beck warned Pete when he tried to get up. His brother turned his head, and their gazes connected.

Beck made sure there were no doubts or hesitation in his eyes. Because there certainly wasn't any of that in his heart.

"I will kill you," Beck promised.

Pete laid his head on the floor and put his hands on the back of his head. Finally surrendering.

Chapter Sixteen

Faith frantically checked Aubrey again.

She hadn't seen any blood, or even a scratch, but she had to be sure that Pete's shots hadn't harmed her child.

"No, no, no," Aubrey fussed, batting Faith's hands away. The little girl rubbed her eyes and yawned. She was obviously sleepy and didn't want any more of this impromptu exam.

Deputy Winston rushed in the door. He had his weapon drawn, and he hurried past them and into the kitchen. A moment later, the Ranger, Sgt. McKinney, followed. Then Deputy Gafford.

Finally!

Even though it'd been only minutes since her nine-one-one call, Beck now had the backup he needed. And once she had the all clear that it was safe to check on him, she would. Well, she would after Marita had taken Aubrey into the bedroom away from Nicole and Pete.

She prayed Beck was all right.

In the distance she heard the sirens from an ambulance. And she heard footsteps. Faith looked up from her now fussy daughter and spotted Beck.

Oh, God. He was bleeding. There was a gash on his forehead. His left cheek. And both hands were bloodied.

"The ambulance will be here any minute," Faith told him.

He looked at her. Then at Aubrey. He seemed to make it to them in one giant step, and he pulled them both into his arms. Faith's breath shattered, and she was afraid she wouldn't be able to hold back the tears of relief.

"Is she hurt?" Beck asked. His voice was frantic. "Are you hurt?"

Faith pulled back so she could meet his gaze. "We're not hurt. You are. I called the ambulance for you."

His breath swooshed out. "You're not hurt." He repeated it several times and drew them back into his embrace.

Aubrey rubbed her eyes again and babbled something. It sounded cranky, and Faith figured she was about to cry, but her daughter maneuvered her way into Beck's arms and dropped her head on his shoulder.

"I'll see if I can be of assistance in the kitchen," Tracy volunteered, trying to give them some privacy.

"Want me to take Aubrey?" Marita asked.

"No," Faith and Beck said in unison.

"All right then. I'll just go outside and let the EMTs know what's going on." Marita took a step and then stopped. Her forehead was bunched up. "What exactly is going on?"

He and Faith exchanged glances. He didn't let go of her. But then she had no plans to let go of him either.

"My brother is about to be arrested for three murders," Beck explained. "Nicole will be taken into custody as well since she tried to assist him with his escape.

And we need to look for Darin. He's out there some-where and needs medical attention."

"Oh. I see." Marita turned pale. She waggled her fingers toward the sound of the sirens. "What should I tell the EMT guys? They'll be here any minute."

"Have then come in and check out Faith," Beck insisted.

Other than some bruises and maybe a scrape or two, Faith knew she was fine. She couldn't say the same for Beck. He'd need stitches for that gash.

"And I want them to check out Beck," Faith added as Marita went out the door.

"I'm okay," he insisted, kissing Aubrey's cheek. He kissed Faith's, too. "At least now I am. For a minute there, I thought I'd lost you."

"Me, too," she managed to say. Her emotion was too raw to talk about.

There was movement from the kitchen, and a mo-ment later, Pete appeared. Handcuffed. Corey had a hold on him. The other deputy had Nicole cuffed and was walking her to the front door.

Pete stopped, and Beck automatically turned so that Aubrey wouldn't be near the man. "There's nothing we have to say to each other," Beck insisted.

But Pete didn't speak right away. He stood there, vol-leying glances among Beck, Aubrey and Faith. "You fell hard for her, didn't you?" He didn't wait for Beck to confirm it. "That's how I feel about Nicole."

"You were ready to kill her," Faith pointed out.

"I wouldn't have. *Couldn't* have," he corrected. "Love really messes you up." His attention landed on Aubrey again. "I know she's Sherry's kid. Sherry showed me her picture. One she'd taken in a park, and she tried to convince me that I was the one who got her pregnant."

That gave Faith another jolt of adrenaline. "Did you?"

Pete shook his head. "Not a chance."

Faith desperately wanted to believe him. "And since you've been so truthful in the past, I should just take you at your word?"

"He's telling the truth," Corey volunteered. "This time, anyway. I saw the DNA results from the Ranger lab. He's not the father. Neither are you, Beck. It's Nolan Wheeler."

Nolan. In hindsight, it didn't surprise her. Not really. Sherry had spent most of her life breaking up and then getting back together with Nolan.

"He might have fathered her," Beck mumbled. "But Nolan was never her father."

Faith couldn't have agreed more. If the man hadn't been dead, his DNA connection to Aubrey would have caused her stomach to go into a tailspin. Because Nolan would have spent the rest of his life trying to figure out ways to use Aubrey to get what he wanted.

"Get my brother out of here," Beck instructed the deputy.

Pete didn't protest. He looked straight ahead as he was escorted out. Nicole was next. She didn't even try to say anything. Tears were streaming down her cheeks, and she made a series of hoarse sobs.

However, Deputy Gafford did stop. "On the way over, I got a call from the hospital. Darin Matthews is back there. He's not hurt, and he wanted me to check on Faith, to make sure she was all right."

Faith was so glad that Beck was holding on to her.

Her brother was safe. Pete hadn't hurt him. And better yet, he was receiving the medical treatment he needed. She would check on him as soon as things had settled down.

Whenever that might be.

It might take her years to forget how close she'd come to losing Beck and Aubrey.

"The other Texas Ranger is with Darin now," the deputy continued. "Will there be any charges filed against him?"

"No," Beck quickly answered. "But I want him to have a thorough psychiatric evaluation."

The deputy nodded and escorted Nicole out.

Faith looked around and realized they were alone. The house was quiet. Her heart rate was slowly returning to normal.

"Are you really okay?" Beck asked.

But the silence didn't last. Before she could answer, there was the sound of hurried footsteps, and she automatically braced herself for the worst.

Roy came rushing through the front door.

He looked at Beck. At Aubrey. Then at her. He'd no doubt passed his other son and daughter-in-law and knew they were under arrest. But his concern seemed to be aimed at Beck.

"Son, you're bleeding," Roy greeted him.

"Just a scratch," Beck assured him.

"He needs stitches," Faith insisted.

Roy agreed with a nod, and he put his hands on his hips. He looked around, as if he didn't know what to say or do. "I just spoke to Corey and the nanny, Marita. They told me what happened in here."

"Yeah," was all Beck said.

"'i," Aubrey babbled to Roy.

There were tears in Roy's eyes, but he forced a smile when he returned the "hi." He hesitated. "I'm sorry. So sorry for what Pete did. I knew about the blackmail and the payoff, but I swear I didn't know he'd killed those people. And I didn't know he would come after the three of you. I'm sorry," he repeated, aiming this one at Faith.

She gave his arm a gentle squeeze. "Thank you."

Roy turned those tearful eyes to Beck. "What can I do? Give me something to do. I can't go home and sit there."

"You can go to my office and call Pete and Nicole a lawyer. They're going to need one."

"Of course. I'll do that. And if you need anything, just let me know."

"I will."

"Make sure he sees the medics," Roy whispered to Faith. He gave her arm a gentle squeeze as well and went back out the door just as the medics were coming in.

Beck held up his hand to stop them. "Could you give me a few minutes?" he asked.

That halted the two men in their tracks, and they looked at her for verification. "Just a few minutes," she bargained. But only a few. She wanted that gash checked.

Aubrey fussed and babbled, "Bye-bye," but Faith didn't think she wanted to go with Roy or the medics. She smeared her fist over her eyes again and whimpered.

"It's okay," Beck said to Aubrey, and he lightly circled his fingers over her back.

"Da, Da, Da, Da," Aubrey answered. Not in a happy

tone, either. But it was a tone Faith recognized. Her baby was on the verge of a tired tantrum.

Beck must have sensed that because he caught onto Faith's arm and led them to the sofa. Once he'd sat down, he moved Aubrey so that her tummy was against his chest. She dropped her head onto his shoulder and stuck her thumb in her mouth. Within seconds, her eyelids were already lowering.

Faith smiled. "Tantrum averted," she whispered. Good. She didn't have any energy left to deal with anything. "I might have to call you the next time she gets fussy."

Beck angled his eyes in her direction and stared at her. She'd thought the light comment would have given him some relief. It was certainly better than the alternative of her falling apart.

"You said you loved me," Beck reminded her.

That kicked up her heart again. She'd planned on having this discussion later. After some of the chaos had settled. "Yes, I did say that." Because she wanted to dodge eye contact with him, she checked Aubrey. Sound asleep.

"You meant it?"

But before he let her answer, he leaned in and kissed her. He winced because his lip was busted. Hers, too, she realized when his mouth touched hers. She didn't care. That kiss was worth a little pain, and it was the ultimate truth serum. She was going to lay her heart out there and let him know exactly how she felt about him.

She hoped he wouldn't laugh.

Or run the other direction.

"I meant it," she answered. "I love you." Beck and Aubrey were two things in her life that she was certain of. "I'm crazy in love with you."

His face relaxed a bit. The corner of his mouth even lifted in a near smile. "Good. Because I'm crazy in love with you, too."

A sharp sound of surprise leaped from her mouth. "Really?" She heard her voice. Heard the shock. "You're sure it's not just the lust talking?"

"The lust is there," he admitted. He reached out and pushed her hair away from her face. "But so is the love. You did me the honor of letting me be your first lover. Now I'm asking if you'll let me be your last."

Mercy. That was not a light tone. Nor a light look in his eyes. Still, Faith approached that comment with caution. "Are you asking me to go steady?" she joked.

"No. I'm asking you to marry me."

Oh. *Wow.*

Her heart went crazy. So did her stomach. Her breathing. Her entire body.

Was this really happening? She wanted it to happen. Desperately wanted it, she realized. But she hadn't expected it.

As if to convince her, he kissed her again. And again. Until he was the only thing she could think of. Beck had that kind of effect on her. He could make even the aftermath of chaos seem incredible. Heat and love just rippled through her.

"I don't want you to call me when Aubrey's fussy because I want to be there, close by, to hear her myself. I want to be her father, and I want to be your husband."

"You're already her father," Faith said. And it was true. "Aubrey chose you herself." She had to blink back happy tears. "She made a good choice."

"I'm glad you think so. Now, to the rest. I want to

be your last lover. Your only lover. What do you think about that?"

Faith didn't have to think. She knew. There was only one answer. "Yes."

* * * * *

TEXAS PATERNITY: BOOTS AND BOOTIES
continues next month with Expecting Trouble,
only from Delores Fossen and
Mills & Boon® Intrigue!

THE 9-MONTH BODYGUARD

BY
CINDY DEES

Cindy Dees started flying aeroplanes while sitting in her dad's lap at the age of three and got a pilot's licence before she got a driver's licence. At age fifteen, she dropped out of school and left the horse farm in Michigan where she grew up to attend the University of Michigan.

After earning a degree in Russian and Eastern European studies, she joined the US Air Force and became the youngest female pilot in its history. She flew supersonic jets, VIP airlift and the C-5 Galaxy, the world's largest aeroplane. She also worked part-time gathering intelligence. During her military career, she travelled to forty countries on five continents, was detained by the KGB and East German secret police, got shot at, flew in the first Gulf War, met her husband and amassed a lifetime's worth of war stories.

Her hobbies include professional Middle Eastern dancing, Japanese gardening and medieval re-enacting. She started writing on a one-dollar bet with her mother and was thrilled to win that bet with the publication of her first book in 2001. She loves to hear from readers and can be contacted at www.cindydees.com.

Chapter 1

If one more person told her that her thirties were going to be the best years of her life, she was going to spend that decade in prison, doing hard time for murder.

Silver Rothchild realized her pasted-on smile was slipping and reinforced it quickly.

Thirty years old. Gamblers all over Las Vegas must be losing their shirts tonight betting over whether or not she'd live to see this birthday. A few years ago, no one would have bet a plugged nickel on her chances of making it this long.

She had to admit that her twenties had been one heck of a wild ride. The holier-than-thou crowd was offended at any hint that she'd actually had fun jet-setting around the world, rocking out in front of huge audiences as a pop singer, partying till dawn and pulling dozens of crazy stunts, any one of which should have killed her. But the fact was, a lot of it had been a blast. Self-destructive in the end and rendering her jaded and cynical far beyond her years, but a blast, nonetheless.

Of course, she'd done a lot of growing up since then. She'd buried enough of her friends by now to know the dangers of the lifestyle, too. Since those days she'd sworn off harmful substances, and she'd made a concerted effort to drop completely off the celebrity radar. Heck, she'd made an appearance in a celebrity magazine a few months back in a "where are they now?" article. How pathetic was that? Thirty years old and she was a has-been.

"You okay, snookums? You look like roadkill."

"I hate it when you call me that," Silver muttered to Mark Sampson, her bodyguard and ostensible boyfriend of the past several months.

"It's cute. Like you and your perky little—"

She stepped away from his hand as he made a clumsy grab at her rear end and hissed through her fake smile, "Stop acting like white trash."

"Now, snookums. Be nice. Wouldn't want me to get all mad and accidentally say something to them reporters over there about our arrangement."

She sighed. He was right. She was the one who'd made the offer to him in the first place—she had no business getting bitchy with him over it. She looped an arm through his and guided him out to the dance floor. Dance nasty in front of Mark and he'd forget all about his threat. Men were such incredibly simple creatures.

Not particularly enjoying either the song or gyrating around in as slutty a fashion as she could muster, she was vastly relieved when a sharp vibration tickled her right hip. Her heart leaped in anticipation. *Could this be the call?*

Shouting over the blaring music, she yelled at Mark, "Phone! I've got to take this call."

He nodded, turned to the nearest half-naked bimbo without interrupting his own hip-thrusting Elvis impersonation, and kept on dancing.

Some bodyguard.

She found a secluded corner behind a potted palm in the hall outside and pulled out her brand-new crystal-encrusted cell phone, a birthday present from her stepsister, Natalie. She hit redial quickly.

"Hello, this is Silver Rothchild—"

"Silver! Hi, this is Debbie, from Dr. Harris's office."

Her blood pressure jumped twenty points right then and there. Oh, God. It was the call. Her test results were back. She let out a long, steadying breath and steeled herself to hear the news either way. "Thanks for getting back to me so quickly. I'm sorry I couldn't stick around the office to wait for the results, but I couldn't be late for my own birthday party."

The nurse at the other end of the phone laughed. "Well, I've got a birthday present for you, Silver. Your results are positive. You're going to have a baby."

A *baby*.

The word washed over her and through her like a warm and gentle blessing, calming all the way down to her soul. Her most cherished dream had finally come true.

"Silver? Are you there?"

"Uh, yes. I'm still here. That's…that's fabulous!"

Jubilation erupted in her heart all of a sudden, an elation that wouldn't be contained. She let out a whoop of joy that startled a couple walking past.

"You'll need to set up an appointment for next week. We need to do a sonogram and get you started on prenatal vitamins. And of course, the doctor's going to want to talk to you about managing your blood pressure. As you know, this pregnancy poses a certain risk, given your tendency to high blood pressure. Write down any questions you have as they occur to you or you'll forget them during your appointment."

"Right. I'll call back first thing in the morning."

Silver floated out from behind the palm tree, her feet several inches above the floor. Her hand stole to her flat belly. A tiny human being was growing in there! It was miraculous.

"There you arc, Silver!" a female voice called out with a hint of irritation from down the hall. "Your father wants to give you his birthday present. You'd better hurry before he changes his mind."

Silver spied her perfectly groomed stepmother, only four years her senior, coming her way in a pair of high heels that mere mortals wouldn't dare attempt. But Rebecca, in true trophy-wife fashion, was a former model and wore the four-inch stilettos like they were an extension of her magnificent legs.

Okay, so sue her. She was jealous of her glamorous stepmother's height. It sucked being five foot two in a town full of six-foot-tall show girls. She looked like a twelve-year-old compared to them.

"I'm coming, Rebecca," Silver called.

A spark of curiosity grew within her. What had her father cooked up for her birthday? He'd been so mysterious about it. Usually, she could coax any secret out of him. But this time, despite her very best cajolery, he hadn't given so much as a hint of what her birthday present was…other than the fact that it was going to blow her mind.

It took a lot to blow her mind. Like right now. She was pretty blown away by the idea of a baby of her own. She loved kids. Always had. Born into another life, she'd have been a school-teacher in a heartbeat.

As it was, her life had gone in a radically different direction. She'd always been a good singer, and with Daddy's money and the resources of a show town like Vegas behind her, she'd been trained into a polished performer. A few Rothchild connections in the music biz, and voilà, she'd become a recording artist and pop star. Whether or not she'd deserved it was open to debate. At twenty-two, she hadn't cared if she'd stolen the dream of someone more talented and less connected. But now…now she wondered about it sometimes.

Given a do-over of her life, it might be interesting to see if she could've made it in the music business without any help at all from her father. Of course that was easy to say with a wall full of gold records and the fame and fortune to go with them.

Not having to fake a smile this time, she joined her party once more.

"There's our birthday girl!" her father boomed.

She made her way to him through the crowd of well-wishers. She hugged several of her longtime partners-in-crime who'd managed to survive their youths and grow up to one degree or another. There was no sign of Mark, for which she was abjectly grateful. Had he actually been her boyfriend, she'd have been furious that he'd vanished to who-knew-where with who-knew-whom. But now that she was pregnant, it was a good thing she'd taken the precaution of setting up their arrangement.

Her father gave her a hand up onto the raised dais along the back side of the room. *Wait till he found out he was going to be a grandpa.* Once he got over the initial shock and got done lecturing her about not being married, he'd be tickled to death. At least, that was the plan. Harold was fiercely loyal to his family, but could be…mercurial. Which was to say, he could be a died-in-the-wool son of a bitch. It made him a great casino mogul, but at times, it made him a difficult father to deal with.

Silver acted appropriately amused as a giant, black-frosted cake was wheeled in. The Rothchild Grand's pastry chef had outdone himself, decorating the beastly thing with miniature fondant coffins, plastic wheelchairs, and tiny blue marzipan bottles of Geritol. It really was ghoulish. As if she needed the reminder that she was no longer twentysomething and in the bloom of her youth.

Then the toasts began. Oh, they were meant in good fun— the references to slowing down, growing up, and getting old. But the underlying message of it all was much, much worse. She'd become safe. Bland. *Boring.* To her, that was a thousand times worse than turning thirty. Where had the adventurous Silver gone? The one who dared to take the music business by storm? The one who didn't give a damn what anyone else thought? Who chased all her dreams, no matter how far-fetched?

The only thing that kept her from waxing suicidal at the black balloons, funeral dirge in lieu of "Happy Birthday," and nonstop old age jokes was her delirious secret. They could say whatever they wanted. She was finally going to have a baby.

When the birthday roast was finally over, her father raised his champagne glass. "A toast to my lovely daughter. May her next ten years be as successful as her last ten, and a lot less hard on this old man's heart."

The crowd laughed, and on cue, she looked appropriately abashed. For all his ranting and raving over the years to get her act together and grow up, he could really get over her twenties any day now. She had. She hadn't done anything to frighten or embarrass him in nearly seven years, but he still took every opportunity to remind her what a screwup she was.

That was Harold personified. Never missed a chance to sink a barb into someone if he could. Some people said it was impossible to love and hate a person at the same time. Obviously, they'd never had him for a stepfather.

Of course, now that she was turning thirty, she probably could get away with distancing herself from him and his overbearing ways. Maybe she should consider moving out of Las Vegas. Out of Nevada, even. Heck, out of the country! It was a shocking thought. Daring. But it took root in her head as surely as a baby had taken root in her womb. A new start. No ties to her past. No Rothchilds. No Harold.

Her father was speaking again. "…better thirtieth birthday present than to give my beautiful and talented daughter a special engagement at the Grand Casino…."

Whoa. Rewind.

Engagement? At the Grand? Her…*perform again?*

Silver's mind went blank. She wanted to resurrect her career almost as bad as she wanted this baby. And he was going to give her a shot? In total shock, she looked up at her father.

She whispered, "Are you serious?"

He laughed heartily. "As a heart attack, kiddo."

"My own show?"

"Yup. Seven nights. On the big stage. Orchestra, backup dancers, pyrotechnics, the works."

She flung herself into his arms and did something she hadn't done since she'd been a little girl. She burst into tears. Even he was startled by that.

"Hey now, what's this, kiddo? You're not unhappy, are you? I can cancel it—"

Oh, Lord. Was pregnancy weepiness kicking in already? Or maybe she was just overwhelmed by being broadsided with two such enormous pieces of news in quick succession. "No! I'm overjoyed, Daddy. It's incredible. I've dreamed of restarting my career for years…I don't know how to thank you…you're the best…"

Who'd have guessed he was capable of such a thoughtful and generous gesture? Maybe Candace's death had affected him more than she realized. Her stepsister's recent murder had hit everyone in the family hard.

Damn. Just when she'd resolved to cut the apron strings for good, he went and did something amazing. Something that would keep her firmly in Las Vegas for some months to come, preparing and rehearsing for her show. The guy's timing was uncanny, as always. Just let the thought of leaving cross her mind, and boom, he roped her back in.

He patted her back awkwardly. "No more tears."

She sniffed and smiled up at him damply. Regardless of his motives, it really was an incredibly generous gift.

Quietly, so the audience wouldn't hear, he said, "One condition, though. You stay out of trouble. Out of the bars and nightclubs. No wild partying, no more stunts, no more of your pop-star shenanigans. And stay out of the freaking tabloids." A hard edge entered his voice. "You go back to your old ways, and I'll yank this rug out from under you so fast your head spins. Understood? Keep it clean, and I'll give you another shot at singing. Screw this up, and I'll see to it nobody ever hires you again."

Ahh. That was more like the Harold she knew and loathed.

Careful to keep her voice even, she said, "That seems fair enough."

Oh, God. The baby. He'd just ordered her not to go off and

do anything impulsive or wild or that would land her in the tabloids…like, oh, getting pregnant out of wedlock. And if he—or the tabloids—found out the real circumstances of this baby's conception, the media would have a field day with it.

A baby or her career? How was she supposed to choose between those?

She took a deep breath. If she played her cards right and Mark didn't go and do anything stupid, maybe she could have them both.

Or maybe she could lose everything.

Chapter 2

Army Captain and Delta Force Team Commander, Austin Dearing, stepped out of the taxicab into the blast furnace heat of Las Vegas. Jeez. And it was only May. He'd hate to see this place in August. Of course, after living in full body armor in parts of the world where daily highs frequently topped one hundred twenty, Vegas wasn't so bad. But he was still grateful to step into the air-conditioned cool of the Rothchild Grand Hotel and Casino.

He looked around the gaudy lobby curiously. He liked his creature comforts well enough, but the job he'd been sent here to do overshadowed his appreciation of the beautiful, leggy women cruising the joint, sharklike, in search of fresh meat. In his world, this was what was known as a target-rich environment.

A silicone-enhanced bleach-blonde purred at him, "May I help you, sir?" She was almost tall enough that at six foot four, he didn't have to look down at her.

"I'm looking for Harold Rothchild."

A startled look flickered across her face, but she replied smoothly enough, "Is Mr. Rothchild expecting you?"

"Yes, he is."

"One moment, sir."

She pulled out a cell phone and made a discreet phone call. "He's at his daughter's birthday party at the moment. Would you care to wait in his office?"

"I'm under orders to report to him as soon as I get here, no matter what he's doing." The actual phrase Rothchild had used was more obscene and involved interrupting him even if he was having intimate relations with his wife. Austin snorted. Even an Army grunt like him was couth enough not to repeat such a thing to a lady, though.

Another discreet phone conversation.

"Mr. Rothchild's assistant says you're to go to the party. Would you like to check into your room first? Maybe freshen up a bit?"

He clamped down on his impatience. His orders were to see Rothchild immediately. Not after he took a nap and got pretty. Fingering the beard stubble of his past twenty-four hours' worth of travel, he said firmly in his commanding officer voice, "No. I'll see him now."

The blonde twittered, signaling how turned on she was by his display of manly resolve. *Groupie alert.* Women were forever hanging out at the places Special Forces soldiers frequented, trying to land guys like him. Usually, he could spot 'em at a hundred paces. But this one had snuck up on him. He'd lost his touch. Been out in the field too damned long. Two years since he'd taken a minute off. Only reason he was on leave now was because of his busted left eardrum. He'd blown it when an explosion had gone off too close to him a few weeks back. The doc said it would take several months to heal. Which meant he was left cooling his jets for a while.

Thankfully, his commanding officer, General Sarkin, knew him well enough to know that sitting on his butt for months would drive him completely crazy. With his entire unit deployed overseas, it wasn't like there was anything on a stateside Army post to keep him busy. So, Sarkin had arranged for this special assignment.

Austin had never heard of Harry Rothchild, but he damned well knew who Silver Rothchild was. Her father, eh? Austin sympathized. His daughter was possibly the most notorious wild child of the past decade. The dossier Sarkin had given him said that Rothchild was worth hundreds of millions and the Grand Casino was the crown jewel of his hotel empire. He had a big family, which he kept close by, including several daughters. One of them, Candace, had been murdered a few months back, which was why Austin supposed he'd been hired to play nursemaid to Rothchild's third daughter—the troubled Silver.

He'd fought the cream puff assignment, but Sarkin had been adamant. Ultimately, he'd been a good soldier and sucked it up. It wasn't an official job, of course. The military didn't make a practice of babysitting spoiled little rich girls, thank you very much. But when a man with the stature of General Sarkin, who held the future of a guy's career in his hands, asked him to do something off the books, the guy did it, like it or not.

And it was only for three months. Just until his ear healed and he was cleared to go back into the field. He could put up with pretty much anything for three months.

The busty blonde opened a door marked Private, and the sounds of a party in full swing slammed into him. The shock of it was a physical blow. He couldn't remember the last time he'd been in a gathering of people this large and boisterous. Claustrophobia closed in around him. So accustomed was he to the desolate, wide open mountains of Afghanistan that he'd been patrolling for the past two years, he could barely force himself into the crush.

Three months. He could do this.

He waded into the crowd. Using his height to look over the partiers, Austin searched for the florid face of Harold Rothchild from the dossier. There he was. On the far side of the room on some sort of raised platform.

A hand groped Austin's rear end, and he pivoted sharply, prepared to take out the assailant. A brunette leered up at him. He stood down, relaxing his hands from their knife-blade rigidness. *You're back in the real world, Dearing. Cool it.*

Easier said than done. Those lightning fast reflexes, the total lack of hesitation to kill, were the reason he was still alive and kicking. Lecturing himself about the rules of engagement for this particular type of jungle, he managed to cross the dance floor without causing anyone bodily harm.

Austin touched Harold Rothchild lightly on the shoulder. The older man spun around, startled. *Hmm. The Rothchild patriarch was plenty edgy.* Not to mention he was hiring ridiculously overqualified bodyguards for his kids. What was going on? The dossier hadn't said anything about why the mogul suddenly wanted someone like Dearing—who specialized in guarding heads of State—watching out for his daughter.

"You must be Captain Dearing. Your commander described you to a tee, I must say."

At least Rothchild sounded relaxed enough. "Call me Austin, sir. I'm not on the Army's clock at the moment."

Rothchild snorted. "You don't have to tell me. I'm the guy who wrote your first paycheck. It has already been wired into the Singapore bank account you gave my secretary."

Austin nodded, annoyed. Why did men like this think that men like him gave a damn about money? Just because Rothchild worshipped at the altar of the almighty dollar didn't mean everyone did.

He schooled himself to patience. Growing up poor had probably made him more cynical than most. But his family had gotten by. And he and his brothers had all turned out fine. They were all hardworking, law-abiding citizens who enjoyed their work. Sure, he could make more money as a civilian bodyguard—a lot more than his Army pay—but that wasn't remotely why he did his job. He loved his work.

Rothchild bellowed, "Silver, come over here. There's someone I want you to meet,"

A fist in his gut couldn't have knocked the wind out of Austin more thoroughly than his first glimpse of Silver Rothchild. Wow. He couldn't help it; he stared as the pop star made her way to them. Her face, familiar to him from newsstands around the world, wasn't the most beautiful he'd ever seen, although she was genuinely pretty. She didn't have the best body he'd ever seen— she was too petite to achieve beauty queen stature—but she was in great shape and shaped great, not to mention he didn't spot a hint of silicone or surgery. She was one of those rare women with innate sexual charisma, a woman whom men couldn't peel their gaze away from and didn't want to. A genuine blond bombshell.

It was, of course, the reason she'd been such a sensation on the pop music scene. Belatedly, it occurred to him that she was actually wearing a perfectly modest dress, not showing a hint of cleavage, nor an inch of extra thigh. Her signature platinum blond hair was twisted up in a clip of some kind behind her head, and her makeup was understated.

Those silver-blue bedroom eyes of hers penetrated right through him as she looked up at him politely. She held out a perfectly manicured hand. "Hi, I'm Silver. It's nice to meet you." Her voice was honey sweet, hinting at the million-dollar sound that had made her famous.

Suppressing an urge to stammer, he replied, "Austin Dearing, Miss Rothchild."

One graceful brow arched at his shift of her name into the formal. She glanced over at her father questioningly.

"This, my dear, is your other birthday present."

Silver's startled gaze shot back to his. Chagrin abruptly warmed his cheeks. He was a *birthday present?* An elite-trained, highly-decorated war hero who led men into the jaws of death on a routine basis? Harold made him sound like a damned trained monkey!

His brows slammed together. Favor or not, General Sarkin could take this job and shove it. He wasn't *anybody's* pet.

Silver murmured in an appalled undertone, "What are you up to, Daddy?"

"Austin is a bodyguard."

The rosy blush in Silver's porcelain face drained away, lending a faintly gray cast to her complexion. Austin frowned, his internal alarm system exploding to life. He was missing something, here. Silver Rothchild was deathly afraid of something. Or *someone*. His protective instincts roared to the fore, jolting his every sense onto high alert. He abruptly didn't like the press of people around her, didn't like how exposed she was up on this raised dais above the crowd. He needed to be in front of her, between her and the balcony to his left that was a perfect perch for a sniper.

She choked out, "I already have a bodyguard, Father."

"And he's an idiot. Captain Dearing comes highly recommended by a friend of mine. He's the best. After Candace…"

Rothchild trailed off. Silver closed her eyes in pain, obviously understanding her father's veiled reference. Austin's brain kicked into overdrive. Was there more to the Candace Rothchild murder investigation than met the eye? Was the killer targeting other members of the Rothchild family? That would certainly explain daddy bringing in a high-powered bodyguard to protect his most famous child.

Silver seemed to gather herself together. She said more strongly, "I appreciate your concern, Dad, but I don't need another bodyguard. I'm perfectly safe with the one I have."

"What about that incident last week?"

"Brakes fail on cars. And Las Vegas is as flat as a pancake. I coasted to a perfectly safe stop."

"You were supposed to drive up into the mountains that day. What if your brakes had failed then?"

"Well, I didn't go up into the mountains and everything was fine."

Austin had to give the girl credit. Her father was a big, intimidating guy, and she was showing pluck to stand her ground like this.

Brake failure, huh? In his experience, the brakes on any reasonably well-maintained vehicle never, ever failed of their own volition.

Rothchild turned to him. "Ignore her. She needs a decent bodyguard, and I'm signing your paycheck."

Austin glanced over at the singer, who looked more than irritated. For just a second, her wonderfully expressive eyes looked…haunted. What in the hell was going on that had a wild woman like her looking like that? No doubt about it. She put his protective instincts on full combat alert.

He turned back to her father and nodded firmly. "I'll protect her with my life, sir."

"But—" Silver began.

Harold cut her off. "No buts. Austin Dearing is your bodyguard now. Consider him part of our earlier deal."

Whatever that deal was, Silver subsided immediately. But this time, resentment simmered at the back of her transparent gaze. Didn't like being pushed around by daddy dearest. But she was thirty years old according to the banner over her head. She could tell the guy to go to hell if he was that big a pain.

Rothchild gestured at one of the waiters passing by. "Take Mr. Dearing's bag. Check him into the New Yorker Villa and see to it his gear gets up there." Rothchild glanced over at Austin. "As of now, you're on duty."

For his part, Austin nodded and kept his thoughts to himself. Good thing he'd slept most of the way back from Afghanistan on the various flights that brought him here. Jetlag going east to west wasn't that bad, but he was twelve time zones out of sync at the moment. Of course, Harry Rothchild wasn't in the business of caring about anyone's comfort other than his guests'. For his part, Austin was used to the uncomfortable demands of guarding someone else's life.

Speaking of which, Silver turned away from her father and pushed heedlessly into the crowd. But not before Austin caught the flash of naked fear in her eyes. What was going on with her? The currents of mystery and danger swirling around her were palpable. And it was his job to decipher those currents and deflect them away from her at all costs. Of course, Rothchild hadn't exactly helped him get off on the right foot with his famously willful daughter. Austin sighed. Time for some serious damage control. And to think, he'd been on the job a grand total of thirty seconds.

Chapter 3

Silver glanced over her shoulder as a deep voice growled from behind her, "We need to talk, Miss Rothchild."

At least her father'd had the decency to pick a jailer who was easy on the eyes. He was a big man wrapped in muscle. Good looking in a chiseled, all-American kind of way. Totally not her kind of guy. She liked them dark and dangerous, and always seemed to end up with lean, jaded Europeans. He was all tawny and bronze, with a deep tan and sun-streaked blond streaks. His eyes were dark. Mysterious. Smoking hot, in fact. He looked like a male model for sailing attire.

She *so* wasn't stopping to talk to him. He was the living embodiment of everything she hated about how her father was forever manipulating and controlling her life. If Austin Dearing wanted to play bodyguard, he could darn well keep up with her.

She needed to be alone. To assimilate all that had happened in the past few minutes. To figure out how she was going to juggle her secret pregnancy and this incredible opportunity to perform. And then there was Mark. Now she'd have to string him along for even longer, perhaps most of the way through her pregnancy. It would depend on when the shows were scheduled. Yep, that was the key to pulling this thing off. How pregnant would she be by the time the shows happened? No doubt the promoters would want her half-naked and gyrating like she always had. Might be a teensy bit hard to do that looking like Shamu.

She hurried toward the casino, praying that no one would waylay her so Austin could catch up. Thankfully, she'd grown up in this place and knew every slot machine, every twist and turn, like the back of her hand. She zigzagged across the casino practically at a run and made her way to Saul Morgenstern's office by the Grand Theater. He was the vice president in charge of entertainment and the man who would schedule her gig.

Skipping his anal retentive secretary, Silver used her master key card to let herself directly into his office's private entrance. He looked up, startled, phone to his ear, then waved her to a chair in front of his desk.

He shouted into the phone, "Christ, Nigel! These changes are going to cost me a million bucks. Newsflash, your boys aren't worth it… No I'm not giving them an entire floor of the hotel. Just because your band is British doesn't mean they're the freaking Beatles!…and you can procure your owned damned call girls for them. I'm not a pimp… Yeah, well use the phone book. Prostitution's legal in this state, you moron."

Wow. He didn't often get that worked up. Some band had really crossed the line, apparently.

Saul slammed down the receiver, took off his spectacles and pinched the bridge of his nose before he finally said more calmly, "Silver Girl. I gather your father has sprung his little birthday surprise on you?"

He'd called her Silver Girl since she'd been a child. The two of them used to be as close as a beloved uncle and an adored niece. But that relationship, too, had been a casualty of her wild years. He'd overlooked her atrocious behavior far longer than anyone else, but even his patience had run out eventually. Ever since, he'd maintained a frosty distance from her that she'd respected as her just desserts. But she missed him.

"Hi, Saul. I'm sorry you couldn't make my party. Daddy really went overboard." She added wryly, "I expect he was trying to make the point to me that, like it or not, I'm an adult now."

Saul's mouth twitched, but he didn't crack the smile that had once come so readily for her. She sighed. "Harold told me about the show here at the Grand. I never thought he'd do something like that for me. I mean, it's not like I deserve it or anything."

That sent Saul's gray, shaggy brows up.

It was exceedingly uncomfortable having to maintain the entire conversation by herself like this, but apparently doing this gig was going to involve swallowing a healthy dose of crow, too. She continued doggedly. "He didn't tell me what you had in mind for the shows. Am I penciled in yet?"

Saul studied her inscrutably. "How soon can you be ready to go onstage? You'll need to be in tip-top shape, maybe take a few singing lessons. After all these star search shows, singers today are expected to really blow out a song."

The criticism stung. She'd always had plenty of range and power for any song her record label had given her. She replied evenly, "I've been singing again for a while. And I've been working out. I'm ready now, Saul. The sooner we do this thing, the better."

He leaned back, frowning, and said doubtfully, "You're gonna have to find new material….backup singers…you can use the hotel's band and orchestra, but they'll need arrangements… costumes and choreography…"

Her stomach was quickly filling up with lead. What he was talking about could take *months*. In the past, she'd had an entire crew of handlers who had taken care of all the details of putting together one of her tours. Frankly, she'd done little more than learn the songs and show up for a few costume fittings. But this time, it sounded like Saul expected her to do the bulk of the preparatory work herself. An hour ago, she'd have leaped all over the idea of getting to design her own show. But then she'd found out she was pregnant, and a time bomb—in the form of a looming baby bump—had suddenly started ticking.

She took a deep breath. "Saul, I need to do this show right away. I don't have time to develop big production numbers or manage a cast of thousands."

His bushy eyebrows came together over glaring eyes. "Do you want to *blow* this shot?"

She winced. "No. I really, really want to restart my career, and I fully understand how much is riding on this. But I *can't* spend months and months pulling this thing together."

"Why the hell not, missy?"

She closed her eyes. Much more even than her father, Saul could make or break her comeback based on how he supported her show. The good news was that, in many ways, Saul had been more of a father to her over the years than Harold had been. The bad news was he might very well be out to sabotage her comeback.

As Saul stared down at her hands, she realized she was wringing them until they were an angry red. She stopped. "Saul. I swear I have a life-shattering reason why I have to do this show now. But I can't tell you. I don't have any right at all to ask you, but could you please just trust me on this one?"

Skepticism glittered in his eyes.

She sighed. "I've changed. I've grown up. I'm not that spoiled, snot-nosed brat I was a few years ago." Did he remember the night he'd called her that? When she'd called him to bail her out of jail before the paparazzi got wind of it, and he'd come down to the police station and told her she could rot in the slammer for all he cared?

The memory of that night gleamed in his gaze, too. "You're so grown up and committed to your career that you won't sacrifice your personal plans to do this show right?" he bit out sarcastically.

Desperation made her throat tight. "I hear what you're saying. You're absolutely right. But I can't work around this one. I'd give up anything—everything in the world—except one thing, to perform again. And that one thing makes it necessary for me to do this show in the next few months."

Saul stared at her long and hard. If he'd figured out what she was making veiled reference to, he didn't comment on it. Finally, he reached into his desk and pulled out a leather day planner. Saul was old school. No computers or PDAs for him. He did everything on paper. "Lemme take a look at the schedule."

She exhaled on a massive sigh of relief. This could work if he'd cooperate with her.

"You're booked for Valentine's Day next year."

She did the math fast. Good Lord, she'd be over eight months pregnant by then. "What have you got that's sooner?"

He thumbed through the pages. "I always book a year or more in advance. But there is one possibility…" He trailed off as he turned to a page near the front of the planner. She peeked across his desk and saw June in block print at the top of the page. That was next month. Hope sprang through her.

"That phone call you walked in on was the manager for Metal Head Dead."

They were a rock band currently topping the charts. Their reputation was already worse than hers had ever been. And yet, because they were guys, they got away with all the rotten stunts that had deep-sixed her career. In fact, their careers were helped by their wild antics. She put aside her bitterness. The double standard was just part of the business.

Saul was talking again, mumbling to himself. "…would put their knickers in a twist if I canceled their leather-clad butts. And tickets for their show are set to go on sale in three days… We could call a press conference…make a big announcement about your comeback…tickets could go on sale immediately and we could capitalize on the buzz…"

He looked up at her. "You'd have only six weeks to pull the

entire thing together. You won't be able to scrimp on anything…
it's going to have to be a top-notch production or you'll be a
worse has-been than you are now."

Ouch.

He continued, "I'm telling you, I think it's impossible to get
a decent show together by then. Plus, June isn't the big tourist
season on the strip."

She replied hopefully, "But it's hot enough that everyone
who is in town is inside and going to shows."

He shrugged. "I can't promise sellout crowds with only a few
weeks to promote the gig. But if you're hell-bent on doing this
thing right away, I can book you for June."

She darted around his desk to lay a big hug on him, just like
the old days. The tears of gratitude that came to her eyes seemed
to surprise him as much as they surprised her. She whispered,
too choked up to speak any louder, "Thanks, Uncle Saul. I
promise I won't let you down this time."

For just a moment, he returned the hug. Then he cleared his
throat and set her away from him. "Now. About music," he said
briskly. "I'd better be the one to make the call to your old label.
The way I hear it, you didn't part on the best of terms."

Silver grimaced. Now there was an understatement. She'd
been fired and escorted out of the record company's building by
armed guards. In retrospect, she'd probably deserved worse. As
she recalled—vaguely—she'd been stoned out of her head at the
time.

She took a deep breath. "Actually, Saul, I've been writing
some of my own stuff. Maybe we could use some of that—"

He cut her off with a slashing hand through the air. "Nobody
ever builds a decent career on their own stuff. Three or four big-
name, girl pop singers have taken time off recently. There'll be
plenty of good songs lying around waiting for a big, sexy voice."

"But—"

"No buts. Your father told me to launch your second career,
and that's what I aim to do. You leave the music to me, baby doll."

She wanted to tell him she wasn't a baby doll anymore. She was a grown woman, dammit, and she didn't want to do the same old music she'd sung the last time around. She wanted to do something new. Something more soulful, more…grown up. But Saul was first and foremost her father's man. And, he'd been a dear about the scheduling problem. He'd canceled a huge act for her. Like it or not, she was probably going to have to go along with him on the music thing.

She sighed. Time for more of that maturity stuff.

"…stop by tomorrow, and I'll show you the stage. We've made quite a few changes to it since you last were on it."

She winced again. The last time she'd sung on the Grand stage seven years ago, she'd been too fried to hit a note, had forgotten lyrics left and right and had topped off the disaster by being booed offstage. Not one of her more stellar moments in her meteoric fall from grace.

"I'll be here first thing tomorrow. And Saul…thanks. For everything. This means the world to me."

He gave her his first genuine smile. "I'm counting on it, Silver Girl. If you don't fill the house every night, I'm gonna lose a fortune. Those British prima donnas would've sold a lot of tickets."

"Gee. No pressure there."

He quirked a pragmatic brow. "Music's a tough business. Art be damned—this is about dollar signs. You sure you want back in the game?"

She took a deep breath and answered, certain for the first time in a long time about something. "Yes. I'm sure. This is exactly what I want to do." The only thing in the world she wanted to do as much as be a mother was sing. Good Lord willing, she'd find a way to do both.

She let herself out of Saul's office, blissfully happy, and ran smack dab into a living wall of muscle. "Whoa, I'm sor—" she started. And then she looked up. *Austin Dearing.* "—Oh. It's you."

"If you want to play games with me, Miss Rothchild, I'm telling you now you're going to lose. Please don't try to ditch me again."

"I didn't try to—"

He cut her off. "I'd highly recommend never fibbing to me. I have an alarming tendency to turn into a serious bastard when I get lied to."

She muttered under her breath, "You're already there." Rather than stand around arguing with this mountain of a man, she turned and stalked back toward the casino. If he wanted to tag along, that was fine with her.

Austin tagged along all right. He was half tempted to jack her up against a wall by the shirt front and explain a thing or two to Miss Fancy Pants. She didn't seem to grasp that it was not part of his job description to chase around after his subjects like a puppy on a leash. She might be a celebrity, but her life now rested in his hands…not the other way around.

She barged out into the explosion of color and sound that was the casino's gambling floor, and his irritation intensified. The place was a security nightmare. Cut-throughs and niches were *everywhere,* and an assailant could be lurking in any of them. There was so much commotion in here that a guy like him couldn't possibly see a threat coming with his vitally important peripheral vision. Surely there was a way around the casino in a hotel this size. She needed to take an alternate route, dammit!

A low-level hum of panic vibrated in his gut. As a security man, this place made him feel like he'd already failed. Clamping down on the anxiety clawing its way up his spine, he lengthened his stride to catch up to Silver as they neared the front of the place. His impulse was to pick her up, throw her over his shoulder, and get her the hell out of here. Now. He exhaled carefully. *Must go easy on this particular client. Break her in gently to the idea of having a bodyguard, without alienating her if at all possible.*

"Hey, slow down," he murmured casually from just behind her. He needed to get in front of her, pronto!

She blatantly ignored him and continued marching on.

"I mean it, Silver. You need to move more slowly so I can clear the area in front of you for threats."

She spared him an irate glance over her shoulder and didn't even break stride.

His gaze narrowed. Several extremely unkind names for her flashed through his head. Fine. He could play that game, too.

He grabbed her by the arm and swung her around sharply to face him. She was a tiny little thing, and her weight was nothing in his hand. He took an aggressive step closer and glared down at her. "I tried to do this the nice way. But now we're gonna do it my way. I'm heading for the nearest exit and getting you under cover, and you're going with me whether you like it or not. Got that?"

She nervously eyed a cluster of people near the front entrance, most of whom wielded big cameras. "Don't make a fuss," she hissed.

"Too late," he retorted. "I'm making as big a fuss as I damn well feel like. And you are not going anywhere else in this hotel until I say so."

"I have to go see Stella. She's the head costume designer," she insisted. "She's expecting me."

"You're not seeing anybody until you and I get a few things straight," he replied grimly.

Her eyes snapped and sparks all but flew off her, singeing his fingertips.

She bit out, "Let's get *this* straight. I'm the boss. I say where I go and when, and you follow along like a good employee and do as you're told. You *don't* make public scenes in front of tabloid reporters—of which there are a dozen behind me, right now," her voice rose slightly in volume, "and you *don't* do anything to embarrass me. Got that?" She actually had the temerity to poke him in his chest for good measure.

He was so aggravated he could strangle her right then and there. He scowled down at her and loomed even more assertively. "I am *not* your employee. I work for your father. You're under my protection, and you'll damn well do what *I* tell *you* to do when I tell you to do it and how I tell you to do it. Have *you* got *that?*"

She blanched. "You and me—this is never going to work."

His jaw clenched. "I'm *entirely* inclined to agree with you."

If hate at first sight was possible, this was it. The woman drove him crazy, and he'd known her for two minutes.

He became aware of a surge of movement behind her. The paparazzi had apparently noticed their altercation and were closing in like a pack of hungry hyenas. He swore under his breath. Men in his line of work despised the press almost as much as the public figures they protected did. The last thing he needed was to have his face splashed all over the front pages of the tabloids.

"Let's get out of here," he muttered at Silver.

"Ya think?" she snapped back.

"Hey, Silver!" one of the reporters shouted. "Did you hear that the Tears of the Quetzal is in police custody?"

Another piped up. "Yeah. Luke Montgomery's fiancée found it in her purse. Do you believe that story?"

Austin frowned. What were these guys talking about? He opened his mouth to ask Silver, but just then, someone moved forward out of the crowd of reporters, jumping abruptly toward her. Austin registered dark hair and a black, burning gaze, a uniform of some kind. Something about the set of the man's shoulders, the intensity of concentration in his eyes set off warning bells in Austin's head. Time slowed as the guy lunged in Silver's direction, and Austin went into high threat mode. If he'd told his men once, he'd told them a thousand times, don't question your instincts. Act first. Ask questions later.

The guy lowered his shoulder and rammed it into Silver, spinning her around as their bodies collided. Hard. Dear God. The guy had an open shot at stabbing or shooting her at point-blank range in a vital organ! Austin went airborne, flinging himself full length through the air for Silver.

He wrapped his arms around her in a move worthy of the NFL. His momentum knocked her off her feet. While they were still airborne, he twisted to cover her with his much larger body. He released her at the last moment before they hit the floor, catching most of his body weight with his arms so he didn't crush her.

An explosion of flashbulbs went off nearby.

Austin twisted to look for the assailant, and the guy was rushing past, his right shoulder hunched to hide his face from Austin.

And then the strangest thing happened.

A wave of heat passed over Austin, a tangible thing tingling across his skin. He saw flashes of purple and green behind his eyelids, brilliant, jeweled prisms of color momentarily blinding him. His blood rushed, pounding in his ears until frantic thumping was all he heard. Suddenly he became intensely aware of the feminine softness below him, molding to every contour of his body as if she'd been made for him. Oh, yeah. A promise of sex, hot and sweaty enough to boggle the mind, pored off her.

Silver looked up at him, her gorgeous eyes wide with surprise, fear and something else. Something…aware. Of him. As a man.

Their gazes locked and nothing short of unbridled lust roared between them. All that friction of a few seconds ago had abruptly morphed into something so steamy it set him on fire. She looked ready to come apart in his hands. In fact, a moan slipped out of her throat that was all about raging pleasure. Unseen by the press, her hips undulated beneath his, and he realized his male flesh was so hard he was in danger of busting his trouser zipper.

He swore under his breath.

Her pupils dilated until her eyes were nearly black with raw need. He wasn't in any better shape, himself. Small problem: he was the bodyguard, and a whole bunch of cameras were very publicly recording every second of this.

"You okay?" he muttered.

She nodded, looking shell-shocked.

"I'll get up first, then I'll help you to your feet and pull you

behind me. Keep my body between you and the photographers, okay?"

She nodded again.

He started a quick push-up when a voice shouted from nearby,
"Get the hell off my girlfriend!"

Austin came smoothly to his feet and turned to face this new
threat. A beefy guy a little shy of six feet tall was barreling
toward them. Austin assessed the threat in an instant. More beer
gut than muscle. Had barroom brawled just enough to think he
was a hotshot, but lacked the balance of a trained fighter. This
guy would use bluster and bullying to hide his actual lack of
physical skill. A lot of noise, but not a lot of true threat.

Austin reached down and lifted Silver, as light as a feather,
to her feet. He tucked her protectively against his side away
from the cameras. The paparazzi had already turned their lenses
on the loudmouth, and predictably, he was preening for them.

"Who the hell are you?" Austin growled.

"I'm Mark Sampson." Bluster Boy jabbed a finger toward
Silver. "Her boyfriend. And take your hands off her, jerk wad."

Jerk wad? He hadn't been called that since junior high. Austin
allowed his amusement to show on his face. Interestingly
enough, Silver huddled more closely against his side, making no
move to distance herself from him in front of this boyfriend of
hers. Most women would be leaping away from another man, especially with a hotheaded idiot like that for a boyfriend.

Sampson bristled. "Get away from her before I make you do it."

A new round of flashes exploded. He could see the headline now.
Brawl Over Pop Singer. He sighed. Seemed as if he was getting off
on the wrong foot with everyone on this assignment. But Bubba
could damned well come and try to make him unwrap his arm from
Silver, who was now trembling beneath his protective hug.

"Please," she whispered frantically from beside him. "Don't
make a scene."

As if they hadn't already made a big scene? But then he
glanced down at her. Abject terror shone in her face. She was

really scared. For him? Surely not. For Bubba? Maybe. But that didn't feel right, either. What then? Did this have to do with her sister's murder and the unspoken reasons he'd been hired to protect her in the first place?

He murmured under his breath, "For you, I won't kick this guy's ass right now. Let's get out of here, though."

"That'd be great," she murmured back gratefully.

He guided her toward the lobby. Or at least he started to guide her. Sampson stepped forward aggressively and blocked their way before they'd gone two steps. "Get your hands off my girl!"

Austin gave the guy a withering stare but spoke calmly enough. "I've been hired to protect Miss Rothchild. I'm not making a move on your lady, so relax already. You're making a scene and you're making Miss Rothchild uncomfortable."

If anything, Sampson got even redder in the face and swelled up into an even bigger bullfrog. "*I'm* her bodyguard! Now, for the last time, get away from her!"

Sampson reached up and grabbed Austin's hand, physically throwing it off Silver's shoulder. Were it not for the paparazzi eating this whole thing up, Austin would've ripped the guy's arm off then and there. But as it was, Silver threw him a panicked look, and he didn't have the heart to make her any more miserable than she already was.

He took a step away from her. But not before murmuring, "I'm going to go talk to the hotel security guys for a few minutes, and then I'll meet you at the costume lady's office. Don't leave the hotel without me, okay?"

She nodded, trust shining in her eyes. He didn't question it, nor did he examine too closely the surge of protectiveness that bubbled up in his chest. He just knew that something big had happened between them, lying together on the floor a few moments ago.

Sampson elbowed him aside, and Austin stepped back readily, without giving the guy the satisfaction of a response. The paparazzi closed in on Silver and Sampson like a pack of sharks in a feeding frenzy. Austin frowned. Sampson ought to be doing something to keep them back. It was a blatant breach of personal security to let that many strangers surround a subject so closely. But the guy seemed more interested in getting his own arm around Silver's shoulders and posing for pictures than in keeping his girlfriend safe. The pair stepped out onto the front steps of the casino and paused again for another round of pictures. Sampson seemed acutely aware of the best lighting and camera angles for the paparazzi and more than happy to give the press exactly what it needed.

Austin shook his head. Surely guarding celebrities wasn't that different from guarding heads of state. No matter how famous and camera-worthy a subject was, no self-respecting bodyguard let would their principal stand still in an exposed position like those steps for this long.

And why wasn't the guy's gaze scanning the area in search of possible threats at a minimum? Bubba was supposed to be her bodyguard! Silver actually looked eager to go…and if he wasn't mistaken, it was Sampson holding her back. No bodyguard would physically stop their subject to pose for the press! It was insane! What kind of training had this guy—

A fast-moving target hurtled out of the shadows off to one side of the lobby toward the front door.

Silver and Sampson had their backs to the attacker!

Austin lurched into motion, sprinting for all he was worth. But his heart sank even as his thighs churned frantically, propelling him forward. *He was too far away to save her.* Time slowed as the horror of an attack on his principal unfolded before him. He couldn't get between her and the attacker in time. Her beautiful eyes, her smile, her soft body beneath his flashed helplessly through his mind's eye.

He opened his mouth to scream at Sampson to throw himself on top of her.

But it was too late.

The deafening report of a gunshot exploded in the lobby.

Chapter 4

Silver froze as the world went mad around her. She registered a flash of motion. A shout of warning from behind. And then an explosion of noise so loud it made her teeth hurt. A giant sheet of glass crashed down a few feet behind her, showering her with shards of exploding glass.

People screamed and were running and ducking and falling everywhere. She didn't know what to do. Everyone around her melted away, leaving her standing all by herself in a sea of glass, marble and glittering chrome. The torrent of crystal prisms fell like rain around her, each with its own rainbow of slivered light trapped within it. *So pretty.* The thought floated through her head, completely detached from reality.

Mark was a dozen feet away, cursing at the top of his lungs. He was turning in circles, as if he was looking for somewhere to run and hide but couldn't decide which way to go.

And then something hit her from behind. It felt like a freight train had just slammed into her at seventy miles per hour. It drove her to the ground, face first, crushing her in darkness and suffocating weight. Panic struck her then. She couldn't breathe! She had to run! To get out of here, away from this insanity. To protect her baby!

"Let me up!" she tried to scream. It came out no more than a breathy gasp devoid of sound.

"Are you hit?" a deep voice asked sharply in her ear.

Austin. A wave of relief washed over her, so powerful and warm it nearly made her faint. "I don't think so."

He shouted from above her, "Sampson! Clear the lobby! Set up suppression around the exterior perimeter so the subject can be evacuated!"

"Huh?" Mark obviously didn't have the slightest idea what Austin had just told him to do.

Violent swearing erupted in her left ear, much of it dealing with Mark's questionably human parentage and complete lack of training. Then Austin was giving her instructions, urgent and low. "We're getting up and running like hell. We're gonna zigzag back and forth so the gunman has less of a shot at you."

Gunman? *Gunman?* Was that what that noise had been? A gunshot? Ohmigod.

"Let's go!" Austin bit out.

All of a sudden his bulk was gone, replaced by light and air and an awful sense of exposure that made her want to curl up in a little ball with her hands over her head and never move again. But then Austin was pulling at her, yanking her to her feet. She managed to stay vertical and keep up with his zigzagging run until they burst out from under the covered overhang into the blistering late afternoon sun. Austin paused, looking around quickly.

"Hey! Let go of her!"

Mark again.

"Give it up, Bubba. You don't know a damn thing about being a bodyguard. Get out of my way before you get your girlfriend killed. Let me do my job." Austin sounded like he'd about had it with Mark.

Austin was dragging her forward again, toward a long, black stretch limo parked on the far side of the sweeping circular drive.

"That's it, pretty boy!" Mark shouted. "You and me, right here, right now—"

"Shut the hell up, Sampson." And with that, Austin yanked open the back door of the limo and surprisingly gently pushed her inside. Her heel caught on the thick carpet and she stumbled, landing on her knees on the carpeted floor as something big blocked the light behind her. The door slammed shut, and yet again, Austin banged into her.

"Oomph," she grunted as she went down on her side.

The glass panel between them and the driver was sliding down. A pale, shocked face stared at them from under a chauffeur's cap.

"Get this car moving if you don't want to get shot!" Austin ordered the driver in a tone of command that brooked no disobedience. The vehicle lurched into motion violently, dumping Austin on the carpet beside her. Tires screeched, and the vehicle made a sharp turn before accelerating powerfully.

She blinked over at Austin, lying no more than a foot away from her. His eyes were green, a deep, shadowy shade like the darkest part of a forest. She said dryly, "We have to stop meeting on floors like this."

He grinned back at her. "I haven't been horizontal this many times with a woman without being in bed with her since…ever."

In bed with him? Whoa. Now there was a thought. A tingle of that same electric attraction that had about jolted her out of skin the first time he'd tackled her shot through her now.

His pupils dilated hard and fast. All of a sudden, his gaze went so black and hot she could hardly bear to look at him. Other details started to register. His arm, heavy and muscular, lay across the indentation of her waist. And his leg was thrown across hers. If she leaned forward just a little bit, she could cuddle up against that big, brawny chest of his. Her face would fit in the strong curve of his neck, and his shoulder would make a perfect pillow for her head. A lock of his hair had fallen across his forehead, and her fingers itched to reach up and push it away.

"Are you okay?" he asked so tenderly it made her heart ache a little.

"Yeah." And then an awful thought hit her. "Are *you* okay?" she blurted, alarmed. Her hands splayed across his chest of their own volition, searching frantically for injuries.

He grinned then, a lopsided thing oozing so much charm it ought to be illegal. "I'm fine. I'd have been glad to take that bullet for you but no, I'm not hit. Thanks for asking, though."

Her hands stopped, somewhere in the middle of all those acres of muscle. "Take a bullet for me?" she repeated blankly.

"Yes. I'm a bodyguard. It's what I do."

"Get shot?"

Another one of those lethal grins. "Well, the idea is to avoid either one of us getting shot in the first place, but if it comes down to you or me, it's my job to take the hit."

She shuddered at the thought of deadly lead slamming into this man and erasing that smile forever. "Don't take a bullet for me, okay?"

He drew her closer against him, and funny thing, she had no desire whatsoever to resist. That volcano of heat and lust that had erupted between them back in the casino exploded again, spewing steam and fire and molten images of sex with him all over the back of the limo. She'd been no saint in her day and had certainly partaken of meaningless sex just for the sake of it now and then. But never, ever, had she been bowled over by an attraction to any guy this instantaneous and this incendiary.

Her entire body felt liquid, flowing over and around him, seeking to engulf every inch of him. His arms tightened around her like tempered steel bands, and his desire rose to meet hers, towering every bit as powerfully as hers. For an instant, fear flooded through her. What had she unleashed between them? It was so big, so overwhelming, she wasn't entirely sure she could handle it. She looked up, and Austin was staring down at her, looking every bit as stunned as she felt. Well, that was something, at least. Somehow, the idea of him being blown away, too, calmed her.

She relaxed once more in his arms, her trust restored. This was not ops normal for him, either. Something gigantic *had* happened between them. She hadn't imagined it.

Wonder filling his dark gaze, he murmured, "I'll do my level best not to have to take a bullet for you. But rest assured, I will do it if necessary. I'll die for you."

The import of those simple words slammed into her like a boulder. She stared at him for a long time, trying to absorb what it truly meant. Finally she managed to mumble, "Nobody's ever said anything like that to me. Ever. Do you really mean it?"

His gaze locked with hers, as he clearly weighed what she'd just said. Was he trying to figure out if she was talking about other bodyguards, or about more? Much more. All of a sudden, she wasn't sure, herself, just how much she'd meant by the question.

He answered so low she almost didn't hear him over the sound of pavement beneath the tires. "Yeah. I *do* mean it."

Now, that definitely sounded as if he was talking about more than keeping her alive. And darned if her pulse didn't race even faster, her heart pounding even harder against her ribs.

He reached up to push a strand of white-blond hair out of her face. He whispered, "You're even more beautiful in person. And I've always secretly thought you were a knockout. Are you really real?"

Her breath caught in her throat. "I'm just a normal girl who's been lucky enough to live an extraordinary life."

He smiled as if he didn't quite believe her. If she didn't know better, she'd swear the guy was a little starstruck. "How 'bout you? Are you real? I thought superheroes only live in comic books."

His grin was a little unbalanced. "I'm just a regular guy who's been lucky enough to get some extraordinary training."

"I think there's more to you than that, Austin Dearing. A whole lot more."

"I could say the same of you, Silver Rothchild."

She gazed deep into his eyes. Shockingly, she didn't see deception. Not an iota of greed or social climbing or self-interest. Was this guy for real? Everyone always wanted something from her—money or fame or a leg up on an entertainment career. Was it possible that he liked her just for her? That all those sparks zinging back and forth between them were real?

A rumble of laughter vibrated deep in his chest. "I have a sinking feeling that you're going to lead me on a merry chase before this is all said and done."

She grinned up at him. "Sounds like fun."

He sighed, but the smile didn't quite leave his eyes. "If I'm going to do my job, we need to get a few things straight between us."

She couldn't resist. She snuggled her hips against his—and gasped at the feel of him, huge and hard between her thighs. "Everything feels straight to me."

He closed his eyes tightly for a moment. When he opened them, she was disappointed to see that he'd shifted into business mode. "I was trying to talk to you about the rules of engagement we're going to operate under when you kept running away from me."

"I wasn't running away from you!"

He quirked an all-too-knowing brow. "What would you call it?"

She replied defiantly, "Creative avoidance."

His crack of laughter inexplicably warmed her heart. She liked making this man happy. Wanted to get to know him better. To explore this thing between them. What was up with that? He was her father's lackey. She ought to hate his guts. But somewhere in the past five minutes, in the midst of their heated argument and diving for cover, something had changed between them. Radically. It was almost as if someone had waved a magic wand and cast a spell over the two of them. Talk about going from zero to sixty in two seconds flat…

Weird.

His arm lifted away from her waist. The movement felt reluctant, like he didn't want to let her go. That was lovely. He sat up and helped her twist around and sit up without coming out of her dress. And that was lovely, too. Considerate. Far too few people in her life showed her simple courtesy not because she was a rock star but because she was a human being.

She scowled at her dress as she gave the dowdy thing one last tug. It figured that she'd meet the man of her dreams the one day she was wearing something this goofy looking—her, the ultimate fashion diva, who never appeared anywhere without looking like the cover of the latest pop culture magazine. But her father had a cow whenever she wore anything even remotely sexy, and she hadn't wanted a fight with him at her birthday party. So she'd chosen this high-necked, long-hemmed, multilayered affair in a demure shade of pink.

"Shall we go for the gusto and actually try using the seats?" he asked wryly.

She felt her dimples pucker up. "If we're gonna hijack a limo, we may as well enjoy it before we go to jail."

He grinned. "Good point." He knocked on the glass partition, which had closed sometime during their exchange on the floor.

The chauffeur looked back at them in his rearview mirror. "We safe now?" the guy asked.

Austin nodded. "Yes, thanks to you. Mr. Rothchild's going to be very grateful that you saved his daughter's life."

The guy snorted. "Mr. Coddington's going to be very *not* grateful that I took off with his limo."

Silver knew Albert Coddington. She jumped in, waving a casual hand. "Albert's a dear. Once he knows what happened, he'll be delighted to have helped."

The driver muttered, "Maybe. But Mrs. Coddington sure won't like having to wait for her ride."

Silver laughed. "I give Mrs. Coddington-Number-Five six more months before she's outta there. No need to worry about her. Albert's determined to be just like Henry VIII, and he has one more wife to go."

Austin's gaze swiveled to hers. "The man's had five wives? What's wrong with him?"

She grinned at him. "He has a weakness for gold diggers and gets suckered, like clockwork, every ten years. But give the guy credit for style. The current Mrs. Coddington is younger than I am. By a lot."

"You're not exactly an old lady."

She shrugged. "It's not like I can lie to you about my age. After all, you met me at my birthday party."

"You'll like being thirty—"

She cut him off. "Don't tell me my thirties will be my best decade yet. I made a pact with myself that I'd murder the next person who said that to me."

He shrugged. "Okay, how 'bout this? My thirties have been great to me so far. Wouldn't trade 'em for the world. I hope yours are the same for you."

"I'll let you know in six weeks," she replied ruefully.

"What happens in six weeks?"

She opened her mouth to tell him about her upcoming gig at the Grand, when the driver spoke from up front. "Sir, when do you want me to head back to town? We're gonna have to turn around now or go straight for about a fifty miles and get gas before we turn around."

Austin frowned. "Let's head back to town. Does the Grand have a private entrance?"

Silver and the driver answered simultaneously, "Yes."

Austin looked over at her. "I forgot. You grew up there, didn't you?"

Indeed, she had. She was plenty familiar with the underground loading dock for the many deliveries it took to keep the Grand running. Rather than have trucks constantly clog the busy streets around the hotel, they unloaded underneath it, out of sight and out of the way. Which also made for an ideal entry for celebrities in search of privacy—or safety.

"We'll have to call ahead to use it. Security's very tight down there," she said. "Particularly in the late afternoon. The casino gets its shipments of cash in at about this time of day."

Austin pulled out his cell phone. "What's your dad's personal phone number?"

She rattled off the number and Austin dialed it quickly. She listened unabashedly.

"Hi, sir. This is Austin Dearing. I wanted to report that your daughter is unhurt and with me…that's correct…what are the police saying about the shooting? Any trace of the gunman?" Austin listened a long time, then commented dryly, "With all due respect, sir, that Bubba who calls himself her bodyguard doesn't know his nose from his ass. You made an exceedingly wise decision to hire me."

Silver's jaw dropped. Mark would go ballistic if he heard Austin say something like that! Everybody knew to tiptoe around his hair-trigger temper. She thought she heard tinny laughter emanating from Austin's phone.

"We'll be arriving at the underground entrance of your hotel in…driver, how long till we're back at the Grand?"

"Twenty minutes, sir."

"…in twenty minutes. Right. Thanks. No sweat." Austin pocketed his phone.

She liked to think of it as healthy inquisitiveness, but nosiness was one of her greatest weaknesses. She liked to know everything that was going on around her. When Austin made no comment, her curiosity quickly got the best of her. "So, what did my father say?"

"He'll have someone waiting at the gate for us."

She huffed. "No. About the shooting? Did the police catch the guy?"

"No."

"Who was he shooting at? Was anyone hurt? C'mon, Austin. Gimme the scoop."

Amusement glinted in his green gaze. "I don't need the police to tell me the gunman was shooting at you. I saw the guy make his move. And, no, no one was seriously hurt. Some guests and staff have cuts and bruises from twisted ankles and falling glass."

She was still stuck on his first sentence. "The gunman was shooting at *me?* Are you sure?"

That earned her an annoyed look. "Yes, I'm sure. It's what I do, remember?"

"How do you know?"

He sighed. "I saw the gunman dart out of hiding and pull out his weapon. He timed his move for when Bubba had stepped away from you to give the cameras his best profile. He really is a jerk, you know."

"The shooter or Mark?"

Austin grinned. "Both of them."

She rolled her eyes. The guy was trying very hard not to be informative with her. She prompted him again. "Then what did the gunman do?"

Austin crossed his arms. "He took aim at you with a large-caliber handgun and fired. One thing we know about him—he's a crappy shot. He should have nailed you cold. Any eighteen-year-old raw recruit could make that kill."

"Well, thank God for small favors," she replied dryly.

He glanced over at her. "Seriously. It tells us a lot about the guy. If he were a professional hit man you'd be dead. This guy's an amateur with something personal against you. Can you think of anyone who might want to kill you? Maybe get revenge for some past wrong?"

She frowned hard, not liking the turn this conversation was taking one little bit.

"Any old boyfriends you had ugly breakups with? Anyone you crossed swords with during your career? Anyone who might feel slighted by your success?"

She gifted him with an annoyed look of her own. "Yes to all of the above. Times about a hundred. In case you didn't know it, my former singing career was…slightly tumultuous."

He laughed. "The way I hear it, that's an extreme understatement."

Sometimes it got really old having a public past like hers to live down. With a long-suffering sigh, she replied, "There you have it. The list of people who want to see me dead is long and distinguished. Take your pick of who the gunman could be."

For a moment sympathy shone in his eyes. But then his gaze went flinty hard. "Never fear, honey. I'll figure out who he is and take the bastard out. Nobody shoots at someone I'm responsible for and lives to tell about it."

She sank deeper into the plush seat, taken aback at his abrupt shift of mood. Maybe Mark was the one who ought to be worrying about ticking this man off, and not the other way around.

"What's the Tears of the Quetzal?" he asked abruptly.

"It's a diamond. It's set into a ring, and my father calls it his most prized possession." As Austin quirked a skeptical eyebrow, she added, "It's a super-rare stone that changes color. It's called a chameleon diamond. When you heat it up it changes from violet to green."

"Cool." A pause. "Why do the police have it?"

She sighed. "Candace borrowed or stole it—depending on who you talk to—the night she was murdered. The ring was gone when her body was found."

Austin's face lit up. "So if the cops have the ring, maybe that means they've got a lead on her killer."

Silver replied fervently, "I hope so. That would be great news."

"Yeah, but if the police are closing in on her killer, the guy's probably hiding or on the run."

His question sobered her sharply. "I dunno."

"No idea at all?" he asked.

"Nope. None."

Austin went silent, tugging absently at his left ear and staring out the window broodingly. She didn't interrupt his thoughts, whatever they might be. She'd like to think a little of his steely resolve to keep her safe had to do with their two intimate exchanges, but that was probably wishful thinking. Now that she was sitting up in her own seat, not in physical contact with him, the crazy attraction of before seemed a little hard to believe. She'd been scared and high on adrenaline and had overreacted. Yeah, that was it. Her temporarily heightened senses explained it.

But they didn't explain the thick sludge of disappointment that abruptly chugged through her veins. It had been an amazing feeling while it lasted.

A few minutes later the driver swung smoothly past the Grand's acres of swimming pool and tennis courts and into the black maw of a gated entrance that looked like it led to a parking garage.

Before their rear fender had barely cleared the entrance, a reinforced steel gate was already sliding closed behind them. Darkness closed in. The limo spiraled down a long ramp, and then light flared ahead. She spied a familiar silhouette and started. Her father was down here personally to meet them? Either she was in big trouble for her display to the press, or Austin was about to get fired.

Reluctantly she reached for her door handle. Time to face the music.

A big, warm palm clamped down lightly over her hand. "Lesson number one in being a good protectee. Never get out of the car first. I will always get out before you and have a look around. Please don't come out until I tell you it's safe. Ever. Got it?"

She looked up at him, startled. Mark had never made her go through any routine like that. "So you're pretty much always going to be a gentleman and get my door for me? I think I can get used to that."

That killer grin of his flashed briefly, then was replaced by an expression more akin to sympathy. He seemed to understand that she was joking about this security procedure to hide her dismay at the seriousness of the situation.

His finger brushed her temple, pushing back that pesky strand of hair again, and then the quick, light touch was gone. But the earthquake it left behind continued to shudder through her for several long seconds. Whoa. No adrenaline heightened senses could explain away that.

Eventually her breathing restarted as she stared at the back of his head. Who was this guy whose casual touch made her all but orgasmic?

"Here we go," he muttered.

As advertised, Austin stepped out of the vehicle and paused directly in front of the door. Heck, she couldn't have gotten out even if she'd wanted to. It did, however, give her an excellent and isolated view of his buns. Tight. Muscular. Made for driving into a woman strongly enough to know she was with a man—

Good grief! She had to get control of herself! Heat climbed her cheeks just as he murmured, "Okay, you can come out."

Her heart all but palpitating, she took the hand he offered and climbed out of the limo. Sheesh. She was a mess.

Her father exclaimed, "How'd you get her to do what she's told like that? I've been trying for twenty years and never got her to behave."

Without stopping to think, she snapped, "He said please."

She wasn't in the habit of sassing her father—she never won and it wasn't worth the hassles to follow. But it had been a rough day. She braced herself, waiting for his explosion. But today Harold made no comment at all. Which was testament to just how upset he must be over the shooting.

She was stunned when he merely turned to Austin and said quietly, "I suppose it goes without saying that I'm grateful to you for pulling my little girl out of there."

Her jaw dropped. Her father never said things like that! She frequently wasn't at all sure he actually felt softer emotions like love or concern for his family.

Harold passed a small white object to Austin. "Your room key."

Austin nodded his thanks. "You understand that nobody is to

know that she's with me. Nobody. The staff can just think that I eat like a horse and like to make my own bed for a few days."

Harold nodded. "It's taken care of."

"And maybe you could thank Mr. Coddington for letting us commandeer his limo like that."

Harold grinned. "I know just the thing. I'll give the guy a fat stack of thousand dollar chips, which he'll promptly lose back to me at the tables."

Silver snorted. That was vintage Harold. Give someone a generous gift that he knew was going to come right back to him. But then he did surprise her by pulling out his wallet, extracting a thick wad of hundred dollar bills and handing them to the limo driver. "Here's a small token of my appreciation for helping save my daughter's life."

Silver stared as the driver stammered his thanks. Well, knock her over with a feather!

Austin said, "Oh, and one more thing, Mr. Rothchild," Austin said. "Fire that Sampson guy. He's worthless as a bodyguard."

Harold grimaced. "Believe me, I'd get rid of him if I could. But I don't employ the guy. You'll have to take that up with Silver. He works for her."

Austin's eyebrows shot up, but he made no comment to her. She got the distinct feeling they were going to converse more on the subject very soon, however.

While Austin steered her toward the elevator, she chewed on her father's vehement comment about Mark. She'd had no idea Harold disliked him that much. Why hadn't her father said something to her about it before now? Although, to be brutally honest with herself, if she'd known it would tick off her father, she might have made the relationship with Mark real just to get her father's goat.

Maybe Harold wasn't as dense as she thought he was. Maybe he'd finally learned not to push on the subject of her boyfriends and let her discover their schmuck-like qualities for herself. And they always turned out to be schmucks in the end. The sad fact was she had terrible taste in men. It was why she'd taken the drastic measures she had to have a baby.

As the elevator door slid shut, Austin called, "Thank you for your help, Mr. Rothchild." Examining both sides of his plastic key, he asked, "Where's my room?"

"Lemme see." She took the card and turned it over. Wow. The New Yorker villa. It was one of the Grand's four incredibly swanky penthouses that shared the roof of the forty story tall hotel. "You've got one of the penthouses. You put your key card in this slot to activate the elevator to the top floor." She demonstrated, and then passed the key back to him. With a quiet, powerful whoosh, the elevator shot upward.

The metal encased space took on a heavy silence she had no interest in disturbing. At some point, Austin was going to start asking her questions—lots of them—and not a one of them was going to be easy to address.

The door opened on a quiet, oak paneled hallway lit by lamps on console tables. Fresh flower arrangements and thickly padded carpeting added to the overall ambience of European style.

"Let me guess. You want to get out of the elevator first, too," she mused.

"Fast learner," he murmured as he stepped out and took a hard look around.

"Your suite's the one to the left."

He nodded and gestured for her to follow. He all but ran down the hall, and for a man as tall as him, that was really moving. She had to break into a jog to keep up. Note to self: wear flats around this guy. She would only come up to his armpit that way, but at least she wouldn't be forced to run in heels.

Austin hustled her into the suite and closed the door quickly behind them. His mental sigh of relief was nearly audible. She knew the feeling. The last hour had been a heck of a ride. Literally. Man, she was getting old. There was a time when this amount of excitement wouldn't have fazed her. But now, the danger and racing around in fear for her life were simply exhausting.

A single thought exploded across her mind. *I'm pregnant.*

She really shouldn't be doing crazy stuff like getting shot at anymore. Her wild days were, indeed, officially over. Now, they just had to convince an unnamed gunman of that fact.

"You hungry?" Austin called from the far side of the living room. He'd been looking carefully out of each of the floor to ceiling windows—probably checking for snipers or something.

Actually, she was vaguely nauseous. "Not really. You?"

"Starving. Adrenaline always makes me hungry."

"Typical man."

"Honey, I'm a lot of things, but typical isn't one of them."

She grinned over at him. "I gather modesty isn't on your list of major attributes, either."

He shrugged. "I call it as I see it, darlin'."

"Want me to order up a steak for you from Room Service? The prime rib here is to die for if you're a carnivore." She started to reach for the phone, and Austin moved to her side so fast he was practically a blur.

He snatched the phone out of her hand. "*Nobody's* to know you're here. As of now, you're officially in hiding."

A moment's relief at the idea of being safe gave way to dawning horror. "Small problem, big guy. I don't have *time* to hide. I have only six weeks to pull together the show of my life."

He scowled down at her. "Sorry. Not happening. What part of 'someone just tried to kill you' didn't you get?"

Chapter 5

Silver stared up defiantly at him. Taking temporary precautions in case her sister's killer tried to harm her was one thing but screwing up the rest of her life by ruining her comeback was another thing entirely.

He had to be wrong about someone from her past coming after her. Sure, she'd stepped on a lot of toes in her early days. But that had been a long time ago. Anyone who'd had it in for her had had more than enough time to get even with her before now. And as for Candace's killer? Her stepsister had made plenty of her own enemies through hard and selfish living. Besides, the past several years her path and Candace's had barely crossed. Silver had a very hard time believing that she and Candace shared any enemy in common. Yeah, there'd been a shooting downstairs, but incidents like that weren't unheard of in this town. Gambling did funny things to people.

Austin pulled at his ear again, looking impatient. But he said evenly enough, "What exactly do you think happened in the lobby?"

"We were in the wrong place at the wrong time. Nothing more. Somebody snapped under heavy gambling losses or got ditched by one of our showgirls."

"Silver, I'm not just your run-of-the-mill bodyguard. I guard heads of state. I train the people who guard heads of state. I'm one of the top personal security experts in the entire world. And I'm telling you that shooter was aiming for you."

She sat down heavily on the nearest sofa as she reluctantly acknowledged the possibility that he might be right. "But… why?"

"That's what you and I are going to figure out."

"How?" she pressed.

"You're going to tell me everything about your life, and I'm going to develop a list of people who might want to see you dead."

Everything? She had no intention of telling this man everything about herself! She said lightly, "If you want to know *everything,* it's going to take a while."

He looked around the suite. "We've got nothing but time, kiddo. You and I aren't going anywhere anytime soon."

"About that. I've got things I have to do. Urgent, time sensitive things that can't wait."

"Like what?"

"Well, I never made it to Stella's office today."

"The costume lady?"

"Don't let her hear you call her that. Her client list is a who's who of the entertainment industry."

He looked unimpressed. "I suppose I can arrange a meeting for you with her in the next few days. I'll scout out a secure route to get you down to see her. What other meetings were you hoping to have?"

"I told Saul I'd take a look at the stage tomorrow morning. Then, I'll have to meet with executives from my old record label, the set designer, choreographers, the Grand's band leader. I need to audition and hire backup singers and dancers, start rehearsals, do costume fittings, press conferences, publicity appearances—"

"Whoa, whoa, whoa. What are you talking about?"

"My father gave me a one-week headliner gig here at the Grand for my birthday. The show's in six weeks. It's going to take scrambling every waking minute between now and then to get it ready."

"I'm sorry. I can't approve it."

She stared. Closed her hanging jaw. And then laughed in patent disbelief. "I'm not asking for your permission, Austin."

His dark gaze drilled into her. "That's good, because you don't have it."

"I don't need it. I turned thirty years old today, remember? I'm an adult. I can do what I want."

"I am responsible for your safety. And that gives me the final say over what you do and don't do."

Outrage at his high-handedness surged through her. "Do you tell the president of the United States what to do like this?"

"I'm not in the Secret Service. But if I were assigned to his security detail, I most certainly could—and would—tell him what to do regarding his security. I tell foreign princes and prime ministers what to do all the time."

Panic threatened to choke her. He had to stay out of her way! This show was incredibly important. Everything rode on it! If she got her career going again, she'd never have to worry about financial security for herself or her child, let alone the fact that singing was in her blood. She couldn't imagine her life without it.

"Why don't you go back to work for some foreign dignitary and quit bugging me?" she snapped.

A pained shadow crossed his features. "Sorry. You're stuck with me."

"I'll call my father and have him fire you."

"By all means, make the call. I have no interest in working with someone who's got a death wish. With this attitude, you won't last a week—even with me here to guard you. You're dead already."

The stark words stopped her cold. Dead? Her? But…she was going to have a baby! She finally had something truly important to live for! Her fury drained away as suddenly as it had exploded. She wandered over to the plate glass windows and, hugging herself, gazed out at the glittering skyline. Night was falling. How could a place as hot as Las Vegas look so cold? And why did this have to be so bloody hard?

She took a deep breath and let it out slowly. Without turning around, she said, "I'm sorry I snapped at you. I'm under a lot of pressure, but I have no right to take it out on you." She would have in the old days. Heck, maybe she was finally growing up a little, after all. She continued doggedly, "There has to be a way for me to get my work done and still let you do your job. What do I have to do to make that happen?"

He spoke from so close behind her she about leaped out of her skin. "Have dinner with me, and let's talk it over."

She ventured a glance back at him. His jaw rippled as he stared out over her shoulder into the night, his gaze roving constantly, always seeking, always testing for threats. Lord, he was attractive. There was something incredibly sexy about having a man like him—a warrior in his prime—totally focused on her and her well-being.

Behind them, a quiet knock sounded on the hallway door.

"Into the bedroom," he ordered her under his breath.

As Austin closed the door on her, she murmured, "Have the waiter lay out supper by the pool. It's beautiful out there, and there's a privacy wall so you can skinny-dip."

Her last sight of him before the door shut was his eyebrows quirking. It dawned on her what she'd said, and her face exploded with heat.

"You can come out now."

That was Austin's rich baritone. If he put his diaphragm behind that voice, she'd bet he wasn't a half-bad singer. The door opened, and his tall silhouette completely filled the door frame. She breathed a sigh of relief. Since when had she turned into such a thunder chicken? Oh, yeah. When she heard she was going to have a baby and someone tried to kill her.

She followed him outside onto the elegant, Zen-inspired pool deck. The simple granite block walls, oiled teak decking and spare bamboo plantings soothed her. The pool sparkled like a turquoise jewel beneath the descending blanket of night. It was still close to ninety degrees, but the temperature was dropping fast. In another hour, she'd need a sweater.

Austin frowned down at the linen-covered table. "There's only one place setting."

She shrugged. "I'll take the salad fork and the dessert spoon, and you can have the rest."

He grinned. "All I really need is a sharp knife. If you know your way around a blade, you can skin and carve just about anything."

She shuddered in mock horror. "That sounds so…carnivorous."

"You wimp."

She nodded firmly. "Yup, that's me. I like a steak well enough, but I don't need any reminder of where it came from."

He shrugged. "I can't tell you how many times I've had to hunt and kill my supper. You get used to it if the alternative is starving."

She examined him closely. "You don't look like a cold-blooded killer."

Without comment, Austin fetched a second dining chair from inside and held it for her. Smiling up at him, she sank down into it. For an instant, his eyes glowed back with a heat that was anything but restrained and gentlemanly. She blinked, and the look was gone. Had she imagined that?

Still standing over her, he asked quietly, "So tell me, Silver. What exactly does a cold-blooded killer look like?"

"I dunno. Just…not you."

"In my experience, the sheep and the wolves all look pretty much the same. The key is to trust no one. Then nobody can sucker you."

"That's a pretty cynical view of the world," she murmured.

"Call me cautious. Comes with the job."

Wow. That was a pessimistic take on life. It was completely

unlike her own positive and generally trusting opinion of her fellow man. "How do you manage to make friends or have faith in anyone with an attitude like that?"

"I trust the guys in my unit."

"No one else?" she probed.

"My boss. The support team for my unit."

"And?"

He frowned down at her. "Who else do I need?"

"What about women? Do you have any girlfriends or just simple female friends?"

"There aren't many women in my field."

"Don't you have *any* friends or social acquaintances outside of your work? Family that you're close to?"

He frowned. "No. And no, I don't feel I'm lacking anything in my life because of it."

As exasperating as her own big, messy, extended family could be, she couldn't imagine life without them. And although admittedly fewer these days, she couldn't imagine life without her friends' laughter and gossip…acceptance and understanding. "You're missing out on what makes life most worth living."

He crossed his arms defensively. "You have your measure of worth in life, and I have mine. I believe in honor, duty and country. I serve those three things above all else. And before you accuse me of being brainwashed, let me add that I do it freely and derive deep satisfaction from it."

"You're an odd duck, Austin Dearing." She'd never met a man who actually put something like honor above his own well-being. Oh, she'd met plenty of guys who talked the talk, but this guy walked the walk. She didn't know whether to eye him with new caution or new respect. Either way, he was an anomaly in her experience with men.

As he slid into his seat, his knee rubbed intimately against hers. Her breath hitched as his leg jerked away. *Drat.* She'd rather liked the contact, and it was disappointing that he didn't seem to share her attraction.

"Sorry," he mumbled.

"Don't apologize," she replied quickly. In a desperate bid not to sound quite so desperate, she added lamely, "It's nice of you to share your supper with me."

He shot her a sidelong grin that all but melted her insides. "In my experience, hungry women are grumpy women. When in doubt, feed 'em, I say."

She laughed and reached for a fork. And immediately encountered a problem. Neither the steak nor the lobster was cut into bite-sized pieces, and he'd already picked up the only knife.

Austin grinned down at her. "Need me to cut up your meat, oh squeamish female consumer of meat products?"

"It's either that or I'm picking up the whole steak and gnawing at it with my teeth. This squeamish girl is *hungry*." It had hit her all of a sudden, but she'd gone from nauseous to ravenous sometime in the last sixty seconds or so.

He cut off a bite-sized chunk of the juicy, pink beef and held it toward her with his fork. She realized he was waiting for her to open her mouth. He fed her the succulent prime rib, and flaming heat reddened her cheeks. Next, he held out a piece of lobster. She had no choice but to open her mouth quickly or else drip butter all over her dress. There was something so personal about him feeding her supper like this. So…intimate.

A little freaked out by how fast they were becoming so *involved* with each other, she slid her chair around to the far side of the table to face him. A pair of candles flickered between them, casting a dance of light and shadow across his rugged features. It struck her yet again what a handsome man he was. Exasperating in the extreme at times, but definitely easy on the eye.

He glanced up at her. As if he'd captured her very thought, he murmured, "The candlelight is good to you."

Son of a gun if her face didn't get even hotter. She mumbled, "Candles hide a multitude of flaws. They're good to all women."

"Trust me, you didn't need the help to begin with. Maybe you should do your show by candlelight. You wouldn't have to worry about what the stage looks like that way."

She laughed. "That's a great idea."

"Why not do something simple? Maybe just you and a spotlight."

"I'm known for big productions. Elaborate stage sets, a bunch of dancers, fireworks."

He shrugged. "I mostly listen to my favorite singers over the radio. I never see 'em. Seems to me a concert should be about great music and not all that other stuff."

She gave him a thoughtful look. It actually was an interesting concept. A one-woman show. Just her and the music. No bells and whistles. One thing she knew for sure—it would be a complete departure from her past image.

"Want some of this cake?" Austin asked. "It looks like German chocolate."

Usually, she loved the Grand's version of the smooth milk chocolate cake, smothered in a rich butter frosting crammed with fresh-grated coconut. But tonight, the idea of all that gooey, über-sweet richness made her stomach churn. Great. Did she have to start feeling pregnant already? She reminded herself quickly to embrace the burbling nausea. It was all part and parcel of the miracle growing inside her.

"What were you just thinking about?" Austin asked.

She glanced up, startled. "Why do you ask?"

"Your face…glowed…all of a sudden."

Yikes. She was going to have to be careful around other people if she was going to keep her secret. "Uh, nothing. I'm just relieved you're willing to work with me. This show means the world to me."

"Why?"

"Are you by any chance familiar with any of my past?"

"I've seen what was in the newspapers," he answered noncommittally.

"You mean the tabloids?"

"Well, yeah. For a few years there, you were hard to miss in the grocery checkout line."

She sighed. "I wasn't nearly as wild as the tabloids said, but the things they published weren't entirely lies, either. I did a real number on my career and my life when I was too young and stupid to know what I had. I've been laying low for the past seven years, trying to regain a little privacy."

"It didn't look like that was going too well today in the casino. The paparazzi were all over you."

"They heard us arguing and smelled a story. And then when Mark showed up, they saw a love triangle and went into a feeding frenzy."

"Speaking of Bubba, what possessed you to hire him as your bodyguard? He's an idiot."

She chewed on her lower lip. Privately, she had to agree with him. But Mark was supposed to be her boyfriend, and she couldn't very well admit he was an idiot. She settled for mumbling, "He had a résumé."

"He lied."

"Why do you say that?"

"He didn't have the faintest clue what to do today when bullets started flying. Then, he committed the mortal bodyguarding sin. He left your side. Failed to use his body to protect you. He should've stuck to you like glue. Instead he ran around screaming like a woman."

"Okay, so he probably doesn't have any formal training. Truth be told, my sister, Candace, recommended him to me."

"And she was some sort of security expert, I gather? That's why she's dead, right?"

Silver flinched at that.

He swore under his breath. "I'm sorry. That was out of line." He reached over and laid his hand on top of hers. "I've been out in the field with a bunch of soldiers for way too long. I don't stop and think about what I say like I should. I'm sorry your sister died. I shouldn't have spoken ill of her."

Silver shrugged. "Why not? She was mostly a bitch and a bully. Being dead doesn't change that."

Austin blinked, clearly taken aback. Then he said noncommittally, "I've always wondered about people's tendency not to be honest about the dead, no matter how flawed they were in life."

She sighed. "Apparently, it's time to air some of that past history you're dying to hear all about. Candace and Natalie are my twin stepsisters. Well, they were until Candace died."

"How are you related to them?"

"Their mother was Harold's first wife. She died from complications during their younger sister Jenna's birth. My mother was his second wife. Mom and Harold got married when I was about ten years old."

Austin nodded. "And how did they feel about you coming into their lives?"

"They were jealous of the attention Harold paid to me. I wasn't his blood daughter and they were. It only got worse as we got older. Sometimes I wonder if he played us off against each other. It would be his style."

"Why do you say that?"

"He believes in jungle rules. Survival of the fittest. He wouldn't hesitate to pit his daughters against each other to see who came out standing and who buckled under the pressure."

"Who blinked first among you three?"

She sighed. "I did."

"But you're the rich and famous celebrity of the three of you."

"I was well down the road to self-destruction when I bailed out on the fast life. Natalie bailed out next. But Candace never slowed down. She was wild till the end. She'd use anyone or anything to get her way. You should have seen how she used her kids…"

Faced with the prospect of becoming a mother herself, she didn't understand how Candace could've treated her sons the way she had, ignoring them when they were inconvenient and using them like pawns to squeeze money from her father.

"Tell me more about how it was between you and your sisters."

"When Harold put a lot of money and backing behind my career, they resented that. In retrospect, I see how Candace in particular set out to sabotage me. She led me into the heavy Hollywood party scene, introduced me to booze and drugs and hooked me up with a whole lot of people who were lousy for both me and my career."

Austin's expression was unreadable. But at least it didn't contain outright condemnation.

"In my sister's defense, I was gullible. I didn't have to go along with any of it. At the end of the day, what happened to my career—to my life—was my fault."

He made a sound of acknowledgment. Leave it to a military man like him not to make any attempt to let her off the hook. She appreciated his forthright worldview, even if it did sting her in the crossfire.

She continued grimly, "If you're looking for people I pissed off with my success in all fairness, you'd have to put those two at the top of the list."

"Except now Candace is dead."

"Yeah, and Natalie's totally past her resentment of me. In fact, we've grown a lot closer since Candace's death." She smiled proudly. "She's a cop now, you know."

That made Austin start. "How does Harold feel about that?"

"About like you'd think. That it's too blue-collar for his daughter and it's beneath a Rothchild. But she seems to really like it, and she's good at it." Silver stirred her ice water with her finger, chasing a stray cube around the glass. "Matt—he's her fiancé—was a godsend. He really helped center her. But truth be told, since Candace died, she's changed. It's as if losing Candace was a wake-up call for her to truly appreciate her life and her family."

"Are you positive Natalie's not behind the attacks on you? As a cop, she certainly has access to resources and people who could come after you."

Her gaze jerked up in surprise. "Not a chance. Not Nat. We're sisters, blood kinship or not. And besides, she's too direct for all these sneak attacks. They're not her style." She added ruefully, "If Natalie wanted to kill someone, she'd do it herself."

Austin nodded. "I have to agree. Tampered brakes…shooting ambush…those don't feel like sibling rivalry gone bad."

"Mark thinks it's a stalker fan."

"Wow. An intelligent thought from the Neanderthal. Who'd have guessed he had one in him?"

She sighed. "At least he's good at keeping the photographers away."

Austin snorted. "Like today? Hell, he was posing for them more than you were. He did his damnedest to draw them to you."

She blinked, surprised. "He did not—"

"Think about it. Who shouted and turned the whole thing into a big scene? Who made threats and slapped my hand off your shoulder?"

She studied him in the dim light. "You could just be saying that to cover your butt for your part in the incident."

He took a slow, appreciative sip from his glass of wine. She noted with interest that, although he'd been sipping at the wine steadily through the meal, the level of the liquid in his glass had only gone down by about an inch. "Are you always this suspicious?" he asked.

"You get a little jaded when you've lived a life like mine."

He studied her for a long moment. "Fair enough. And for the record, I have no reason to push blame onto Bubba. I'm man enough to fess up if I screw up."

She believed him on that one. He'd been much more restrained than she'd expected him to be in the face of Mark's truculence. Speaking of Mark. It was strange that he hadn't been trying like crazy to call her. He was fond of micromanaging every last detail of her life if she let him.

She pulled out her cell phone to see if it was turned on. Yup, and the battery indicator said it was fully charged. That was really strange. Not that she minded the break from him, though. She hadn't realized what a relief it would be to be away from his overbearing presence until he was gone.

No way could she ever actually get involved with him the way he was pushing her to do. The guy drove her around the bend. He actually had the temerity to tell her that a 'little woman' like her couldn't raise a baby on her own. The rugrat needed a daddy. Like him. As if he was actually a viable candidate for parenthood. The very thought made her cringe.

When she'd asked him to help her out with her baby plan, she hadn't known him like she did now. Candace had said he was "cool" and "knew the score." And fool that she was, she'd believed her stepsister. Candace said he was the kind of guy who would scratch your back if you scratched his. Except he'd decided that he wanted to scratch her back literally, and he'd been furious when Silver refused to enter into a real relationship with him.

She'd been crystal clear in her requirements, and he'd agreed to them up front. It was only later that he'd tried to change the rules of the game on her. She could smell a gold digger at a hundred paces, and he was double-dog, big time after a piece of her fame and fortune.

She sipped at a club soda in silence while Austin took his time finishing the cake.

With a satisfied sound, he laid down his fork. "For what it's worth, I did my best to avoid provoking Bubba this afternoon. Not that I didn't want to deck him. He really is a deserving jerk. But you were already upset, and I didn't want to make it any worse for you."

Austin had been worried about her feelings? That was a first for the men in her life. Most of the people who surrounded her were takers, always asking what she could do for them, not the other way around. Unfamiliar warmth suffused her at his consideration.

Her gaze faltered as he looked back at her steadily. Good

Lord. He'd see right through her to the ridiculous crush she was fast developing on him. Abashed, she mumbled awkwardly, "Call him Bubba to his face and he'll deck you."

Austin let out a snort that spoke volumes. "He can try to lay a hand on me, but he'll fail. Besides, Bubba's a far sight better than the other names I've come up with for him. Wanna hear a few?"

"No," she laughed. Frankly, Bubba fit him just fine. She dared not voice the opinion aloud, though. After all, Bub—Mark—was supposed to be her boyfriend.

"What can I say to convince you to fire him?" Austin asked seriously.

"Nothing. I'm not going to fire him."

"Why the hell not?" Austin sounded ready to get all worked up again.

She laid her napkin beside her plate and stood up. Stars dusted the sky overhead, and the silence was deep and dark around her. She wandered over to the edge of the pool. On impulse, she kicked off her shoes and sat down on the rough granite coping, dangling her feet in the inviting water.

"Wanna go for a swim?" Austin asked.

"I don't have a bathing suit."

A chuckle. "Don't let that stop you. You were right. This is a perfect spot for skinny-dipping."

The old Silver—or rather the young Silver—would've taken him up on that dare in a second. She missed that girl. She'd lived life with gusto and hadn't second-guessed her decisions, hadn't lived in fear of paparazzi or headlines. She'd done what made her feel good. Over the years, she'd learned to have a care for hurting other people with her impulses, and that was probably a good thing. But somewhere along the way, all the fun had been ground right out of her. Darn it, she wanted some of it back before her fortieth birthday snuck up on her in shades of gray and boring.

She stared at Austin in one last second of indecision. And then she grinned at him…and slid into the water.

Its pleasantly cool embrace felt amazing against her skin. The spontaneity of it felt even better. She hadn't done anything remotely like this in years. Her skirt floated around her like a pink lily pad. She submerged, dragging it down with her until it was a sodden mess around her legs.

She'd done it. She'd taken back a tiny piece of herself. And she had Austin Dearing to thank for it. He challenged her like no man she'd met in a very long time. Challenged her to do more. To *be* more.

She saw a dark shape looming by the edge of the pool and surfaced for air, laughing, pushing her seaweed-hair out of her face. "Come on in. The water's great."

He scowled. "Unlike some people, I don't jump into swimming pools fully clothed."

She grinned up at him. "Then take off your clothes and go for that skinny-dip."

He stared down at her for several endless, heart-stopping seconds. Then he stunned her by saying evenly, "All right."

She gaped up at him. He was going to strip and jump in with her? Ho. Lee. Cow.

All of a sudden she felt in way over her head, and she wasn't talking about the swimming pool.

Chapter 6

This is madness. But in spite of his misgivings, Austin's fingers moved to the hem of his shirt. He stripped the soft cotton off over his head.

It's totally unprofessional. The bare night air felt cool on his skin. Liberating. He was completely out of line to get in the pool with her. He reached for his belt buckle.

But who would see? It was just the two of them up here on top of one of the tallest buildings in the city. There wasn't a sight line anywhere for a sniper to get an angle on her. She was safe. They both were. He started to push his pants down his muscular thighs.

She gasped.

One corner of his mouth curled in amusement. She didn't know yet that he had on Lycra biking shorts beneath his pants. Interesting that she didn't ask him to stop, though. A bit of the old wild child peeking through her newly pious and mature exterior, perhaps? He liked the hint of daring in her. She wore it well.

He particularly liked throwing her off balance. She was less…guarded…when she wasn't on familiar ground. It was good for her. She was entirely too predictable and bland in this persona her family—specifically her father—had forced on her. While the rebellious, twenty-two-year-old diva no doubt would've driven him crazy, he would almost prefer that version of Silver to the strangled version of her that remained.

Fame sure had done a number on her. It seemed to have driven all the spontaneity out of her. She took no risks lest a cameraman jump out of the nearest potted palm and capture her humiliation for all the world to see. A need to challenge her, to shake her up, coursed through him. Being with her was like being around a puppy that didn't know how to play. It was sad and somehow not natural. A desire to teach her how to chase her tail again overcame him. And hell, he wouldn't mind chasing her tail, either.

Jumping into a swimming pool with their clothes on was a good start on waking her playful side. Except his cell phone, earpieces, gun and various other gadgets were all in his pockets. It was easier to just strip off his clothes, the contents of his pockets intact.

He knifed cleanly into the water. He hadn't been swimming in several years—it wasn't a favored pastime in the remote parts of Afghanistan. Not to mention water was too scarce over there for anyone to even contemplate swimming in giant vats of it. He stroked toward the far end of the pool, relishing the slide of water over his skin, the muffling silence and weight of it. Damn, he'd forgotten how much he loved to swim.

The water was cool but did little to dissipate the heat that woman stirred up in him. She'd be irritating if she weren't so damned interesting. And sexy. And funny. And…cute. She sure was a little thing, all sparkly and bright, like a shiny new coin. Her name fit her.

He surfaced beside her. "You gonna just hang onto the edge or are you coming swimming with me?"

She laughed and took off for the far end of the pool. He caught up and passed her easily. Not only was he trained to swim for hours on end in rough oceans but that dress of hers added serious drag to her hydrodynamics. She ought to take it off—

Slow down, there. No trying to get the client to strip. Although she'd look hot in just her bra and panties. *Stop that!*

She reached the far end and surfaced beside him, panting. "Man, you're fast. Are you some sort of Navy SEAL or something?"

He grinned. "Something like that."

"Seriously?"

"Yeah. I'm part of an Army unit called Special Operations Detachment Delta. We specialize in urban counterterrorism, surveillance, indigenous recruitment and liaison work, establishing and running intelligence networks…" Her eyes had glazed over somewhere around the word *surveillance.* He amended, "Would it be clearer if I just said I do scary stuff involving guns?"

"Much."

She gazed up at him with something akin to awe gleaming in her ethereal eyes. For the first time, he understood how his men could enjoy the groupies who chased after them with this combination of admiration and adoration. It almost made a guy feel like a hero.

Except he knew what a real hero was. They were forged and tested and proven on the battlefield. Under fire and in the face of death. He'd been privileged to serve with more than a few of them.

At a loss for what to say to her, he mumbled, "I can't believe you jumped into the pool in that dress."

"I never liked it anyway. I was happy to ruin it."

"It's not so bad. You look nice in it."

She huffed. "Let's just say it's not me, okay?"

"How so?"

"It's too…pink. Too frilly."

"You're not exactly an old lady."

"I'm not a little girl, either."

He grinned at her. "As a man, may I say—with gratitude—that's an absolutely true statement."

He thought he caught her cheeks reddening as she dived under and swam away from him. He knocked out a mile or so in laps while she mostly floated on her back and stayed out of his way, smiling up at the stars. He wondered as he pulled strongly through the water what put that dreamy expression on her face. It was the kind of look a guy would love to put on a woman's face. The kind of look he'd love to put on *her* face.

High up above Las Vegas like this and isolated behind the thick glass panels that made up the walls of the courtyard, most of the city's noise stayed well below. Of course, with his busted eardrum, he wasn't hearing all that well anyway. At least not in his left ear. Only a faint ringing came from it right now. The doctor said the tinnitus ought to clear up and the hearing recover. Eventually. Maybe.

He ground his teeth together and swam harder. He hated words like *eventually* and *maybe*. He wanted to be in control of his life, dammit! It was hell waiting around like this to see if his ear healed up well enough for him to go back to his unit or not. If not…

He forced himself to finish the thought. If not, his career was over.

It was Silver who climbed out of the pool first, pale silk clinging revealingly to her body. He probably shouldn't have looked, but he did. Had there been any question about her having a dancer's body, fit and toned and sleek, that dress erased any doubts.

He tore his gaze away, climbed out of the pool and went inside to towel off and change into dry clothes. He grabbed a couple towels and his largest T-shirt and handed them to Silver, shivering in a chaise lounge by the pool.

She stared at the garment for a moment. "Aren't we going back to my place to get some of my clothes?"

"Not a chance. Anyone who's out to hurt you will have your apartment staked out."

She sighed and took the sloppy T-shirt. "Can we at least go shopping tomorrow?"

"As long as we don't go to any of your usual stores."

She nodded, a fearful look back on her face. Damn. He said, "Why don't you go take a hot shower? The blue tint to your lips does nothing for your coloring."

Laughing, she disappeared into one of the guest bathrooms.

While she was showering, he ordered up a pot of hot chocolate. It arrived just as the blow-dryer in the bathroom cut off. Good timing.

In short order, he installed her on one of the matching leather couches in the living room with a cup of steaming cocoa. When she was settled in, her bare feet tucked beneath her and all but purring in contentment, he succumbed to envy of his T-shirt and how it rubbed intimately against her rosy body.

"So, Silver, why did your father hire me? Why does he think you're in danger?"

She frowned. "According to you, someone shot at me today. Doesn't that say it all?"

"Harold hired me before that. Why did he think you were in danger a week ago?"

Her normally expressive features shut down, taking on a stubborn cast. Before she could refuse to talk or, more likely, lie to him, he commented, "I'm as close to a priest or a lawyer as you can get without me actually being one. Nothing you say to me will go any farther than this room, I swear. But to do my job, I have to know what's going on."

She studied him for a long time, obviously weighing what to tell him. Finally, she said quietly, "You know my sister was murdered, right?"

"Affirmative. That's not exactly breaking news since the story has been splashed all over the tabloids for weeks now."

Silver nodded. "When it became obvious there'd been foul play, my father and the police initially tried to keep that out of the news. But that didn't last long. And then the threats started—"

She broke off as if she'd said too much.

"What threats?" he asked quickly.

A sigh. Then, "The usual for rich, powerful men. Vague,

anonymous threats. Some crazy guy claiming the Rothchilds wronged his family and vowing revenge."

"Who's investigating this threat?" Austin asked.

She shrugged. "Natalie knows about it. Problem is it could be practically anyone. Do you have any idea how many people my family has walked on or over to get to where it is today? Las Vegas doesn't exactly have the most savory past…particularly the casino industry. Back in the day, it was a rough business."

"What exactly is this person threatening to do?"

"To kill every member of my family one-by-one. He didn't specify how. "

"Has anybody else been shot at or had any attempts made on their lives?"

"My sister, Natalie, was ambushed and nearly shot. But her attacker turned out to be her fiancé's crazy aunt and not Candace's killer."

"Is this crazy aunt in police custody?"

"She's undergoing psychiatric treatment in a facility right now. The police and her doctors say she's not a danger to anyone anymore."

Austin frowned. "Is today the first time you were shot at?"

"Shot at? Yes."

"But…" he prompted.

She continued reluctantly, "But there've been a couple other incidents in the past few weeks. Nothing this serious, though. My car's been sideswiped, and the brakes failed—but you knew that. My apartment was ransacked—"

Austin cut her off. "Anything taken?"

She shuddered over her hot chocolate. "Yes. Some of my sexiest underwear."

A frisson of apprehension and possessive fury rippled down his spine. The would-be killer was a pervert, too? That was never a good combination. But it did help explain why Silver and her sister were the first targets. It also gave him a better idea of what kinds of attacks to expect. This assailant would try to isolate

Silver. Terrorize her before he killed her. Maybe sexually assault her, which involved restraint and imprisonment. The guy would want her to suffer before she died. It also told Austin this guy was capable of long-term planning and complex organization. This was no garden-variety stalker.

"I'm afraid that until this guy is caught, you and I are going to be spending a whole lot of time together," he said quietly.

Her eyes went wide, but he didn't know how to interpret the expression. Hopefully, that was pleasure at the idea of being with him and not dismay.

A cell phone vibrating on the coffee table startled them both. Silver started to reach for it, but Austin said quickly, "I'll get it."

"It could be Mark."

He replied grimly, "Then I'll definitely get it."

"No!" Silver retorted sharply. "You'd be rude to him!" She looked at the face of her phone, and the color drained from her face. As much as he wanted to snatch that phone away from her, he restrained himself. What in the hell did she see in that cretin, anyway?

"Hi, Mark. How are—"

The guy had obviously cut her off. Austin heard shouting as she held the phone slightly away from her ear. His urge to grab the phone and tell the guy where to go grew even stronger.

When the jerk eventually paused for breath, Silver interjected hastily, "I'm so glad to know you're all right. I was worried about you."

That sent Austin's eyebrows up. She hadn't acted worried that he'd seen. She hadn't even attempted to call the guy. If anything, she'd acted relieved not to have to deal with the bastard for a while.

She did sound sincere, though, when she said she'd been worried about Sampson. Although Austin couldn't for the life of him figure out why. She must just be a soft touch when it came to undeserving sons of bitches. No wonder she was throwing out interested vibes in his direction, then.

And what was up with that if she was so involved with this

Sampson character? Something was definitely off in this relationship of hers. Did she actually perceive him like Sampson? A down on his luck bastard in need of being thrown a bone in the love department? It tasted bitter in his mouth to think that she might actually include him in the same class of man as Mark Sampson.

More screaming emanated from her cell phone before she managed to interject, "How about tomorrow morning? Saul's giving me a tour of the Grand Theater stage at ten—"

That was as far as she got, because Austin snatched the phone out of her hands. Unceremoniously, he cut off the call without a single word of explanation.

"What did you go and do that for?" she exclaimed. "Now he'll be *really* mad!"

He growled back at her, "What part of no one is to know where you are didn't you get?"

"He's my bodyguard, for goodness' sake—"

"He's not fit to guard a smelly Dumpster full of week-old trash," Austin snapped. "I'm your bodyguard, now. I'm responsible for your life, and you'll follow my instructions and no one else's from here on out. Got it?"

That earned a glare out of her. Ignoring her, he powered down her phone, which gave a trilling note of warning and went black.

"What are you doing?" Silver cried. "I need to be available in case Saul or someone associated with my show calls me."

"It's ten o'clock at night. They can call you tomorrow."

"The music business doesn't observe normal working hours."

"If folks in the biz want you bad enough, they will from now on."

"But that's the problem," she half-whispered. "I don't think they want me that bad."

"Don't sell yourself short. You were a hell of a singer. For what it's worth, I liked your songs."

She looked up at him sharply. "You're just saying that to be nice."

"Do I look like the kind of guy who'd admit to liking a teeny-bopper pop princess just to be nice?"

"I wasn't a teenybopper!"

"Fine. You were a teenaged bad girl."

She subsided, grinning. "Guilty as charged."

"I don't know about you, but I'm beat. I flew twenty hours to get here. What say we hit the sack?"

"Now that you mention it, this *has* been a big day." She stood up, starting across the living room toward the second bedroom.

"Where are you going?" he asked.

"To bed?" she replied questioningly.

"Bed's that way," he said, pointing at the master bedroom on the other side of the suite.

"That's the master suite. You take it. I'll take one of the other bedrooms."

"Didn't you hear me earlier? I said you don't get to be out of my sight for a while. That's a 'round the clock proposition, darlin'."

She turned and stared at him. "You want me to *sleep* with you?"

"In the same room, at any rate. You can have the bed. I'll take the recliner."

"That's ridiculous. I'll be fine in my own room."

He crossed his arms and stared at her implacably. "You wanna die, be my guest."

Her gaze wavered. Fell. Her hand stole to her abdomen, and she reluctantly nodded her acquiescence at him. He said more gently, "It's just for a few weeks. Until the cops catch this guy. The police have been notified of the attacks on you, right?"

"I suppose so. Mark said he'd take care of it."

Austin grunted skeptically. "Great. In that case, I'll call the LVMPD first thing in the morning to make sure they're aware you've got a stalker."

"Mark's not that awful. You just caught him having a bad moment today."

Austin snorted. "He had a number of bad moments today. And a couple of them could have cost you your life."

Silver walked away from him across the expanse of plush carpet. Her legs were surprisingly long in proportion to her diminutive height. She might be small, but everything was emphatically in exactly the right place.

Without warning, she glanced back over her shoulder and caught him red-handed staring at her juicy little tush and made-for-sex legs. Damned if the corner of her mouth didn't tilt up knowingly. *Little flirt.* If he wasn't mistaken, there was an extra sashay to her hips as she continued on into his bedroom.

While she climbed into the king-sized bed and snuggled in under the down comforter, he pulled the heavy drapes across both walls of floor-to-ceiling windows. He had a great view down the Strip from here, but that represented danger. If he could see all those other hotel windows, it meant a whole lot of people could look back at him. Or at Silver.

He grabbed a blanket and pillow out of the closet and stretched out in the large leather recliner next to the window. It might not be the luxury bed Silver was enjoying but compared to a canvas camp cot or the cold, rocky ground of Afghanistan's harsh mountains, this chair was heaven on earth.

Silver's voice came out of the darkness. "I feel bad about this. You ought to be sleeping in your own bed."

"Honey, I haven't been this comfortable in two years."

"All the more reason you ought to be over here."

"With you?" Why the words popped out of his mouth, he had no idea. Silver went dead silent, and the darkness lay heavy between them all of a sudden. He sighed. "I'm sorry. That was out of line."

Her voice floated thoughtfully out of the dark. "No, it wasn't. And in answer to your question, why not with me? We're both adults, and this bed could sleep six. Heck, given some of the parties that have happened up here, it probably *has* slept six."

He chuckled, grateful for an excuse to cover his shock at the invitation to join her. Surely she didn't have a long night of hot sex in mind. Even he wasn't that lucky.

"I'm serious, Austin. If my life depends on you, I want you to be well-rested and ready to go in the morning. You're a big man, and you're not going to be comfortable in that chair all night. Come stretch out in bed. I trust you."

Ahh. Well-rested. She was interested in him *sleeping* with her and nothing more. He mumbled under his breath, "Maybe you shouldn't trust me."

"I beg your pardon?"

"Nothing," he replied quickly.

"Don't make me get up and come over there to drag you to bed."

He laughed at that. "A little whisper of a thing like you? You couldn't budge me if you tried."

"Is that a dare?"

"What if it is?"

His sharp eyesight made out her shape rising out of the bed, and if he wasn't mistaken, that was a mischievous grin on her face. Uh-oh.

Her legs were pale in the dark, and he focused on them as she prowled toward him, catlike. It was either that or look at the way the soft cotton of his T-shirt clung to her high, firm breasts and skimmed across her narrow waist and lush hips. Nope, the legs were a better bet. But damned if he didn't wonder what they'd feel like wrapped around his hips, clinging tightly to him, urging him deeper into her—

She stopped beside the chair, and he stared up at her warily, hardly daring to breathe.

She purred, "So, if you won't get out of the chair, I guess I'm getting into it with you."

"But there's no room—"

"Wanna bet?" She flung one leg across his lap and straddled his hips, her knees sinking into the cushions on either side of him.

"Uh, okay then. So I lose that bet."

She reached down and used one finger to trace a random design on his chest through his T-shirt. "I dunno. From where I'm sitting, it looks like you might just have won the bet."

He grinned up at her until her realized his hands had come to rest on her hips. He jerked them away. But where to put them?

The armrests put his hands perilously close to her rear end. Frankly, he feared for what she'd do next if he simply let his arms drag along the sides of the chair.

She solved his problem by leaning forward until she fell against his chest and his arms shot up reflexively to catch her.

New problem. Soft parts of her were rubbing against hard parts of him that really didn't need that kind of encouragement at the moment. "Ready to come over to the bed and join me yet?" she murmured.

"You're not fighting fair!" he protested.

"Is there a rule in the bodyguard handbook that says I have to fight fair? Because I distinctly recall in the single girl's guide to men that it says the girl doesn't have to fight fair."

"Where is this guide? I think I need to study up on it."

She laughed up at him. "That's not how it works. We women know the rules we play by, and it's your job as a man to figure them out for yourself."

Her laughter rocked her against him in ways and in places that *seriously* didn't need to be rocked against. He groaned under his breath. "I'm getting a real good idea of the rules of engagement you're operating under."

"Excellent." And then the minx kissed him.

Not a first, chaste getting-to-know-you kiss, not even a flirty, slightly-drunk-and-you're-cute kiss. Nope. This was a check-out-your-tonsils, hot-sex-to-follow, I'm-gonna-eat-you-alive kiss. And having not been kissed in far, far too long, it was more kiss than he could handle and manage to stay calm.

His entire body temperature spiked, and his hands suddenly developed a mind of their own, roaming up her back restlessly. They slipped under her T-shirt, and silky flesh slid beneath his palms so smooth and sleek it stole his breath away.

And her mouth…oh my, her mouth. She sucked on his lower lip, her tongue playing across his flesh, all wet and slick and hot. He about shot out of the chair, it turned him on so intensely. And then her hands were on either side of his head, and she angled her head so she could plunge that clever tongue of hers into every nook and cranny of his starving mouth.

He was absolutely prepared to devour her whole and not think twice about it. Not that the lady seemed to find that an unpleasant idea. She was squirming all over him, making little sighing and moaning sounds that were going to cause him to embarrass himself if she didn't slow down a bit here. After all, it had been a *very* long time since he'd been with a woman.

She breathed his name on a note of wonder. "Austin. Who'd have guessed a man like you could kiss like this!"

"What do you mean, a man like me?"

Her smile flashed down at him. "You know. Straightlaced. Square."

"Square? I'm not square. I'm as wild as the next guy." Besides. Who was she to talk about being straightlaced?

Her laughter tinkled around him like silver bells. "You are not wild. You're Mr. Law-and-Order, do-the-right-thing guy. I bet you sort your socks by color and fold your underwear in perfect squares. You're the epitome of not-wild."

"Hey!"

She shrugged, and the movement made his breath catch as her breasts rubbed tantalizingly against his chest. "Trust me. I know wild. And you're not it."

If only she knew some of the things he'd done in his life. He could tell her about missions so daring they'd curl her toes. He couldn't count the number of times he'd dived into death defying stunts without a second thought. He murmured. "You think messing around with fast cars and dabbling in a few drugs makes a guy wild? You have no idea what wild really is, little girl."

"Oh, yeah? And are you gonna show me?"

Man, he was tempted. Really, really tempted. But from somewhere way deep inside him, a kernel of the self-control she'd accused him of reared its ugly head. He answered her lightly, "Honey, you couldn't handle it."

"Hah! Chicken!"

He smiled up at her knowingly. "I'm not going to bother responding to that because even you know I'm no coward."

Her expression softened, and her gaze grew serious. Aww, jeez. Did she have to go all feminine and sweet on him? That was so much harder to resist than the brazen hussy. "You're right," she murmured. "You're no coward, Austin Dearing."

He couldn't help it. He tugged her close. He had to kiss his name on her lips.

It tasted sweet, like peach ice cream on a lazy summer day. And he was lost.

Chapter 7

Silver's breath hitched as Austin looked up at her like she was some kind of goddess—whom he was about to devour for lunch. It was a heady thing to be looked at like that. Maybe he was right. Maybe she had underestimated him. A thrill of trepidation raced through her. She'd thought all those guys in her youth were wild and dangerous…but suddenly, she wondered. Maybe they'd been the pretenders. Maybe she'd finally found the real deal.

A struggle broke out on Austin's shadowed face and she watched it play across his features in fascination. "What?" she murmured.

He blinked up at her. "I beg your pardon?"

"Ever the gentleman, my dangerous Austin. What's wrong?"

"Wrong?" He sounded startled. "Nothing's wrong."

She smoothed her fingertips across his furrowed brow. "A word of advice. You can't lie for squat."

He lurched between her knees. "I can, too. I'm highly trained in the art of dissembling. I know all the body language that conveys sincerity. I know how to hide the signals of a lie. I even know how to fool a lie detector machine."

"Sorry. I'm not buying it. So give. What's wrong?"

He sighed. "I can think of several things wrong with this scenario."

She felt him pulling away from her, and panic erupted in her gut. Not him, too! He wouldn't leave her, would he? Her fingers tightened convulsively on his shoulders.

"Easy, honey," he murmured low. "I'm not going anywhere. You're safe with me."

As her death grip on him relaxed, it belatedly occurred to her to wonder how he'd known why she'd panicked. She became aware of his big hand stroking down her spine like he was gentling a skittish wild animal. In spite of herself, the tension drained from her under his soothing touch.

"What's so wrong with this…scenario?" she asked.

He sighed. "First, I work for you. It's not ethical to fool around with you."

"You work for my father," she countered. "I figure that means you and I can do whatever we want."

He ignored her argument and pressed on. "Second, I'm only here for a few months, and then I'll go back to my job overseas."

Darn it! She'd finally plunged in and dared to take a chance, and now he was rejecting her? He was the guy who'd emboldened her to do something like this in the first place. She just couldn't win for losing. Especially when it came to love.

Trying—and failing—to keep desperation out of her voice, she replied, "All the more reason not to waste time tap-dancing around each other and just do what feels good."

Doggedly, he continued. "You're a celebrity. I've spent the past decade watching your life unfold in the tabloids. I look at you and I see this face I know, but I have no idea who the person underneath is. It's like you're not even a real person. I've gotta say, I'm not interested in being with a plastic pop star."

That made her pull back. Plastic? Her? She was a lot of

things, but that was *not* one of them. "So because you've seen my face before, you don't want a relationship with me?"

He scowled. "That's not what I said."

"Is it because I'm famous? I can't help being Silver Rothchild. I belong to a rich, notorious family. So sue me. I happen to be a halfway decent singer, and I happen to be successful. So sue me again."

"But that's the point. I don't want to be with the surface image of you. I want to know the real person beneath."

"I am a real person! Right here. I'm me. Silver. I have thoughts and opinions and feelings and dreams in here."

He replied gently, "And I need to know those parts of you before I jump into bed with you. I'm not interested in sleeping with a Rothchild heir or a famous pop singer. I want a real woman."

The arrogance of the man! She was a real woman, dammit! She climbed off him angrily. "I offered myself to you, and all you can say is I'm not a real woman? Well, to hell with you, Austin Dearing. I don't care how dangerous and wild you are. You have no idea what you're missing out on!"

She stormed out into the living room, too furious to stay in the same room with him.

His voice came from directly behind her, and she about jumped out of her skin. "Honey, I know exactly what I'm missing out on."

She whirled to face him, hurt coursing through her. "Then why are you turning me down?"

"What about Bubba?"

She stared at Austin, frustrated. *Mark again.*

"Our relationship is less serious than the press portrays it. And," she added with a certain desperation, "neither of us thinks of it as exclusive." She crossed her fingers and prayed Austin bought her explanation.

His hands came up as if to gather her into his arms but fell away without touching her. "I told you. I'm only here for a little while and then I'll go back to my real life. You're a pop star and I'm a soldier. This thing between us—it would never work."

"You *are* a coward, Austin. We'll never know if it could've worked between us or not because you're too afraid to take a chance on us. That's a shame because I happen to think we could've been dynamite together." Tears clogged the back of her throat all of a sudden. She finished lightly, "Your loss, big guy."

"Silver…"

She turned away from him. She didn't want to hear anything he had to say right now.

Thankfully, he fell silent. She padded over to the refrigerator and pulled out a can of tomato juice. She slugged down its thick tartness, and her stomach gave an ominous rumble. "Ugh." She grabbed the edge of the wet bar to distract herself from the burgeoning urge to run for the bathroom.

Austin was beside her in an instant. "You okay?" He did touch her then, his hands skimming up her arms in concern.

She closed her eyes in pain. This was what she'd sacrificed by choosing to go this pregnancy alone—a partner and lover to share these moments with. The magnitude of doing the whole parenthood thing solo struck her full force in that moment of Austin's quiet concern.

"No," she mumbled, "I'm not okay." As Austin took a step closer, preparatory to wrapping her in his arms, she stepped away hastily. "But I will be okay." She straightened her spine determinedly. "I'll be just fine on my own."

She moved away from the comfort of his big, warm hands and marched back toward the bedroom. She'd made her choice, and now she had to live with it. She didn't need any man's help, thank you very much. They all ended up bailing out on her anyway.

At least Austin had been decent enough to tell her up front that he'd be abandoning her. She probably ought to be grateful to him for sparing her the pain when he just disappeared one day. He was right. They weren't meant for one another. Falling for him would be a very, very bad idea.

But did he have to be such a damned gentleman about it?

Didn't he understand that it would've been so much easier to hate him if he'd been a bastard?

Rather than start another fight, she climbed back into his big bed. Predictably, Austin was right behind her, gliding into the master bedroom on silent bare feet. Except instead of settling in the recliner, he moved over to one of the windows and pulled the curtains back just enough to be able to look down on the Strip. He lounged against the wall and stared out into the night for a long time, his jaw hard and his gaze harder.

For once, she was a little afraid of him and what he might be thinking. She'd been an idiot to throw herself at him. She couldn't blame him for thinking the worst of her. Not to mention, he thought she'd thrown herself at him even though she was involved with Mark Sampson. He must think she was the lowest form of slut.

She sighed and rolled over, turning her back to him. She tried her darnedest to go to sleep, but it wasn't happening. The realization that she was pregnant loomed huge in her mind. Was it a boy or a girl? What color hair would he or she have? Would he or she be small like her, or built more like his or her father? All of a sudden, she understood all those expectant parents who, when asked if they wanted a boy or a girl, fervently answered that they just wanted their baby to be healthy.

And then there was the show to think about. She'd love to do some of the songs she'd written. They were completely different than anything she'd ever sung, more soulful, more meaningful than the pop tunes she'd belted out a decade ago. But Saul was undoubtedly right. If she was going to make a comeback, she had to do what people expected of her. And that was the old Silver, hot and hip and naughty.

To think she'd spent the past seven years doing her level best to shed that image. And now she had to pick it back up again. How was she supposed to do that at the ripe old age of thirty? Heck, even Austin wouldn't jump into the sack with her, and he hadn't been near a woman in two years! She was never going to pull this off. It would be Harold's last and greatest revenge on her for all the crap she'd pulled on him and that he'd never really forgiven her for. He was going to ruin her career once and for all.

She sighed. It was a mean thing to think of him. But she'd seen him exact worse vengeance on people who wronged him far less than she had. She honestly wouldn't put it past him. Not unless he'd changed a whole lot recently. Was it possible that Candace's death really had changed him that much? She had a hard time believing it.

Her thoughts in turmoil, she finally drifted off into restless sleep.

The sound of a baby—her baby—crying in terror jerked her harshly from her dreams, disoriented and frightened. She sat up wildly, looking around in the dark in panic. Where was her baby? Where was she? This pitch black room was not hers. The bed was too hard, the pillows too soft. And, good grief, someone was breathing smoothly beside her! Please God, let it not be Mark! She squinted down at the large form sleeping beside her.

Austin.

She sagged in relief.

And then it all came back to her. This was his bed. His suite. He was protecting her from whoever was trying to kill her. One man against unseen and unknown forces of unknown strength. She couldn't die! Her baby deserved a chance at life!

So much for being relieved.

"Bad dream?" Austin murmured from beside her.

She exhaled slowly. "Yeah."

She looked down at him, and he gazed back up at her sympathetically. "I'm not surprised. You had a rough day."

He had no idea.

"Breathe nice and slowly. Concentrate on long, even exhalations."

Following his soothing instructions, her heartbeat slowed and her breathing returned to a semblance of normal. But the idea of lying down and going back to sleep, back to that horrible sound of a desperate baby, kept her sitting upright.

The bed shifted slightly beside her, and she glanced over at him. Wordlessly, he held out his arms to her. And without a second thought, she went to him, cuddling against his warm, solid, *naked* chest. She didn't dare move any closer and find out if he was wearing another pair of those biking shorts of his—or not. The idea of 'or not' made her pulse pound. Hesitantly, she draped an arm across his broad rib cage. Springy chest hairs tickled her nose. She nuzzled her face against him, enjoying the sensation.

Man. It had been a long time since she'd been with a man like this. She really had withered and dried into a prune of her former self in the past few years.

"Comfortable?" he murmured.

"Uh, yeah. You?"

"Not particularly."

She started. "Why not? Am I poking you?"

He sighed. "I've been in the field a long time, honey, and you're not exactly chopped liver."

"Gee, thanks," she laughed. "That's the nicest thing anyone's called me in years."

"What do you want me to say? That you're possibly the sexiest woman I've ever met, and I can't help thinking all kinds of dirty thoughts about you and wondering what you'd feel like underneath me? That I've been lying awake here all night fighting like hell to keep my hands off you and wishing like crazy that you'd roll over and have your way with me?"

Something in the timbre of his voice told her he was being dead honest with her. Whoa. "Uh, that's better. Much better," she stammered.

Silence fell between them. What was she supposed to do now? Roll back over like she ought to and go to sleep? Crawl up his chest like she wanted to and kiss him senseless? He'd already told her that it wouldn't work between the two of them. And he was absolutely right. But dang, she got tired of being alone, sometimes. She had so much on her plate right now and not a soul in the world to share it with. The least she could do was allow herself to scratch this particular itch.

They were both grown-ups. They knew the rules for these things. One night. Hot sex with no promises of anything more. Mutual pleasure. Mutual release. No more, no less.

A sigh rattled in Austin's chest beneath her ear. "It's late. You need your sleep."

Desperation erupted in her gut. Their moment was slipping away. Like the coward she'd become sometime in the past seven years, she was turning away from going after what she wanted… from really living…again. "No!" she blurted.

Austin started beneath her. "I beg your pardon?"

God, she was an idiot. She was messing this all up. "I…I don't want to sleep."

"Uh, okay. You wanna talk? Or I can make you some hot tea?"

She squeezed her eyes shut in mortification. Where had the aggressive, confident young woman she used to be gone? She hadn't even known that other Silver had disappeared until this man had barged into her life, challenging her at every turn. Heck, it wasn't like he was daring her to bungee jump off a cliff. It was just the two of them. Mostly naked in bed already, and she still couldn't bring herself to go for what she wanted.

He shifted beneath her, partially sitting up. "What's the matter? Talk to me."

A simple request. Just tell him what she wanted.

"I…I…" she forced it out all in an awkward, jumbled rush. "I want to do more than just sleep here with you. I want to get naked and feel your skin against mine. I want to be alive again. To take risks. To be brave. To grab what I want and not always be looking over my shoulder for someone to catch me or disapprove of me. I don't want to care what they all think anymore. I…"

She sat up, looking down at him miserably. "I'm not making any sense at all, am I?"

"If I'm not mistaken, I think you're asking me to make love to you."

She exclaimed in abject relief. "Exactly!"

"All the reasons I stated before not to do that are still in place."

"I know. I'm not asking for a long-term relationship. Heck, I'm not asking for any relationship at all. Don't you ever…" she paused, searching for words "…just need to feel alive?"

"Yeah. I know the feeling. More than you know."

The sigh that escaped her came directly from her heart. "Thank God." She draped her arms over his shoulders and her body over his chest. "You're gorgeous, you know."

His hands roamed up her back, under his T-shirt she was wearing, neatly slipping it over her head. He sighed in satisfaction as her naked breasts came into contact with his chest. Profound relief flooded her. Maybe she wasn't on the verge of dead and buried after all.

"You're not so bad yourself," he murmured.

She kissed her way across his chest, tickling her nose with his chest hairs again. "I've wondered what being with you would be like since the moment I met you."

His hands came under her armpits and he commenced dragging her ever so slowly up his chest until his mouth nearly touched her breast. His breath was a tantalizing caress on her skin as he rasped out, "Ditto, darlin'."

That made her laugh. "Really? Even in that stupid pink dress?"

"You could wear a nun's habit and still be sexy. Demure isn't a bad look on you. Not that much of anything could be a bad look on you."

And then his mouth closed on her flesh, and she lost all capacity to form words. Wave after wave of sensation broke across her as his mouth traveled from one breast to the other, via the valley between, all of it thoroughly explored with his tongue and teeth.

When he surged beneath her she rolled with him, glorying in his weight as his lower body pressed her deep into the feather ticking over the firmer mattress below.

"You sure you want to do this?" he muttered as he trapped her wrists over her head and inserted a knee between hers.

She'd never been more certain of anything in her life. She ached for him from a place deep inside her, from a dry well of desire that desperately needed him to fill her, to replenish her. "If you don't ravish me pretty soon, I'm gonna ravish you."

He laughed richly. "Next time, you get to be on top. Time after that, I want to go back into that swimming pool with you. And that sofa by the windows looked about the right height to bend you over—"

She heaved beneath him, dislodging his knee and capturing the length of his male member between her thighs. She simultaneously squeezed and undulated, drawing forth a hearty groan of pleasure from him. He turned her hands loose and reached between them to skim a hand down her body, following the curve of her belly to where she held his flesh.

"Open for me, Silver. Let me pleasure you, too."

Her thighs fell apart as she pulled his mouth down to hers. He tasted like cinnamon, spicy and hot on her tongue. His teeth clicked against hers, and she tilted her head, fitting herself more comfortably to his voracious need. She grasped at his mile-wide shoulders, reveling in the power of the muscles flexing beneath her palms. His control hung by a thin thread, and she reveled in her power to snap it.

But then his finger took a long, intimate stroke across her swollen, slick flesh, and she all but unraveled on the spot. There was no need to pretend pleasure with this man, no need to live up to her reputation as a wild child, no need to force the sex to meet some celebrity standard. This was *real*.

Shock broke across her awareness. After all those guys, all those casual flings, had she never found real sexual pleasure before?

His fingers danced across her skin, rubbing in maddening, wet circles that drove her out of her mind with need. His knee was back, anchoring her to the mattress, holding her in place for his explorations.

His blunt fingertip slipped inside her and her internal muscle clenched convulsively around him. The pad of his finger pressed forward, rocking against the wall of her passage, and sudden, hot wetness flowed within her. Her limbs went liquid, and her entire being narrowed down to needing him inside her. Now. Filling her with his size and heat. Riding her into oblivion.

She gasped, "What are you doing to me, Austin?"

He murmured against her mouth, "Pleasuring you, I hope."

This pulsing desire, this building torrent of electric sensations dancing across her skin, this sense of impending explosion were unlike anything she'd ever experienced before. How could Silver Rothchild, bad girl extraordinaire, have failed to discover *this* for all those years?

"Do it some more," she begged. "I want…"

His finger drove deeper within her, sliding in and out until she could hardly form words. "What do you want?"

"I want you inside me. I want you to feel this, too. I want to share this with you. It's incredible!"

He rolled away for a moment, his finger never leaving her, never breaking that mesmerizing rhythm that had her shamelessly riding his hand, seeking more and more of that incredible pleasure building deep in her core. His chuckle mostly masked the sound of latex, and then he was back, using his knees to lever her thighs apart.

"Sing for me, Silver."

And then he was over her and in her and around her, filling her so full she thought she might burst. Smelling of man and pleasure, gloriously heavy on her, Austin was all heat and muscle, driving into her with just enough violence to match her surging hips.

And sing she did. She cried out as an explosion of intense

ecstasy such as she'd never dreamed of broke over her. Her vision went black as he transported her out of herself for a moment, and she keened her pleasure on a long, shuddering note he wrung from her very soul.

He froze, his eyes closed in a cross between bliss and agony as her muscles pulsed around him. And then he began to move again, his fingers reaching between them to rub the swollen nub of her overly sensitive flesh. In a matter of seconds, another orgasm clawed at her, flinging her against him in an excess of abandon in her search for release.

And this time, when it broke, he went over the edge with her, his shout mingling with hers, his flesh pulsing as hard and long as hers, his awed collapse into a state of complete, boneless satiation as thorough as hers.

Her mind was blown. Totally, irrevocably blown. His heart thumped like a series of sonic booms beneath her ear, and her own pulse raced double-time in sync with his.

He found his voice first. "Wow."

"Yeah," she managed to breathe. "Wow."

"Did I hurt you?"

That made her laugh. "If that was pain, I want to be tortured to death just like that."

"I think you killed me."

That made her lift her head—a monumental task—to stare at him in the dark. "I'm sorry. I didn't mean to—"

He laid a finger across her lips. "I meant that as a compliment of the highest order."

"Oh." She let that sink in for a moment. "Do all guys get that much pleasure whenever they have sex?"

"I dunno. In my experience, there are degrees of enjoyment. On a scale of one to ten, most sex is somewhere between a five and an eight. But this…" A smile crinkled the corners of his eyes. "This was a twenty-two."

Relief made her feel even weaker. Thank goodness. It wasn't just her. She would've felt like a huge idiot if she'd experienced her first ever orgasm—and her second—and it had turned out to be only average sex for him.

"Only a twenty-two?" she asked lightly. "Next time I'm aiming for a thirty in honor of my birthday."

His chest vibrated with a chuckle. "I hereby place myself at your disposal for the effort."

"Such a noble guy."

A shadow crossed his face. "I'm not so noble. I needed the reminder that I'm still alive. Thanks for giving it to me."

She stared down at him. "What happened?"

He didn't answer right away. She wasn't sure he would at all, in fact. But then he spoke quietly. "A couple weeks back I was guarding a guy. A would-be assassin wired with explosives blew himself up, and I barely got between my guy and the bomber. I thought I was a goner."

The thought of Austin blown to smithereens made her shiver in horror. She wrapped her arms tightly around him. "Thank God you're all right."

He shrugged beneath her cheek. "It's all part of the job."

Suddenly, vividly, she understood exactly what it was he did. He threw himself in the path of *death* for a living. "How can you do that?" she exclaimed.

"Do what?"

"Throw yourself in front of bombs? That's insane!" She lifted her head to stare down at him, to communicate to him the absurdity of such behavior. He had to stop. She couldn't lose him! Not like that.

He stared up at her, a perplexed look on his face. "Somebody's got to do the job."

"But it doesn't have to be you. Let someone else do it!"

"I've got the training and I'm the best."

"Stop being the best, then. Can't you retire or something?"

He dumped her on her back and loomed over her, leaning on one elbow and staring down at her. "What's gotten into you?"

She couldn't exactly tell him he was the first guy who'd ever given her an orgasm and she was desperate for him to stick around and do that some more. A lot more. She stammered, "I don't want anything bad to happen to you."

He smiled broadly. "Thanks."

She swatted his upper arm. "It's not a joke."

"You're right. It's not. And I've got a busted eardrum to show for it."

Ahh. The left ear he was prone to tugging on.

"Why don't you quit?" she asked reasonably.

"I like what I do."

"You *like* it?"

"Yeah. I give people peace of mind. Safety. Hell, I give them their lives. That's a pretty cool gift to give someone, don't you think?"

Almost as cool as multiple orgasms. All right. More cool, dammit. She was being selfish. But in her defense, her motives weren't all self-centered. He was an incredible man, and it would be a tragedy if something bad happened to him.

He interrupted her turbulent thoughts. "And I'll keep you safe and alive, too. I promise."

That's what she was afraid of. How could she ever live with herself if he came to harm on her watch? "Don't you dare die on me. I'll never forgive you if you do."

"If I die, I'm not likely to much care whether or not you forgive me."

"I'll haunt you," she threatened.

"Well, then." Chuckling, he leaned down until his mouth nearly touched hers. "By all means, I'll do my best not to die on you. Not tonight, at least. You still owe me a skinny-dip."

"And the couch," she added sternly.

His laughter rose into the night, balm to her troubled soul. "And the couch."

And then, as much as it was going to kill her to do it, she had to find a way to send him away from her.

Chapter 8

Austin stared at Silver in disbelief in the early morning light. So much for intimate morning-after pillow talk. He could not believe she'd just tried to fire him! "We've already been over this. Your father hired me and pays me. You can't fire me," he replied in a clipped tone.

"But you said it yourself," she argued. "We're too involved for you to do your job effectively."

She might be right, but it wasn't the real reason she was trying to dump him. He was dead certain of it. He'd come to know a thing or two about her last night, and it was clear that she was using a smaller truth to hide a bigger truth.

Not that the smaller truth wasn't a problem in and of itself. How in the hell was he supposed to stand in front of Harold Rothchild and explain that he had to quit this job because he'd leaped into the sack with the guy's daughter at the first opportunity? Plus, he'd have to face General Sarkin. And wasn't that going to be a fun ass chewing? The hell of it was that he knew better. He'd *told* Silver they had no business getting involved.

But had that stopped him when she poured out her heart to him so sweetly and innocently last night? Oh, no. It had turned him on like a raging bull to think that she—Silver Rothchild—wanted and needed him that bad.

So much for the notion of her as a plastic pop star. She'd turned out to be a flesh-and-blood woman who'd made him laugh one minute and stole his breath away with her passion and honesty the next. He'd even gotten comfortable enough with her to bare his soul over the whole business of nearly dying. And that wasn't the sort of thing he talked about with anybody. Ever. Men in his line of work couldn't afford to dwell on such thoughts, let alone admit to having them.

He'd even spilled his guts about his worry that he might not get to go back out into the field if his eardrum didn't heal. To her credit, Silver had been sympathetic about that. She'd already begged him to stop being a bodyguard, but she'd understood him well enough to grasp that his job was more than what he did. It was who he was.

She really was a hell of a woman. Not many like her came along in any guy's life. Especially his, where he spent months on end in the field with his social life drastically curtailed. She was the kind of woman who made a guy think about foreign concepts like commitment. Settling down. Hell, engagement rings.

If Silver were his woman, he'd get a ring on her finger so fast it would make her head spin.

But she wasn't his. As much as it set his teeth on edge to remember it in the light of day, Mark Sampson had first claim on her. Except…

He studied her speculatively across his scrambled eggs, bacon and mixed berries, minus the toast, which she'd snagged and was nibbling on cautiously at the moment.

She did not strike him as the kind of woman who jumped into the sack with one guy while she was involved with another one. Her loyal streak ran a mile wide if he judged her correctly.

If she and Sampson truly had anything at all going on—which he was beginning to be seriously skeptical of—she clearly didn't consider it to be much of a relationship with Bubba.

Silver startled him by pushing her chair back abruptly. "I've got to go get ready," she announced, making a beeline for the second bathroom.

He poured himself a cup of coffee and strolled out to the pool to drink it in the clear, sharp morning light. If she and Bubba weren't an official and exclusive item, then that meant the field of battle was open to other players. He'd be a damned fool to pursue her for himself…but he might just be a bigger fool not to.

The porcelain bottom of his coffee mug gleamed white, and still no solution to his quandary presented itself to him. However, he'd come to the reluctant conclusion that his problem was actually very simple. He wanted Silver for himself. He could absolutely take her away from Bubba if he tried. But the thing was, should he? Was it the best thing for her, or was it grossly selfish of him to go after her?

"Ready to go?"

Silver's voice startled him. He'd been so lost in his thoughts that he hadn't heard her approach him from behind. "Uh. Yeah. Let me go get my SIG Sauer."

"Your what?"

"My SIG Sauer. My sidearm." As incomprehension remained on her face, he added, "My pistol."

Comprehension dawned. Either that or a random shadow had just obscured the brilliant azure of her gaze. "I'm serious. Austin. I'm going to talk to my father today and ask him to remove you from my protection."

Pain and frustration slammed into him. "What flimsy reason are you going to give me next? The fact that I carry a gun? Why don't you just come clean and admit you want me off this case because you're embarrassed about last night and want to get rid of me?"

She murmured in a husky half whisper that sent shivers up and down his spine, "I don't want to get rid of you. Exactly the opposite, in fact."

Huh? He stared at her, confused.

She continued. "Isn't it obvious why I want you off my security? Austin, I'd die if something bad happened to you because of me."

Beneath his exasperation, a kernel of something warm and…and happy…sprouted. She cared about him? Enough to push him away to see him safe? Son of a gun.

More calmly, he responded, "If you send me away, I'll just go back to another bodyguarding job. Most likely someone in a hell of a lot more dangerous situation than you're in. My odds of dying will go up dramatically."

"Yes, but then it wouldn't be my fault. Like I said last night, I couldn't live with it if you died for me."

He shrugged. "This life is my choice. I'm responsible for the results of my job. No one else. Me. Not you."

"Sorry. Not buying it. In my mind, it would be my fault—no matter what you say."

"Stubborn woman."

"Mule-headed man."

"Wench."

"Jerk."

He did a quick flip with his hands to toss her grip off his forearms and pulled her against him too fast for her to protest. "I love you, too, darlin'."

He closed his eyes and kissed her before she could reply. Before he could see if she took his words at face value or treated them as a joke. Hell, he didn't know if he meant them or not. They'd just slipped out. Lord knew, she was the kind of woman he'd have no trouble loving. None at all.

She relaxed into him, melting against him, her mouth opening under his. Welcoming him in, her tongue coaxing him to come and play in their own private garden of sensual delight.

And maybe that was answer enough for now. She definitely enjoyed being with him and was clearly hungry for more of what they'd shared through most of last night. It didn't take a rocket scientist to read the little sounds she was making in the back of her throat. She'd be all kinds of amenable to turning their one-night stand into a two-nighter…or more.

That did it. Mark Sampson was history. This woman was entirely too special, too spectacular for a guy like Sampson. Silver Rothchild was his, effective now.

They'd figure out the details later. She'd get used to his work once she realized how good he was at it. He'd take more time off and be with her every chance he got. He was all over coming home on leave if he had someone like her to come home to.

Exultation filled his heart as he gave in to the inevitable. The two of them were meant to be. She might not have realized it in her head yet, but her body recognized him as her true mate. It was only a matter of time until her conscious caught up with her subconscious.

He could be patient. He'd give her time to adjust to the idea of the two of them. Plus, it would give him time to show Sampson the score and run him off—far, far away from Silver. The worst of it was going to be restraining his protective impulses enough not to drive Silver crazy. She was no big fan of restrictions on her life. Not that he blamed her after having met Harold Rothchild and having seen firsthand how the press hounded her.

He lifted his mouth away from hers and gazed down at her. "Have I told you this morning how beautiful and special you are?" She blinked up at him rapidly. If he wasn't mistaken, those were tears pooling in her eyes. "Hey, why the tears?"

She batted away the moisture, smiling up at him. "You're the most amazing man."

He dropped a kiss on the tip of her nose. "And don't you forget it, either."

"Amazingly arrogant."

"Amazingly confident," he corrected.

She gazed up at him, emotions racing through her eyes too

quickly to name. But most of them looked good for the home team. Hope spiraled through him. By golly, the two of them might just pull off this miracle together.

His voice inexplicably gruff, he muttered, "C'mon. Let's get going. You don't want to be late to your first day of work."

She shook herself out of her thoughts and nodded. "You're right. The new Silver is responsible and on time."

"I like you just the way you are, darlin'. Don't change a thing."

As he paused in front of the door to peer out the peephole, she murmured behind him, "Keep telling me that, and I might just believe you one of these days."

He glanced over his shoulder and grinned broadly. "You've got it."

Silver stared thoughtfully at Austin's back as he led the way down the hall to the elevator. What had gotten into him this morning? He'd been so quiet. And so thoughtful toward her. Not that she was complaining. Thoughtful was almost as new an experience for her as multiple orgasms—of which she was now a proud veteran of several. Yes, it had been a long and informative night.

It was darned hard not to be more than a little shocked by him and what he'd taught her about pleasure and about her body. She literally felt like a new woman this morning.

The elevator door slid open, and after checking to be sure it was empty, he held it for her to step inside. She moved to the back automatically, and he took his place in front of her, a veritable wall of muscle. She couldn't resist. She reached out and ran her hands down the long, powerful V of his back, every contour of the expanse as familiar to her now as her own body.

"Silver—" he rumbled warningly. "I'm working."

"So stop working for a minute. We're alone in an elevator. What can possibly happen to me in here?"

"It's about being alert. In the moment. I have to be ready for anything."

"Mmm. I like the sound of that."

He threw a glare over his shoulder at her that lacked any real heat. "You're incorrigible."

She grinned up at him. "I've been called worse."

He grinned back at her reluctantly. She thought he might have started to turn toward her with a kiss on his mind, but the elevator dinged just then to announce its arrival on Subfloor 1. He whipped back around to face the door, danger abruptly pouring off of him as he stepped outside.

"Clear," he announced briskly.

She slipped in close behind him as he walked swiftly down the basement hallway. They used the orchestra entrance to the Grand Theater, winding through various practice rooms for the musicians and out to the actual pit where they sat unseen during shows. Austin moved up the narrow steps to the main stage and she followed him, admiring the view.

"*There* you are, snookums. I've been *waiting* for you."

She winced at both the nickname and the aggravated tone. Bub—Mark. "Good morning to you, too," she replied evenly.

"What the hell have you been doing all this time? Where were you? Were you with *him?*" Mark's whining was quickly giving way to strident jealousy.

She answered vaguely, "Austin took me someplace safe while the police sorted out what happened yesterday."

"Did they catch the shooter?" Mark asked urgently. She couldn't tell if it was just a case of his usual nosiness or if that was fear vibrating in his voice.

She shrugged. "I don't know. Austin took care of everything." Speaking of Austin, she smiled over at him, and his eyes lit with an answering smile.

Mark looked back and forth between the two of them and thunder gathered on his brow. It didn't take long for the storm to break. About a second-and-a-half. For some reason, this morning his tirade bugged the living heck out of her. She usually let it roll off her back. But today, she saw Mark through Austin's eyes—and the view was not pleasant.

What was she going to do with him? She couldn't get rid of him, but she couldn't stand being around him, either. How much would it cost to just buy him off? He was desperate to get his hands on wealth and fame, and if she gauged him correctly, he didn't care how he got either.

His initial plan had clearly been to marry her. She'd been stunned when he'd proposed to her barely two weeks into their arrangement. That was the day he'd popped the 'little lady couldn't raise a rugrat by herself' line on her, in fact. It had also been the day she'd made it crystal clear that she never intended to become romantically involved with him.

Would a million dollars do the trick?

She wasn't made entirely of money, and that was no small sum to her, but if it would make him quietly disappear, it might be worth it.

Usually Mark ran out of things to yell at her about by now, but this morning, he seemed inspired to new heights of ranting and raving by Austin's presence. She had to give Mark credit. He had being a bastard down to a fine science. Absently, she gazed around the stage, estimating its dimensions and playing with various possibilities for using the space in her show.

Mark continued to yell, and she registered the various stage-hands and technicians drifting off to places unseen. Which was just as well. It was embarrassing having to stand here and take this.

If he'd been mad at her for worrying him sick or for not letting him know right away that she was okay, she might have had more sympathy for his tantrum. But as it was, he was chewing her out for choosing the other bodyguard over him and making him look bad. She was appalled when the phrase "selfish pig" actually floated through her head.

What on God's green Earth had she been thinking to choose him to be the father of her baby?

Speaking of the other bodyguard, Austin stood in the wings of the theater, his arms crossed. At first, he'd seemed amused, possibly even pleased, by Mark's truculent behavior. He probably got a kick out of Mark showing his true stripes to her. Not that she needed the demonstration to know that Austin was exactly right about Sampson.

But now, as Bubba's tantrum wore on, a black scowl had settled on Austin's brow. Apparently, his patience had its limits, too. She knew the feeling.

She noted that in spite of his apparent irritation, Austin's gaze still roved everywhere, never settling in any one place for more than a few seconds. She got the distinct impression he wasn't missing a thing that was going on in every last corner of the cavernous theater. At least one of her bodyguards was doing his job.

A few stagehands still milled around, repairing and touching up the current stage set—part of a traditional Vegas production with lines of showgirls and a vaguely over-the-hill headliner act. Would that be her fate? To do occasional gigs in Vegas for her aging fans? She was so sick of all the phony glitz and glamour. Why couldn't she just do what Austin suggested and come out on stage and sing her songs?

"Silver? Are you listening to me?" Mark snapped.

"Yes, Mark. I'm listening," she replied dryly. "I believe you left off at 'what the hell do I see in that arrogant bastard?'"

Out of the corner of her eye, she caught the upward quirk of Austin's mouth. He was certainly chipper this morning, especially given how little sleep he'd gotten last night after a very long journey the day before. At least he'd gotten to eat and enjoy a hearty breakfast this morning. She hadn't managed to get down more than a slice of dry toast, and even that had come right back up. It had been a close thing to make it to the bathroom before she'd turned green and started heaving.

Speaking of her non-breakfast, all of a sudden, she was ravenously hungry—light-headedly so. Mark could really quit yelling at her any time now. The beginning of a headache commenced throbbing in her temples.

Thankfully, Saul bustled out on stage just then, and the

number of visible stagehands suddenly picked up considerably. And even more thankfully, Mark finally shut up.

Saul glanced down at his watch and she did the same. Hah. She was not only on time, but she'd gotten here a few minutes early. He sounded faintly surprised when he said, "Silver Girl. Glad you could make it."

"I said I'd be here. I keep my word these days," she replied evenly.

That earned her a thoughtful look. Then, without further comment, he launched into a tour of the upgraded features the stage had acquired in the past few years. She'd be interested to see what the lighting guys could do with that digital laser system when it came time to design that part of the show.

Mark tagged along, making snarky comments, until Silver finally turned to him and snapped, "Mark, this is my job. If you can't keep your nose out of it, go somewhere else."

He puffed up, offended, but shut his mouth and disappeared for the remainder of the tour. Unfortunately, when she stepped out to center stage once more, walking through various options for dance numbers and staging with Saul, he reappeared and started up again.

"Let's get out of here, babycakes. You've got the money to hire other folks to do all this work for you. There's no need for you to stand around here all day. You've seen it, now let's go. I made a reservation for us at La Bamba for lunch."

That got her attention. La Bamba Cantina was paparazzi central, with big windows that gave ridiculously easy access to photographers with telephoto lenses. More to the point, a sniper would have a clear shot at her anywhere in the place, too.

"Mark, I don't think it's a good idea to go someplace that public to eat. After the attack yesterday—"

He cut her off. "Nothing's gonna happen today. I guarantee it."

"What? You had a little talk with my stalker and told him to take the day off?"

He went beet-red. "I'm the bodyguard, and I say it's all right, dammit—" His voice was rising quickly to a bellow, and she winced. Dumb, dumb, dumb. She knew better than to set off his temper by being sarcastic.

All of a sudden, a large, menacing presence loomed beside her. Austin. Hovering protectively over her, perfectly still. Poised. Waiting. Threat rolled off of him in palpable waves. "Is there a problem here, Maynard?"

Mark shouted, "My name's Mark, you son of a—"

"Perhaps you should step outside and collect yourself until you can focus enough to do your job. I'll take over protecting the lady until you've calmed down."

Amusement flared in Silver's gut. She didn't for a moment doubt that Austin knew how infuriating his calm and reasonable advice would be to Mark. Sure enough, Mark turned several shades closer to purple and took an aggressive step forward.

Reluctantly, she tamped down her amusement and stepped between the two men. "Mark, it's okay. I'll go to lunch with you."

"You will not—" Austin started behind her.

She whirled to face him. "Stay out of this. Mark's waiting here until I'm done looking at the stage, and then he can guard me at lunch. It'll give you a little time off to rest and eat yourself. After all, you didn't get much sleep last night—" She broke off. Whoops. Probably shouldn't have said that.

"Whaaat?" Mark squawked. "What the hell?"

Oh no. Not good. Mark would rush Austin any second now, and in turn, Austin would break Mark in half. The press would find out about her feuding bodyguards and have a field day with it. And Harold would kill her show before it ever got off the ground. Must do damage control. Now!

She spun to face Mark quickly. "Never mind. He told me he was having trouble with jet lag." It wasn't working. A vein throbbed in his temple, and he looked apoplectic. His fists came up and he all but pawed the ground like a bull.

Crud. Time for drastic measures. She raced forward, plastered herself against Mark's beer gut and wrapped her arms around his vaguely rounded shoulders. After Austin, he felt…flabby. Distaste coursed through her. She forced herself to keep her arms around him, though. Nothing distracted him like a display of affection from her. Sure enough, she caught the smug leer he threw over her shoulder at Austin. She braced herself as he squeezed her too tight and tried to kiss her.

She simply couldn't bring herself to tolerate his wet, foul-tasting mouth on hers. She turned away as subtly as she could but feared he'd noticed anyway, given how his arms tightened cruelly around her.

"You're crushing me," she managed to gasp.

As much as she tried to stand it, she had to pull away from him. She wriggled free of Mark's reluctant arms and sighed in relief. She got the distinct impression that had Austin not been there, he wouldn't have let her go and might even have forced himself upon her further. A frisson of alarm skittered down her spine.

She turned and was just in time to catch Austin's tall form fading silently into the shadows of the velvet folds of curtains. Damn, damn, damn. It was all she could do not to run after him. To explain why she'd had to put up with Mark's pawing. To tell him about the secret arrangement, about why it was necessary to keep Mark happy, at least until after her show. It wasn't forever. Just six weeks.

Then she'd be in the clear to tell the whole world how she felt about Austin Dearing. She'd shout it to the rooftops. She just had to get through the show without a scandal. And to pull that off, she dared not alienate Mark. She needed him. Even if it meant pushing away Austin and hurting him. Unfortunately, it felt like she'd just buried a knife in her own heart, too.

Saul broke the tense silence that had fallen over the stage when Mark started to blow. "Silver, do you remember any of your old songs? I had the sound boys cue up the instrumental tracks from a few of your hits so you could try out the speaker system."

Halfheartedly, she smiled at the older man. His timing

always had been impeccable. "That'd be great. Have you got a mike for me?"

In no time, she was wired up with a barely there earpiece and mouthpiece attached to a wireless battery pack in the back pocket of her jeans. The familiar chords of one of her biggest hits started, and she closed her eyes, trying to imagine herself back in the good old days. The dance moves came back to her effortlessly, and she fell into the sequences. The sound system was great, with practically no feedback on the stage.

But there was something missing.

She didn't feel this music anymore. It didn't speak to who she was or what she thought about. She wasn't nineteen and only worried about having fun and dancing till she dropped. Who'd written those lyrics, anyway?

The next song started, an even more upbeat piece. Automatically, she started into the choreography. By the second verse, she was starting to feel nauseous. By the third chorus, the lights were spinning, and the rows of seats were wavering like a roller coaster. She launched into the last big dance sequence, and the entire stage heaved beneath her. And then everything went black.

Chapter 9

Austin lurked in the darkest shadows just offstage, watching in disgust as Sampson leered lewdly at Silver. What *did* she see in him? She was so out of that guy's league. She had more class in her pinkie finger than Sampson would amass in his entire life.

Her energetic dance number brought her over to this side of the stage, and Austin took advantage of his training to make himself invisible behind the various curtains, ropes and pulleys clustered beside him. He frowned. Silver looked pale, and that fine sheen of perspiration on her face didn't look like the honest sweat of exertion.

She finished singing the chorus and danced her way up a ramp and onto a raised platform. She squinted out at the theater, like she was having trouble making out the rows of seats. A hum of alarm low in his gut had him frowning as she wobbled and then took a definite misstep.

His protective instincts fired, and he didn't hesitate. He darted forward, out onto the stage. He peripherally registered Sampson, standing at the other side of the stage, his tongue all but hanging out with lust. But Austin's focus was on Silver. Time slowed as she staggered toward the edge of the platform. Not good.

He put on an extra burst of speed and reached the front of the raised stage just as she toppled over in a dead faint. She collapsed to her knees and then pitched forward into his arms. He grunted beneath her weight but caught her safely.

Sampson was just now getting his butt in gear to move forward. Lousy reflexes—must've had way too much beer over the years to be that dull.

"Hey, Dearing—"

"Not now," Austin snapped, turning to Saul. "Is there a dressing room I can lay her down in?"

"This way, son."

While Sampson blustered behind him, Austin hustled offstage, carrying Silver limp in his arms. Panic made him preternaturally strong, and she felt featherlight. His mind raced frantically. Please, don't be anything serious. Had he missed something yesterday? Had someone poisoned her? Had she eaten anything he hadn't?

They wound their way to a row of closed doors, and Saul opened the first one on the right. Austin brushed past him and into the cluttered space. A chaise lounge in the corner was covered with sequined costumes, which he pushed onto the floor with his foot before laying Silver down.

He glanced up just in time to see Saul slam the door shut in Sampson's face. "Thanks," Austin bit out.

Saul nodded grimly as he locked the door for good measure. "How is she?"

"I think she just fainted." He took her pulse quickly and pressed his ear to her chest. "I hope," he muttered.

Saul volunteered, "She has a history of high blood pressure, but as far as I know, she's always been good about taking her medicine."

Austin commenced chafing her wrists. "Call the hotel doctor. I want a blood pressure cuff on her *now*."

The older man pulled out his cell phone and made a quick call. As he hung up, a god-awful pounding started on the dressing room door, accompanied by Sampson bellowing unintelligibly outside.

Silver's eyes fluttered but didn't open.

He glanced over at Saul, who was looking worriedly at the rattling panel. Austin sighed. "I'll take care of him." He stood up and moved swiftly to the door. He yanked it open. "Quit making a fool of yourself, Mick. The doctor's on his way. Go be useful and show the guy back here when he arrives."

"My name's *Mark*—"

Austin cut him off. "Go get the doctor and quit making so much noise. My four-year-old nephew has more control of himself than you do." And on that note, Austin closed the door—firmly—in the guy's face.

Saul was grinning when he turned around. Grinning himself, he headed back to Silver's side. Her eyes fluttered again, opening partially this time. She asked vaguely, "Did you just call Mark a four-year-old?"

She was conscious. Relief flooded him. It might have been a simple faint, but he'd still been sick with fear. "Actually, I called him worse than a four-year-old."

A hint of a smile crossed her ghostly pale features as her eyes drifted closed.

He knelt beside her and asked gently, "Honey, have you taken your blood pressure meds for the past several days?"

She opened her eyes again, their delicate blue piercing him straight through the heart. "Yes. Like clockwork. Especially now…"

"Why now?" he prompted when she didn't continue.

Her gaze slid away from his. "Especially now that I've got this show to do. Can't afford to mess it up." She lurched in alarm. "Saul, there weren't any reporters around, were there?"

"The theater's closed and locked. We were alone. Just my staff. And they know better than to blab to the press if they want to keep their jobs."

Austin frowned. What was he missing here?

He glanced up at Saul, who obligingly explained. "Tabloids eat up stuff like this. Pop star collapses while attempting comeback." He got a thoughtful look on his face. "But maybe we ought to let it leak. You know what they say. Any publicity is good publicity."

Silver lurched on the couch and blurted, "No!"

Both men looked down at her questioningly.

Reluctantly, she explained, "Harold said he'd cancel the gig if I show up in the tabloids again."

Austin and Saul "ahhed" simultaneously, and then abruptly exchanged alarmed looks. *Sampson.* "I'll go take care of it," Austin murmured.

"You're a good boy," Saul murmured back as Austin headed for the door.

"Where are you going?" Silver cried. "Don't leave me!"

He paused, his hand on the doorknob. She looked as frantic and scared as a kid who'd just lost her puppy. "I'll be back in a minute, honey." When her expression didn't ease, he added, "I promise."

The frown on her brow smoothed out a little, and he stepped out into the narrow hall. It didn't take long to find Sampson. The guy was in the middle of the stage throwing a hissy fit over what was taking the doctor so long.

Austin strode out to have a private word with the man.

Sampson turned to face him and drew a breath, but Austin cut him off before he could utter a word. "Don't get started with me, Mack. Nobody's here to stop me from smashing you into a million pieces this time."

Interestingly enough, Sampson clammed up. Give the boy credit for having a sliver of self-preservation at any rate.

Austin continued, "So here's the thing. Silver really doesn't want this little episode to show up in the newspaper. Saul assures me his staff won't spill the beans, which means, if I catch wind anywhere outside this room of her fainting, it's your ass I'm kicking into last week. Got it?"

"Are you threatening me, Dearing?"

Austin considered Sampson like he might a mildly interesting insect. He reached out to flick an imaginary piece of lint off Sampson's shoulder. Then he answered evenly, "No, my friend, I'm not threatening you. I'm merely telling you what's going to happen if you don't keep your mouth shut."

"I'll press charges. I'll get you tossed in jail, and they'll throw away the key! I have contacts in this town, you know—"

Austin took a gliding step forward, casually invading the guy's personal space even more. "Do you seriously think I'd be stupid enough to leave behind any evidence of your existence? I have friends, too, Sampson. The kind who can and will make you disappear so your remains are never found. You catch my drift?"

The guy's eyes went wide. He took a step back. But when Austin didn't follow, he seemed to regain some of his bluster. "This isn't over, Dearing. I'll show you. I'll show you all. I'll get the girl and laugh all the way to the bank, and you'll be wondering what the hell happened."

A chill chattered down Austin's spine. What did this guy have on Silver? Surely he was holding something over her to be this confident. Certainty that Sampson was blackmailing her washed over him. And if she hadn't come clean and run screaming from this guy yet, it was something big. Something she didn't want to face.

Determination to help her washed over him. But first, he'd have to get her to confess her secret to him. Austin spoke grimly. "Stay away from her, Sampson. If I catch you around her again, I'm going to hurt you. Bad. And that's a promise."

One of the theater's doors opened, spilling a shaft of bright light into the huge, dim space. A man carrying a leather bag hurried down the center aisle.

"Are you the doctor?" Austin called.

"Yes."

"She's backstage. This way." Sampson forgotten, Austin led the doctor quickly to Silver.

She'd regained a little color, which was to say she'd gone from gray to ghostly pale, but she still looked terribly weak. Nonetheless, she waved a wan hand at him and Saul. "Go away, you two."

Reluctantly, he left her to the doctor's care. Saul grinned at him as he paced the hall outside. "She'll be okay, young man. She's stronger than she looks."

Worried, Austin turned on the man. "How do you know that?"

"She holds her own with her father and that boyfriend of hers, doesn't she? She's tough, I tell you."

"Yeah, well, she shouldn't have to be. She should have someone who gives a damn to look out for her and take care of her."

"Like you?"

Yeah. Exactly like him. Thing was, he got the distinct impression that Silver valued her privacy above just about all else. He'd be no better than Sampson if he announced to Saul that he intended to make her his at the first available opportunity. Austin mumbled, "No, not me. I'm only here for a few months, and then I'm going back to my real job."

Saul's gaze narrowed almost threateningly. "Don't you break my girl's heart, you hear? She's had a lot of bad luck in her life, and she's working hard to make a new start. Don't you mess this up for her."

Austin stopped pacing. Stared at Saul, who looked as fierce as a bear at the moment. "You're really worried about her, aren't you?"

"She's like my own daughter."

Austin nodded respectfully. "I won't do anything to hurt her." Except he already had. He'd taken her to bed despite it being foolish and selfish in the extreme. He'd never forget that wounded look on her face last night when he'd called her a plastic pop star. He hadn't meant it the way she'd taken it, but he hadn't thought about how it might sound to her. And then there'd been the blow to her when he'd reminded her he'd be leaving in a few months; he'd seen that flash of *knowing* in her eyes. Men had left her before. Probably without warning and without a goodbye if that look was any indication.

She deserved better than him.

And that was the thought uppermost in his mind when the dressing room door opened a minute later, to reveal the doctor, with Silver standing behind him.

His eyes never leaving her lovely face, Austin asked lightly, "Is she going to live, Doc?"

"I think she might pull through. It was just a combination of fatigue, lack of food and a little stress. Nothing to worry about."

Silver murmured her thanks to the doctor and Austin added his as well.

As they stepped out into the hallway, she asked, "Where's Mark?"

She might as well have punched him in the gut. Sampson was so freaking lucky to have a woman like this give a damn about him. "If he knows what's good for him, he's not here," Austin growled.

"Please tell me you didn't pick a fight with him."

He snorted. "If I pick a fight with him, you'll know it from the blood and Sampson body parts strewn all over the place."

"Did you two argue?" she pressed.

"We had a…conversation. Came to…an understanding."

Alarm blossomed on her face. "Did you make him mad?"

"Kinda hard to talk to him and not make him mad, it seems."

"What did you say to him?" she asked urgently.

Austin frowned. "I told him to stay away from you."

Silver wrung her hands in agitation. "I told you to stay out of it! Oh, Lord. There's no telling what he'll do now."

"He'll do nothing now, or else he'll answer to me." Austin retorted.

"You have no idea what you've done!" she wailed.

Heads were starting to turn among the stagehands, and Saul and the doctor were looking uncomfortable. He said quietly, "Why don't we go someplace a little more private and you can explain it to me."

She looked around suddenly, as if she'd become aware of their audience. She nodded, abruptly silent. Sheesh. What a way to live. Always having to look over her shoulder for journalists or people who'd sell her out to one. He was already craving a little anonymous privacy, and he'd only been living her life for a single day.

Of course, in his line of work, it was all about being invisible. Unnoticed. Sliding in and sliding out unseen and unheard. It was the polar opposite of her existence. She could have this fame and celebrity stuff. He'd take the obscurity and complete absence of recognition of his work over her life.

"Let's blow this joint," he muttered.

"I need to swing by my dressing room and pick up my purse first."

He nodded and led the way backstage, stopping outside the room she'd changed in earlier. She stepped in to fetch her bag.

A muffled scream had him shooting through the door before he was hardly aware of moving.

She stood frozen in front of her dressing table, her hands pressed to her mouth, a look of horror on her face. He glanced up and swore. Scrawled across the mirror in some red, greasy substance were, "YOU DIE NEXT."

He moved around the space fast, checking it for intruders. Thankfully, there weren't any hidey-holes that could conceal a person. He turned to Silver and gathered her trembling form in his arms.

"I've got you, baby. You're safe. Nobody's gonna touch you on my watch."

She shuddered and burrowed against his chest, her face buried in his shirt.

He muttered, "Let's go. I'll call the police and have them come check this out. Can you walk or do you need me to carry you?"

She leaned back far enough to stare up at him. "You'd carry me?"

"If that's what it takes to get you out of here."

"You're in luck. I can walk."

He kept his arm tightly around her shoulders, her body tucked against his side as he turned for the door. He saw Saul standing there, gaping at the scrawled threat. "Lock this door and don't let anyone in until the police get here. Tell the cops to come in plain clothes, through a back entrance," Austin ordered quietly. "If you can manage to keep hotel security out of this for a day or two, that'd be helpful. LVMPD will appreciate having the breathing space to do their job before Harold crawls up their—" He broke off. "Well, you get the idea."

Saul nodded knowingly and pulled out his cell phone. As Austin whisked Silver out of the room, the older man was already on the horn to the police.

He rushed her out a backstage exit, emerging into a service hallway leading to the hotel's laundry. She directed him to a service elevator, and he ushered her inside with a quick look in either direction down the deserted hall. He randomly punched a button and the elevator whooshed upward quickly.

"Are you okay?" he asked in concern.

She nodded, but she still looked badly shaken.

"I gather writings on your mirror are not common occurrences?"

She smiled halfheartedly at him. "Not so much."

"You're not gonna faint on me again, are you?"

She replied bravely. "Thanks for worrying about me, but I'll be fine. Everything's proceeding as it should."

He frowned. Strange way to describe her health. She looked momentarily alarmed, then asked quickly, "What's on the twentieth floor?"

"Huh?" He glanced over at the elevator's control panel. "Oh. We'll transfer to an elevator that will take us up to the penthouse. Nothing special about twenty. I just punched any old button. Odds of someone being there waiting for us are close to zero."

"You really take this security stuff seriously, don't you?"

Surprised he glanced down at her. "I spend most of my life around people who will die if I don't do my job to perfection. I don't get assigned to the popular guys who are beloved by their people. I guard the guys everyone wants to kill."

She shuddered. "That sounds *so* dangerous."

He shrugged. In point of fact, it was more dangerous than she knew. Daily, he lived in real danger of being shot or blown up in an assassination attempt. The fact that he was only sporting a busted eardrum after the latest attempt to kill one of his principals was a minor miracle.

"Have you actually come close to dying before?" she asked curiously.

He snorted. "You're joking, right?"

She looked up at him innocently. What must it be like to be that unaware of how deadly the world could truly be? A need to protect her naiveté surged through him, to keep her just like this—sweet, trusting and sheltered from life's harsh realities.

Except this was Silver Rothchild he was talking about. The way he heard it, she'd seen a whole lot of life's harsh realities already.

He blurted, "How did you stay so innocent through all the stuff you did?"

She stared up at him, saved from answering by the elevator door opening. He stepped out quickly, cleared the empty halls and gestured for her to follow him. It was a short jaunt down a hallway to a guest elevator. He swiped his key card and the elevator leaped upward toward the penthouse level.

He turned to look down expectantly at Silver. For her part, she looked disappointed that he hadn't forgotten his question.

Finally she answered. "What makes you think I'm innocent? I've done some pretty wild things in my day."

He frowned. "Then how do you maintain your positive outlook on life?"

Her hand drifted to her stomach as she laughed shortly. "The alternative is to slit my wrists. And I'm too much of an optimist to give up that easily."

The elevator jerked faintly beneath his feet, but it was nothing compared to the jolt coursing through him. "Is your life really that bad?" he asked. "You have wealth and fame and a family that cares about you."

"My family meddles in everything I do. Living with the press hounding you 24/7 sucks. My career is dead, my personal life is nonexistent and money isn't everything. Next argument for how great my life is?"

He laughed. "Ahh. There's the cynicism I expected out of you."

She sighed as he opened his door and ushered her into his villa. "I'm sorry. I try not to go there if I can help it."

"Why not?"

"It's toxic to my soul. I have a ton of things to be grateful for, and I'm not about to whine about my life. It's no more perfect than anybody else's life, though. Everyone's got problems of their own—rich or poor, old or young, the problems may be different, but we all have garbage to deal with."

"True. So what garbage fills your plate?"

"Nothing you'd care to hear about, I'm sure."

"On the contrary. I want to know everything about you, Silver Rothchild."

She threw him a startled look. Then the expression cleared. "Oh. So you can figure out who's trying to kill me."

No, because he was fascinated by her and becoming more so by the minute. But he bloody well wasn't about to admit that to her. Not yet. She was still far too distant from him to hand her a weapon like that. The first order of business was to test her interest in him to see if she reciprocated any of his desire to take this relationship further.

He commented, "You're gonna have to cancel your lunch date with Bubba. No public places for you today. Not after that message on your mirror."

"Gee. Darn."

He frowned over at her. "What the hell's going on between you two? You've got no chemistry, you've obviously got nothing in common and, if you have a lick of sense, the guy has to drive you crazy."

She sighed. "No comment."

Maybe not now. But he'd get her to tell him the truth sooner or later.

"Speaking of meals, I've got dinner with my family tonight. But never fear. It's at my dad's house. Do you think you can handle the whole Rothchild clan?"

"If you can, I can, darlin'."

She rolled her eyes. "Sometimes they're too much for me."

"If you need to bail out, just give me the signal, and I'll pull you out of there."

She blinked up at him. "What signal?"

He grinned back at her. "Just throw me one of those come-hither looks of yours that I can't resist, and we'll be out of there before you know it."

"You mean like this?"

He squeezed his eyes shut. That had been a mistake. A *major* tactical mistake to admit she had that kind of effect on him. He gathered her in his arms, ignoring the startled look she gave. "Yeah. That look, little minx."

She looked up at him, gazing through her thick lashes, blatantly flirting with him.

That was better. He couldn't stand that haunted look of terror lurking in her eyes. "What am I going to do with you?" he murmured.

She mumbled against his chest, "Keep me safe and never let me go."

If only he could do both.

If only.

Chapter 10

Silver gazed up at the Rothchild estate as Austin whistled under his breath beside her. The mansion was daunting even to her, and she'd spent a good chunk of her childhood there. Not that she'd ever felt that she truly belonged in the place. Candace and Natalie had seen to that. When her mother had married their father, they'd made sure she felt like the ugly stepsister she in fact was. In her opinion, it was a vast karmic joke that she'd grown up to have the striking looks and talent that she had.

To Austin she murmured, "It's just a house."

He grinned over at her. "Yeah. Twenty thousand gaudy square feet of just house."

She shrugged. "There is that." They walked up the front steps to the columned, Italianate half circle of the front porch. "I never can quite shake the feeling of being an intruder here."

Austin looked over at her in quick surprise. "Why do you say that?"

"Harold's not my biological father. When he married my mom,

he adopted me and I changed my name to Rothchild. He said it would serve me better in life than my father's name would have."

"What happened to your father?"

"He made some bad business decisions. Couldn't face the music and killed himself when I was little."

Austin swore quietly, then said, "I'm sorry, Silver."

"I don't remember him much. Harold's as close to a father as I've ever had."

"Then I'm doubly sorry for you."

Startled, she started to ask him why he'd said that, but the front door opened just then to reveal Harold himself. She blinked, stunned. Since when did he open his own doors? It was almost as if he'd been waiting for them!

And then, over the next few minutes, Harold was shockingly cordial to Austin. Usually her father treated the hired help like, well, hired help. But he fawned on Austin as if the guy was some kind of rock star. Which was ironic, because she actually was a rock star and merited only an absent kiss on the cheek.

Most of the clan was already assembled in the billiard room, sipping on cocktails and snacking on canapés before supper. The shrimp salad and curried-something petit fours did nothing for her, and she opted for a club soda while the others arrived.

Jenna Rothchild, Natalie and Candace's younger sister, drifted over to say hello. She was yet another tall, gorgeous female with the capacity to make Silver feel like an inadequate midget. But in Jenna's defense, she had always been kind to Silver. Although they were several years apart in age, they'd been good friends over the years and throughout their various antics.

As a blissfully happy-looking couple strolled toward them, Austin's hand came to rest possessively on the small of her back. His familiar touch ruffled and soothed her at the same time, and she was abruptly aware of how good he smelled. It wasn't the sort of thing she usually noticed in a man. But then, there wasn't much about Austin Dearing that she didn't notice. The guy completely filled her senses, commanding every bit of her attention.

"Austin, this is my sister, Natalie, and her fiancé, Matt Schaffer. He's in charge of security for a major casino chain, which I might add is a competitor of The Grand's. But we forgive him because he makes my sister so glowingly, obnoxiously happy. Nat…Matt, this is Austin Dearing—my new bodyguard compliments of Daddy dearest. He's some sort of military officer."

The two men nodded in mutual recognition like a pair of fellow warriors.

Eyeing Austin appreciatively, Natalie commented, "I gotta say, sis, this model's a vast improvement over the last one."

Silver tensed at the jab at Mark but forced herself to relax under Austin's all-too-perceptive hand. Okay, so it hadn't been the smartest thing she'd ever done to recruit Mark to help her with the whole secret-baby thing. But the deed was done. There was no backing out on their deal, whether she liked it or not.

Desperate to change the subject, she asked Matt, "Any progress on the investigation of Candace's murder?"

Austin went on full alert beside her. Mission accomplished. The boy was officially distracted from the subject of Mark Sampson.

Matt frowned. "The FBI forensics folks are certain from the angle of impact that Candace was pushed forcefully to have sustained her head injuries. But as for who did it, there's not much to go on."

"Are there any suspects?" Austin asked quickly.

Matt shrugged. "Since my Aunt Lydia was ruled out as a prime suspect, our best lead is whoever wrote those letters to Harold."

"What letters?" Austin asked ominously, looking pointedly at Silver.

She winced. "The threatening ones Dad got recently saying that all of the Rothchilds are going to die one by one."

Austin's jaw clenched. "That's the sort of thing guys like me need to know about, Silver. Have you got any more juicy little tidbits along those lines that you haven't shared with me yet?"

Like, oh, she was pregnant and he was guarding two lives, not one? Aloud, she replied, "Nope, that's it."

"You're positive?"

The significant undertone in his voice didn't escape her. What was he hinting at? Surely he didn't know…

She sighed. "Yes, I'm positive."

Thankfully, Matt laughed, breaking the tension between her and Austin. "You gotta be on your toes with these Rothchild women, buddy. They'll lead you on a merry chase."

Austin glanced down at her wryly. "So I've noticed."

She muttered in an undertone pitched for his ears alone, "Good thing you're not chasing me, then." It was a petty thing to say, but it really bugged her that he'd made such a point of telling her he had no intention of getting involved with her. It was apparently all well and good to have wild bunny sex with her but only as long as she knew up front that he was going back to his military life at the first possible opportunity.

He replied teasingly, "Don't knock it. You probably couldn't handle me, anyway."

Hah. She darned well could handle him! He'd loved it when she'd handled him last night, thank you very much. She stuck her tongue out at him and held out her empty glass. "Make yourself useful, and get me another club soda while I catch up with my sister."

Austin took her glass without comment, but he did cast a thoughtful look down at it and back up at her before he turned away. His being so observant might be a good thing when he was looking for bad guys, but it was a pain in the rear when he was nosing into her personal life.

"Wow, Silver. He's a hunk. Where can I get a bodyguard like that?"

"Hey," Matt protested. "What about me?"

Silver laughed along with her sister. It felt good to be getting along with her like this. For too long, she'd been at odds with Natalie. In retrospect, it had been mostly Candace leading the way with Natalie following her forceful twin's lead. Now that Candace was gone, Natalie seemed to have settled down considerably. Candace had always portrayed Nat as the instigator, but Silver had recently revised her opinion on the subject. Now that Natalie was operating on her own, it had become clear that Candace had been stirring the pot all along to sabotage Silver's career and reputation.

Of course, she'd long ago accepted her own part of the blame in letting Candace get away with it. Ever since they'd been children, she'd secretly wanted to be like her flamboyant sister, and it had been her enduring Achilles' heel. Candace had always been the center of attention and the center of the action. So cool. So hip. Funny how, even at the height of her own fame and popularity, she'd always felt like a fraud compared to Candace.

Maybe all that time she'd been chasing Candace's idea of the perfect life and not hers. In a flash of insight it occurred to her that maybe that was why Candace had always been so jealous and vindictive toward her. So, if being a rock star had been Candace's dream, why was *she* diving back into the pop music game again? Guilt over her sister's death, maybe?

She rolled the idea over in her head. *Nah.* She was sorry Candace was dead, but she didn't feel any lingering debts or regrets toward her.

Her hand crept to her as yet flat belly. If she'd learned nothing else from watching how Candace had lived, always hovering on the edge of broke, living off of nothing more than the notoriety of being a Rothchild, using and abusing everything and everyone around her, it was that she was not going to follow Candace down that path.

She'd do the shows at the Grand out of respect for the generous gift that they were. But that was where her obligation to Harold—or anyone else—it ended. She'd do the shows her way, with her music. She made a silent promise to herself. From here on out, her career—her *life*—would go forward strictly on her terms and no one else's.

"Earth to Silver, come in," a voice said laughingly nearby.

She looked up, startled, at her sister. "Sorry." She added quietly, "You look good, Nat. You seem at peace with yourself."

"I am. I wish you the same happiness I've found." She glanced adoringly at Matt.

Simultaneously, Silver and Natalie stepped forward and hugged each other. Silver couldn't remember the last time they'd been so close. It was a shame that it had taken Candace's death to finally bring them together like this.

They drew back, and awkwardness settled between them. There was so much to say, but Silver had no idea where or how to get started. Finally she asked, "How are Candace's boys? I keep meaning to drop by Jack's place and see them." Jack Cortland was Candace's ex-husband and the boys' father.

Natalie sighed. "They're confused. They don't understand why Mommy won't come play with them. But thankfully they're too young to really understand what happened. Maybe it was a blessing in disguise that she didn't spend all that much time with them."

Silver nodded on cue, but she made another silent vow. No way was her baby growing up with an absentee mother too caught up in partying and living large to spend time with him or her. She was going to change diapers and do 2 a.m. feedings and pace the floors with colic...the whole nine yards. She was going to be there for her baby. It was a tragedy that Candace's toddler boys would never know their mother—no matter how flawed and distant she might have been.

Before she could wax any more maudlin and start boo-hooing, Austin returned with her club soda. She sipped at it while Austin and Matt sorted out exactly what sort of military man Austin was and then made small talk about their favorite guns. She was saved from the technical details of some newfangled pistol that both men were excited over by the butler stepping into the billiard room to announce that dinner was served.

Rebecca, looking stunning in emerald satin next to Harold, said dramatically, "Oh dear. Conner's not back from the police station with the Tears of the Quetzal yet. But dinner mustn't get cold."

Harold solved her dilemma brusquely. "If he can't fetch a simple ring in two hours, that irresponsible boy can eat his supper cold."

Silver's mouth twitched. Conner was thirty-four years old and a highly regarded criminal attorney. Hardly a boy, and definitely not irresponsible. Of all her various Rothchild cousins, he was perhaps her favorite.

Austin murmured sotto voce in her ear, "You do realize I'm never going to get everyone in your family straight, don't you?"

Her pulse leapt at the intimacy of his nearness, familiar and protective at the same time. She was tempted to crawl inside his shirt then and there. Whatever woman this man eventually gave his heart to was going to be one lucky lady, indeed. She sighed. What she wouldn't give to be that woman. She'd never met another man even remotely like him.

"Never fear. I can barely keep them all straight, and I've lived with them for twenty years," she muttered back.

The smile he flashed her all but melted her shoes off her feet. Lord, that man was sexy. Sheesh. He had to stop doing that or she'd never make it through supper.

"Doing what?" he murmured as the family commenced heading toward the exit.

She jolted. Had she said that aloud? Apparently. In a millisecond, panic flashed through her head. Should she play it safe or throw caution to the wind? What the heck.

She replied under her breath. "You have to stop smiling at me. Just think how scandalized the family will be if I have to throw you down on the dining room table and have my way with you between the main course and dessert?"

A grin spread across his handsome face. "I dunno. They look like they could use some shaking up."

She suppressed a laugh. "Believe me. You don't want to be around when Harold gets wound up. His temper is legendary."

"Being ravished by you would be worth it."

Her jaw dropped.

Austin pasted on a bland look, offered her his elbow formally and proceeded to decorously lead her into the dining room. Not a single decorous thought rattled around in her head as they filed down the long hall.

The grandkids and nieces and nephews materialized noisily from upstairs, and the entire bunch trooped into the dining room.

Silver was pleased to see Austin's place card beside hers. She started to reach for her chair but caught the glare Austin threw her and let her hands drop. As he stepped forward to pull it out for her, his hand came to rest on the small of her back, a fraction lower than was polite. His fingertips hovered just above the crevice of her buttocks, scorching her through the thin silk of her dress.

As she sank into her chair, grateful that her legs hadn't given out before she was seated, her father glanced down the long table and made eye contact with her. She smiled carefully, doing her darnedest to hide just how flustered she was.

No matter how hard she tried to stay mad at Austin for announcing that he would eventually leave her, she couldn't do it. His mere touch had her all but hyperventilating with lust. She glanced sideways at him as he took his place beside her.

A private smile for her glowed in his rich, green eyes as he glanced back at her. Almost as if he knew and relished the effect he had on her.

Oh, yes. A girl could definitely get used to having a man like him around. Too bad that was the one thing he'd promised he couldn't give her. The whole falling for someone just in time to get dumped bit sucked rocks. And she ought to know. She was the queen of getting dumped.

She made it through the salad course okay, but when the butler served her a plate of lamb chops, quivering green mint jelly and baby vegetables smothered in some kind of sauce, her stomach gave an ominous heave. She picked up her knife and fork and commenced picking at the sumptuous meal in a halfhearted effort to look like she was actually eating the too-rich food.

Her father boomed from the end of the table, "So, Silver, I hear you visited the Grand Theater today."

Oh, God. What else had he heard? Had someone felt obliged to tell him about her fainting episode? The last thing she needed was for him to decide she wasn't up to doing a show. She gulped and replied, "Uh, that's right. I love the improvements you've made to the stage. The digital lighting system is incredible."

"It ought to be. It cost me a bloody fortune. Saul said you ran through a few of your old tunes. How did that go?"

With an apologetic glance at Austin, Silver opened her mouth to utter a bald-faced lie, but a commotion in the doorway distracted everyone. Her cousin, Conner, burst into the room like a minor tornado.

"It was stolen! Right out of the police evidence locker! The Tears of the Quetzal!"

Silver's jaw dropped as her gaze skittered to her father. The Tears of the Quetzal was Harold's pride and joy. Her father swelled up like an angry puffer fish before he finally bellowed, "Whaaat?"

Conner continued, agitated, "They said a man in a police uniform signed it out of the evidence locker earlier today. It was signed back in just a few minutes before I got there to pick it up. Except a paste copy got left in its place."

Silver started as Conner dropped a heavy ring onto the table in front of Harold. Her father picked it up and examined it closely.

Conner went on. "They're reviewing the security videos to see if they can get an image of the guy. But it's gone. The Tears of the Quetzal has been stolen *again*."

Harold swore violently and flung the piece of jewelry the length of the dining room. Thankfully, his aim was true and he didn't bean any of the children seated at the far end of the table with it. The heavy ring slammed into a delicate porcelain vase, which toppled off the buffet and crashed to the floor, exploding into a hundred pieces.

Heavy silence fell over the room.

Rebecca finally broke the frozen vignette, suggesting in a soothing voice, "Why don't we retire to the library and discuss this more calmly."

Silver was surprised. Normally, Rebecca wasn't exactly the Rothchild she'd expect to be a pillar of strength in a crisis. But her stepmother's uncharacteristic calm seemed to penetrate Harold's rage, and he simmered down enough to shove back his chair and storm out of the room. Conner followed on Harold's heels, while the others trickled out more reluctantly. Austin gestured her subtly to remain seated until most of the others had left the room. As a result, the two of them were the last to leave.

Austin paused beside the shattered vase, bending down and scooping up the fake ring out of the shards of porcelain. "How did Harold recognize that this is a copy?"

"I don't know. Lemme see."

He handed her the piece, which had similar heft and weight to the original. The chameleon stone was priceless, shifting in color from purple to green and back again based on its temperature. It was the largest of its type in the world, a one-of-a-kind piece. She turned the stone, studying as it threw off the same peculiar lavender light of the original diamond.

"It's really quite a good copy. It captures the resting color of the original to a tee."

"Resting color?"

"Yes. When this stone is heated up, it turns a brilliant green for several hours. In that state, it's slightly darker than a typical emerald, close to…say…a green tourmaline in color. They're ferociously rare. Hence their value."

"And hence the reason it was stolen, I gather?"

She shrugged. "I don't know why someone would steal it. The stone's so unique you'd have a heck of a time fencing it without getting caught. And I can't imagine too many collectors wanting to risk the wrath of Harold Rothchild to possess the thing for themselves. If Dad ever found out anyone had it…"

Austin nodded and finished for her. "They'd wish they'd never laid eyes on the rock. Never steal from a man with the means and capacity to make you pay for it in blood."

"You've got it." She slipped the ring on and held it out to study it at arm's length. She frowned at a faint roughness against her flesh. She took it off to peer inside the band. "See this jeweler's mark inside the band? The original's band is completely smooth and has no markings inside it."

Examining the jeweler's mark closely, Austin murmured, "Do you know if Harold had a copy made of the ring at some point?"

She nodded. "I believe there is one. My father kept the original under lock and key, refusing any of us access to it."

"How come?" he asked curiously.

She rolled her eyes. "He believes there's some crazy curse attached to it."

"Excuse me?" he asked, his right eyebrow creeping up.

"According to Mayan legend, the Tears of the Quetzal is supposed to bring true love to anyone who possesses it."

"Doesn't sound like much of a curse to me," he mused wryly.

"There's more to it than that," Silver explained. "You see, if the ring falls into the wrong hands, misfortune is sure to follow." She took a deep breath. "Two months ago Candace was wearing the Tears when she was killed. The killer stole it." She sighed. "So of course my father now believes that the curse came true."

Austin stared at her, suddenly comprehending. "So that's why your family suspected right away that she was murdered. Let me guess. You've kept this theft from the press to help the police investigation, too?"

She nodded. "But I can't imagine Harold cooperating too much more now that the police have lost the ring again. He's going to have a stroke if the police don't get it back. He went completely nuts when it was stolen the first time. When he wasn't ranting about catching Candace's killer, he was raving about getting the diamond back."

Austin peered inside the ring's band again, before passing it back to Silver. "Whoever made this fake sure knew what they were doing. Is this perchance the copy your father had made?"

"I don't know. You'd have to ask Rebecca. I expect the copy would be in her jewelry box, or maybe in the safe upstairs." She studied the stone again. "It really is a remarkable copy. If all of the Rothchilds hadn't grown up knowing every intricate detail about the original ring, we wouldn't have known the difference."

"That's probably what the thief was counting on," he said. "He probably won't expect the copy to be discovered for several days at a minimum, which would give him plenty of time to get away with the real one."

She shivered. "I guess we're not dealing with your run-of-the-mill jewel thief."

"You've got that right." Austin's eyes darkened. "Call me paranoid, but the timing of the murder, theft and that threatening letter your father got seem suspicious to me. There's no doubt in my mind that someone's out to get ole Harold."

"But why do you believe that he's the specific target?"

Austin stared down at her grimly. "Correct me if I'm wrong, but wouldn't his daughter and this fabled diamond be two of his greatest treasures?"

She gulped, realizing where his logic was leading. "You think Candace's death and the theft of the diamond were acts of vengeance against my father?"

Austin shrugged. "Or acts of rage." He escorted her out of the dining room and into the hallway where Natalie and Matt, last in the line of family members, were just disappearing into the library. He looked down at her thoughtfully. "Why did you mention vengeance specifically?"

"The letters said the writer was going to get even with the Rothchilds for wronging his family."

He nodded slowly. "It fits. And now, according to our lunatic killer's message in your dressing room, you're next on the list of precious things he's planning to take from Harold."

The thought that Austin was right shuddered through her.

"Did you have to remind me? Now I'll never get to sleep tonight!"

His mouth quirked into that boyish smile that made her toes want to wiggle. "One of the rules in my unit is that if you cause a problem, you're in charge of fixing it. I guess I'll have to help you get to sleep tonight, then."

Okay, that tied her toes right up in tight little knots of antici-pation. She could *so* go for more of the same from last night. She could go for more of that every night for a long time to come. But it wasn't in the cards for her. He was leaving, and she'd be an idiot to get more attached to him than she already was. As it was, she couldn't imagine how empty her life was going to seem without him at her side around the clock.

Reluctantly, she replied, "Thanks, but no thanks."

The light left his gaze abruptly. She physically felt his emo-tional withdrawal from her, as sharp as a knife to her own gut.

She was *such* an idiot. She should've thought before she blurted out a flat refusal of his offer. He deserved an explanation at the least, but she couldn't exactly give him one in front of her assembled family. She tried to stop in the hall where they still had a modicum of privacy. Tried to tell him why she was turning him down. But he put a firm hand in the middle of her back and bodily propelled her forward. Obviously, the man didn't want to talk.

With her heels all but skidding along the marble floor, they rounded the corner into the library, a vaulted space filled with carved stone and floor-to-ceiling shelves of leather-bound books no one had ever read. Austin might be stronger than her, darn it, but he wasn't more stubborn. She owed him an explanation, and he was going to get it whether he wanted it or not. Now.

"Austin—"

"Not now."

"But—"

"No." She had no idea how he managed to make a single whispered syllable into a sharp command she had no desire to disobey.

Irritated enough to draw a little blood, she muttered, "Fine. Be that way. But if Mark found out we spent another night together, he'd kill you."

Austin sighed as if he knew it for the taunt it was and finally looked down fully at her. "And how would he find out? I bloody well wouldn't tell him. I told you. Your secrets are safe with me. Would *you* tell him about us?"

Her female instincts fired strong and clear. He was testing her. Checking to see if she'd slept with him because she liked him or just to get Mark's goat. So Austin was human after all. Sometimes she wondered.

In response to his question, she snorted. "Why would I say anything to Mark about us? It's none of his business. Besides, I'm not in the habit of waving red flags in front of bulls. His temper scares me."

Austin stopped dead in his tracks. He stared down at her in what she would swear was satisfaction tinged with relief.

Then he leaned in so close that her breath caught in her throat and he whispered in her ear, "Don't worry anymore about Mark blowing up. If Bubba ever tries to tangle with you again, he'll have me to answer to. And I promise you, he'll be so dead so fast he'll never know what hit him."

The sexy heat of his breath on her skin distracted her so completely that she barely registered his words. But then she jerked back, stunned by the casual threat in Austin's voice. "You can't kill him!"

Austin straightened up, a fake smile pasted on his face as a few heads turned their way. Behind it he growled, "Why the hell not? I've never met a guy more deserving, if for no other reason than the good of the human gene pool."

Panic climbed the walls of her stomach. "I'm serious, Austin. Don't you hurt him. I need him—" She broke off, appalled at what she'd almost revealed.

"What the hell for?" Austin burst out, abruptly drawing the attention of the rest of her family.

"Hush," she muttered urgently. "Can we talk about this later? *Not* here?"

"Promise?"

"Sure. I promise. Just *please* smile nicely and change the subject."

"All right." He added darkly under his breath, "But I'm holding you to that."

The next hour was a trial, listening to her father bluster about what he planned to do if he ever caught up with the bastard who'd stolen the Tears of the Quetzal not once but twice.

Austin and Matt agreed that the thief in both cases was probably the same guy. And that idea made her intensely nervous. What thief robbed the same victim twice? That spoke of the rage and vengeance Austin had mentioned earlier. Surely, any sane thief would cut his losses and run after losing the ring the first time.

Thankfully, Austin didn't bring up the scrawled message on her dressing room mirror, and word of it seemed—miraculously—not to have reached Harold's ears yet. Of course, it was only a matter of time before her father found out about it from the hotel security staff and had a conniption. She'd just have to convince him that Austin was good enough at his job so she could go on with her show anyway. Piece of cake. *Not.*

"Will Harold be mad if we slip out of here early?" Austin murmured.

Gratitude flooded through her. He seemed to anticipate her needs before she was hardly aware of them, herself. "He's so upset by the theft, he'll hardly notice. Let me just go say goodbye. I'll claim that I have to get up early to rehearse."

"Early rehearsal. Got it."

She grinned up at him as his green eyes twinkled down at her. "I don't make a habit of lying, I'll have you know. But sometimes with Harold, it's so much less complicated to just gloss things over a little."

"I completely understand. Go do your thing with Daddy. I want to have a quick word with Rebecca. And Matt."

It felt weird to step away from Austin. Like part of her was suddenly missing. She'd become so accustomed to his big, safe presence plastered to her side that she felt naked without him. How was she going to manage without him once he went back to whatever war zone he'd come from? The thought was too awful to contemplate. She forcefully pushed it out of her mind.

And then Harold was looming before her, still blustering and cranky.

Taking a cue from her surprisingly adept stepmother as she hugged him goodbye, she murmured sweetly, "Thanks for arranging to have Austin guard me, Daddy. He's wonderful. You're the best."

Harold fussed and acted gruff, but she could tell he was pleased. Hmm. Who'd have guessed that he would be susceptible to feminine flattery? Apparently, old dogs could learn new tricks after all. Or at least they could when a madman was threatening them and all they held dear. But then she caught the calculating gleam in Harold's eye as he glanced back and forth between her and Austin.

No. He wouldn't.

He would.

Could he really be scheming to throw her and Austin together? The idea sent a jolt of exultation through her.

Whoa, there. No Silver and Austin sitting in a tree, K-I-S-S-I-N-G. Austin had made it perfectly clear he wanted nothing to do with a relationship with her.

But dang, it would be nice if he were interested in her. He was a heck of a catch, the kind of man she could see herself being happy with forever.

Sighing, she turned to join him. And her pulse raced. Austin was looking straight at her. Studying her intently, in fact. Her skin warmed and her insides felt mushy all of a sudden. And what was that look in his eyes? Was that actually a spark of desire, calculation even, that she'd glimpsed before he carefully masked his expression?

Could it be?

Was it possible?

No way.

Were Harold and Austin in cahoots to tear her away from Mark? If so, what did that say about the night she'd spent with Austin?

Chapter 11

Austin watched Silver in the shadows of the limousine's interior. An evening with her family had been good for her. She seemed more relaxed, more open, in spite of the drama over the stolen ring. The Rothchilds hadn't been what he'd expected. He hadn't expected them to be that…nice…in the midst of the opulence they lived in. Silver suddenly seemed much more like a regular girl to him. Approachable. Hell, touchable. His life would've been a whole lot less complicated if the Rothchilds were snooty, pretentious socialites and Silver one of them. But no such luck.

At least he'd had a stroke of luck with Rebecca. Sure enough, her paste copy of the Tears of the Quetzal had disappeared not long before Candace's murder. She hadn't thought anything of it when it came up missing; apparently the Rothchild jewelry collection was extensive, and it wasn't uncommon for a piece to be removed from the safe for cleaning or appraisal. It did explain how Candace's appropriation of the original was spotted so quickly, however. With both pieces gone, their absence was perfectly obvious.

And wasn't that an interesting little tidbit about Candace? Not too many women would waltz into their father's safe and help themselves to a priceless ring. Ballsy woman. Rule breaker. Make that a dead rule breaker.

When he'd asked Rebecca about where and when the copy of the ring had been made, he'd struck out. It predated her marriage to Harold, and that was all Rebecca could tell him about it. At least he'd made out the name of the jeweler stamped inside the band. Delvecchio's. If he was lucky, that would turn out to be a local outfit. And just maybe the thief had inquired about the Tears of the Quetzal there.

He knocked on the blacked-out glass partition behind his head and it lowered immediately. "How long until we reach the Grand?"

"Fifteen minutes, sir."

"Thanks. And don't sir, me. I'm hired help, too."

The driver grinned at him, and the partition started back up.

"Wait!" Silver called out, startling Austin. "Turn up the radio!"

The driver did as she asked, and she closed her eyes, listening intently to the now blaring country music tune.

Austin didn't recognize the song. Unfortunately, the remote corners of Afghanistan didn't offer much by way of American country music radio stations. Silver began to hum and then to sing along, her eyes still closed. As she gained confidence with the tune, her voice grew in strength and volume. She began ad-libbing harmonies in a pure, clear tone that soared above the melody, weaving in and around the male artist's voice as seamlessly as if the song had been meant to be recorded that way.

Austin was stunned. He'd known she was a good singer, but he had no idea how good until hearing her in person like this. She didn't sound the slightest bit like the pop star he knew her to be. Gone was the street slang, the riffs, the urban rasp. Her voice seemed tailor-made for this unapologetically mournful ballad of love and loss.

The song ended, and her singing trailed away to humming and then to silence. Her eyes fluttered open and she didn't look like she knew exactly where she was. The glass quietly slid closed, and they were alone again.

"Wow," he said in awe. "That was gorgeous. You ought to record a duet with whoever was singing on the radio."

She smiled ruefully. "Nobody who listens to country music has the faintest idea who I am. Besides, a star that big would never record with me."

"Methinks you underestimate how famous you were in your day."

She shrugged. "'Were' being the operative word. The music business moves fast. You're last week's news in a year or two. I've been out of the game for a lifetime."

"All the more reason you could get away with going in a new direction," he countered.

She laughed lightly. "I can't exactly picture myself prancing around the Grand Ole Opry mostly naked, doing vulgar hip thrusts all over the stage."

"I dunno. It worked pretty well for Elvis. Although the white jumpsuits would be a radical change of image for you. But you do sound like you were born to sing love songs to a twangy guitar in the back of a pickup truck."

"I don't even own a pair of cowboy boots!"

"We're in Nevada for God's sake. A girl has to be able to get a decent pair of boots around here, somewhere. And aren't we going shopping in the morning anyway?"

She shook a playful finger at him. "You're a bad influence, Austin Dearing. My record label and Saul would kill me if I did something that different. My fans wouldn't stand for it, either."

"I'm not so sure of that. They're all seven years older, too. They've gotten married and started having kids and are holding down mortgages and real jobs, now. You might be surprised at the kind of music they're listening to these days."

"Good grief, you make me sound ready for the Lawrence Welk show."

He laughed. "Hardly. I'm just saying I think you could get away with growing up. Your fans have."

She studied him intently, as if the concept were intriguing.

And then it dawned on him what he'd just said. He'd just made another plastic pop star gaff. "Hey, I'm sorry. I didn't mean that the way it came out. You're plenty grown up. I was talking purely about your performing image."

She nodded. "I caught that. But thanks for clarifying. Most thirty-year-old women wouldn't be too thrilled at being told to grow up."

He huffed. "I'm a man of action, not words."

One of her graceful eyebrows arched humorously. "I'm not so sure about that. I haven't gotten all that much action out of you today."

His jaw dropped for a moment before he realized she was intentionally baiting him, then his gaze narrowed threateningly. "You're not challenging my manhood, are you?"

"If the shoe fits…"

"You are a brave woman. Or else a very foolish one."

She waved a breezy hand at him. "I dare say I'm the latter."

Whether he slid forward off his seat first or she slid off hers first, he couldn't rightly say. But before he knew it, they'd met in the middle of the cavernous vehicle on their knees—hands plunging into each other's hair and tearing at each other's clothes, heads tilting for a voracious kiss.

Damn, he couldn't get enough of this woman. His body was already hard and ready. Of course, it didn't hurt that she was crawling all over him like she couldn't get enough of him, either. One of her legs wrapped around his waist, and he growled deep in his throat as her heated core scalded him through his slacks. The smell of her desire, spicy and sweet filled his nostrils, and then her hands slipped around his waist, joining her leg in urging him closer.

"Honey, we're in a car…"

"You've been rolling around on floors with me ever since we met," she murmured back, laughing. "You gonna do something about it or are you wimping out on me?"

He conceded reluctantly. "I've never met another woman who'd bait a man capable of the things I'm capable of like you do."

"I'm not afraid of you," she laughed. But then she lifted her mouth away from his to gaze up at him seriously in what could only be interpreted as adoration. "Seriously. I've never felt as safe as when I'm with you. I love that about you."

He was such a sucker for those soulful eyes of hers. One look like that from them and he was putty in her hands. "The floor, huh?"

Her mouth curved into a vixen's smile. "Actually, I was thinking more in terms of you on the floor and me on you."

"Come here, baby. Show me what you had in mind."

He carried her down to the carpet with him, stripping her out of her panties as he went. He guided her knee across him, relishing the sight of her panting lightly over him, her eyes glowing with desire.

But then she took over, unzipping his pants and catching his flesh as it sprang forth from its confinement. Her eyes took on a look of sleepy anticipation that all but undid him. Smiling down at him, she stroked him into a frenzy of red-hued lust that all but drove him out of his mind. Brazen and beautiful, sexy and innocent all at once, she literally stole his breath away.

As she continued squeezing and stroking him, his pleasure turned to torture of the best possible kind. Gritting his teeth, he hung onto control by the most fragile of threads. And then he begged. Shamelessly. Laughing, she positioned herself over him, her moist heat lapping at the tip of his throbbing flesh.

In a blinding and truly painful burst of belated rational thought, he swore violently under his breath.

"What?" she asked, alarmed.

"I don't have any protection with me."

She laughed. "Not to worry. I've got the birth control angle completely covered. You don't have any diseases, do you?"

"After two years in the field without a woman? Nope. You?"

"I don't get enough action these days for it to be an issue, but no, I just had a physical. I'm good."

And with that, she slid him home. He gasped as sensation exploded all through him. He released his breath on a long, low groan of pleasure. Her dress pooled around them as she began to rock, a slow lullaby at first, building gradually to a frenzied ride that had her clapping both of her hands over her mouth to muffle the cries.

He grabbed onto her hips and hung on for dear life, thrusting helplessly into her, his body desperate to touch the very core of her. She met every thrust with one of her own, her internal muscles gripping him until he thought he was going to die from the pleasure of it. And when his release came upon him, her body milked him relentlessly, drawing out the exquisite agony of bliss until he actually did black out for an instant.

And then light and heat…and joy…came crashing back in on him all in a rush that was almost too much to stand—almost better than the orgasm itself.

Damn, that woman was something else.

She lay collapsed on his chest, breathing hard, her delicate skin flushed with sex and bursting pleasure, a smile of satiation radiant on her face. *And he'd put it there.* Soul-deep satisfaction flowed up from someplace deep within him, filling him with a sense of undeniable *rightness*. No doubt about it. She was The One.

She murmured lazily, "Am I squishing you?"

Hardly. He opened his mouth to tease her about weighing a ton, but the words died in his throat as her cell phone trilled in her purse.

Both of them went tense.

It would be just like Sampson to ruin this moment of delicious afterglow for them.

Silver sighed reluctantly and sat up. She swung her leg over his hips and went digging for her phone in her purse.

Reluctantly he sat up, setting his clothes to rights. He lounged back, still sitting on the floor, and watched her with hooded eyes. How was it that he felt like he was cheating on Mark Sampson with the guy's girl? Silver had made it crystal clear that whatever was between her and Mark wasn't meaningful to her.

And Lord knew, she couldn't keep her hands off him any more than he could keep his hands off of her.

Sampson was a pig and treated Silver like dirt. The guy didn't deserve to wipe her shoes, let alone date her. Austin swore under his breath. To hell with scruples and keeping his hands off another man's woman. Any man who treated his woman that lousy deserved to lose her.

"Hello?" Silver all but whispered into the phone. A pause, then her voice rose to a normal tone. "Oh. Hi, Conner. Is there news on the ring?"

She listened for a minute, a frown gathering steam on her brow the longer he talked. Finally she replied tartly, "Just because I used to hang out with Darla St. Giles doesn't mean I still do. In case you haven't noticed, Conner, I haven't been arrested or peeled off a sidewalk drunk off my butt in years." She shook her head. "Candace and Darla stayed close, but not me. I haven't even spoken to Darla for a couple of years."

Another silence while Conner spoke, followed by a sigh out of Silver. "Last I knew, she lived over on the west side of town in the Mountain View Villas. Number 24."

Conner got off the phone fast after that, and Silver disconnected the call pensively.

"Everything okay?" Austin asked.

"I don't know. Conner thought he saw an old acquaintance of mine, Darla St. Giles, hanging out across the street from the police station when he came out of it. He thinks she might know something about the theft of the Tears of the Quetzal. He wanted to know where she lives."

Austin nodded, immensely relieved that the call hadn't had

anything to do with Sampson. He held out his hand. "May I have your phone for a minute?"

She passed it to him and he flipped it open and started rapidly pushing buttons.

"What are you doing to my phone?"

He looked up grimly. "I'm blocking Sampson's phone number."

Her eyebrows shot up. "Why?"

"So I don't have to sit through you talking to him." And so he didn't have to see that haunted look on her face every time her damn phone rang. Sampson was holding something over her as sure as the sun rose and set. The trick with blackmail victims was to get them to realize that no exposed truth was as bad as a secret eating out their guts.

Really. How bad could it be? Some pretty nasty things had been revealed about her in the tabloids over the years, and he was still crazy for her. In his line of work, he saw some seriously eyebrow-raising stuff. He was damned hard to shock. Now he just had to convince her of that.

The limo turned into the private, underground entrance to the Grand and commenced winding down the ramp. He couldn't make out her expression in the sudden dark. First order of business—get her to admit that Sampson was blackmailing her. "Tell me what you see in him. Please," he said quietly. "I'm completely at a loss to explain you two."

She shook her head. "I can't."

"Can't because you don't know yourself, or won't because there's no good reason for it?"

"Oh, there's an excellent reason for it. It's just none of your business."

He sat back, frowning. It wasn't exactly an admission that she was being blackmailed, but he could work with the tiny opening she'd given him.

As the limo pulled to a smooth stop, he said, "Honey, everything about you is my business. There's no corner of your life that isn't my business if you expect me to keep you alive. I've already told you I'll keep your deepest, darkest secrets, and I mean it. But you can't hold out on me if you expect me to do my job."

Looking dismayed, she stared him down, finally breaking the stalemate by murmuring, "Aren't you supposed to get out of the car first?"

Damn. He'd almost had her there. Scowling, he climbed out of the vehicle and looked around carefully. Just because he was frustrated didn't mean he got to be sloppy or lazy. After trading nods with the hotel security man standing at the hotel door, Austin spoke over his shoulder. "It's clear, Silver. You can come out."

She stepped out of the limo lightly, her movements elegant. Classy. No sign of their recent sex or their more recent conversation showed on her face. She merely said politely, "Thank you, Austin."

They walked inside, where another security man held an elevator door open for them. Austin whisked her into the small space and scanned his room card. The elevator jumped upward into the night. What the hell. Time to go for the jugular.

"What's Sampson got on you, Silver? The guy's got to be blackmailing you because there's no way you would voluntarily spend two minutes in the same room with him otherwise."

She stared blankly at him, her face a perfect mask that revealed nothing.

"Talk to me. I can help you, Silver."

A sardonic smile finally flitted across her features. "You can't fix everything, Austin."

"Maybe not, but I can damn well try. And I do succeed a whole lot more often than I fail."

She replied wistfully, "That must be a nice way to live life. I have a knack for screwing up most of the things I try."

"That's ridiculous. You had a massively successful career once, and you will again. You have a terrific family, and you're a kind and decent person. I'd say you've gotten more right than most people manage to."

She shrugged as the door slid open. He stepped out, did his security thing and walked her down to his suite. They stepped inside and he froze, his hand on the light switch. Silver bumped into him from behind.

"What?" she breathed. "What's wrong?"

"Someone's been in here."

"Of course someone has. This is a hotel. The cleaning staff goes in and out of all the rooms."

His instinct said it was something else. He pushed her back into the hall and bit out, "Stay here unless that elevator door opens. In that case, dive into the suite and close and lock the door as fast as you can." God, he wished he weren't working this detail solo. He could really use a couple more guys to cover her from an attack coming down the hall while he cleared this place.

Cautiously, he flipped on the lights and spun inside low and fast. He took a quick look around. No one moved. He practically sprinted around the room, checking in closets, under the bar and behind the sofas. A quick check of the bedrooms and bathrooms, a quick circuit around the pool and then back to the front door.

"Okay, you can come in." He all but ripped her arm off pulling her into the room, but he was tense as hell at leaving her outside alone like that. "I've got to show you some self-defense moves," he muttered. "Soon."

"You can relax, now, Austin. We're in your room safe and sound, and no one tried to kill me." She walked farther into the living room. "Oooh, look! Flowers!"

He hadn't noticed the elaborate arrangement other than to note that nobody had been hiding behind it when he swept the room.

She went over and pulled out the small white envelope tucked under a lily the size of his palm. "Let's see who it's from." She opened the envelope, then muffled a cry as she dropped the card onto the table.

He darted forward, scooping up the card in the same movement that wrapped her in his arms protectively.

Over her shoulder, he flipped the card over and read the scrawled words, "I'm coming for her. You can't keep her safe from me."

He swore foully and, keeping Silver tucked under his arm, yanked out his cell phone. He punched out the number of the florist printed on the bottom of the card, but there was no answer. He'd have to wait until morning to find out what they could tell him about who'd sent these flowers. He studied the card more closely. The neat handwriting looked exceedingly feminine. Either Silver's stalker was female, or most likely, a clerk at the florist's shop had written the note for a phone-in client.

"Why is this happening to me?" she wailed into his chest.

"Because you had the misfortune of becoming a Rothchild. Just remember, all this stuff seems aimed at Harold. Whoever's doing it hates him, not you. It's nothing personal."

"Gee. That's comforting."

"Believe me, it's better than someone having a vendetta against you directly."

Not that hearing something like that did a damned bit of good to stop her from shaking like a leaf in his arms. He suggested gently, "Why don't you go take a nice hot bath while I make a few phone calls?"

"To whom?"

"The police for one. The bell captain's station for another. Maybe they can tell me something about who delivered these flowers. It's a long shot, but you never know."

"Could you keep the hotel staff out of it? Daddy hears about everything that's going on around here, and if he knew I was getting these threats, he'd cancel my show for sure."

Austin grunted. "It's not like it's any surprise to Harold that someone's gunning for you, darlin'."

"Why do you say that? You yourself said he believes the shooting in the lobby yesterday was the random act of a deranged gambler."

His reply was somber. "I'm here with you, aren't I?"

She studied him a long time. "Are you really as good as you say you are?"

He looked her dead in the eye. "I'm the very best there is, and no amount of modesty is going to make that any less true. Your father knew exactly the caliber of bodyguard he was getting when he hired me. Believe me, with what I charge for civilian jobs, he knows he's paying for the best of the best."

He hated to be the one to put that haunted look back in her eyes after she'd finally lost it. But there it was again, and it was all his fault. "Go run yourself that bath. I've got your back, honey. You're safe."

"Keep telling me that, and maybe in a decade or so I'll believe you."

That was sounding better and better to him. The more time he spent with her, the more tempting she was. Tempting enough to pull him out of the field, though? Away from his men? His mission? His duty?

Twenty-four hours ago, he'd have said there wasn't a chance she'd manage that. But now? Guns or the girl? The scales looked pretty even from where he stood.

He waited until she'd retreated to the master bath to go for a swim in the giant tub there, and then he made his calls. As he'd expected, the bell captain said a local delivery service had dropped off the flowers using its usual delivery driver. The stalker was careful to cover his tracks. Which meant the flowers were no doubt going to turn out to be a dead end.

And that made him jumpy. Thwarting a psycho killer was one thing. Thwarting a *smart* psycho killer was another entirely.

Following his earlier hunch, he fished the Las Vegas yellow pages out of a desk drawer. No listing for a Delvecchio's Jewelers.

He looked up other jewelers who advertised making paste replicas of jewelry. The first store didn't answer, nor the second. But a man at the third store did. It turned out this very store, now part of a national chain, used to be known as Delvecchio's. When Mr. Delvecchio passed away a few years back, his widow had sold the place. Hot damn.

Even better, the clerk remembered someone coming into the store recently and asking about a copy of a big purple diamond. The clerk didn't know the name of the customer, but maybe the store's goldsmith would know it. He'd be in tomorrow morning. Bingo. Not a home run, but it was a lead. At a minimum, he ought to be able to get some sort of general physical description of the suspect.

Pleased, Austin hung up the phone. And now, to go extract from Silver whatever secret Sampson was using to force her to pretend to be his girlfriend. She wasn't avoiding him this time. He was going to get answers out of her and get to the bottom of whatever was going on between them, and that was that.

The water had turned off a while ago. She ought to be dressed by now. He tested the doorknob to the master suite, and it was unlocked. Perfect. He took a deep breath. Here went nothing. Mentally girded for battle, he turned the knob and stepped inside.

Curled up in a shaft of moonlight like a contented kitten, Silver lay sleeping in the middle of his bed. He swore under his breath.

He moved quietly over to her side to look down at her. Her beauty stole his breath clean away. She was one of those women whom it was hard to believe really looked like she did until you got close to her and saw her like this, with no makeup, no fancy hairdo, no artifice. Just the pure, lovely lines of her face kissed by moonbeams.

As beautiful as she was, lying there, disappointment coursed through him. He really was ready to get to the bottom of this mystery with her.

Man, she'd crashed fast. Poor kid must be exhausted after all the morning's excitement and then facing dinner in the lion's den. Except she was young and healthy…the day hadn't been that strenuous. Unless she was finally sleeping well after days or weeks of sleeping poorly. Sampson really did deserve to be run over by a locomotive or two.

Tomorrow.

Come hell or high water, Silver would tell him what was going on tomorrow.

Chapter 12

Silver was in heaven as she walked down the sidewalk. She was out of the hotel, she was going shopping and best of all, she was with Austin. It was a beautiful, cool morning, likely the last one of the year before the furnace-heat of summer packed in for the next four months. She hadn't felt sick at breakfast and had chowed down a substantial chunk of Austin's omelet, which was a relief.

He'd tried to bring up Mark, but she'd deflected him by gulping down a glass of orange juice, grabbing her purse and announcing that it was time to go. No matter that he was sulking now. Austin could get over it. It was too gorgeous a day to spoil it by thinking about Mark.

And then there was the shopping. She had the perfect excuse to buy a whole new wardrobe—her upcoming show and renewed public image—and she got to go shopping for it with a gorgeous hunk who couldn't take his eyes off her. Oh sure, Austin's assessing gaze moved all over the place like it always did, but every time she stepped out of a dressing room to model something new, his gaze snapped to her and he drank in the sight of her hungrily. It was sweet balm for a girl's ego.

"What do you think of this one, Austin? Is it country enough for you?"

He frowned. "You're actually planning to pay for a pair of jeans that beat up? Those have more holes than cloth."

"Aren't they great?"

He studied her legs intently. "Turn around. Let me see what they do for your caboose."

She turned around, the part in question burning at the idea of him blatantly ogling it. She seriously hoped he liked what he saw. All those hours at the gym had to be good for something, after all.

"Buy them," he said decisively. "But lose that shirt. I like the white one you had on two shirts ago better. It's sexier."

The shirt he liked was a sheer cotton knit so fine you could all but see through it. It buttoned up to a high collar but then fell in soft, figure flattering drapes. Now that he mentioned it, the shirt's very demureness had added to its overall sexiness. It was more understated than she was used to but with the right belt, and paired with these edgy jeans…

She nodded to the clerk who scurried off to fetch the shirt in question out of the reject pile.

Silver studied Austin curiously. "Any other recommendations, oh great guru of fashion?"

He shrugged. "I'm only the bag-schlepping guy today."

"And a fine job you're doing hauling around my bags, too," she laughed. "But you are a guy. You know what looks good on a woman, right?"

One corner of his mouth turned up. "I know what looks good on you."

"Do tell."

She listened in amusement and growing respect as he shredded her fashion choices with painfully accurate comments about what looked good—and not good—on her and why. Before he was done, she'd exchanged nearly half of her original choices for other ones. It wasn't that she blindly bought what he told her to. It was the fact that he made such sensible arguments for what complimented her and what fit the image of a hip, but definitely grown up, star.

At the end of the spree, she stood back and took a hard look at the hanging rack of clothes that had passed muster with him. She had to admit that he'd done well. She'd wear anything on that rack with pride and know she looked not only hot in it but also mature. Chic. That was the difference. She'd tried to duplicate her pop-star, early twenties clothes, and he'd chosen things fitting not for a girl but for a woman. A sexy one, thankfully.

"You know, Austin, if you ever get tired of throwing yourself in front of bullets, you'd make a fine fashion stylist."

He laughed heartily at that. "The only fashion I can fit folks out in is the latest bulletproof vest."

"You did great with me."

He shrugged. "That's different. I've made a thorough study of your body, and I happen to give a damn about how you look."

That made her stare. "Why?"

A hint of red climbed his neck. He harrumphed uncomfortably before finally coming back with, "Hey, I have a rep to maintain. Any woman I'm seen with in public, client or otherwise, has to uphold my usual standards."

She rolled her eyes, amused. "That is such a lie. But I'm having fun and you're behaving nicely for a man dragged along on a shopping trip, so I'll let you off the hook this time."

He rolled his eyes back at her as she pulled out her wallet to pay for her latest additions to the haul.

She vaguely heard some sort of commotion behind her and felt Austin slip into place at her back as she signed the credit card receipt. As the clerk separated the copies and thanked her profusely for the business, Silver murmured without turning around, "Everything okay back there?"

"Looks like we've been spotted. Either that or a whole bunch of skanky guys with cameras are out for a morning stroll and just happen to be mobbing the sidewalk in front of this store."

She peeked around him. "What do they want with me today? I'm just out shopping for some clothes. That's hardly tabloid-worthy news." She punctuated her disgust with a muttered oath.

He glanced back at her, grinning. "I didn't know you knew that word. Shame on you, Miss Rothchild."

"I know worse words, and they all apply to that pack of hyenas out there." She looked over at the clerk. "Is there a back way out of here?"

"No, I'm sorry. That's the only exit."

"Great," she muttered. "Looks like we get to go swimming with the sharks."

"How aggressive do you want me to be with these guys?" Austin asked.

"What are the options?"

"We can pose nicely and let them have their pictures, then we invite them to let us through, so we can clear out as quickly as we can. Then there's the jacket-over-your-head, no-pictures-today-please approach. Which gets a picture of you with your coat over your head printed on the front of a tabloid anyway. Then there's the one where I go out first and threaten to start cracking skulls if they don't back off. They'll use their telephoto lenses and get their pictures anyway, but they won't be directly in your face about it."

She sighed. "What do you recommend?"

"Do you recognize any of those guys?"

She studied the crowd of photographers and tipsters. "Actually, I know most of them. It's the usual gang."

He winced. "As much as I hate to say it, given that your father doesn't want you to get splashed all over the tabloid headlines, you probably ought to take the polite and cooperative approach. And at least that way they'll choose the more complimentary pictures of you to publish. Good Lord willing, some other poor schmuck celebrity will land in a scandal this week and you won't get the tabloid covers."

She appreciated his feeble attempt at humor. It was a kind gesture. "You'll stick close to me?"

"Wouldn't have it any other way, darlin'. And a word of warning. If I see anything that looks remotely like a threat out of any of them, I'm going to pull you out of there at lightning speed."

"Got it," she said with a smile.

"Your hair and makeup perfect?" he murmured.

She checked herself over in one of the many mirrors placed around the boutique and made a few adjustments. This was just like the good old days. Except back then, Candace would've barged out, started a brawl, blamed Silver for it and enjoyed watching Silver get accused all over the tabloids of throwing a tantrum at the press.

Eternally grateful for Austin's level head, she nodded her readiness at him.

He nodded back. "Let's do this, then. I'll go first. Stick close behind me while I talk to them."

Resolutely, she followed him to the front door.

Austin gestured for her to stay in the shadows while he addressed the reporters. "Miss Rothchild will be happy to pose for you for five minutes, but then she's got an appointment. Is that fair, guys?"

A murmur of surprise passed through the crowd. Poor guys weren't used to her cooperating with them. She hoped it took every last bit of fun out of them doing their jobs.

She took a single step forward, and the paparazzi immediately started pushing and shoving one another, all the while snapping pictures of her. What was up with that? They acted like they were in a full feeding frenzy. She hadn't done anything to merit this kind of enthusiasm! They acted like a million-dollar sale rode on them getting the best shot of her.

And then they started to shout out questions. "Is it true? Are you pregnant? How far along are you, Silver? Show us your baby bump!"

They shouted other questions about yesterday's shooting and

the Tears of the Quetzal, but all of those faded away in the face of her shock.

How in the world…

A vaguely familiar face leered at her—swarthy, dark haired and dark eyed, his gaze burning with maniacal enjoyment at this attack on her. Was he the guy who'd jumped at her in the casino two days ago?

He shouted maliciously, "Who's the father of your baby, Silver?"

Her brain shut down. Completely.

An overwhelming urge to flee overtook her. She looked left and right in panic. Nowhere to go. Bodies and camera lenses and flashbulbs hemmed her in on all sides, pressing closer and closer to her. She was cornered. Trapped!

"No. No, it's not true!" she cried. This was exactly the sort of scandal her father had forbidden her to fall into. Her scheme with Mark would be exposed. Harold would yank the gig out from under her. She'd lose everything and everyone who'd given her this second chance. Even Austin. Especially Austin.

Her gaze locked on his back in horror. She watched as, in extreme slow motion, he half-turned and looked over his shoulder at her, accusation written in every line of his face. Terrified, she lifted her gaze to look him in the eyes.

The crowd was shouting too loud for her to hear a thing, but as clear as day, she saw him mouth the words, "It *is* true, isn't it?"

Dear God.

Now what was she supposed to do?

Panicked, she mouthed back to him, "Help."

Thank God, he appeared to put aside his personal fury and nodded grimly at her. Squaring his shoulders, he turned briskly and faced the crowd, the picture of the professional he was. Politely, but firmly, he announced, "Picture time's over boys. Let us through."

When the wall of cameras didn't budge, and the din of shouted questions only got louder, Austin called to her over the din, "Grab my shirt and don't let go!"

She barely managed to catch the soft polo knit before he plunged into the crowd, his hands moving in a blur in front of him. She caught only glimpses of whatever he was doing, but the paparazzi fell back from him like magic, forming a narrow passageway that Austin wasted no time diving through. Flash-bulbs exploded inches from her face, but she put her head down and hung on grimly as Austin dragged her through the gauntlet. Then, all of a sudden, his back dipped down and strong, familiar hands reached out to drag her into the dark interior of their limousine.

"Go, Jimmy!" Austin called.

The car lurched into motion beneath her. It took her a couple of minutes to catch her breath and collect herself. Her brain whirled in frenzied circles as she tried to make sense of what had just happened.

How in the world had the press gotten wind of her pregnancy? Dr. Harris had sworn his staff was the soul of discretion and had promised her that professional medical ethics prohibited him or his staff from speaking about her pregnancy to anyone without her permission. Who then? Nobody else knew!

"Here. You look like you need this."

Austin shoved a can of orange juice from the limo's tiny refrigerator into her hand. She opened it gratefully and sipped its contents. Thankfully, her stomach was still behaving itself, and the juice went down without problem.

"We need to talk," Austin announced gruffly.

She squeezed her eyes shut in dismay. Oh, God. Here it came. He was going to blow his stack at her and dump her the way they all did. Her heart felt as if it was breaking in two already. And suddenly she was terribly sick to her stomach, but it had nothing whatsoever to do with her pregnancy.

Aiming for a flippant tone and failing miserably, she said, "Gee. It seems like I've heard that line out of you before."

"Yeah, it does seem to be a recurring theme with us, doesn't it?" he replied dryly.

She risked a glance up at him. His expression was completely unreadable. "Can we at least wait until we get back to your place? Privacy for this conversation would be a good thing."

He glanced in surprise at the closed partition behind him. No way was she talking where anyone else had even a chance of overhearing them. Not for this talk. He glanced back at her and must've caught the stubborn tilt of her jaw, because he nodded tersely and sat back, his arms folded across his chest.

The limo rolled along for several minutes in stony silence.

Too nervous to stand the strain of the tense silence any longer, she ventured, "Thanks for getting me out of there. You're really good at clearing a path through a crowd."

He didn't bother to reply. Rather he threw her a look that communicated a loud and clear, "Duh."

Okay, so she'd stated the obvious. The least he could do was acknowledge her attempt at breaking the ice between them. She tried two or three other innocuous comments, but he steadfastly refused to bite on any of them and maintained his silence. Harold would've been screaming his head off by now. Which, by comparison, would've been easier to put up with than this.

Betrayal and anger emanating off of Austin was made all the more palpable by his refusal to give vent to either. Maybe control wasn't always all it was cracked up to be. At least once Harold blew his stack he usually calmed down relatively quickly. She had no idea what to expect out of Austin. And that scared her to death.

So terrified she could hardly walk, she followed him through the usual routine up to his suite, waiting just inside the front door while he checked the place out. But this time he added a twist. He went into his room and emerged with some sort of handheld electronic device about the size of a cell phone. He ran it quickly over the walls and furniture before finally speaking.

"No bugs. We can talk now."

Well, she'd wanted complete privacy. The guy had certainly delivered it in spades. But she wasn't even close to ready to deliver on her end of the deal. How could she ever explain it to him?

"Are you hungry?" she asked in transparent desperation.

"Nope. Talk now. Food later."

Great. He wasn't even communicating in complete sentences with her. In resignation, she trudged over to one of the fawn-colored leather sofas that faced each other on the far side of the room. She sat down glumly, her gaze downcast. She felt him sit down across from her, but as always, he moved in uncanny silence and she heard nothing.

She took a deep breath. The only way to begin was to just start talking. The story would come out one way or another. "You understand that everything I'm about to tell you is in strictest confidence."

One eyebrow cocked at that, as if her saying it aloud was some sort of insult to his honor.

"Okay, fine. I know. You promise not to tell anyone anything." She took a deep breath and plunged ahead. "Yes, it's true. I'm pregnant. But I don't have the faintest idea how the press found out about it. Nobody knows. And I mean *nobody*. Me and my doctor and his nurse."

She flinched, waiting for Austin to blow.

But he merely sat there. And stared at her. Yet another silence grew between them. Stretched to the breaking point. And then, shockingly, he repeated relatively calmly, "You're pregnant?"

She nodded miserably and went back to staring at her toes, bracing herself for the explosion to come.

"Well. That certainly explains a lot."

He sounded almost *relieved*. What was up with that? She looked up quickly. "Like what?"

"Like why you fainted yesterday and why you can't eat any rich foods and why you passed up a glass of the hundred-dollar-a-bottle wine your father served at supper last night."

"I don't usually drink anyway," she retorted to that one.

"You didn't even let the butler pour you any. You didn't want to smell it, did you?"

"Well, no."

All of a sudden Austin lurched up, half off the sofa, before settling back, as if an intensely disturbing possibility had just occurred to him and then been as quickly dismissed from his mind.

"What?" she asked in alarm.

Austin asked, his voice dangerously quiet, "Who's the father?"

"With all due respect, that's not exactly any of your business."

He all but came across the coffee table at that. As she pressed back against the cushions of her sofa, violently startled, he waged a visible struggle with himself before settling back down on his own cushions.

His voice was thin with strain. "It's Sampson, isn't it? This is what he's been blackmailing you with."

There it was. The sixty-four-thousand-dollar question.

She had to say yes. The story was already in place. It was a done deal. Mark would take credit for being the baby's father, and she'd avoid the embarrassment of the real story coming out. Sure, an affair with her hick bodyguard was tawdry, but it would keep the press mostly off her case.

And as soon as she admitted that Mark was the father, Austin would back away from her for good. He'd leave her to Mark, no questions asked. He was too honorable to do anything else. He'd do his job, keep her safe and turn her back over to Sampson safe and sound in a few months. For once, she'd be the one doing the dumping and not the other way around.

Of course, he'd also walk out of her life forever and never look back, just like every guy who'd ever loved her and then left her. Of course, she'd learned not to look back, either. Sometimes pride was all a person had left to cling to. And Austin's formidable pride wouldn't allow him ever to forgive or forget this.

Something in her heart cracked at the thought. Pain shot through her. The kind of intense, emotional agony that few people had ever managed to cause her. In a moment of prescience, absolute certainty came over her that a whole lot of guys might have walked out on her over the years but none had ever hurt like this one was going to.

She and Austin could've had something really special between them, given a chance. Of that she was equally certain. In another place, another time, another set of circumstances…the chemistry was unmistakable. This was a man she could love. Deep and hard and forever.

She took a deep breath, prepared to say the words that would drive him away for good. And then she made the mistake of looking up.

The disappointment gleaming in his eyes was more than she could bear. And she was about to stab him in the gut with another lie. She *so* didn't deserve him.

But then something bubbled up within her. A kernel of hope. Maybe…just maybe…he'd understand if she told him the truth.

But what right did she have to dump the whole sordid story of her pathetic life on him? He hadn't asked for it. It was too much to ask of him.

"Silver?" he prompted. "Is this what Mark's been holding over you? Is he the father?"

She opened her mouth. She couldn't tell the lie. But neither could she bring herself to confess the truth. No sound at all came out.

And then Austin's control snapped. He surged up off the sofa. "Forget it. You're right. It is none of my damned business. I had no right to go after you when I knew you were involved with another man."

He cursed violently as he stalked across the room and back. "You're having his baby, for God's sake. Hell, I'm sorry, Silver. You tried to tell me, and I was so set on having you for myself that I didn't listen." He shoved a distracted hand through his hair, setting it akimbo.

It was the first time she'd seen him anything other than perfectly turned out—a measure of just how upset he must be.

"I thought we—" He broke off. "Hell, I didn't think. I'm sorry." He whirled and strode toward the door.

"Austin! Wait! It's not what you think! I—"

But then the door closed behind him.
He was gone.
He'd walked out on her after all.

Chapter 13

She hadn't been wrong. Nothing in her life even began to compare to the pain of Austin's leaving. With the closing of a single door, her life became bleak and colorless, a sawdust-dry existence she walked through numbly.

Sometimes it sucked being right.

A tall, taciturn man named Warren showed up at the penthouse door late that evening. She was so distraught that she'd thoughtlessly opened the door to his quiet knock without even checking to see who it was. She already knew it wouldn't be the one person she desperately wanted it to be.

"Miss Silver Rothchild?"

"That's me," she'd answered dully.

"My name is Warren Bochco. Captain Dearing sent me. I'll be taking over your protection detail…"

And that had been when her heart well and truly broke. He'd left her for good. Of course, he'd never shirk a responsibility. He'd promised to keep her safe, and he'd see that promise through. But if he'd sent this tall, silent man to guard her, he had no intention of ever seeing her again.

Warren was speaking. "…briefed me on your upcoming show and the problems your family's been having. He said you knew the drill. I'll stay out of your way as much as I can as long as you let me do my job."

Warren was built like Austin, tall and crazy fit, but where Austin had been all tawny and bronze and smiling, Warren was a study in black. Black hair, black eyes, black clothing. Quintessential bodyguard material. And the guy had all the personality of a telephone pole.

The next month passed by in a blur. Grief and going through the motions of preparing for her show were all she registered.

She went along with every song Saul and her newly re-signed record label fed her. The mindless drivel they chose for her was right up her alley; she had no heart left to put into her music. A couple of the songs inspired a certain spurned-female anger in her and were pronounced her likely next hits. Probably because they were the only songs she could find any spark of emotion to relate to.

Interestingly enough, Mark dropped completely off the radar. He never contacted her, although she made no effort to unblock his cell phone number from her own cell phone, either. But he never showed up at any of her rehearsals or planned public appearances. For the first several press junkets she kept an eye out for him, waiting for him to pop up and announce that he was the father of her rumored baby. Why he hadn't done that already, she had no idea.

At first she wondered if maybe Austin had gotten to the guy and managed to apply a little blackmail of his own. It would've been like the old Austin—the one who had looked at her like he wanted her for himself and who'd been fiercely protective of her. But the Austin who'd turned his back on her and walked out— would he bother to shut Mark up to protect her reputation and her privacy? Somehow, she thought not.

Her morning sickness got worse but thankfully settled down to a predictable routine. She didn't eat before 10 a.m., scheduled her rehearsals for the afternoon, avoided all rich foods and she muddled by.

The prospect of a baby was still a miracle to her that she anticipated with immense joy, but her child's actual arrival was still such a distant event that her current agony greatly overshadowed it.

Warren followed her around like a grim shadow, muttering occasional orders that she followed woodenly. Every time he did or said something bodyguard-like, it inevitably reminded her of Austin and piercing pain would stab through her all over again.

The one anomaly to her stoic bodyguard was the daily cell phone call he got. It had a custom ring tone that was more of a subliminal rumble than an actual ring. It usually came in the early evening, and it always made him take a quick look to clear the area around her and then turn his back on her. He'd plaster his hand over his wireless earpiece and mutter in a near whisper into his collar microphone. It was all very secretive and spooky.

It took her a few days to sidle close enough to hear what he was saying without him noticing, and she was stunned to hear him give a quick report on her day's activities and security concerns. *Austin.*

She knew it in her gut with absolute certainty. She didn't even have to ask Warren if she was right or not. She *knew.*

At first she clung to desperate hope that his calls meant there was still hope for them. But after a few weeks and still no word from him whatsoever, her hope died. Eventually it turned to anger and then from anger to grief to dry-eyed acceptance.

People began to fret over her losing too much weight, but she didn't have the energy to fake caring about anything.

She slept terribly, and Austin constantly haunted her dreams, but that was her secret. She'd moved into the spare bedroom in the San Antonio suite, where she'd asked to be moved with Warren.

Thankfully, the man didn't insist on keeping watch on her through the night. She heard him get up conscientiously each night to prowl the suite—Austin had sent the very best to protect her—but Warren never intruded upon her privacy in any way.

The threats against her tapered off. Either that or Warren was very good at keeping them from her. And knowing the guy, that would be exactly his style. He was extremely stingy when it came to sharing information of any kind with her.

About a week before her show, there was some kind of a flap over her dressing room, and Warren hustled her out of the theater in the middle of a full dress rehearsal for no apparent reason. She spent a tense hour huddled in the hot laundry room with him until a man she didn't recognize came and declared the scene clear. *Whatever that meant.* Then Warren had whisked her to a regular hotel room on the twenty-third floor and told her curtly not to leave the room.

He'd come back a few minutes later with a haphazardly packed overnight bag of clothes and toiletries for her and had offered no further explanations.

In a better frame of mind, she'd have bedeviled him mercilessly until he spilled the beans and told her what the heck was going on. But as it was, she crawled into one of the two double beds, pulled the blankets up over her head and went to sleep. She didn't hear whether or not Austin called to check on her that night.

Two days before her premiere, Saul was waiting for her in the theater when she arrived to do a last run-through of the dance sequences and a final costume change rehearsal. "Good news, Silver Girl!" he announced jovially.

"What's that?" she asked with no great interest.

"Every show is sold out. You did it! You filled the biggest theater on the Strip for seven nights!"

She nodded. That was good news. "Now all I have to do is keep them in the seats all the way through the show."

"Stop being such a worrywart. Your show is fantastic. You're going to be back on top of the industry in no time."

She gave him the smile he expected but didn't feel it in her heart.

"Have you decided on your encore songs?" Saul asked. "If the media buzz is any indication, you'd better have several songs picked out. Maybe an old one or two. Your fans are coming out in force to see you again."

That was going to be weird. All those stoned college kids who'd screamed their way through mosh pits at the front of her audiences were going to be here? She wondered if they had receding hairlines and office-cubicle paunches yet. Would they bring their kids? She hoped not, because her show was distinctly R-rated. It was definitely more grown up than her early material. But the record label had interpreted her request for more mature content to mean that she would do more explicit material now than she used to.

The songs they had given her weren't that bad, really. The problem was with her. Only long years on the road, doing nightly shows when she'd been drunk and wasted and burned out, saved her now. Somewhere along the way, she'd apparently picked up enough professional savvy to deliver a decent show even if her heart was not in it. Who'd have guessed her misspent youth could some in so handy after all?

The day of the show dawned, and she slept in late, praying that she'd sleep through her regularly scheduled bout of breakfast hurling. She would have a busy afternoon. She had a surprisingly large list of things to do, from a quick press conference to last-minute appointments for hair and nails, a massage and stretch by her trainer and then a hearty meal. She never could eat less than four hours before a show. The nerves usually started about then, and she didn't stand a chance of keeping anything solid down once she started getting keyed up.

Warren was as he always was—vigilant, silent and completely disinterested in her state of mind.

She really missed Austin today of all days. She was half tempted to snatch Warren's phone out of his hand when Austin's daily check-in call arrived. She desperately needed to hear his voice. There was nobody else she wanted to share this moment with but him.

She was pathetic, moping over a man who'd probably already forgotten what she looked like. As soon as his three-month promise to keep her safe expired, he would no doubt cut her totally out of his life. And here she was, mooning over him like some lovesick moron.

Oh, wait. She *was* a lovesick moron.

Austin stepped off the private jet, pausing for a moment to get over the shock of the afternoon heat slamming into him. It felt like he'd stepped into hell's oven. Damn, Las Vegas was hot in the summer.

He checked his watch quickly. He only had a few hours before Silver was scheduled to perform. Warren's team of investigators had finally gotten a lead on the elusive Mr. Mark Sampson, and Austin was personally running the guy down before Silver's show started. It was the least he could do for her.

Hell, it wasn't hardly enough.

He'd gone over to Sampson's place the day he walked out on her to have a little man-to-man chat with the guy about stepping up to his obligations and being a man for Silver's sake. But Sampson had been gone. Not as in out on an errand. As in cleared out. Fled the scene for good.

The Tears of the Quetzal and its thief had disappeared, as well. The goldsmith didn't remember anything about the man who'd asked for information on the diamond other than having told the guy that he wasn't allowed to share information about clients' pieces. The florist shop had received the order for flowers online. Despite getting his own support team's best computer guys on the trail, they weren't able to discover anything about the sender. All the trails to Sampson and the diamond went cold all at once. Which was suspicious in and of itself.

Despite Harold's protests, Austin had gone to the local police and the FBI with everything he'd had. Natalie continued to work on the case as much as she could, but because of conflict of interest issues, her hands were largely tied. A guy named Lex Duncan in the FBI's jewelry/gem theft division had been brought in on the case, too, and he seemed sharp.

But Austin had an unshakeable, niggling feeling in the back of his mind that it wasn't enough. His gut said Mark Sampson wasn't done messing with Silver yet. He snorted. Where she was concerned, though, his instincts hadn't proven to be worth a hill of beans.

How could he have missed the fact that she and Mark were not only involved but expecting a *baby* together?

A stab of piercing regret—hell, of uncontrolled jealousy—tore through his gut. It did every time he thought of her holding a baby in her arms. She'd be a beautiful mother. A good one, too. She was funny and fierce and loyal and loving…everything a mother ought to be.

Everything a woman ought to be.

Everything a wife ought to be.

And he'd walked out on her.

But what else could he have done? She was having another man's baby, for crying out loud. He had no right to encroach on Sampson's turf like that. It flat out wasn't honorable to put a move on a pregnant woman. No matter how much he'd wanted Silver for himself, he wouldn't stoop that low. It was beneath him—and beneath her. She deserved better than that.

But damn, losing her had been like ripping his heart out with a spoon. A dull one. With rust on it.

He'd never been a man who gave his friendship or loyalty easily, let alone his love. But once given, he'd always been the most steadfast of companions, never wavering in his support. But not so with Silver. He hadn't been strong enough to stand by her in her time of need. He'd been too hurt, too angry, too betrayed to handle being with her.

He'd failed her.

Sure, he'd brought in Warren Bochco, who was arguably the finest bodyguard in the business, so technically he'd kept her safe.

But if he didn't miss his guess, he'd done a real number on her heart and her head. The woman Warren described to him daily was quiet, withdrawn and impassively cooperative with everyone around her. That wasn't the sexy firecracker he'd fallen for like a ton of bricks.

He didn't doubt for a second that her change was all his fault.

He nearly broke down and went to her the day there was a bomb scare at the theater. An anonymous caller said there was a bomb in her dressing room and that she was going to die in a blaze of glory.

If it had been the stalker who'd murdered Candace, it made no sense for the guy to call and warn his intended victim to get out of harm's way. But what if it had been Sampson? It sounded just like his style. Make a fuss so he could rush in and be the hero.

Austin had played and replayed that first day he'd met Silver over and over in his mind, examining every remembered detail for some evidence of who the stalker was. He had the sneaking feeling he'd seen the guy but not known at the time who he was looking at. This stalker was brazen enough to show himself to the Rothchilds and their would-be protectors.

While the mental exercise had revealed no hint of the stalker's identity, something else significant eventually had come to him. Sampson had not been alarmed when the first attack had happened on Silver—the guy who'd jumped her out of the blue. Sampson's only real reaction had been fury that he hadn't been the guy at her side to heroically protect her.

Bubba knew the attack was going to happen.

Given Sampson's comments about getting the girl and laughing all the way to the bank and given that Silver clearly hadn't agreed to marry the guy even though she was carrying his baby, his guess was that Sampson had decided to apply a little extracurricular pressure to get her to turn to him for protection.

Except Sampson's plan had backfired. Harold had thrown the guy a nasty curveball and hired Austin to protect Silver. When she felt threatened, she'd turned to him and not to Sampson.

But it had been more than that between them, dammit. There'd been something special there. They'd almost had it all.

Swearing under his breath, Austin took the suitcase the copilot handed down to him. He headed across the sweltering ramp for the car he'd arranged to have meet the plane.

That second attack in the hotel lobby—the shooting—had scared the living hell out of Sampson. The guy had flatly panicked. He clearly hadn't been expecting that attack. Austin was convinced the shooting had been the work of the real stalker.

The only question that remained to be answered was whether or not Sampson and the shooter were in league with each other. More than one partnership-in-crime had suffered a case of crossed wires before. It was possible that Sampson's crone wasn't supposed to take that shot, or not at that time and place.

The fastest way to find that out was to go to the source directly. And that meant finding and talking to Sampson. Forcefully, if necessary.

Austin's gut said the guy hadn't left the local area. Silver was the guy's golden goose, and he didn't see Sampson walking away from her without making one last effort to get his hooks into her.

The one silver lining to the whole mess—pun intended—was that she hadn't made any attempt as far as Warren could tell to contact the guy. She hadn't even mentioned Sampson, in fact.

While Austin was privately relieved that the scum bucket was apparently out of her life, intellectually he wished for her sake that the guy would've stepped up to the plate and been there for her. Lord knew, she had a lot to deal with right now, and she could've used a strong shoulder to lean on.

Like his.

Damn, damn, damn.

He punched the address Warren's guys had obtained for Sampson into the car's GPS system. It was supposedly a dive on the unlucky side of town where a guy matching Sampson's description had been spotted entering and exiting over the past few days. If Austin got lucky, he could have this whole mess quietly cleaned up and out of the way before Silver's big night.

Some parting gift. But it wasn't like he could do any more for her. He'd pretty much cut off his chances of that when he'd walked away from her. For the thousandth time, he reminded himself it had been the right and noble thing to do. And for the thousand-and-first time, he thought grimly that if losing the woman he loved was the price of his honor…*it wasn't worth it.*

Silver looked up hopefully as her dressing room door opened. Her hopes wilted when it was only Saul and her mother. Harold, Natalie, Conner and various other relatives had stopped by to wish her luck.

"Ready, Silver Girl?"

"As I'll ever be."

"Break a leg, kiddo," her mother added.

"I thought that only applied to actors."

Anna grinned. "I dunno. Just don't actually do it, eh? You've got six more shows to do."

After those, she looked forward to sharing her baby news with her mother. Recently, she'd been feeling a deeper bond with Anna as becoming a mother herself became more real in her mind.

Silver turned back to the makeup artist who was just finishing applying the heavy-duty, waterproof makeup she needed so as not to sweat it off during the first dance number.

Saul continued to hover. "How are you feeling?"

She frowned at his reflection in the mirror. There was no way he knew she was pregnant. But it almost sounded like…"I'm fine. Nervous. Okay. Sick to my stomach and thinking about bolting. My hands won't stop shaking, my knees are knocking, and my teeth are about to start chattering. But I always get that way before a show."

He nodded sagely. "I recall. But I see you're not taking chemical measures to calm yourself this time."

She laughed. "I keep telling you—I'm not that irresponsible kid anymore."

He came over and rested a hand on her shoulder. "Believe me, I've noticed. And the change suits you. I've put the word out in the biz that you were an angel to work with on this show. I made sure your label knows it, too."

She blinked up at him through sudden tears. Whether it was stray eyeliner or emotion putting them in her eyes, she wasn't sure. Either way, she murmured, "Thanks, Saul." A pause, then she asked quietly, "Are we square, then?"

He gave her a long, considering look. "Yeah. We're square."

Well, at least one relationship in her life was back on track. Speaking of which, she asked, "Any messages for me? Any visitors?"

"Your father tried to come backstage again. I told him you were too busy getting ready."

"Bless you, Saul."

The older man grinned at her knowingly.

"Anyone else?"

"Like that young man of yours? No."

She didn't have the guts to ask him which young man he was referring to—Mark or Austin. The one she could do without. The other…

A stagehand poked his head in the open door. "Ten minutes, Miss Rothchild."

She couldn't do this. Not without Austin. He was her strength. She was weak and frightened and incomplete without him.

"Where's Warren?" she called out suddenly. "I need Warren!"

The tall man stepped inside her room immediately. He must've been standing guard just outside. "What's the problem, ma'am?" he bit out.

"Everyone else, out. I need to speak to my bodyguard alone."

The crowded space emptied quickly, leaving behind an island of quiet amidst the last-minute chaos.

"What's up, Miss Rothchild?"

"I need your cell phone."

He blinked at that and actually looked faintly surprised. "May I ask why?"

"I need to make a phone call."

He glanced at her crystal encrusted cell phone, sparkling conspicuously on the corner of her dressing table. "What's wrong with your phone?"

"Please, Warren. I've never asked you for anything before. Do me this favor."

Frowning, he pulled it out and handed it to her. She stared down at its unfamiliar face in dismay. "How do I retrieve your recently received calls?"

Comprehension broke across his face. And then a grin. "'Bout damn time you two got over what's been going on between you."

Her jaw dropped. In the first place, Warren never smiled. And in the second place, he *knew* about the two of them?

In answer to her unspoken question he rolled his eyes. "It doesn't take a rocket scientist to see how miserable you two are apart. You've been moping around like a zombie ever since I took over for him, and he's not in much better shape."

Okay, that put her jaw on the floor. "He's upset?"

Warren actually laughed. A rumbling sound from deep in his chest. "He's a bloody wreck. Gimme that phone. I'll get him on the horn for you."

Thank God. She was actually light-headed with relief at the idea of finally getting to talk to Austin again. Whatever it took—pleading, begging, crawling on her hands and knees—she had to get him back. She couldn't live without him.

The revelation broke over her, cool and refreshing, and as inevitable as spring following winter. She loved him.

And that was exactly what she was going to tell him.

The apartment door opened, and Austin went on full battle alert behind the wheel of his car. His hand drifted to the door handle. The guy looked like Sampson. Maybe a little slimmer than before. If he took off that baseball hat, Austin could be sure. As soon as Bubba turned back to the door to lock it, Austin slid out of the vehicle quietly. He moved fast and low across the parking lot toward his target, ducking between cars and using a tall cactus for cover.

Sampson turned and walked the opposite direction. Perfect. Austin put on a burst of speed to close the final gap. It would've been a piece of cake, except his cell phone rang just then. Sampson threw a startled look over his shoulder and took off like a jackrabbit.

Swearing, Austin ignored his phone and gave chase. The bastard wasn't getting away from him this time, no sir. With Silver's face firmly in mind, Austin gave chase. It really wasn't much of a chase. His superior fitness, training and motivation made short work of the distance between them. Austin made a flying leap and tackled Sampson in a move his high school football coach would have been proud of. In short order, he straddled Sampson, who was facedown in a patch of dried-out grass with one arm cranked up high between his shoulder blades.

Swearing erupted beneath him as Sampson struggled against the restraint. The baseball hat flew off, and Austin looked down grimly at the profile, half-ground into the grass.

It was not Sampson.

"Who the hell are you?" Austin burst out.

"Who the hell are *you?*" the guy snarled back.

"Name's Dearing. What's yours?"

"Call me Dingo."

Austin let up a little on the guy's twisted arm. "I'm looking for a guy named Mark Sampson. Ever heard of him, Dingo?"

"That son of a bitch. I'll kill him myself if I ever catch up with him…" The guy devolved into a spate of angry curses.

Surprised, Austin demanded, "What did he do to you?"

"Stiffed me on a deal. I did some…jobs…for him, and he was gonna pay me ten grand for the package. I came over here to his place to collect, but the bastard's skipped out on me again."

Austin squeezed his eyelids shut in frustration. "Any idea where he's gone?"

"You think I'd be here if I did?"

"What kind of job did you do for him?" Austin asked.

The guy's chattiness evaporated in an instant. "Just a job," he muttered.

Something illegal, obviously. Ten grand worth of illegal. Which meant it was something major. Possibly dangerous. Like, oh, stalking Silver? "Ever heard of a girl named Silver Rothchild?" Austin asked darkly.

Dingo lurched violently beneath him, struggling frantically to free himself. Austin nodded to himself. Uh-huh. Exactly what he'd thought.

"Sampson paid you to harass her, didn't he?"

Dingo went perfectly still this time. Like a deer in a hunter's headlights.

Oh yeah. He'd nailed this one spot on. Given some time and some…gentle…persuasion, this guy would no doubt sing and give him all he needed to put Sampson away for a good long time. But time was the one thing Austin didn't have right now. "I'll pay you ten grand to tell me where he is."

The guy sighed. "Man, I'd tell you in a second if I knew."

Austin reached into his jacket and pulled out a plastic strip. He looped it deftly around the guy's wrists and gave a yank.

"Oww! What are you doing?"

Austin pushed to his feet and quickly gave the same treatment to the guy's ankles. "I'm making sure you're still here when the cops get here."

"Aww, man. I swear. I don't know where Sampson is."

This guy didn't strike Austin as being sophisticated enough to be the stalker who'd murdered Candace, stolen the Tears of the Quetzal and shot at Silver. But that wasn't up to him to decide.

"Ask to speak to a cop named Natalie Rothchild," he advised grimly. "Tell her how Sampson hired you to stalk Silver and cooperate your ass off with her, and maybe she'll cut you a break."

"What the hell did Sampson do to bring all this heat down on him?"

"He messed with the wrong girl."

"Looks to me like he messed with the wrong guy," Dingo grumbled.

Austin laughed shortly. "That, too."

He turned and headed for his car. He pulled out his cell phone and called the LVMPD to tell them about the little fish he'd caught and left all tied up with a bow for them to come collect. That done, he climbed into his car. What the hell was he supposed to do now? The idea had been to catch Sampson before he hassled Silver again.

Silver.

Austin swore violently. Her show was about to start. And Sampson was still on the loose. Three guesses where the bastard would be right now, and the first two didn't count.

Austin gunned the engine and pointed it toward the Strip. As he drove, he checked his cell phone to see who'd called him earlier and nearly screwed up his ambush. This was a work phone, and he didn't get social calls on it.

Warren? What was Bochco doing calling him?

Panic leaped in his gut. Oh, crap. Had something happened to Silver?

He punched out Warren's number fast and plastered the phone to his ear. It rang. And rang. And rang, dammit. Warren either couldn't hear the damned thing…or worse, he was too occupied to answer it.

Austin stood on the gas pedal. Hard.

His thoughts devolved into complete turmoil. What would he do if something happened to Silver? He couldn't lose her!

Hang on baby, I'm coming.

Chapter 14

Through the scaffolding and the fireworks, Silver made out the cheering crowd. The lift had about eight feet to go and then she'd begin to rise out of the top of the stage set. The violins started on cue, buzzing like a swarm of hornets. Six feet to go. The guitars wailed a chord. The audience cheered even louder, all but drowning out the drums. Four feet to go. The hiss of Roman candles all around her started up, their heat enveloping her. And then her head cleared the floor. Her claustrophobia subsided and a single thought filled her head.

Showtime.

She spread her arms, welcoming the wildly screaming mass of humanity below her. It was a heady moment. Silver, the rock star, was back.

Too bad Austin wasn't here to share it with her. It would've been perfect then.

Get your head back in the game!

On cue, she stepped off her mark and commenced the dan-

gerous race down a narrow set of steel stairs in her high stilettos. The backup singers laid down the introduction, and Silver
launched into the first song.

She reached the stage and danced over toward stage right.
Quickly, she scanned the faces backstage. Maybe she did it out
of habit, or maybe desperation. But there was no sign of Austin's
familiar features.

Singing gustily, she and the dancers spun their way across the
stage so she could wave at the left side of the audience. No
Austin in the front rows of the crowd.

Stop that.

Throughout the entire song, she searched for him. She'd been
so sure he'd be here. After Warren admitted how unhappy Austin
had been after their split, certainty had lodged in her gut that he
would come. He knew how important this night was to her. He'd
be here for her, to share her big moment with her.

The second song came and went with no sign of him.

Then the third.

And something went out of her. Her enthusiasm drained in a
slow leak she was powerless to stop. She forced herself to keep
going through the motions of the show, but it just wasn't the
same. The lovesick moron in her head had misled her heart yet
again. When *was* she going to learn? Austin was done with her.

And something in her was irrevocably broken.

Hmm. That would be her heart.

After the fifth song, she slipped offstage while the dancers and
backup singers finished the last chorus to one of her old songs
with the audience bellowing it out in a giant sing-along moment.
Saul had decided that instead of a traditional intermission she'd
take breaks every half dozen songs or so to make quick costume
changes and keep the show going in a continuous flow. It was
ambitious and strenuous, but it kept the show's energy sky-high.

She raced for the changing area, where Stella and her two as-
sistants stripped off the first costume and crammed her into the
second one. She had one minute and forty seconds to make the

change, assuming the band didn't speed up the chorus like they had a tendency to do.

Saul poked his head around the screen after she was decent again. "Pick up the energy, Silver. You started out great, but you're losing steam."

He was right. But she just couldn't find it in herself to care. She closed her eyes. She could do this. If not for herself, for her baby. For his or her future.

Stella ordered, "Turn around, honey. Time to curl your hair."

They'd rehearsed this until they had it down to a fine science, and Silver made the required one-eighty spin.

And that was when she saw him.

Standing way back in the darkest shadows at the back of the stage. Staring at her fixedly. His arms crossed, his face as potently handsome as ever. When they made eye contact, some turbulent emotion passed across his face. What was that? Anger? Relief? Anguish? Or maybe it was just the shadows and her imagination.

She jerked free of the curling irons and lurched toward him.

Stella squawked behind her, "We've only got fifty-five seconds left!"

She called back over her shoulder, "So my hair'll be straight! This is more important!"

She screeched to a stop in front of him. And just looked up at him. Her vocal cords tangled in hope and fear until she couldn't speak. Please let him be glad to see her. Please let this not be just business. Please let him forgive her. Please let this not be a lovely hallucination.

"Hey." His voice sounded abnormally tight. Could it be? Was Warren right? Had Austin missed her, too?"

"Hey," she murmured back.

Time stopped, and it was as if a cone of silence descended around them.

He jammed his hands into his pockets. "How've you been?" he finally asked roughly.

She reached out to touch his chest. He drew in a sharp breath but didn't move away from her touch. Yup, he was real, all right. Warm and strong and as solid as ever. "I've been okay—" She broke off. Tried again. "No, strike that. I've been terrible."

"Is the baby all right?" he asked quickly.

She blinked, startled at the depth of concern in his voice. "Junior's fine. Still making me sick every morning."

A frown flickered across his face. "What's wrong, then?"

Shouting from behind her penetrated the fog that shrouded her brain. "Thirty seconds!"

She gazed up at him, hungrily drinking in the sight of his features. Lord, she'd missed him. She answered simply. "You were gone."

The old fire leaped in his eyes, fierce and protective, for just a moment. He opened his mouth to say something.

"Silver! Let's go! You'll miss your mark!" She scowled as the stage manager rushed up to her and took her by the arm. She started to resist his urgent tug.

"Go," Austin bit out.

She let the stage manager drag her away but called back over her shoulder, "Hold that thought! I'll be back in six songs and I want to hear it!"

She knocked the next set of songs out of the park. Not a person in the house was sitting down, the crowd screamed wildly after every song and even Saul was beaming and tapping his foot with the music in the wings offstage.

Her feet barely touched the floor, and she rode a wave of exhilaration that she could hardly contain. He'd come back. He still had feelings for her. He hadn't said anything yet, but it was written on his face as clear as day. The only problem with her show now was that it was taking too blessed long to get to the next costume change.

But finally it came.

She jumped down a hidden hatch in the stage floor to the screams of the crowd and slid down the short slide, landing on a crash pad. She'd barely stopped moving before Stella and her girls went to work. She got decent, the privacy screen went down—

—and Austin was standing there, looking almost as impatient as she felt.

Stella looked back and forth between the two of them. "Straight hair again?" the costumer asked in resignation.

Silver answered briskly, "Yup." To Austin, she said, "Come with me."

She grabbed his hand and pulled him toward the tiny lift that would reposition her for her next entrance. They stepped into the cramped space, and the doors closed behind them. Oh, God. He still smelled as good as ever. She hit the stop button. In deference to the show in progress on stage, the elevator had no alarm bell, and relative silence enveloped them.

They both started to speak simultaneously. Then they both laughed, which cut a little of the heavy tension between them.

"You go first," he said.

"That day when you walked out—"

He interrupted in a rush. "About that. I'm sorry, Silver. It was selfish of me. I couldn't handle it and I bailed out on you—"

She reached up quickly and pressed her fingers against his lips. "I've only got a few seconds. Let me get this out. I was trying to tell you when you left that Mark isn't the father of my baby."

Austin stared at her, stunned.

Urgently she pressed on. If only there was more time to explain it all. To break this to him more gently.

"I used artificial insemination. I wanted a baby, but I didn't have a man in my life. At least, not the right man. I used an anonymous donor. But to avoid ending up in the tabloids over it, I asked Mark to pose as the father of my child." She exhaled sharply. "I swear, I didn't know him at all when I asked him to do it or I never would have chosen him. Candace told me he was…different…than he turned out to be. She was good at sabotaging me that way—" Silver broke off. That didn't matter anymore.

She heard faint voices outside yelling through the elevator door, asking if she was okay and announcing ten seconds until her next mark. Reluctantly she took her finger off the stop button. The lift lurched into motion.

Austin was nodding. "So that's what he had on you."

She shrugged. "It wasn't one of my more brilliant moments."

"It wasn't a bad plan. You just didn't have the right man for the job."

Her gaze snapped up at the sexy timbre abruptly vibrating in his voice. Austin was staring down at her. The elevator stopped and the doors started to open.

"So you never were romantically involved with Sampson?"

She snorted. "Hardly."

The screams of the audience burst in on them and Austin lurched around, startled. Apparently he hadn't realized they were riding up to the back of the stage proper. The scaffolding of the set was a steel jumble directly in front of them.

Austin swore quietly beside her. Whether he was reacting to the news that she'd never been involved with Sampson or the fact that he was practically on stage with her, she couldn't tell.

"Gotta go," she told him quickly. "Promise me you won't leave again until we talk more."

"I promise."

Her cue sounded, and she raced forward into the lights through a shower of sparks.

Austin watched her go, dumbfounded. Son of a gun. Sampson had never been her boyfriend. Relief and exultation all but knocked his legs out from underneath him. A stagehand dressed in all black slipped into the elevator and started almost as violently as he did to find Austin in the lift.

"I'm Silver's bodyguard," Austin said quickly.

The guy nodded and punched the down button. Austin stepped out below. Stella and her girls were packing up. "How do I get up to the stage?" he asked the woman.

She gave him directions, and he made his way to the staircase and up into the wings of stage right. Silver was on fire out there, and he relished watching her lithe form as she performed. The music wasn't half-bad, either. He still preferred her singing a soulful ballad, but she had a great voice no matter how she used it.

He scanned what he could see of the audience carefully. No sign of Sampson. His gut said that if the guy was still in town, he was here tonight. And furthermore, his gut said Sampson's bag of tricks wasn't quite empty yet.

Austin's jaw rippled. Now that he'd found his way back to Silver, he wasn't letting her out of his sight for any length of time. Not until Sampson was caught and his role in the Rothchild stalkings uncovered.

Had the guy actually been smarter than he seemed? Was Sampson capable of murder? Of the clever theft of the Tears of the Quetzal from a police lockup? Of the calculated and well-planned moves of the stalker?

Was Sampson so smart that he'd successfully pulled the wool over people's eyes and convinced everyone he was a dimwit? The thought chilled Austin to the core.

He spied Warren across the stage, and the two men made brief eye contact before going back to their respective scans for threats.

Silver was a free agent. Available for the taking. He *so* wanted her for himself. And a baby? Did he want an instant family, too? What about his job? Was it fair to Silver and the baby to go back out in the field for months on end? To put himself in harm's way day in and day out? How was he supposed to choose between his career—which was more than a career, more like his identity—and love? Did he have to choose? Could he have both? Possibly, but was it fair to Silver to ask that of her?

The questions continued to roll through his head, and damned few answers were forthcoming. He clenched the bulky rope beside him in frustration. He knew for sure that he didn't want to lose Silver again. And she seemed pretty intent on not losing him, either. They'd find a way to make things work between them. They *had* to. He'd burn up from the inside out if they didn't, leaving behind only a hollow shell of his former self. He'd lived that way for the past six weeks, and he couldn't do it for a lifetime.

The rope vibrated faintly in his hand, and he frowned. Nothing had happened on stage to explain it. He looked up, following the rope into the darkest recesses of the black-painted ceiling overhead. It led to the lighting system. Each of those big spotlights up there weighed several hundred pounds, and there were dozens of them. What was heavy enough to jiggle all of that tonnage? Elaborate scaffolding suspended the entire lighting system from the ceiling, a massive affair that stretched all the way across the stage. All the way across the stage—

Ohdamnohdamnohdamn…

He looked around frantically for a way up there. He spied a narrow ladder and dived for it, swearing in a steady stream around his sudden, choking certainty. He knew exactly where Mark Sampson was planning to make his final strike at Silver.

Question was, would he get there in time to stop it or not?

Chapter 15

Silver fell backward into the arms of her dancers. They turned her in a slow circle while she gazed up at the ceiling, catching her breath. Something moved overhead, and she started. That was odd. It looked like someone was up there. One of the stage-hands, no doubt. There must be a problem, because all the light sequencing was done digitally. Even the spotlights were operated by remote joystick.

The dancers put her down and she sashayed off, keeping one eye peeled on the lights to make sure she didn't need to make any on-the-fly adjustments.

The song ended, and she made her way to the front of the stage to introduce the next song. It was actually a scheduled pause to let all the performers catch their breath after that last number. She asked the audience if they were having fun and got a gratifying scream of approval back.

She turned to face the band and cue up the next piece. As she strode to the back of the stage, she glanced up.

And did a double take. There was definitely someone crawling around up there. More than one someone.

She spun to face forward and took one more look up into the rafters.

Oh. My. God.

That was Austin up there. And that could mean only one thing. He'd spotted a threat.

"Silver!" the drummer hissed.

Crud. She'd missed the cue. The band did a smooth repeat of the last few bars of the music, and she started the song on time this time. It was an effort to remember the lyrics and stop herself from looking up every two seconds. But the audience would figure out that something was wrong if she did, and it would take them out of the show.

She ran to stage left and up the ramp to the second platform and took the moment to see what was going on above. She spotted Austin immediately…and he was grappling with someone else. *So not good.* He was a good three stories above the stage. If he overbalanced the slightest bit, both men would crash down. And there was no safety net.

She pasted a smile on her face, prayed the audience was far enough away not to see the panic in her eyes and pressed on with the show.

Above, Austin hung on fiercely, trying futilely to get enough purchase to subdue his opponent. Sampson was fighting like a crazy man, and that made him a great deal more dangerous than he'd otherwise be. He seemed to understand that the jig was up and this was the end for him. The guy acted prepared to make a suicidal last stand.

A seam on Sampson's shirt gave way and the bastard tore out of his grip, spurting away down a narrow catwalk. Austin gave chase, swearing. He didn't much like how the heavy scaffold was wobbling under the force of their gymnastics up here. The planks under foot were maybe eight inches wide, and he pounded after

Sampson's fleeing form carefully. At least if Sampson was occupied getting away from him, the guy wouldn't have time to harm Silver.

Sampson dodged to the right, down one of the side access walks. Austin skidded around the corner and accelerated hard. Time to put an end to this foolishness. Sampson reached the end of the planks and paused momentarily in indecision, looking right and left. And that was his fatal mistake.

Austin went airborne, laying himself out flat. His arms wrapped around Sampson's waist, and his momentum carried both men straight forward, down to the very end of the plank they stood on. He felt himself tilting to the left. Air loomed under his left side. In a survival reflex, he wrapped his legs tightly around the narrow catwalk he straddled.

Sampson started to fall, and as strong as Austin was, he wasn't powerful enough to stop the guy's body weight. Nonetheless, he hung onto Sampson's waist with all his strength. The guy flung out his arms and managed to snag the perpendicular catwalk. With Austin's help, the other man dragged himself back up onto the planks.

"Give it up, Sampson," Austin grunted. "You're gonna kill yourself up here."

"If I can't have Silver, who cares?"

"Get over it. You never gave a damn about her. You just wanted her fame and fortune."

"Go to hell, Dearing."

"Your life's not over. You still have a lot of years to score the big one and get rich. Don't throw it away."

"You've got nothing on me. Back off!"

"Ever hear of a guy named Dingo? He and I had a little chat earlier today. He's in the custody of Las Vegas's finest as we speak, singing his heart out."

That took the remaining starch out of Sampson.

"If you make a full confession, maybe the district attorney

will go easy on you. Come quietly with me now, and I'll put in a good word for you."

"I didn't shoot at her that day," Sampson blurted. "I had nothing to do with that."

"You willing to say that hooked up to a lie detector?"

"Yeah, I'm telling you. It wasn't me!"

Somehow, he believed the guy's whining. But he wasn't about to give Sampson the weapon of that knowledge. "Tell it to the cops. You and Dingo cut her brakes. You had Dingo assault her. You sent her threatening notes—"

He broke off as Sampson frowned, perplexed. So he hadn't been behind the bouquet and the death threat that came with it? Damn. Aloud, he commented, "It doesn't matter. With what Dingo's telling the cops, they'll still nail you cold. You're hosed."

Sampson uttered another foul suggestion for what he could do to himself. Time for a little reverse psychology.

Austin shrugged. "If that's the way you feel, there's no sense in my trying to save you. You should go ahead and jump. The publicity for Silver will be spectacular. She'll make global head-lines. You'll make her millions of dollars in record sales."

Sampson snarled something about not giving her a red damned cent. Austin didn't catch the rest of what the guy called Silver, which was probably just as well. He would've hated to have to toss Sampson off the scaffold himself.

Austin loosened his grip slightly and glanced below. "I'd rec-ommend you go off the back of that plank you're on. It's a longer fall on that side, and there's some sound equipment down there. The combination ought to kill you nicely." He gave Sampson a little push in that direction.

"Are you crazy?" Sampson hollered.

Austin's voice dripped with anger when he replied coldly. "Buddy, I'm stone-cold sane. But I am getting you out of Silver's life for good one way or another tonight."

Sampson's eyes widened fractionally as he realized that Austin meant business.

Austin continued emphatically. "I really don't give a damn if you climb down from here or fly down. But you're done stalking Silver. As of now. It's over. What's it gonna be? Stairs or airborne?"

Silver looked up yet again, watching in horror at the drama unfolding over her head. She had to do something! Mark was volatile and unpredictable, and Austin could get hurt or killed up there!

She stumbled and missed a couple steps but did her best to cover it.

She couldn't lose Austin now, just when she'd finally found him again. She sang through the song's chorus, and as the last verse approached, the words didn't come to her. Damn. What came next?

She looked up again. And gasped. Austin dived for Sampson and both men crashed down onto the scaffold, which started to swing ominously. She missed the first line of the verse, but thankfully the backup singers were also belting it out at the same moment, neatly covering her gaff.

The two men looked to be struggling. She couldn't make out who was winning, but she had to believe Austin had the upper hand, given his fitness and training. Assuming Mark didn't pull them off the scaffold and kill them both. He was vindictive enough to do it.

She searched frantically off to her left. There. Warren was still lurking offstage. In the guise of waving at the audience, she desperately gestured at the bodyguard until he glanced her way. She made frantic eye contact with him.

He started to move forward, but she shook her head. He stopped, looking confused. She pointed up, looking up as she did so. It wasn't the choreographed movement for the song, but fortunately she was the star of the show, and she could deviate from the routine the backup dancers were grinding out without looking strange.

Warren, thank goodness, correctly interpreted her movements. Frowning, he looked up, peering into the blackness of the stage ceiling. Suddenly he jolted and reached into his jacket for his pistol. He must've spotted the two men. He spun and took off running into the bowels of the theater.

She executed a couple of spins across the stage, glanced at the dancers to see what they were doing, got in front of them where she belonged and picked up the routine again. An urgent prayer for Austin's safety ran through her head in a continuous loop of near panic as she continued the performance. It was the best she could do.

Austin waited tensely while Sampson blustered for a few more seconds, but then the guy went limp.

All the fight went out of Bubba and sullen defeat entered his eyes. "Stairs, you son of a bitch," Sampson snarled.

Austin laughed shortly, without humor, a hard sound even to his ears. "Your misfortune was to run into a son of a bitch who wanted the girl just a little bit more than you. Let's go."

He dragged the guy to his feet and, as much as was possible in the narrow, dangerous confines up here, goose-stepped him to the ladder that led offstage.

Sampson stopped abruptly at the top of the ladder and muttered, "Who the hell's that?"

Austin glanced down. Praise the Lord. Warren. His worry about how to maneuver Sampson down the ladder without the guy pulling something stupid evaporated. He answered, "That's my partner. And if you think I'm a badass, you ought to tangle with him. He'd kill his own mother to get the job done."

Sampson grumbled under his breath. Uh huh. As Austin had thought. The guy had been planning to do something on the way down.

"Here's how this is gonna work, Mike. You're gonna go down in first, and my buddy down there's going to keep his gun on you. Try anything and he'll shoot you off the ladder like a juicy little pig in a shooting gallery."

"My name is Mark, dammit," Sampson ground out.

Austin leaned close and murmured in the guy's ear. "I've got a friend named Mark. Good man. Saved my life a few times. You don't deserve the same name as him, you slimeball. Now get moving." He gave Sampson's arm a sharp twist that drove the guy to his knees.

For the first time, true fear entered Sampson's gaze. Was the jerk just now starting to figure out how dangerous a man he really was? Austin snorted. *Gee, Maynard. A little slow on the uptake there.*

On stage, Silver spied Austin standing at the top of the ladder with Sampson kneeling in front of him and nearly sobbed her relief into her microphone. Thankfully, she was due for her last costume change before the grand finale, a medley of her greatest hits. She was supposed to exit stage left, but there wasn't a chance she was going anywhere but stage right to meet Austin.

She all but ran off the stage at the end of the song, while the lead guitarist held a "Which side of the theater can cheer louder?" contest.

Across the stage, she spotted Saul and Stella flapping in consternation like a pair of wet chickens, and a flurry of activity as they tried to pack up, no doubt, with the intent to race over with the last costume. Whatever. She so didn't give a darn about any old outfit right now.

She raced behind the big velvet curtain to where Warren was just finishing slapping handcuffs on Mark. With a wordless cry she flung herself at Austin. He heard her coming in enough time to turn around before she barreled into him, which was probably what saved them both from tumbling to the floor.

"Oh my God," she cried. "Are you okay?"

"Easy, darlin'. I'm fine. I spotted me a rat up in the light rig and went on a little hunting expedition."

She twisted in Austin's arms to stare at Mark. "What did I ever do to you to make you want to hurt me?"

The guy opened his mouth, but Austin cut him off. "Don't answer that, Sampson. In fact, don't say anything at all. You scared Silver tonight, and that's all the reason I need to break your neck." He added in disgust, "Get him out of here, Warren, before I hurt him or worse."

The other bodyguard nodded tersely and dragged Sampson away.

Silver buried her face against Austin's chest and let out the sob she'd been desperately holding in ever since she'd realized what was going on overhead.

"Hey, sweetheart. Why the tears? Everything's okay now."

She sniffed, smiling up at him damply. "That's why I'm crying, you big oaf. I thought I was going to lose you again, and I flipped out."

He pulled her close and buried his face in her hair, murmuring unintelligibly beneath the roar of the crowd. But she didn't need to hear the words. She felt his relief that she was okay in the way he crushed her against him, felt his caring in the way he nuzzled her hair with his nose, felt his emotion in the way his heart pounded against hers.

She'd almost lost him tonight. The realization flowed through her like a glacier, freezing everything in its path with stark terror. Suddenly, nothing else mattered. Not some stupid costume change, not her career, nothing. She'd been out there shimmying around and he'd been overhead, putting his life on the line for her. It made what she did seem so blessed shallow.

Heck, she'd spent all these weeks assuming he'd left her for some selfish reason of his own. He probably had some noble reason for doing that, too! "Why did you leave?" she blurted.

He lifted his head to look down at her solemnly. "You were having another man's baby. A man you were involved with. What kind of lowlife would I be to break the two of you up? I cared about you too much to do that to you. I had to leave. It was the only right thing to do."

Yup. Noble to the core. And she'd been too blind to see it. She'd been busy thinking all kinds of terrible things about him and he'd done it all for her. She *so* didn't deserve him. How was she ever going to live up to his sense of honor and decency?

She'd sold out on him. Given up on him—and on them. She'd sold out on her career. Sold out on everything. She'd just rolled over and done what everyone around her told her to, whining all the while about how miserable she was. Meanwhile, he'd made a giant sacrifice for her, an ultimate gesture of caring, without a word of complaint. How could she possibly make that up to him?

And then what he'd just said truly registered on her over-wrought brain. He'd cared for her enough to leave. Cared.

Past tense.

It was too late. He'd come back to nab Sampson, not to be with her. She was in the middle of her big show, and he was gentleman enough not to dump her until it was over. But his return had nothing to do with her. She'd truly blown it.

The floor might just as well have opened up and swallowed her whole at that moment. Apparently, somewhere deep in her subconscious, she'd been holding out some small hope that they'd get back together, for that spark just blinked out of existence. And her world went black. All desire to go back out on that stage drained away.

She had to leave. Go somewhere far, far away from here, and never come back.

Austin frowned down at her, and all of a sudden, the light disappeared from his gaze, too. He knew. He'd realized that she'd figured out why he was here and that he could drop the pretense now. She spun away. "I've…I've got to…go," she mumbled. Where to, she had no idea. Just away. Now.

Vaguely, she became aware of her name being repeated over and over. "Silver! Silver! Silver!" It was the crowd chanting—screaming at the top of its lungs, actually—for her return.

Austin gave her a push toward the stage. "Go. Your fans are waiting for you."

Blindly, she stumbled forward. And realized the spotlights had picked her up. She was back on stage. She stared out at the audience numbly. *Sing. She was supposed to sing.* But she had no idea what song came next. She didn't care what song came next.

One of the guitarists whispered urgently to her, prompting her with the line for the beginning of the final medley.

She heard Saul behind her, asking Austin urgently what the hell he'd just said to her. Austin murmured back that he hadn't said anything at all. *And that was the problem. He had nothing to say.*

Nothing to say.

That was the title of the song she'd written right after Austin left. It talked about how there weren't words to describe her love and loss.

"Sing, Silver!" Saul hissed at her angrily.

Sing. Right. As if coming out of a trance, she walked out to the center of the stage and reached behind her waist to flip on her microphone pack. "Everybody, with your indulgence, I'm going to change up the pace, now."

She gazed up toward the back of the theater where the lighting director and his men sat in a concealed booth. She couldn't see them, but she knew they were there. "Gentleman, if you could cut all the lights and give me a single white down-spot, center stage?"

The party atmosphere in the audience faded as the lights went down, and the crowd buzzed, clearly perplexed.

She glanced back at the band. "Jerry, may I borrow your acoustic Gibson?"

The lead guitarist looked stunned but nodded and turned to the stand behind him. He picked up the plain, wooden guitar and passed it to her.

She looked offstage. "Is there a stool around, by any chance?"

After a few seconds, a stagehand ran out with a bar stool. She directed the kid to place it in the wash of light shining down from the spotlight above. She glanced over the wings of stage right. Saul mouthed furiously something to the effect of "What in the hell are you doing?"

And Austin—he had faded back into the shadows, but she still recognized his tall form, nearly invisible behind Saul. Already pulling away from her, huh? Her heart broke a little more. Well, at least she was now in approximately the same frame of mind she'd been in when she wrote the song.

She perched on the stool and gave the guitar an experimental strum. She looked up at the audience but couldn't see even the front rows in the blackness now enveloping the theater.

"You know, folks, a lot of time has passed since I was last onstage. And I've done some growing up since then. To pass the time, I've been trying my hand at a little songwriting. If you don't mind, I'd like to play one of my songs for you now. It fits my mood better than what was up next on the playlist. I hope you like it."

And with that, she closed her eyes, strummed the opening chords, and began to sing. It wasn't so much a song as a confession. The ballad told the story of her long search for and finally finding the right man. It told how she'd taken him for granted and how she'd lied to him and lost him. She sang of her loss and pain but also of her regret and sorrow. She poured out all the anguish in her soul into the music, her voice soaring into the silent void all around her.

And then the song was over. The audience was dead silent. The moment stretched out eerily as she opened her eyes in slow motion and looked up. And then the spellbound quiet broke as thunderous applause erupted, shocking her out of her reverie. The applause swelled to cheering, then to screaming and to a standing ovation that was deafening.

But that din was nothing compared to what came next. A massive explosion slammed into her, throwing her off the stool, flattening her on the stage. It was so loud that the impact of the noise ripped the air from her lungs. Sharp pain burst in her ears, ringing through her head until she couldn't see.

She registered screams. Then a crunching, creaking sound of metal tearing.

And then the entire lighting scaffold crashed down on top of her.

Chapter 16

The explosion sent ice picks of agony stabbing into Austin's left ear, driving him to the floor along with the concussion of the blast. *Holy—* Before he could finish the thought, his instincts took over and he rolled back to his feet all in one lightning fast motion. *Silver. Must get to Silver.*

He jumped for the stage just as the light system came crashing down before his eyes, burying Silver somewhere beneath tons of lights and wires and steel beams.

Right then and there his life flashed before his eyes. Except it wasn't his past scrolling through his mind's eye…it was the future they could've had together. Laughter and fireworks and sweet memories. The exciting roller coaster of her career. Laid-back retirement for him. Kids playing in the backyard. Fourth of July picnics with sparklers and burnt hot dogs. Lazy moments together in bed. And the love.

Oh, God. The love.

Oblivious to the screams and chaos around him, he leaped

onto the twisted pile of steel, thinking frantically. She'd been sitting slightly forward of where he was now. He shifted over that way, searching furiously. He threw pieces of twisted metal in all directions, dodged bundles of wires that might or might not be hot, all the while bellowing, "Silver! Silver! Where are you?"

The noise in the theater was deafening. People screamed, feet stampeded and the roaring aftereffects of the explosion still echoed in his skull.

Quickly, he was waist deep in the pile. Still, there was no sign of her. What was she wearing? He cast his mind back frantically. Pink. Hot pink. He looked around in the deep shadows cast by the emergency lighting system across the stage.

"Light! I need light over here!" he shouted. No telling if anyone heard him or would respond if they did.

He grabbed the lip of a mangled spotlight and laboriously rolled the thing, weighing easily two hundred pounds, to the side. It crashed off the stage, causing squeals and more localized panic. He didn't care. Silver was under here somewhere, hurt, maybe dying. Please God, not already dead.

He jumped down into the new opening. Squatting, he was finally able to catch glimpses of the stage under the overarching pile. He looked around carefully, squinting to make out something, anything, resembling a human being.

Over there. Could it be—

He crawled to his right, snagged his trouser leg on something and ripped it free impatiently. He looked again. A hint of color caught his eye in the gloom. Studying the pick-up-sticks pile above him, he carefully pulled free a long metal pipe. The pile shifted slightly above him, then settled again. He released his breath.

He crawled another few feet. Oh, yes. That was definitely a splash of pink.

"Silver! Can you hear me?"

Nothing. The inert pile of cloth didn't move. It looked like she was lying in a pocket surrounded by stacked railings and girders. But she didn't look crushed.

He managed to draw a breath. Now, if she only hadn't taken a blow to the head or neck. He ought to wait for firemen to get here. They had extraction training for collapsed structures. But what if she was seriously injured? Dying? He couldn't afford to wait.

Eyeballing the stack overhead and doing his best not to bump or dislodge anything, he slithered mostly on his belly under the worst of the pile and toward where she lay, still and silent.

Finally, a lifetime later, he reached her.

He plastered a hand to her throat. Nothing. Oh, God. He moved his hand slightly to the side and something jumped under his fingertip. He held his breath. Come on. Be a pulse. Another thump beneath his finger. *Yes.* She was alive.

It was awkward checking her over for injuries because of a pair of steel poles between them, but he managed. Her limbs seemed intact. The floor beneath her felt dry. No bad bleeding, then. Carefully, he ran his hand down her spine, checking for any bends or bumps that shouldn't be there. It felt all right.

It was a risk to move her, but did he dare leave her under here, where the pile could shift and crush her at any time? And what about the baby? What if it was in distress?

That decided it for him. He maneuvered around to the left, positioning himself above Silver's head. Sitting on his behind, he leaned forward, hooked her armpits and eased her toward him. As petite as she was, he was only able to move her a few inches at a time, lest her clothing snagged on something and brought the house of cards tumbling down upon them both.

Finally, she was lying mostly in his lap. He scooted backward, pulling her along with him. He didn't come out the way he'd come in, for he'd spotted a clearer route out the back of the pile. It still took him several minutes to work his way to the edge of the mess.

As he neared the light now shining down on the stage, he heard male voices shouting. "Austin, Silver, can you hear us?"

"We're here!" he called back. "I've got her. She's alive but unconscious. Get an ambulance!"

"One's already here," somebody called back. "Wave your hand if you can. I think I've spotted you."

He lifted his hand through a small gap overhead and waved it back and forth.

"Gotcha. Sit still. There's an unstable area between us and you. We're shoring it up now."

He acknowledged the instruction and used the pause to catch his breath and to stroke the tangled hair off of Silver's face. She looked surprisingly peaceful and unscathed. "Wake up, honey," he murmured. "You're scaring me. I need to know how you are. If anything hurts."

Maybe it was a trick of the flashlights playing across the pile from behind him, but he could swear her eyelids fluttered. He called her name more urgently, but she didn't respond.

In a matter of minutes, a big guy in a canvas jacket and fireman's hard hat put a hand on his shoulder from behind. "Lemme carry her out, buddy. You crawl behind me."

Austin didn't want to give her up, but the fireman was best qualified to evacuate Silver from this mess. Reluctantly, he laid down on his back and dragged her up and over his body to the fireman behind him.

In moments, he was free of the hellish nightmare of the pile. Silver was just being laid on a gurney by a pair of medics. Austin leaped to his feet and rushed over to her.

"I'm coming with you," he announced to the EMT.

"Are you family?"

"Yes," he lied. "Her fiancé and father of her baby." He registered gasps of surprise around him but ignored them. They could split hairs with him about his relationship status with Silver later.

"C'mon," the paramedic said without ceremony.

Austin sprinted down the hall beside the racing gurney and climbed into the back of the ambulance outside. It was a fast, noisy ride to the hospital and another sprint into the emergency room, which was filling up fast with frantic Rothchilds. The bad news was Silver was still unconscious. The good news was the medic had found a heartbeat on the baby using the sonogram in the ambulance.

Anna and Harold closed in on him to grill him about the baby, but he put them off by telling them to ask her when she woke up.

Austin was not allowed to accompany her into the trauma unit, however, and was relegated to the waiting room to pace impatiently. It was the longest half hour of his life. And then a nurse came out. "Mr. Dearing?"

He whirled quickly. "That's me. How is she?"

"Come with me."

The nurse smiled. That was good news, right? She wouldn't smile if something terrible had happened, would she? He all but ran the poor woman down as they headed down the hall.

He turned into a room full of electronics and monitors and skidded to a halt. Silver was sitting up in the bed…smiling at him. Swear to God, he went light-headed. His knees went weak and he felt crazy hot all of a sudden. He grabbed the door frame to steady himself until his vision cleared and he could breathe again.

"Hey, beautiful," he managed to murmur.

"Hey, you," Silver murmured back. "I hear you saved my life."

He shrugged and moved over to the bed, almost not daring to believe that she was okay. "Nah, I just dragged you out from under the lighting scaffold." He took her hand gently. "How're you feeling?"

"Woozy."

"Woozy? What the hell is that? Weak? Sick? Or is that some kind of pregnancy thing?"

She laughed and then winced. "It means I'm a little nauseous and my head's swimming a little. And I have a headache, too."

"And the baby? Junior's fine?" he asked in concern.

Silver glanced over at the doctor, and Austin's heart skipped a beat. Oh, God. Not the baby…

"Her baby's fine, Mr. Dearing," the doctor said soothingly.

He about fainted again. Big, tough him, who faced down assassins without blinking and leaped in front of bullets for fun. This business of being in love was hard on a guy. *Being in…*

Son of a gun.

Sure enough, he was slam-dunk, out-for-the-count, no-doubt-about-it, in love with Silver Rothchild. His heart did a flip.

"Sir," the doctor said firmly, "where is that blood on your collar coming from?"

Blood? What blood? He cranked his chin down and noticed a bright red stain along his left shoulder seam and running down the front of his shirt. "No idea. I'm fine."

"Sit down on this stool and let me have a look."

He sat. The doctor did a quick examination of his head and neck but stopped abruptly after he stuck a light in Austin's ear and elicited a sharp yelp from his patient.

"Nurse, call in Dr. Whitney." To Austin, the doctor said, "He's the best ear, nose and throat guy we've got around here."

Austin frowned. And then comprehension dawned. Oh no. His bum eardrum. Had he busted it again? It had bled the last time he ruptured it, too. This could delay his return to the field for weeks or even months, dammit. Although, on the upside, it would give him more time to spend with Silver and convince her to marry him.

Marry…

Damn! His brain had to quit throwing these heart-stopping thoughts at him like this!

Marriage? To Silver?

Oh, yeah.

No doubt about it.

Now to do a better job of convincing her to go along with his plan than Mark Sampson had…

Another doctor interrupted his strategy planning, whisking him out of the room over Silver's protests and taking him upstairs to an office full of more equipment, most of it designed to poke him in the ear and cause as much excruciating pain as possible.

After about fifteen minutes, the doctor quit poking and took a seat on a stool in front of Austin. The guy had just opened his mouth to speak when a knock sounded on the door. A nurse stuck her head in.

"I tried to keep her downstairs, but the E.R. doc said we'd better let her come up here or she was going to cause a riot. She insists on seeing Mr. Dearing right away."

The woman stepped aside, and Silver barged into the room, her eyes blazing and her arms akimbo. She looked like a minor tornado.

Austin came up off the table. "What's wrong?" he bit out.

"Nothing. I just want to be with you and make sure you're okay. And those tyrants downstairs told me I had to wait there for you. It's been forever, and I got worried—"

He laid his fingertips on her mouth, gently cutting off her babbling. "Dr. Whitney was just about to give me the verdict."

She turned to the doctor. "How bad is it? Can he still be a bodyguard? He's a Special Forces soldier, you know. A captain. He has a team of men and does all kinds of cool things…" She trailed off, glancing over at him, abashed.

Surprised, Austin asked, "How do you know all that about me?"

"I read up about Delta Force on the Internet. You guys do some amazing stuff. It scares me to death to think of you doing it, but if that's what you want to do, I guess I can live with it."

Dr. Whitney cleared his throat, and Silver and Austin turned simultaneously to face him.

"I don't think that's going to be an issue for Captain Dearing, young lady. You see, his eardrum's basically shredded. Best case, I'm estimating that by the time it heals, we're looking at a fifty percent hearing loss. Worst case, it could run up to eighty percent hearing loss in the left ear. I've done some work with the military doctors over at the air force base across town, and my understanding is that this will disqualify Captain Dearing for combat."

Austin heard the words with his good ear. But they failed to register. *No more combat?* "Ever?" he asked in disbelief.

"I'm sorry, son."

Silver gasped beside him and her hand came to rest comfortingly on his shoulder.

Well, hell.

This was certainly not how he'd envisioned ending his career. He'd always thought to go out in a blaze of glory. To do something wildly heroic and go down in the annals of the Delta Force as one of the great ones.

Although, saving the life of the woman he loved wasn't too bad a way to go out.

"Oh, Austin. I'm so sorry. I know how much your job means to you." He heard tears in Silver's voice and looked up in surprise.

"I thought you hated what I do."

"I do. But it makes you happy. Made you happy. I'd never wish for you to lose something that you love."

He gathered her close and buried his face in his hair. "I almost lost the thing I truly love tonight when those lights came down on you."

She froze in his arms. Small hands pushed at his shoulders, backing him up until she could look at him. They were almost eye-to-eye with him sitting on the table like this. She whispered, "What did you say?"

"I said I love you."

"Seriously?" she asked.

He gave her a withering look. "Do you take me for the kind of guy who'd joke around about something like that?"

"Well, no. But…really?"

"Yes, really, you silly vixen. I love you. I love your music. I love your temper. Your smart mouth. Your giant heart. Your laughter. All of you."

"*All* of me? Including the fact that I'm pregnant?" she replied hesitantly.

"Speaking of that." He winced. "Back at the theater, when you were unconscious, I might have let it slip that you're expecting."

Alarm made her jolt. "Who heard you?"

"Uh, I imagine pretty much everyone in the place. I sort of bellowed it at the top of my lungs."

She groaned. "You didn't."

"'Fraid so. The cat's out of the proverbial bag."

She laughed ruefully. "Well, it was bound to happen sooner or later. At least I got the first show under my belt before that bombshell exploded in my face."

"Uh, Silver?"

"Hmm?"

"I, uh, also sort of let it out that I'm, uh, your…" he trailed off.

She frowned down at him. "If I didn't know you better, I'd swear you look a little afraid. What in the world did you say?"

He closed his eyes. Opened them. Took a deep breath. "I claimed to be the, uh, father of your baby."

Her jaw dropped. She stared at him, speechless for several long seconds.

"I swear, honey, I'm not pulling a Sampson on you. I'll recant the statement if you want me to. But I would love to be the father of your baby. I was thinking maybe I could adopt Junior if you'd agree to it…"

Even to his good ear, that sounded too lame for words.

She frowned at him, clearly perplexed. "But to adopt the baby, you and I would have to be married."

"Well, of course we would—" he burst out before stopping abruptly. "Whoops. Got ahead of myself. You do that to me, you know."

He slid off the table, landing on one knee on the floor in front of her. "Silver, would you make the happiest man alive and marry me? I'm hopelessly, helplessly in love with you and can't think of anything I'd rather do than spend the rest of my life with you. And that includes my career." Now he was the one babbling, but he didn't care. "Frankly, I'm glad my eardrum is shot. That way you can't send me back into the field when I drive you crazy. Because I'm sure I will, now and then. I apologize in advance, but I'm just so crazy about you. I want to wrap you up and keep you safe and never see that haunted look in your eyes again. The one you get when you're scared—"

He broke off. "Lord, woman, you make a blubbering idiot out of me. Put me out of my misery and agree to marry me. Please!"

A tinkling sound, like little silver bells ringing, intruded upon his senses. Was it another one of Dr. Whitney's hearing tests?

And then it hit him. It was Silver. Laughing. And crying. And falling to her knees in front of him and flinging her arms around his neck.

"Is that a yes?" he mumbled into her hair.

"Oh, yes. Yes, yes, yes!"

It hit him like a ton of bricks. A wave of joy so damned big and powerful it blasted him plumb off his rocker.

"Hot damn!" he yelled as he jumped up, dragging her with him and spinning her around in joy. He staggered to a halt, dizzy.

Dr. Whitney intruded dryly, "You might want to go easy on the spinning, there, fella. Your sense of balance won't return to normal for a few weeks."

Austin grinned widely. "Doc, with this woman for my wife, I'm not ever gonna regain my balance."

"Hey!" Silver protested, laughing.

He grinned down at her. "Don't get me wrong, honey. I think balance is highly overrated. Marriage to you is going to be more fun than ought to be legal."

She grinned back up at him. "Right back at ya, big guy."

Another nurse poked her head into the now-crowded office. "Miss Rothchild, a man named Saul sent me up here to let you know that, and I quote, 'The entire Rothchild clan is waiting for you downstairs, and there's going to be a revolt if they don't see for themselves pretty soon that you're all right.' I might add that about fifty reporters are also down there. They're asking for a statement regarding rumors of your pregnancy and the identity of the father of your baby."

Silver glanced over at Austin. "You're sure about this?"

He nodded firmly and looped his arm around her shoulders. "Positive. It's you and me, darlin', from now on. You'll never have to face your family, or the press, alone again."

She leaned into him and said softly, "I love the sound of that."

"I love you, Silver."

"Mmm. I love the sound of that, even more. I may even have to write a song about it. A whole bunch of songs." She smiled tenderly at him. "By the way, I love you, too."

He bent down to kiss her sweetly, savoring everything about her as he did so. They hadn't done too bad together, the two of them. They'd survived Mark Sampson, revived her music career, found each other and were on their way to a family of their own. Sure, Candace's killer was still out there, and whoever had written those threatening letters. But together, he and Silver could face anything life threw at him. Endings didn't get too much happier than that.

He asked doubtfully, "Are sappy love ballads allowed to have happy endings?"

She laughed and hooked her arm around his waist. "All that matters to me is that *our* song has a happy ending."

There was only one answer to that. "Amen, honey. Amen.

Epilogue

Silver sighed in contentment and enjoyed the view of Austin's broad shoulders and athletic grace as he strode out of her father's house. He came over to the pool and handed her a tall glass of iced orange juice. She never got tired of looking at him. He claimed the same thing about her, and she was going to hold him to it when she grew to the size of a house over the next few months. She couldn't wait. She thought she'd spied a little swelling in her abdomen this morning when she was getting dressed. Her hand drifted to her belly as she smiled up at him.

"Thanks. What would I do without you, Mr. Dearing?" she said. His retirement from the army had come through a few days ago.

He grinned down at her. "I don't know, and fortunately, you're never going to have to find out. You're stuck with me for good, Mrs. Dearing."

She loved the sound of that. Their wedding had been a quick, quiet affair with just family attending. The hospital that had treated her and Austin after the accident had its own schlocky wedding chapel—gotta love Las Vegas. They'd scheduled it on ten minutes' notice and been married before they walked out of the hospital at midnight the night of her premiere.

The press had loved it. On top of her triumphant comeback to rave reviews, she and Austin had announced to the world that they were married and expecting a baby all in one fell swoop.

Conner was working on the legalities of making Austin the official father of her baby, but it didn't take a piece of paper to make it so in her heart. In the past two weeks Austin had stepped in the to the role of doting daddy-to-be as if he'd been made for it.

"What are you thinking about?" Austin murmured as he sank into the cushioned pool chaise beside her.

"What a great father you're going to make."

The look in his eyes as he gazed over at her was pure love. "Can't wait."

He reached out and she took his hand, their fingers intertwining between their lounges. In quiet companionship they watched the sun set in a kaleidoscope of crimson and purple.

A jovial voice rang out behind them. "There you are, you two lovebirds!"

Silver glanced up as Conner joined them, drink in hand. "How's tricks, cousin?"

He shrugged. "Could be worse. I got a lead on your buddy Darla. Her landlord says she skips town for a couple weeks at a time now and then, but she always turns up again. He told me about a club where I might find her when she shows up. I'm gonna go check it out later tonight."

Silver scowled. "She was Candace's pal, not mine."

Conner raised his glass and grinned. "So noted."

A new voice came from near the back doors. "Rebecca said I could find all of you out here."

Silver looked up to see Natalie stepping outside. She was in her police uniform—she must have just gotten off duty. It was still strange to see her stepsister wearing a gun. "Defending truth, justice and the American Way, are you, sis?"

Natalie smiled, but her gaze remained serious.

Austin went watchful and quiet beside her. He asked quietly, "Any news?"

Natalie nodded. "Today the FBI ran the polygraph tests on Mark Sampson and his buddy Dingo that they agreed to as part of their plea bargains."

Silver went on high alert, but it was nothing compared to the predatory intensity that suddenly enveloped Austin beside her.

Natalie continued, "The polygraph examiner confirms with high certainty what they've been saying all along. Sampson and Dingo had nothing to do with the shooting in front of the casino. According to the test, they're not lying, either, when they claim not to have left that message on Silver's dressing-room mirror, and neither of them had anything to do with the sabotage of the light scaffolding."

Silver frowned. The police had concluded that someone set small explosive charges at key support points all over the big lighting rig over the stage and brought it down on her intentionally. "If not Mark, then who?" she asked in alarm.

Austin and Conner traded grim looks. It was Austin who answered her. "Whoever's targeting the whole Rothchild clan."

She met his gaze worriedly. "What am I supposed to do about it?"

Austin shrugged. "Exactly what you've been doing. Keep working on your next album. We continue to lie low here at the mansion, and I continue to watch over you."

"For how long?" she asked.

"Until the killer is caught."

Conner piped up, "So you're convinced that whoever murdered Candace and stole the ring is behind the attacks on Silver?"

Austin replied, "Makes sense."

Natalie added, "The threatening letter to Harold suggests it's the same guy."

Conner nodded. "Well, then. I guess I'd better head over to that club and see if I can track down Darla. If she can lead me to the ring, maybe she can lead me to the killer."

Natalie murmured, "You want some backup?"

"Nah. I got this one. I'll give you a call if I need you to charge in, guns blazing, and save the day."

Natalie and Conner wandered into the house, arguing good-naturedly about the kind of trouble he was likely to get into without her there to bail him out.

Silver looked at Austin in concern. He held out his arms, and she didn't hesitate. She crawled into his lap and cuddled close as he wrapped his strong, safe arms around her. She laid her head on his shoulder, and they watched the last vestiges of sunset fade from the sky. Venus came into view overhead and the first few stars blinked into sight.

He murmured, "It'll be okay, Silver. I've got your back now."

"Promise?"

"Promise."

And that was enough for her. Enough to build a family on. Enough to build a life on together. Forever.

* * * * *

*Mills & Boon® Intrigue brings you
a sneak preview of…*

Delores Fossen's Expecting Trouble

*Special agent Cal Rico lives by the rules. He would
never get involved with someone he has sworn to
protect, which is why it comes as a shock that Texas
heiress Jenna Laniere would name him as the father of
her baby. With an assassin hot on Jenna's trail, though,
and Cal falling hard for both mother and daughter, he
faces his most important
assignment yet.*

Don't miss the thrilling third story in the new
TEXAS PATERNITY: BOOTS AND BOOTIES
*mini-series, available next month from
Mills & Boon® Intrigue.*

Expecting Trouble
by
Delores Fossen

A deafening blast shook the rickety hotel and stopped Jenna cold.

With her heart in her throat, Jenna raced to the window and looked down at the street below. Or rather what was left of the street, a gaping hole. Someone had set shops on fire. Black coils of smoke rose, smearing the late afternoon sky.

"Ohmygod," Jenna mumbled.

There was no chance a taxi could get to her now to take her to the airport. And worse were rebel soldiers, at least a dozen of them dressed in dark green uniforms. She'd heard about them on the news and knew they had caused havoc in Monte de Leon. That's why by now she'd hoped to be out of the hotel, and the small South American country. She hadn't succeeded because she'd been waiting on a taxi for eight hours.

One of the soldiers looked up at her and took aim with his scoped rifle. Choking back a scream, Jenna dropped to the floor just as the bullet slammed through the window.

She scurried across the threadbare rug and into the bathroom. It smelled of mold, rust and other odors she didn't want to identify, and Jenna wasn't surprised to see roaches race across the cracked tile. It was a far cry from the nearby Tolivar estate where she'd spent the past two days. Of course, there'd been insects of a different kind there.

Paul Tolivar.

Staying close to the wall, Jenna pulled off one of her red heels so she could use it as a weapon and climbed into the bathtub to wait for whatever was about to happen.

She didn't have to wait long.

There was a scraping noise just outside the window. She pulled in her breath and waited. Praying. She hadn't even made it to the please-get-me-out-of-this part when she heard a crash of glass and the thud of someone landing on the floor.

"I'm Special Agent Cal Rico," a man called out. "U.S. International Security Agency. I'm here to rescue you."

A rescue? Or maybe this was a trick by one of the rebels to draw her out. Jenna heard him take a step closer, and that single step caused her pulse to pound in her ears.

"I know you're here," he continued, his voice calm. "I pinpointed you with thermal equipment."

The first thing she saw was her visitor's handgun. It was lethal-looking. As was his face. Lean, strong. He had an equally strong jaw. Olive skin that hinted at either Hispanic or Italian DNA. Mahogany-brown hair and sizzling steel-blue eyes that were narrowed and focused.

He was over six feet tall and wore all black, with various weapons and equipment strapped onto his chest,

waist and thighs. He looked like the answer to her unfinished prayer.

Or a P.S. to her nightmare.

"We need to move now," he insisted.

Jenna didn't question that, but she still wasn't sure
what she intended to do. Yes, she was afraid, but she
wasn't stupid. "Can I trust you?"

Amusement leapt through his eyes. His reaction
was brief, lasting barely a second before he nodded.
And that was apparently all the reassurance he
intended to give her. He latched on to her arm and
hauled her from the tub. He allowed her just enough
time to put back on her shoe before he maneuvered
her out of the bathroom and toward the door to her
hotel room.

"Extraction in progress, Hollywood," he whispered
into a black thumb-size communicator on the collar of
his shirt. "ETA for rendezvous is six minutes."

Six minutes. Not long at all. Jenna latched on to that
info like a lifeline. If this lethal-looking James Bond
could deliver what he promised, she'd be safe soon.
Of course, with all those rebel soldiers outside, that
was a big *if*.

Cal Rico paused at the door, listening, and eased
it open. After a split-second glance down the hall, he
got them out of the room and down a flight of stairs
that took them to the back entrance on the bottom
floor. Again, he looked out, but he must not have liked
what he saw. He put his finger to his lips, telling her
to stay quiet.

Outside, Jenna could still hear the battery of gunfire

and the footsteps of the rebels. They seemed to be moving right past the hotel. She was in the middle of a battle zone.

How much her life had changed in two days. This should have been a weekend trip to Paul's Monte de Leon estate. A prelude to taking their relationship from friendship to something more. Instead, it'd become a terrifying ordeal she might not survive.

Jenna tried not to let fear take hold of her, but adrenaline was screaming for her to run. To do something. *Anything.* It was a powerful, overwhelming sensation. Fight or flight. Even if either of those options could get her killed.

Cal Rico touched his fingers to her lips. "Your teeth are chattering," he mouthed.

No surprise there. She didn't have a lot of coping mechanisms for dealing with this level of stress. Who did? Well, other than the guy next to her.

"Try doing some math," he whispered. "Or recite the Gettysburg Address. It'll help keep you calm."

Jenna didn't quite buy that. Still, she tried.

He moved back slightly. But not before she caught his scent. Sweat mixed with deodorant soap and the faint smell of the leather from his combat boots. It was far more pleasant than it should have been.

Stunned and annoyed with her reaction, Jenna cursed herself. Here she was, close to dying, only hours out of a really bad relationship, and her body was already reminding her that Agent Cal Rico smelled pleasant. Heaven help her. She was obviously a candidate for therapy.

"I'll do everything within my power to get you out of here," he whispered. "That's a promise."

Jenna stared at him, trying to figure out if he was lying. No sign of that. Just pure undiluted confidence. And much to her surprise, she believed him. It was probably a reaction to the testosterone fantasy he was weaving around her. But she latched on to his promise.

"All clear," he said before they started to move again.

They hurried out the door and into the alley that divided the hotel from another building. Cal never even paused. He broke into a run and made sure she kept up with him. He made a beeline for a deserted cantina. They ducked inside, and he pulled her to the floor.

"We're at the rendezvous point," he said into his communicator. "How soon before you can pick up Ms. Laniere?" A few seconds passed before he relayed to her, "A half hour."

That was an eternity with the battle raging only yards away. "We'll be safe here?" Jenna tried not to make it sound like a question.

"Safe enough, considering."

"How did you even know I was in that hotel?"

Cal shifted his position so he could keep watch out the window. "Intel report."

"There was an intelligence report about me?" But she didn't wait for him to answer. "Who are you? Not your name. I got that. But why are you here?"

He shrugged as if the answer were obvious. "I'm a special agent with International Security Agency—the ISA. I've been monitoring you since you arrived in Monte de Leon."

Still not understanding, she shook her head. "Why?"

"Because of your boyfriend, Paul Tolivar. He is bad news. A criminal under investigation."

Judas Priest. This was about Paul. Who else?

"My ex-boyfriend," she corrected. "And I wish I'd known he was bad news before I flew down here."

Maybe it was because she was staring craters into him, but Agent Rico finally looked at her. Their gazes met. And held.

"I don't suppose someone could have told me he was under investigation?" she demanded.

He was about to shrug again, but she held tight to his shoulder. "We couldn't risk telling you because you might have told Paul."

Special Agent Rico might have added more, if there hadn't been an earsplitting explosion just up the street. It sent an angry spray of dirt and glass right at them. He reacted fast. He shoved her to the floor, and covered her body with his. Protecting her.

They waited. He was on top of her, with his rock-solid abs right against her stomach and one of his legs wedged between hers. Other parts of them were aligned as well.

His chest against her breasts. Squishing them.

The man was solid everywhere. Probably not an ounce of body fat. She'd never really considered that an asset, but she did now. Maybe all that strength would get them out of this alive.

© Delores Fossen 2009

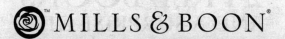

2 FREE BOOKS
AND A SURPRISE GIFT

We would like to take this opportunity to thank you for reading this Mills & Boon® book by offering you the chance to take TWO more specially selected books from the Intrigue series absolutely FREE! We're also making this offer to introduce you to the benefits of the Mills & Boon® Book Club™—

- **FREE home delivery**
- **FREE gifts and competitions**
- **FREE monthly Newsletter**
- **Exclusive Mills & Boon Book Club offers**
- **Books available before they're in the shops**

Accepting these FREE books and gift places you under no obligation to buy, you may cancel at any time, even after receiving your free books. Simply complete your details below and return the entire page to the address below. You don't even need a stamp!

YES Please send me 2 free Intrigue books and a surprise gift. I understand that unless you hear from me, I will receive 5 superb new stories every month, including two 2-in-1 books priced at £4.99 each and a single book priced at £3.19, postage and packing free. I am under no obligation to purchase any books and may cancel my subscription at any time. The free books and gift will be mine to keep in any case.

Ms/Mrs/Miss/Mr _____ Initials _____

Surname _____

Address _____

_____ Postcode _____

Send this whole page to: Mills & Boon Book Club, Free Book Offer, FREEPOST NAT 10298, Richmond, TW9 1BR